图像 IMAGE
历史 HISTORY
存在 EXISTENCE

泰康人寿
保险股份有限公司
成立15周年
艺术品收藏展

TAIKANG LIFE
15th ANNIVERSARY
ART COLLECTION
EXHIBITION

文化藝術出版社
Culture and Art Publishing House

卷首语

有大境界
方有大收藏

陈东升

从1996年创办至今天，泰康人寿历经15年奋斗成为中国前五大人寿保险公司。这15年恰遇中国经济黄金发展，也是中国企业的黄金时间。记得2002年泰康人寿的保费才60多亿，还是亏损的，到2010年底我们总资产近3000亿，税后利润超过20亿。2003年我们的客户才二三十万人，现在泰康人寿累计服务过的客户达到了6000万，那时候我们有5万人的员工队伍，现在是近30万人。这15年来，泰康因时而生、因时而兴、因时而变，实现了超常规的跨越式发展。

泰康的成功彰显我们的实力，更提醒我们不要忘记肩负的责任。时逢盛世，在自身发展的同时，我们从来没有忘记社会，没有忘记回馈社会，多年来我们开展了包括支持重大社会活动、为重大灾害事件捐款、支持教育事业、支持学术研究、支持文化产业发展、保护环境等等很多方面的社会公益事业，泰康和我个人累计捐款1.67亿，捐赠保险金额207亿。首都北京，是中国总部经济基地，是政治文化中心，是文物艺术品之都，有着悠久的文物艺术发展史，雄厚的研究力量和发达的流通市场，文物艺术品资源丰富，大量最优秀的艺术人才聚集在这里，是世界公认的极具高度吸引力、影响力的魅力之都。在和社会共同分享这些资源的同时，我们也积极投身参与到她的发展中。从2001年起公司坚持赞助支持当代／实验艺术发展，10年的时间举办数十个艺术展览，展示200多位艺术家的不同作品。很多员工对艺术家的名字从陌生到熟悉，艺术已经成为泰康不可分割的一部分，成为我们的企业文化传统的重要组成。

这赞助的10年也是泰康收藏艺术品的10年，到今天逐步建立形成了自己的收藏体系，有缘成为很多美术史上重要艺术品的守护者。在收藏的同时，对一些藏品和相关艺术家开展更深入的再学习再研究，并通过展览的方式和大家交流，把我们的工作成果传播开，为艺术的社会化发展尽一份微薄之力，与一些艺术研究机构或学院的合作也即将进一步展开。

经济的发展必将带来文化的繁荣，从1993年我创办嘉德至今近20年，我亲眼目睹和经历了伴随中国经济起飞到资产持续高速增值，中国艺术市场从起步到亿元时代的三级跳发展。从改革开放之初国家外汇极端短缺，为了争取外汇，80年代艺术品交易的主体——文物商店和工艺品进出口公司，把大量的文物低价卖出去换外汇支持国家建设。到现在，中国经济起飞进入到资产增值的快速阶段，艺术品价格持续升高，文物古董和艺术品市场空前繁荣。

财富的高增长，催生中国中产阶层的兴起和社会消费结构的变化，使一个庞大的中等收入群体和高端收入群体正在日益兴起，人们的消费理念和生活观念正在发生根本性的变化，文化消费已经成为新的潮流，中国正产生一批真正的私人收藏家。投资意识的觉醒和投资渠道的多元化，使得一些企业和社会机构也开始把目光投向艺术品收藏，争相介入文物艺术品市场。今天我们正经历着从投资到收藏的又一转变过程，经历从投资进入鉴赏的健康发展，相信未来的民间美术馆将从他们中出现，综合起私人收藏行为和公共美术馆的职责。

艺术的发展从来就是与资本相伴，我们有能力、有意愿承担更多社会责任，为社会发展和子孙后代而收藏。有大境界方有大收藏，未来泰康将建立自己的企业美术馆，使我们的文化财富社会化，我们将变成社会财富的托管者，担负起收藏、整理、研究和传播的职责。与泰康的发展一样，我相信会成长起来一批既有实力会投资，又有审美情趣会长久鉴赏的收藏家群体和民间美术馆，到那时候中国的艺术品市场将更健康，更兴旺，更繁荣。让我们加强交流，互相切磋，为正在崛起的中国文物艺术品市场注入新的活力，为繁荣中国文化艺术产业、丰富世界文化宝库作出自己的贡献。

2011.5.20 于北京

陈东升
泰康人寿保险股份有限公司 创始人 董事长兼CEO
中国嘉德国际拍卖有限公司 创始人 董事长

Preface

It Takes Great Vision to Create a Great Collection

By Chen Dongsheng

Through fifteen years of striving from our founding in 1996 until the present, Taikang Life has become one of the top five life insurance companies in China. These fifteen years have coincided with a golden age in the development of China's economy. It has also been a golden age for Chinese enterprise. The premium income of Taikang Life in 2002 as I recall was RMB 6 billion, it was a loss at that time. But our total assets reached RMB 300 billion and after tax profit was over RMB 2 billion by the end of 2010. In 2003, the number of our clients was 200,000 to 300,000, while the clients served by Taikang Life accumulatively is now 60 million. The staff has increased from 50,000 to 300,000. In the 15 years, Taikang has experienced emerging, growth and change while adapting to the changing times, and has achieved an extraordinary development of large steps.

While the success of Taikang underlines our strength, it reminds us of our responsibility. In the flourishing age, we have never forgotten our social responsibility. Making our contribution to the society during the process of the company's development, we have been engaged in various kinds of social welfares through sponsoring important social activities, supporting academic research and the development of cultural industry and promoting environment protection. The donation made by the company and I myself is RMB 167 million, and the company has donated insurance with the amount of insured reaching RMB 20.7 billion. Beijing is the economic foundation and headquarters of China, the centre of political culture, the capital of heritage artworks with an ancient history of development of heritage arts and crafts, with abundant research power and a developed market of circulation, rich resources in heritage artworks. A great many most outstanding artists congregate here, in a charismatic capital that is acknowledged by the world as being of the highest quality, and as having the strongest attractive force and influence. As we share these resources with society, we are also actively involved in social development. Beginning in 2001, the Company has maintained its sponsorship and support of the development of contemporary experimental art, and in the last ten years we have held scores of exhibitions showing the various works of more than two hundred artists. Many of our employees, who previously had not heard the names of these artists, are now thoroughly familiar with them, and art has become an inseparable part of Taikang, and has become an important component of the cultural tradition of our enterprise.

These ten years of sponsorship have also been ten years of Taikang collecting works of art. This has gradually led to the establishment and formation of our own system of collecting, and it has been our destiny to become the guardians of many important artworks in the history of fine arts. As we collect, we develop deeper levels of study of, and research in, certain works in the collection, and regarding the relevant artists. Through the format of exhibitions and exchanges with the public, we make the fruit of our labours available to the public, and in a modest contribution to the socialized development of art, we progressively develop our collaboration with certain art research organizations and academies.

Economic development necessarily leads to a cultural boom. In the almost 20 years since I founded China Guardian Auctions in 1993, I have seen with my own eyes and personally experienced how, accompanying the sustained rapid increase in asset values in China's economic take-off, the triple leap in China's art market from its first steps to the age of the hundred-million price tag. From the first period of Reform and Opening when the country was extremely short of foreign currency, the object of the trade in artworks in the 1980s was to sell off, through artefact shops and import and export companies dealing in craft articles, a large amount of artworks cheaply but for foreign currency to underwrite national reconstruction. Now that China's economy has taken off and is entering a stage of rapidly increasing asset values, including the value of artworks, heritage antiques and artworks are enjoying an unprecedented flourishing in the market.

The high increase in wealth has given birth to the Chinese middle class, and to changes in society's structures of consumption, producing the current rise and daily increase of vast masses of middle - and high - income earners, and at present causing fundamental changes in people's conception of consumerism and views on living. Cultural consumption has already become a new trend, and China is in the process of producing a group of genuine private collectors. An awakening of investment consciousness, and the increasing pluralism of investment channels, is causing enterprises and social organisations to begin to cast their eyes on the collection of works of art and to become competitively involved in the heritage art market. Today we are experiencing the process of yet another transformation from investment to collection, in the healthy development from investment into appreciation. I trust that non-governmental art museums will appear among these in the future, in an integration of the collecting activities of private persons and the responsibilities of public art museums.

The development of art has always been associated with capital. We are able and willing to undertake even more social responsibility by collecting art for the development of society and for our children and grandchildren and subsequent future generations. Only with great vision can there be great collecting, and in future Taikang will establish an art museum within our own enterprise. To make this cultural wealth social, we will become the trustees of this social wealth and will shoulder the responsibilities of collecting, organisation, research and dissemination. In the same way that Taikang developed, I trust that we shall grow into a number of collectors' groups and non-governmental art museums that have both the power to invest, and the aesthetic interest to sustain long-term appreciation. When that time comes, the art market in China will be even more healthy, prosperous and flourishing. Let us strengthen exchanges, let us learn from one another, let us pour new vitality into the emerging Chinese heritage art market, so as to make our own contribution to the flourishing Chinese culture and art industries and to a treasure house of rich world culture.

20 May 2011, Beijing

Chen Dongsheng
Founder & Chairman & CEO, Taikang Life Insurance Co., Ltd.
Founder & Chairman, China Guardian Auctions Co., Ltd.

前言

历史与收藏的互映
——写在泰康人寿15周年艺术品收藏展之际

范迪安

在泰康人寿15周年庆典的日子里，中国美术馆十分高兴举办泰康艺术收藏展，这是中国美术馆首次与国内企业携手合作举办中国企业的艺术收藏展。毫无疑问，这个展览基于两个原由：一是泰康收藏的艺术品整体上具有高质量的艺术水平和鲜明的学术特色，通过本馆的公共文化服务平台，使这些艺术品得以与艺术界见面，特别是得以让社会各界人士欣赏品鉴，将使企业的艺术收藏发挥应有的社会作用，这是我们与泰康公司在关于艺术品社会价值上的共识。二是在艺术品收藏在中国方兴未艾甚至成为社会热点和全球热议话题的今天，需要缕析和探讨艺术收藏现象自身许多方面的问题，泰康艺术收藏所走过的道路特别是其在企业艺术收藏中所探索的方式，值得关注和交流，借展览举办之机，展开对企业艺术收藏现状、模式、方法等方面的研讨与对话，将具有特别的意义。

进入21世纪以来中国社会经济的高速发展，使艺术创作与艺术收藏、艺术资源与经济资本之间迅速建立起新的关系，艺术品从创作生产到分配占有的过程，形成了丰富且复杂的格局，成为中国经济与文化关系的表征。这种艺术经济学与经济文化学相互关联的状况，在世界各国经济发展的历史上均有体现，但因中国之大，发展速度之甚，又有其特殊的表现方式。由此，讨论企业艺术收藏，在今天的中国就成为一个牵涉多方面的"跨界"话题。

"泰康艺术收藏"的缘起与展开和"泰康人寿"的企业与发展当然是紧密相关的。虽然我们不能够完全了解泰康人寿具体的事业拓展和业绩状况，但在一个社会组织和个体越来越处于社会机能的互动网络之中的时代，人寿保险业的发展必然有越来越充足的需求。在我们的生活现实空间里，"泰康人寿"四个字不时地进入视域，就是泰康人寿事业发展的体现。同样，在中国艺术界和艺术收藏界，泰康艺术收藏伴随着泰康人寿发展历程的步履也是清晰的，艺术界的同仁在谈及艺术收藏这个话题时，"泰康艺术收藏"总是群言乐道之词，甚至可以上升为一种话语，用以指涉和谈论当代艺术收藏的诸多方面。经过10年的积累，泰康艺术收藏有了自己丰裕的存在，而最值得称道的是这份收藏在学术层面上承载了中国美术一些重要的历史，包括一些可以达到"以图证史"作用的经典。因此，当这份收藏品得以展示时，不仅满足了人们对泰康藏品了解的意愿，也呈现出这批藏品的图像学价值，它们在20世纪中国美术历史的"上下文"中，拥有了牢靠的位置。

展示在人们面前的泰康艺术收藏首先具有时间的脉络。收藏是无止尽的，藏品质的价值胜于量的价值，这些都是浅显的道理，但如何能在浩瀚的艺术品海洋里淘金获宝，构建起藏品的时间序列，也即历史的图景，则是对收藏者眼光和意识的检测。在泰康藏品中，那些重要的作品之所以重要，就是因为它们代表了一个时间的节点，一段艺术史的缩影，也是一个时代社会的标识。例如，蒋兆和的《中国人民从此站起来了》一画，表现的就是新中国诞生这一重要历史时刻，画家在作品中明确标记作于"中华人民共和国诞生之日"，到目前为止，确切落款画于"1949年10月1日"的作品还未见于他处，毋庸置疑，这样的"唯一性"为这件作品增加了特别的份量。而同样作于1949年的作品，还有吴作人的《解放南京号外》。这两幅作品，一是油画、一是中国画，作为两大画种的代表，在时间和社会的坐标上占有了历史的价值。同样，陈逸飞1972年创作的《黄河颂》和吴冠中1979年创作的《北国风光》，作为两位画家主题创作的代表，也在时间上为1970年代中国艺术的主题和画家的创造性风格留下了记载。而孟禄丁、张群1985年合作的《在新时代——亚当夏娃的启示》与肖鲁1989年的装置/行为《对话》，极有代表性地反映了85新潮美术运动的起点与谢幕……这些藏品——确切地说——是隐含于藏品背后的收藏动机、收藏信念，让我们看到了泰康艺术收藏的价值，在今天我们普遍讨论艺术收藏应如何持以良好的动机时，泰康走过的道路提供了重要的经验。

收藏艺术史上的作品需要学识，收藏当代艺术的作品则需要方式。依我所见，在当代艺术这部分藏品中，泰康收藏的价值不仅仅在于作品本身，虽然就作品本身而言，也可印证出当代艺术界基本形成的定评，而对于今日艺术收藏来说，或对于评价泰康收藏的价值而言，这些作品得以入藏泰康的方式是更有价值的。在过去十年的时间里，中国艺术生态业已发生了极大的变化，当代艺术资源几近成为群雄四起、资本控制的"新金山"。在这种情形下，泰康是既不喧嚣张扬，也不浮夸表现的，她以泰康空间为平台，严谨地通过举办学术展览推广艺术新作，通过资助青年艺术家实现艺术想法积累藏品，可以说，走出了一条可以称为泰康模式的道路。模式不乏创新，坚守则是考验。泰康空间从长安街到798、从798到草场地，一向秉承着自己的理念，采用自己的方式。我曾经不少次参观泰康空间举办的展览，在那些展览中看到艺术家得以充分地展示自己的艺术理念。在艺术潮流风云涌动、泥沙俱下的景况中，泰康空间举办的展览坚守了学术的纯粹性，由此，我赞佩唐昕这位策展人兼管理者所做的工作，她在学术思考上体现出敏感与缜密相结合的品质，以规范的操作和从容的心态建立起专业信誉，展示了泰康收藏于涛波浪头淡定的风格。

当藏品的积累穿越时间的帷幕显露出它的序列感和重要性之日，一定是收藏者的欣慰之时。泰康人寿的艺术收藏史也可以说是陈东升先生对艺术认知和对艺术价值认知的精神体现。在我和他的接触中，他对艺术的热情令人感动，他对艺术作用的理解更是由衷的。在许多展览的开幕式上我们相逢，他的讲话总是体现了两个尊重：对艺术的尊重和对艺术家创造性的尊重。我相信在这两个同样重要的尊重中，贯串了他的事业理念，也即泰康人寿的事业不仅要见证中国社会的发展、公民的自我尊严，也要见证中国艺术与时俱进的发展。于此可以说，这个展览是泰康艺术收藏新的起点，是泰康人的骄傲，而我们为之高兴。

范迪安，中国美术馆馆长

Foreword

The Mutual Reflection of History and Art – Written on the occasion of Taikang Life 15th Anniversary Art Collection Exhibition

by Fan Di'an

On the fifteenth anniversary celebrations of the Taikang Life Insurance Company, the National Art Museum of China is delighted to hold this Exhibition of the Taikang Art Collection. This is the first time that the National Art Museum of China joins with a corporation in China in holding an exhibition of the art collection of a Chinese corporation. There can be no doubt that there are two rationales for this Exhibition. First, the artworks in the Taikang Collection as a whole are of a high artistic standard and quality, and they present obvious distinctive features of academic interest. In allowing these works to encounter the world of art on the platform of public cultural service of the National Art Museum, and in particular in presenting the general public with the opportunity of seeing and appreciating these works, thereby bringing into play the appropriate social role of art collections in private-sector corporations, we are of the same opinion as the Taikang Company regarding the social value of works of art. Second, now that collecting artworks is on the rise in China, being a social hotspot in China and a worldwide subject of enthusiasm, questions regarding many aspects of the phenomenon of art collecting as such require fine analysis and discussion. In the road that the Taikang Art Collection has travelled, it is especially the format of corporate art collecting explored by Taikang that deserves both attention and an exchange of opinions and experience, and, taking the opportunity of this exhibition, it will be of especial interest to open up a discussion and a dialogue regarding various aspects of the current state, models and methods of corporate art collecting.

The high-speed socio-economic development of China as it enters the twenty-first century is leading to the rapid establishment of new relations between artistic production and the collecting of art, and between artistic resources and economic capital. The process from the original creation of the artworks to their distribution has established rich and complex patterns, which have come to represent the relationship between the economy and culture in China. The state of interconnection between the economics of art and the cultural study of the economy is one that has also appeared in the economic development history of many different countries around the world, but because of China's size and the extreme speed of its development, the format in which it appears in China is unique. Therefore, when we discuss corporate art collecting, it has in today's China become an interdisciplinary topic that involves multiple aspects indeed.

The origin and development of the Taikang Art Collection is of course closely connected with the founding and development of the Taikang Life Insurance Company. Although we do not pretend to any expertise on the expansion of the business and its present performance situation, there will, in an age when social organizations and private enterprises are situated in a more and more interactive network of social functions, necessarily be an increasingly adequate demand for the development of life insurance companies. In our everyday lives, we are constantly seeing the words "Taikang Life", which is a sign of the development of the Taikang enterprise. Similarly, in the world of art and the world of art collecting in China, the career of the Taikang Art Collection that accompanies the development of Taikang Life Insurance is conspicuous, and when colleagues in the world of art come to talk of art collecting, "the Taikang Art Collection" is a popular phrase that occurs often. It can even become a kind of discourse that is used to refer to and discuss many aspects of the collecting of contemporary art. Through ten years of accumulation, the Taikang Art Collection has led its own abundant existence, yet what is most deserving of mention is that at an academic level this Collection is the carrier of some important Chinese aesthetic history, and that it includes some classics that are fit to serve the purpose of "mapping history by means of images". So, showing these artworks does not only satisfy the desire of people to get to know the works in the Taikang Art Collection, but is also a demonstration of the iconological value of the works in that collection. They hold a solid position in the context of the history of twentieth-century art in China.

As presented to the public, the Taikang Art Collection primarily appears in a context of time. Collecting never achieves finality, and the quality of the collected works is more important than their quantity. These are simple and obvious truths, yet how, among the multitude of artworks, does one discover and obtain the treasures? How does one construct a temporal sequence of the collected works, that is, a historical landscape? This is the test of the collector's eye and understanding. The reason why those important works among the items in the Taikang Art Collection are important is that they each represent a critical point in time, and each sum up a period of art history, and are emblems of the society of a particular era. For instance, Jiang Zhaohe's painting *From Now On, the Chinese People Has Stood Up* represents the important historical moment of the birth of the new China. The artist has clearly indicated in the work that it was created "on the day that the People's Republic of China was born" -

and until now, no other work of art has been found with the clear inscription that it was painted on 1st October 1949. There is no doubt that this kind of 'uniqueness' adds to the special weight of this work. Another work created in 1949 is Wu Zuoren's *Extra Edition on the Liberation of Nanjing*.

These two works, one an oil painting, the other a traditional Chinese painting, represent two great genres of painting. Their historical value is due to their positioning in time and in society. In the same way, Chen Yifei's 1972 work *Eulogy of the Yellow River* and Wu Guanzhong's 1979 work *Northern Landscape* serve to represent the thematic creations of these two artists, and leave a record of the themes and the creative styles of painters working in Chinese art in the 1970s. On the other hand, Meng Luding and Zhang Qun's joint 1985 work *In the New Age – The Enlightenment of Adam and Eve* and Xiao Lu's 1989 installation/performance piece *Dialogue* in a most representative way reflect respectively the starting point and the curtain call of the 1985 New Wave art movement. These collection items, or more precisely, the motives and convictions behind the collection, as implied by the artworks in it, allow us to perceive the value of the Taikang Art Collection. When we nowadays commonly discuss how to maintain good motives in collecting art, the path travelled by Taikang offers us the benefit of important experiences.

Collecting works of art-historical value requires scholarship. Collecting works of contemporary art requires a methodical format. In my view on artworks collected under the heading of contemporary art, the value of the Taikang Art Collection lies not only in the works themselves, although, speaking of the works themselves, they can also be used to provide evidence of the fundamental accepted opinion formed in the world of contemporary art. However, for us, when we assess art collecting today, or the value of the Taikang Art Collection, the format by which these works have managed to enter the Taikang Art Collection is itself of even greater value. Over the course of the last ten years, there have been enormous changes in the ecology of art in China, and the resources of contemporary art have become a "New Eldorado" of numerous heroes arising on all sides and of control by capital. In these circumstances, Taikang is neither noisily self-assertive nor does it perform in an exaggerated manner. With Taikang Space as a platform, it rigorously promotes the creation of new works by holding academic exhibitions, and by providing funding to assist young artists in the realization of their artistic a trail that one might call the "Taikang model". This model does not lack innovation, and the test of it is its perseverance. Taikang Space has moved from Chang'an Avenue to 798, and from 798 to Caochangdi, always adhering to its own ideas and using its own methodical formats. I have often attended exhibitions held by Taikang Space, and I have seen at these exhibitions that the artists have managed to fully manifest their artistic ideas. In the stormy conditions of artistic fashion, where the good is mixed with the bad, the exhibitions held by Taikang Space have maintained their academic purity. Therefore, I admire Tang Xin, who combines all the work of a curator with that of managing Taikang Space. In her academic reflections, she embodies a quality that combines sensitivity with careful attention to detail. In her operative dealings and with her calm mentality, she has established a professional reputation as someone who displays the serene style of the Taikang Art Collection in the midst of all the surrounding turbulence.

The day when the accumulated works in a collection display a sense of sequence and importance through the screen of time is definitely a moment that is savoured by the collector. The history of the Art Collection of Taikang Life may also be said to be the spiritual manifestation of Mr. Chen Dongsheng's understanding of art and of the value of art. In my contacts with him, I have found his enthusiasm for art most impressive. His understanding of the role of art is, perhaps even more impressively, altogether whole-hearted. He and I have met at many exhibition openings, and his words generally reveal that he respects two things, namely art and the creativity of artists. I trust that his respect for these two things, which are equally valuable, permeates his professional philosophy, and also that the enterprise of Taikang Life wishes to witness not only the development of Chinese society and the self-respect of its citizens, but also the timely and up-to-date development of Chinese art. We can thus state that this exhibition is a new point of departure for the Taikang Art Collection. It is a matter of pride for Taikang Life, and we are delighted on these grounds.

Fan Di'an
Director of the National Art Museum of China

目录

专文

未几图景——泰康收藏　唐昕	022
作为收藏品的艺术品　汪民安	028
收藏十年，赞助十年　唐昕	034
从民国风度到延安精神——摄影大师吴印咸的"一张座右铭"　斯然畅畅	051
吴作人《捷报》与第一次文代会　吴雪杉	065
从"流民"到"人民"：为表现新中国而努力的一种 ——试析蒋兆和《中国人民从此站立起来了》的重新发现　蒋岳红	076
靳尚谊与毛主席肖像画　姜鹏	086
《黄河颂》——新中国美术创作中的奇葩　贾慧明	097
解读吴冠中《北国风光》画稿　王玛	108
重读《在新时代——亚当夏娃的启示》　秦晓磊	121
聚焦与定格——再论《对话》　胡晓岚	135

革命与启蒙

吴印咸	063
吴作人	074
蒋兆和	085
靳尚谊	095
陈逸飞	106

Contents

Articles

A Select Show of Images – The Taikang Collection By Tang Xin	024
Artworks as Collected Works By Wang Min'an	030
Ten Years of Collecting, Ten Years of Sponsorship By Tang Xin	039
From the Elegant Manners of the Republic to the Spirit of Yan'an - A 'Maxim' of Master Photographer Wu Yinxian By Siran Changchang	055
Wu Zuoren's *Victory!* and the First Cultural Committee Conference By Wu Xueshan	068
From Refugees to The People: An Effort to represent the New China- An Analysis of the Re-Discovery of Jiang Zhaohe's *From Now On, the Chinese People has Stood Up* By Jiang Yuehong	079
Jin Shangyi and the Portrait of Chairman Mao By Jiang Peng	089
Eulogy of the Yellow River – A Wonder in the Artistic Creation of the New China By Jia Huiming	100
Interpreting Wu Guanzhong's Sketch *Northern Landscape* By Wang Yu	112
Another Look at *In the New Age: the Enlightenment of Adam and Eve* By Qin Xiaolei	125
Focus and Freeze - Revisiting *Dialogue* By Hu Xiaolan	138

吴冠中	118
孟禄丁、张群	133
肖鲁	144

多元的格局

王广义	148
余友涵	152
韩磊	156
叶永青	160
丁乙	164
张晓刚	168
曾梵志	172
李山	176
张大力	180
方力钧	184
刘小东	188
曾浩	192
蔡国强	196
刘野	200
周铁海	204
洪浩	208
刘韡	212
洪浩+颜磊	216
阳江组	220

Revolution and Enlightenment

Wu Yinxian	063
Wu Zuoren	074
Jiang Zhaohe	085
Jin Shangyi	095
Chen Yifei	106
Wu Guanzhong	118
Meng Luding & Zhang Qun	133
Xiao Lu	144

Pluralistic Patterns

Wang Guangyi	149
Yu Youhan	153
Han Lei	157
Ye Yongqing	161
Ding Yi	165
Zhang Xiaogang	169
Zeng Fanzhi	173
Li Shan	177
Zhang Dali	181
Fang Lijun	185
Liu Xiaodong	189
Zeng Hao	193

郑国谷	224
黄永砅	228
汪建伟	232
王兴伟	236
没顶公司	240

延伸的视界

蔡东东	246
胡向前	252
刘窗	258
马秋莎	264
裴丽	270
苏文祥	274
王思顺	280
王郁洋	284
辛云鹏	290
徐渠	294
闫冰	298
赵要	302
赵赵	308

Cai Guo-Qiang	**197**
Liu Ye	**201**
Zhou Tiehai	**205**
Hong Hao	**209**
Liu Wei	**213**
Hong Hao + Yan Lei	**217**
Yangjiang Group	**221**
Zheng Guogu	**225**
Huang Yong Ping	**229**
Wang Jianwei	**233**
Wang Xingwei	**237**
MadeIn	**241**

Extended Vision

Cai Dongdong	**247**
Hu Xiangqian	**253**
Liu Chuang	**259**
Ma Qiusha	**265**
Pei Li	**271**
Su Wenxiang	**275**
Wang Sishun	**281**
Wang Yuyang	**285**
Xin Yunpeng	**291**
Xu Qu	**295**

艺术家简历	312
关于泰康人寿	398
版权与致谢	400

Yan Bing	299
Zhao Yao	303
Zhao Zhao	309
Artists' Biographies	**313**
About Taikang Life	**399**
Copyright & Thanks	**400**

未几图景
——泰康收藏

唐昕

彼得·伯克（Peter Burke）在《图像证史》[1]中给图像（image）的定义包含广泛，图画、雕塑、浮雕、摄影照片、电影和电视画面、时装玩偶等工艺品、奖章和纪念章上的图像等所有可视艺术品，甚至包括地图和建筑在内。这个定义比图像学诞生之初宽泛了很多，当代艺术的种种样式构成的视觉呈现基本上都被它涵盖在里面。

泰康人寿自2001年十年以来支持和鼓励国内当代艺术的实验探索，通过企业内部设立的艺术部门——泰康空间，组织、赞助艺术活动，从理念和资金等多方面给予艺术家和他们的创作以很多实际、有效地支持。赞助的十年也是公司收藏的十年，在今天公司成立15周年之际，泰康人寿艺术品收藏首次公开展示，展览以收藏为核心话题从多角度展开，与图像、历史、存在紧密相关。

图像是一种存在。图像作为一种视觉呈现，与文字并存，它们在近百年曲折的中国社会发展中的作用不可小视。特别是当它们在各种民族、阶级和意识形态斗争的指导下被使用，成为传播媒介和工具时，虽然图像没有文字那么深刻、犀利，但它比文字更能深入到社会各个层面，深入到不懂文字或识字不多的广大人民群众的头脑中，发挥意想不到的、极其广泛而成效显著的作用。一方面图像中形象的直观、感性，容易触动人的情感；另一方面阅读图像比阅读文字时在头脑中产生的想象空间要小，也就是给读者的想象和再思考空间要小得多。图像作为传播工具而非艺术欣赏对象时，它的作用不是要激发读者的想象而是要更为精准地控制读者的想象，这时图像远比文字要直接、有效。比如大批判的漫画，利用视觉图像力图把批判者和被批判者的矛盾，通过突出和强化正面和反面形象之种种反差，非常明了地展示给读者，无论面对什么知识结构、什么受教育程度的读者，信息的传递都直白无误，让你不必再思考。但是同样内容使用文字阐释，在阅读的时候，读者对阅读到的文字信息产生主观判断的同时，头脑中是有空间对信息进行再思考处理的。再思考空间的大小和层次的高低会因为读者文化程度差异、不同的思想深度和视野广度而有所不同。也就是说文字产生的效果是因人而异的。也许正因为如此，大量图像在这个历史阶段被使用和普及的程度非常广泛，与社会大众贴近的程度也是空前绝后的，大众也对图像非常熟悉，感情很深。

这里，我们主要谈论的是80年代以来的艺术实践产生的图像，其形式非常多样，几乎包含了彼得·伯克定义的种种。在去政治化的过程中，这些图像在一定程度上获得自身的独立，回归艺术本体，重新调整了与社会现实的关系，不再从宣传、斗争工具的层面作用于社会大众。它反映艺术独立体系的本体存在，又是对社会客观存在的折射，即成为伯克认为的历史证据。

历史是一种存在。不论哲学上对历史的争论如何，这百年之中作为艺术的图像在不同时期与客观现实或并行或缠绕，影响重重，特别是延安整风运动对艺术与革命实践的关系、艺术针对性的整体理念指导，新中国成立对艺术与意识形态关系的进一步要求，"文革"对文化深层的破坏等等。历史承载的社会现实每每深刻地影响文化艺术的产生和发展轨迹，同时也包含了文化艺术的改变对现实的再影响，更加导致了80年代以来实验艺术的出发和方向，便是我们今天谈论的图像构成的景观。

无论社会发展史还是艺术发展史，都不能孤立存在，图像产生和历史存在相互作用间，前一阶段的矛盾导致后一段史的存在表现。想读懂后一段的存在与表现，必须先了解前一段的矛盾，在与前一段的上下文关系中找到因果。80年代以来的实验艺术是我们工作出发的起点，80年代以来的历史当然是决定性因素，追溯之前的历史将帮助我们更深刻地挖掘它的文化根源。历史存在对图像产生至关重要，图像存在也携带或隐藏了有关历史的可思或可考的信息。翻看诞生于几个历史时刻如1942、

---

[1] 《图像证史——作为历史证据的图像》，纽约：康奈尔大学出版社，2001年。

1949、1966、1979、1985、1989年的图像，仔细研读，社会、政治、艺术、个人复杂而微妙的时代喧嚣映入眼帘。

收藏是一种存在。如果说艺术的存在给历史存在以另一种表现，艺术品本身的物理存在更成了一个物证，收集、整理、保护这些物证所构成的收藏行为得到关于艺术存在的集合，同时收获到一个关于历史存在的物证的集合。倘若按照时间脉络整理收藏，就是一个关于文化史和文明史的存在，那么收藏者无异于一个艺术、历史存在的护佑者，其社会文化意义和责任不言而喻。这种体系化的收藏，建构的是一种史的存在，也是一个存在史。

泰康人寿保险股份有限公司与艺术结缘十年，十年赞助十年收藏，逐步理性化、体系化。针对美术史的梳理研究和分析，收藏体系构成目前的定位可以概括为三个阶段：1942-1976，1976年至今，以及青年专项部分。我们希望未来的收藏整体上反映从1942年以来的文化变化、艺术发展，特别是80年代以后中国实验艺术的产生、发展以及未来走向。

前一阶段：1942-1976，是毛泽东时期美术。1942年毛泽东发表《在延安文艺座谈会上的讲话》，文艺走向工农兵，面向大众，面向基层，从此艺术的自由和独立受到限制，开始服务于政治和意识形态。艺术家的创作态度和内容也从主观的、个人的或代表个人的变为政治的、社会的或代表党的，艺术手法和语言也从专业的、曲高和寡的逐渐变成民间化的、为民众熟悉的。大量艺术家被迫放弃自己对艺术主体的追求和主张，转而使创作变成政治宣传工具。这种状态一直持续到1976年"文革"结束。政治化、民间化、民族化成为这一时期美术作品的普遍特点。

第二阶段：1976年至今，是中国美术从现代到当代的发展阶段，艺术实验重新出现。现代阶段从"文革"结束到1989年，是艺术重获自由和独立的时期。感性方面的体现是"伤痕美术"，从人性和情感上得到解放并反思"文革"；理性方面体现在艺术发展的两个主要层面，即审美和社会职能层面。1979年的"无名画会"（为艺术而艺术）和"星星美展"（艺术干预政治）预示中国美术两个自然层面未来发展的两条线索的出现。这两个层面的发展都由于在1942-1976阶段受到人为的压制和限制，致使随后的解放和发展必然首先针对前段历史有反作用力，建立在对它的文化反思上。破坏、反传统、新尝试、借鉴西方、犹豫、彷徨是这阶段作品的普遍特点。

1989年至今是中国美术的当代阶段，是在审美和社会职能双方面按自身规律的实验和探索阶段。这阶段的特点是艺术媒介多元化发展，从传统的"国油版雕"发展到现在包括平面绘画、雕塑、摄影、录像、装置、行为等，从使用媒介的种类上已经赶上了国际艺术发展的现状。

第三阶段："今"，针对未来的青年部分。美术发展的不断前行，使得"今"永远是一个进行中最鲜活的状态，昨天和明天甚至都被涵盖并行，而其中艺术的未来走向永远是一个迷人的话题，对于未来美术的走向也是泰康人寿艺术品收藏一直持续关注的焦点之一。因此，关注和支持年轻艺术家的实验探索并作适当的收藏，形成了泰康人寿青年艺术品收藏的这个专项部分，是我们对未来艺术的价值判断。

今天，我们以"图像·历史·存在"为题呈现的这个收藏展，是泰康人寿十年收藏的一部分，如同一个图像景观，能一定程度上反映上述三个阶段我们的收获。与以回顾、总结为目的的学术展览不同，以藏品为基础的展览比较而言难度更大些。虽说十年坚持在目前国内的收藏界算得开始较早，持续时间不短，但相对所针对的历史和艺术发展，十年还是太有限了。再加上收藏很是讲缘分，有的擦肩而过，有的无缘相遇，我们需要和缺席的作品还很多很多。在有限的积累中组织这样的展览，可操作空间和斟酌的余地都是狭小的。泰康人寿有幸为社会收集和守护这个图景，希望这个展览作为对泰康空间前一段工作的总结，和对公司的一个汇报，督促我们在未来的工作中继续丰富，使之更加完美。

2011.5.21 于北京

唐昕
泰康人寿保险股份有限公司 收藏部负责人
泰康空间 艺术总监 策展人

A Select Show of Images - The Taikang Collection

By Tang Xin

The definition of 'image' in Peter Burke's *Eyewitnessing: The Uses of Images as Historical Evidence*[1] is very wide. It embraces paintings, sculptures, reliefs, photographs, film and television pictures, fashion mannequins and other craft objects, the images on award medals and commemorative badges, as well as all other visual works of art, including maps and architecture. This definition is much wider now than when iconology was born, and the visual offerings made up of the various formats of contemporary art are basically all included in it.

Taikang Life has supported and encouraged experimental exploration in Chinese contemporary art since 2001 through the Art Section established within the enterprise. Taikang Space organizes and sponsors artistic activities, and provides artists and their creative work with many kinds of practical and effective support from concepts to funding and so on. The ten years of sponsorship have also been ten years of collecting. In this fifteenth year of the Company, the Taikang Life Art Collection is shown publicly for the first time, and the Exhibition opens up the close relations between image, history and existence from various angles, taking collecting as its core topic.

Images are a kind of existence. As a visual presentation linked with writing, the use of images over almost one hundred years of tortuous social development in China must not be underestimated, especially as they have been used in the service of various ethnic, class and ideological struggles, becoming indeed a medium and instrument of communication. Although images do not have the penetration and trenchancy of writing, they can reach deeper into all levels of society than writing can. They can enter deep into the minds of those of the broad popular masses who are illiterate or have limited reading skills, and be put to uses which are astonishing, extremely wide-reaching and spectacularly effective. On the one hand the pictures in images are directly experienced and emotional and easily move people's feelings. On the other hand, when looking at images, the mind produces an imaginative space that is smaller than when reading written texts. That is, the space for imagining and reflecting that looking at images gives the beholder is much smaller. As an instrument of communication, when it is not an object of artistic appreciation, the image serves not to stimulate the reader's imagination, but to control it more precisely. In this situation, the image is far more effective and easier to use

---

[1] Eyewitnessing: The Uses of Images as Historical Evidence, Cornell University Press, 2001.

than writing. For instance, the crtitical political cartoons during the radical period before 1980s in socialist China strive to take the contradictions between those criticizing and those who are criticized, and through emphasizing and exaggerating the various dislocations between the positive and negative images, they present these contradictions to the readers with exceptional clarity. Regardless of the intellectual structure and the educational level of the readers they encounter, the transmission of information is direct, frank and unmistakable, and obviates the need for further thought. However, when similar content is explained through writing, the reader simultaneously produces subjective judgments of the information in the written text that is being read, and also has the mental space to carry out a reflective management of the information. There will be differences in the space of reflection and the degree of the layering according to the cultural level of the reader and the variations in depth of thinking and breadth of vision. In other words, the effect produced by writing varies according to the person reading. Perhaps it is exactly because of this that a great number of images are being used at this stage of history. Their reach is particularly wide, and the extent of their closeness to the broad masses is unprecedented. The masses also know images well, and feel deeply about them.

Here, however, we are talking primarily about the images produced artistically since the 1980s. Their forms are extremely multifarious, and include almost all the types in Peter Burke's definition. In the process of becoming politicized, these images to a certain degree acquire their own independence. When they return to being art as such, they readjust their relationship with social reality, and are no longer used on the social masses in the ideology and Propaganda level. They reflect the fundamental existence of the independent system of art, and also refract the objective existence of society, that is, they become what Peter Burke calls historical evidence.

History is a kind of existence. Whatever the arguments of philosophy about history, images as art have, at various times in these last hundred years, either moved parallel to, or been entangled with objective reality. They have had a heavy impact, especially during the overall conceptual guidance by the Yan'an Rectification Movement of the relationship between art and revolutionary practice and of giving art targeted objectives; when further demands were made of the relationship between art and ideology at the founding of the new China; during the radical destruction of culture during the Cultural Revolution, and so on. The social reality that was carried by history in each case deeply influenced the production and the path of development of culture and art, and at the same time contained the reactive influence of cultural and artistic changes on reality, which to an even higher degree led to the appearance and direction of the experimental art of the 1980s, which is the landscape of images that we are talking about today.

Neither the history of the development of society nor the history of the development of art can exist in isolation. In the interaction between image production and historical existence, the thrust of the contradictions of the earlier stage leads to the existential representations of the later historical stage. If one wants to understand the existence and representations of the later period, one must first understand the contradictions of the earlier period, and find the causes and effects in relations within the context of the previous order. Experimental art since the 1980s is the point of departure for our work. The history from the 1980s on is of course a decisive factor, and tracing back the history that went before will help us to excavate and lay bare the roots and sources of its culture. Historical existence has an important relationship with image production, and the existence of images also carries or hides historical information that is worth thinking about and examining. If we review the images born at various historical moments, such as in the years 1942, 1949, 1966, 1979,1985 or 1989, and look at them carefully, the complex yet subtle social, political, artistic and individual noises of the era come within earshot.

Collecting is a kind of existence. If the existence of art gives historical existence a different kind of representation, the physical existence of a work of art in itself becomes to an even higher degree a piece of material evidence. The activity of collecting that consists in the gathering, ordering and protection of these pieces of material evidence, becomes a compilation regarding artistic existence, and at the same time, of material evidence about historical existence. If we order the collection according to the context of time, it becomes an existence that is about the history of culture and the history of civilization. In that case, the collector is indistinguishable from the guardian of artistic and historical existence, a guardian whose social and cultural significance and duty are clearly evident. This kind of systematic collecting is structurally a kind of historical existence, and is also a history of existence.

The shared destiny of Taikang Life Insurance Company Limited with art is ten years old, ten years of sponsorship and ten years of collecting, which have gradually become rationalized and systematized. The formation of the sifting, research and analysis of art, and of the system of collecting, into the present position can be summarized in three stages: 1942 to 1976, 1976 to the present, and the special section devoted to emerging artists. We hope that the collection will, in future, reflect in a general way the cultural changes and artistic developments from 1942 on, and in particular the production and development of Chinese experimental art beginning in the 1980s, as well as its future direction.

First period: 1942 - 1976,
Art of the Mao Zedong Era.

In 1942, Mao Zedong published the *Talks at the Yenan Forum on Literature and Art*. Literature and art were henceforth to address themselves to the workers, peasants and soldiers. They were to turn to the great masses, and turn to the basics. From that time on, the freedom and independence of art was restricted, and it began to serve politics and ideology. The creative attitude of artists and the content of their art changed from being subjective, and individual or representative of the individual, to being political, and social or representative of the Party. The devices and the language of art also changed from being professional, elitist pursuits to becoming popularized activities familiar to the masses. A great number of artists were forced to abandon their subjective pursuit and advocacy of art, and instead had to change their creative work into a tool of political propaganda, and this state continued until the end of the Cultural Revolution in 1976. Politicization, popularization and nationalism became the common characteristics of works of art in this period.

Second Period: 1976 until the Present.

This was the stage of development in Chinese art from modern art to contemporary art, and of the appearance of experimental art. Between the beginning of the modern period at the end of the Cultural Revolution and 1989, art found its freedom and its independence again. Its emotional manifestation was Scar Art, which achieved a liberation of human nature and emotion and reflected on the Cultural Revolution. Its rational manifestation was the artistic development of two main categories, namely aesthetics and social function. The Anonymous Painting Group (practicing art for art's sake) and the Stars Exhibition (art getting involved in politics), were harbingers of the appearance of two natural levels in the future development of Chinese art. The development of these two levels followed the inhibitions and restrictions suffered in the period from 1942 to 1976, with the result that the subsequent liberation and development had first to react against the preceding historical period, and establish itself on a reflection of the culture of that preceding period. Destruction, going against the tradition, new experiments, Western references, hesitation and helplessness were the general characteristics of this period.

From 1989 to the present is the contemporary era in Chinese art, a period of experimentation and exploration in accordance with its own intrinsic laws of aesthetics and social function. The characteristic of this period is the pluralistic development of artistic media, that is, the development from the traditional categories of 'Chinese painting / oils / prints / sculpture' to the present media, including flat-surface painting, sculpture, photography, video, installation, performance art and so on. In the use of these various media, Chinese art has already caught up with the international state of artistic development.

Third period: 'Now'
- the emerging artists section towards the future.

Artistic development is constantly advancing, which means that 'now' is always the liveliest state. It also brings together yesterday and tomorrow, and its artistic direction is an ever-fascinating topic. The future direction of art is also one of the focal points that the Taikang Life

Art Collection has never lost sight of. Accordingly, we have paid attention to and supported the experimental explorations of young artists and made appropriate acquisitions of their work. This forms a special section of the Taikang Life emerging artists' Artworks Collection, which is our value judgment on the future of art.

Today, we present this Collection Exhibition under the title of Image · History · Existence. It is part of the collection assembled over ten years by Taikang Life, and a landscape of images of this kind can to some extent reflect our harvest of the three periods described above. It differs from an academic exhibition with a retrospective or summarizing aim, and its level of difficulty is somewhat higher than that of an exhibition based on the collected works in themselves. Although in the world of collecting in China today, ten years of perseverance may be considered a fairly long time, also having required a relatively early start, in terms of the historical and artistic developments that we are looking at here, ten years is still a very limited stretch of time, to which might be added that collecting is very much a question of chance. Sometimes one just misses out on acquiring an artwork. Other artworks one never encounters, and there are many artworks that we need, and that are missing from the Collection. The operational space allowed us in organizing an exhibition such as this one from a limited set of accumulated artworks is narrow, and there is little room for discretion. Taikang Life is honored to gather and look after this landscape of images on behalf of society, and hopes that the Exhibition will serve as a summary of this first period in the work of Taikang Space, and as a report to the Company, and that it will spur us on in our future work to continue to enrich it and to make it more perfect.

21 May 2011, Beijing

Tang Xin
Head of Collection, Taikang Life Insurance Co., Ltd.
Director & Curator of Taikang Space

作为收藏品的艺术品

汪民安

艺术品的价值在哪里呢？我们可以给出无数的答案。人们会说，它有特殊的风格和美学，可以供人们欣赏；它是历史的产物因而是人们进入历史的方便通道；它是某个人隐秘内心的泄露，可以借助于它窥视人性的秘密，等等。所有这些答案，都是将艺术品的价值和意义置于艺术品内部。但是，我们可以换一个角度说，艺术品的意义就在于它被收藏。一旦没有被收藏，艺术品就没有价值——它如果一直默默无闻地躺在艺术家的画室或者家里，它的命运就到头了——它就像没有来到这世上一样。或许，艺术品一旦诞生，它最隐秘的欲望不是被欣赏，而是被收藏。

艺术品的结局就是被收藏。但是，收藏艺术品，是为了去独自享受和占据艺术品的意义吗？事实上，几乎所有的收藏家都愿意将藏品展示给人，收藏家与其说是去垄断藏品的意义，不如说更愿意同人分享藏品的意义。而且，没有哪个收藏家长久而持续地注视着他的藏品。既然如此，收藏家是出于什么目的去收藏作品的？

对绘画的收藏，显然不单纯是因为绘画本身的内容——一些藏书家甚至乐意去搜集同一本书的不同版本，显然，激发他去收藏的不是文字的内容本身，而是书这一物质本身，是书的各种不同的印刷、装订和纸张形式，是不同年代的书籍形式。搜集一幅画，很可能是出于对这幅画本身的喜爱，但是，一旦搜集到手了，没有哪个收藏家会长久地欣赏这张画，他收藏的意义，在于占有这幅画，在于和这幅画发生一种特殊的独一无二的关系。收藏家的激情与其来自艺术品的刺激，不如说来自他自身对艺术品的占有欲。人们渴望获取一种对象，不是因为这个对象本身，而是因为占有者的渴望。

一旦占有了这幅画，画作本身的图像以及这图像所蕴含的意义，对他而言并不那么重要了，重要的是这幅绘画的物质性：或许，他将目光投射到画作的时候，目光的聚焦点是画框和画布，而不是画的图像本身，不是画面。收藏家哪怕看到一幅画作的背影也够了。就此，收藏家和画作最恰当的关系，不是一种看和被看的关系，而是一种拥有和被拥有的关系——甚至是触摸和被触摸的关系。对收藏家而言，触摸一幅画比观看这幅画能够更深地触动他：触摸，翻检，挪动，展开。一个收藏家在清理而不是在观看藏品的过程中获得极大的满足：往日的记忆纷纷涌现，他和藏品遭遇的那一刻像电影镜头一般地在他的心头回放。清理藏品的行为一再被回忆所打断，时间在悄悄地流逝……收藏家身不由己地将自己交付给了藏品。

藏品变成了他重要的生活伴侣。收藏家同自己的藏品相处的时间越久远，他就越对它们产生感情。他们生活在藏品中，和藏品相依为伴，被藏品所包围。如同一个读书人坐在书房中，只要有大量书籍做伴就可以获得满足，书的内容无关紧要。对于收藏家而言，他真正的享受不是来自对作品的观看，而是因为被众多作品所环绕。因此，收藏，一定在数量上要有所要求。偶然收藏一两件作品不能算是收藏家。只有大量地收藏，只有让自己的收藏品形成一个氛围，成为一个系统，才称得上是收藏家——没有一个收藏家觉得自己的藏品太多了，数量的要求是收藏的基本品质之一——一个真正的收藏家是从来不会罢手的，这既因为收藏行为本身的快乐在不停地驱使着他，也因为收藏本身就意味着一件无止境的行为。收藏是一个无限的行动：收藏家的死亡之日，也就是收藏行为的终止之时。这样，收藏成为收藏家的生活方式。将各种对象想方设法地纳入到自己的怀抱中，这是一件幸福至极的事情，为此，他们睁大眼睛，挑挑拣拣，四处寻觅，同竞技对手巧妙地博弈——收藏不仅是一种职业行为，也是一种生活方式。

收藏就此变成了一种恋物行为。这一行为，几乎将创造性的艺术品都转化成物质性本身。艺术作品的画面内容被悬置了，它们要么只能通过印刷品去曲折地传达，要么只是在公开展示的时候才能现身。一件艺术品，在被收藏和被展示之际，就显现出两个完全不同的意义：在被收藏起来的时候，绘画是一种物质存在，它等待着被触摸，手的触摸和目光的触摸；当被展示（展览）的时候，绘画作为视觉对象的存在物，它等待着被观看和欣赏。

对于收藏家而言，他收藏的画作难道不是一个特殊的物质吗？画作，从历史的深邃之处流淌下来，它们编织了自身的舞台和戏剧，从而镌刻了命运的诡谲。收藏家偶然获得了它，中止了画作的沉浮命运。他触摸着它，实际上也在触摸着历史。这同阅读不一样，阅读是通过文字进入历史，历史的获取是以文字作中介的，文字将历史间接地带到了作者眼前。而收藏家则直接拥有历史的一部分，他和历史发生了身体的连接，直接摸到了历史的物质，触摸到了这物质所镌刻的历史戏剧。他置身于藏品中，仿佛是这舞台剧的最贴近的观众。他的目光缓缓地掠过这些藏品，进入这些历史剧目的核心——这怀旧的目光是对命运的眷恋和爱抚。

但是，收藏也并不仅仅将藏品作为历史的身体来对待。实际上，藏品一旦来到了他这里，藏品在它漫无止境的飘零中又有了新的命运。收藏家将搜集来的藏品重新安顿，为藏品进行排序，将孤零零的藏品安排到一个秩序之中，让它和其他的藏品在收藏的密室中发生关联，藏品就是在这关联中重新获得了意义，藏品就此得到了更新。如同本雅明在谈论藏书的时候所说的："对一个真正的收藏家，获取一本旧书之时乃是此书的再生之日。"这个再生的藏品和其他的藏品发生了对话，一个收藏家的藏品来自五湖四海，每个藏品都包含着一个特殊的世界，这些完全是异质性的时空中诞生的作品，出于各种各样的原因，被收藏家聚拢起来。它们之间必定存在着沉默的抵牾。这种抵牾构成了这个收藏系统的特殊性。任何一种大规模的收藏，都是一种抵牾的体系：它居然将无限广袤的时空压缩在一个狭小的密室之中。置放收藏品的空间，既是封闭的，也是敞开的；既是沉默的，也是喧哗的。它们在倔强的冲突和臣服的协调中左右摇摆。正如艺术家创造了一个世界一样，收藏家也创造了自己的艺术世界，他的收藏过程，就是一种创造过程，他的收藏原则，就是他的创造原则。他建立了自己的风格，正如艺术家也建立了自己的风格一样。

这样，藏品一旦被收藏，它就摆脱了原作者的宰制，从原作者的系统中解脱出来。艺术品通常有创作者的签名，但是，在一个规模庞大的收藏室里，仍旧会为它编排一个序号。就像艺术家总要给他的作品签上创作的日期一样。一个收藏家的序号，乃是收藏家的隐匿签名。一件艺术作品一旦被收藏，它就同时性地获得了两个作者。两个作者——原作者和收藏家——赋予给它的两种不同的意义在它身上交汇。就此，藏品是收藏家和艺术家之间的一条连接线索。这两个人借助藏品发生了特定的关系：既是一种争执的关系——他们潜在地争夺作品的意义；也是一种友谊的关系——他们分享了一件作品，共同创造了这件作品。一件古老的藏品，就会穿越历史的雾霭将收藏家和艺术家连接在一起。

但是，任何一个收藏家都不能终结藏品的命运，藏品比他活得更久。这也意味着，艺术品的创作者只有一个，但是，它的收藏家则有许多人。它的命运就是与不同的收藏家相伴。它不仅将艺术家和某个收藏家联系起来，而且还将众多收藏家串联起来。就此，对于藏品而言，被收藏，不过只是一种临时寄居的形式。相对于自己的不死命运而言，藏品和某个收藏家的关系总是短暂的。收藏家在濒死的时候，要么将自己的藏品留给后代，要么为自己的藏品找到一个很好的继承人。藏品是收藏家最重要的遗嘱。在这个意义上，所有的收藏家扮演的既是继承人的角色，也是传承人的角色。宽泛一点地说，历史总是以收藏的方式延伸下来的。一件久远的艺术品注定会历经很多收藏家。这样，艺术作品在创作出来之后，它的历史存在方式，一方面是同许多读者和观众相遇的方式，另一方面，是和不同的收藏家的相遇方式。但是，人们讨论艺术作品的时候，总是讨论观众（读者）赋予艺术作品的意义，总是讨论艺术作品的展示意义，一部作品的美术史，总是观看的美术史，总是作品图像的美术史。

人们相信，艺术品只有诉诸视觉才能揭开它的意义。但是，在历史的大多数时刻，艺术品是藏在密室之中，它只和某个形单影只的收藏家相依为命。这是艺术品的暗室。但是，我们难道不能撰写这件艺术品的暗室的历史？我们难道不能从收藏的角度来写一部作品的艺术史吗？我们可以为一部作品写另一个传记，不是艺术家创造的传记，不是画面意义的传记，不是各个时期人们对于绘画进行解释的传记；而是它的收藏传记，它的旅行传记，它的流浪传记，它的沉默传记。这传记的情节就是它和收藏家的遭遇，它在藏家这里的寄居，离开，向另外藏家的转移，再次寄居，再次离开——这循环往复的寄居和离开的传记。这个传记之所以重要，是因为每一个物质都有其传奇人生；同时也因为，艺术作品同不同的收藏家相遇，它会打开不同的意义，它有不同的人生际会。每一次相遇都是唯一的，是不可复制的，因此，这相遇以及相遇打开的意义也是不可复制的。每个藏家激活的意义都是唯一的。一部艺术作品的收藏史，同样是这部作品的意义史。人们总是从艺术家的创作历史中去看待一件艺术品，但是，人们为什么不能将一件作品放到收藏家的收藏脉络中去看待呢？艺术作品和收藏家的相遇，既确定了收藏家的存在——一个收藏家是靠艺术品而存活于世的；也确定了艺术作品的存在——一个艺术品没有被收藏，即便它是一件杰作，也一定会在历史中销声匿迹。

真正的收藏家同公共收藏有根本的区别。在公共收藏——即博物馆和美术馆的收藏中，收藏者的个人趣味降到了最低。美术馆和私人收藏的一个重大差异在于，私人收藏完全取决于个体自身的选择，而美术馆（博物馆）收藏则取决于美术馆的公共功能——美术馆排除了个人趣味，有自己固定的冷漠规则——美术馆就是一个收藏和展览的机器，而艺术作品则是美术馆的功能配件，艺术作品的意义，不在于它自身，而在于它促发了美术馆机器的运转。美术馆一旦运作起来，艺术品就陷入了这运转机器的程序之中。艺术品服从于美术馆的制度。同人们所想象的相反，一个强大的美术馆，并不是对艺术品的庇护，而是对艺术品的调配，它并非艺术品的最好归宿——在美术馆中，没有一个人像收藏家那样对待和理解自己的作品，没有人像收藏家充满深情地将眷恋的目光缓缓地掠过这些作品——美术馆中的人是作品的看护者，而不是作品的拥有者。他们外在于作品，和作品并不构成一种私密关系。美术馆中的作品，尽管有时候享有被千万人目睹的巨大虚荣，但它一旦从展厅撤回到库房的时候，它便无人光顾，郁郁寡欢。这些作品，尽管它们会遭遇无数观众，无数和它有过肤浅接触的陌生人，但是，它和这所有的人之间都间隔着某种不可逾越的沟壑——它在孤独和虚荣之中摇摆。而收藏家的作品，尽管很少示人，但它并不孤独，相反，它自豪地拥有收藏家的全部激情，全部人生。

而收藏家呢？我们还是用本雅明的话来作结吧——也把这句话献给泰康在中国美术馆的收藏展——"闲人真幸福，收藏家真幸福。"

汪民安　哲学家，北京外国语大学教授

Artworks as Collected Works

By Wang Min'an

Where does the value of a work of art reside? We can answer this qustion in countless ways. People might say that it has a special style and aesthetic, and it provides people with enjoyment; it is a product of history and therefore it is a convenient way for people to enter history; it reveals the secret heart and mind of some person and can therefore be a way of peeping into the secrets of the human character; and so on. All of these answers place the value and meaning in the work of art itself. However, we can also say, from another angle, that the meaning of a work of art lies in its being collected. As soon as it is not collected, the work of art has no value. If it lies forever silently in the artist's studio or home, its destiny is over, and it might as well never have come into the world. Perhaps the most secret wish of a new-born work of art, is not to be appreciated, but to be collected.

The destination of a work of art is to be collected. However, is collecting works of art just for private enjoyment and possession? In fact, almost all collectors are willing to show their collected items to others. Rather than saying of collectors that they are monopolizing their collections, one should say that they are more willing to share them with others. Besides, no collector sits and gazes at his or her collection for long. This being so, what is the purpose of collecting artworks from the collector's point of view?

For collectors of paintings, it is clearly not purely about the content of the paintings-some book collectors will even happily accumulate various editions of the same book. Clearly, what stimulates them to collect is not the content of the words as such, but the book as a physical object, the various ways of printing and binding the book, the format of the paper used, and the forms of books of various periods. Collecting a painting is very possibly born of a fondness for that painting in itself, but as soon as it is in one's hands, no collector will enjoy looking at it for long. The meaning for the collector lies in possessing the painting. It lies in forming a unique relationship with it. The excitement of the collector and the stimulation that comes from the work of art should be considered to come from the desire of the collector to possess the work of art. People's yearning to obtain an object is not for the sake of the object itself, but for the desire of possessing it.

Once the painting is in one's possession, the image of the painting itself, and the meaning contained in that image, are no longer all that important to the collector. What is important is the materiality of the painting. Perhaps, when the collector looks at the work, the focus of the gaze is on the frame or on the canvas, and not on the image of the painting in itself. It is not about the painting. The collector might just cast a glance at the background of the painting, and find that enough. Therefore, the most appropriate relationship between the collector and the artist, is not one of looking and being looked at, but is one of possessing and being possessed, or even of touching and being touched. For the collector, it can be more exciting to touch a painting than to look at it: to touch it, flick through it, move it, open it up. A collector derives more satisfaction from the process of cleaning a collected work than from that of looking at it. Memories of the past well up, and the moment of the first encounter with the collected work is replayed as if with a film projector in the collector's mind. The action of cleaning the work repeatedly recalls what has been broken. Time is flowing stealthily by⋯and the collector involuntarily delivers him-or herself to the collected work.

The collected work becomes an important companion in the collector's life. The longer the collector spends with the work, the more feeling the collector generates towards it. Collectors live in their collections, relying on them as companions. They are surrounded by their collections. In the same way, a reader can sit in this or her study and achieve a feeling of satisfaction as long as there are a large number of books for company, the content of the books being of no significance. As for collectors, their real enjoyment does not come from looking at the works, but from being surrounded by a great number of them. Therefore, collecting definitely makes demands in terms of quantity. Collecting one or two works at random cannot be considered enough to make you a collector. Only if there is collecting on a large scale, only if one can let one's collection become an ambience, become a system, can one qualify as a collector. No collector thinks that his or her collection is too big. The demand for quantity is one of the basic characteristics of collecting. A true collector never gives up. This is both because the pleasure of the activity of collecting in itself ceaselessly spurs the collector on, and also because collecting as such is an activity without end. Collecting is an unlimited action: the day the collector dies is the day the activity of collecting ceases. Thus collecting becomes a way of life for the collector. Getting various objects into one's embrace by all the means at one's disposal is a thing of extreme happiness. It is for this that their eyes widen, that they pick and choose and look around in all directions, as if taking part in a game against a skilful competitor. Collecting is not just a professional activity. It is also a way of life.

Because of this, collecting has become a kind of fetish activity. This activity almost transforms the creative character of the work of art into a kind of physicality as such. The surface content of the work of art is suspended, and can either be conveyed through the tortuous process of going through published materials, or when it is publicly exhibited. Between being collected and being exhibited, a work of art only manifests two completely different meanings: when it is collected, a painting is a kind of material existence, it is waiting to be touched, touched by the hand and touched by the gaze; when it is exhibited, the painting exists as a visual object, and is waiting to be looked at and appreciated.

As for the collector, how could the collected painting not be a special substance? Flowing forth from the deep recesses of history, a painting weaves its own stage setting and drama, and thus fashions the intrigues of its destiny. The collector obtains it by chance, suspending the ups and downs of its fate. In touching it, the collector touches history. This is different from reading. Reading is entering history through the words, and history is obtained through the medium of words. Words indirectly bring history before the eyes of the agent. The collector on the other hand directly holds a part of history, and there is a bodily contact between history and the collector, who directly grasps its substance and touches the historical drama forged by this substance. The collector placing him-or herself in the collected work seems to be the most intimate audience of this stage drama. The collector's gaze sweeps past these collected works, and enters the core of their historical repertoire. This reminiscent gaze is an attachment and a fondness for fate.

However, collecting also does not in the least mean just treating the collected piece as a historical body. In fact, as soon as the collected work has arrived here, it has found a new destiny in its endless drifting. The collector re-settles the sought-out collected work, sorts it out anew and places the orphaned work in an orderly matrix, letting it establish connections with the other pieces in the collection chamber. In these connections, the collected work obtains a new meaning, and the collection is also renewed by this means. As Benjamin said about books: "I say that to a true collector the acquisition of an old book is its rebirth." A dialogue arises between the re-born collected work and the other works in the collection. A collector's pieces come from all over, and each piece contains a special world. These are works born in completely heterogeneous times and spaces, and they have arisen for all sorts of reasons before being gathered in by the collector. Between them there necessarily exists a silent discord. This discord forms the special character of this system of collecting. Any large-scale collection is a discordant system. It actually compresses the infinite vastness of time and space into a narrow little chamber! The space in which the collected pieces are placed is both sealed and open, both silent and noisy. In stubborn conflict and in submissive coordination, they swing this way and that. Just as the artist has created a world, the collector too has created his or her own world of art. The process of collecting is also a process of creation, and his or her principles of collecting are his or her principles of creation. The collector has founded his or her own style, just as the artist has founded his or her own style.

Thus, as soon as the piece has been collected, it throws off the domination of the original creator, and escapes from the system of the original creator. The work of art usually carries the signature of the creator, but if the collection is housed in a large space, it will still be given a serial number, just as the artist will usually like to write a date on his or her work. The serial number given by the collector is the collector's hidden signature. As soon as the work of art has been collected, it simultaneously acquires two creators. The two creators - that is, the original creator and the collector - provide it with the intersection of two different meanings. In this respect, the collected work is a connecting thread between the collector and the artist. On the basis of the collected piece, a particular relationship arises between the two: it is one of dispute - they are potentially fighting over the meaning of the work - and one of friendship. They are sharing a work and creating it together. An ancient piece may penetrate the mists of history to connect the collector and the artist.

However, no collector can end the destiny of a collected work. It lives longer than the collector. This also means that there is only one creator of the work, but many collectors. Its destiny is connected to various collectors. It does not only connect the artist with one collector, but also connects many collectors. Because of this, being collected is, for the collected work, just a temporary form of accommodation. In relation to its immortal destiny, the relationship of the collected work with any given collector is ephemeral. When the collector is on his or her deathbed, he or she can leave it to his or her descendants or find a good successor to the collected pieces. The collection is the collector's best testament. In this sense, all collectors play both the part of successor, and that of testator. Expressed more broadly, history is usually transmitted in the format of collecting. An ancient work of art is doomed to experience many collectors. In this way, after the work of art is created, the format of its historical existence is, on the one hand, one of meeting many spectators and audiences, and on the other hand, a format of meeting various collectors. However, when people discuss a work of art, they generally discuss the meaning given to the work by the audience (the spectator), and generally discuss the meaning revealed by the work. The fine arts history of a work of art is generally the fine arts history of beholding it, the fine arts history of its image. People are confident that its meaning can only be revealed by recourse to its visuality. However, at most times in history, works of art have been hidden in chambers. Their destiny has depended only on one solitary collector. This is the darkroom of the work of art. Yet why should we not be able to write the history of this darkroom of the work of art? Why should we be unable to write the art history of the work from the angle of the collector? We can write a different biography of the work, not the biography of the artist creating it, nor of the meaning of the picture, nor of the explanation of the work offered by people of various times, but the biography of its being collected, of its travels, of its roaming, of its silence. The details of this biography are its meeting with the collectors, its accommodation in their collections, its partings from them, and the moving on to other collectors, to their new residences and new departures - the biography of this repeated cycle of taking up residence and leaving. The importance of this biography is due to every substance having its own legendary life. At the same time, it is because, in the meetings with various collectors, a work of art may open up various meanings, and have various human encounters. Every encounter is unique and cannot be repeated. Accordingly, the meeting and the meaning generated by this meeting can also not be repeated. The meaning activated by each collector is unique. A history of the collection of a work of art is also the history of the meaning of this work. People usually look at a work of art from the angle of the creative history of the artist, but why can they not place the work in the context of the collection of a collector and deal with it in that context? The meeting of artwork and collector both confirms the existence of the collector-a collector exists in the world in reliance on works of art-and also confirms the existence of the work of art - if a work of art is not collected, even if it is a masterpiece, it will definitely disappear in history.

There is a fundamental difference between the true collector and public collections. In public collections, that is, collections in museums of art and art galleries, the personal taste of the collector is minimized. A great difference between art museums and private collectors is that private collectors rely complete on their personal choice, whereas art museums and museums in general collect in accordance with the public function of the art museum - art museums eliminate personal tastes. They have their own set of dispassionate rules. An art museum is an entity that collects and exhibits, and works of art are accessories of that function. The meaning of a work of art is not inherent in the work itself, but in its precipitation of the mechanical operation of the museum. As soon as the museum operates, the work of art falls into the operational program of the museum. The work of art submits to the system of the art museum. Contrary to what people imagine, a powerful museum does not protect works of art, but deploys them. It is not the optimal place for a work of art. In the museum, there is nobody who treats and understands the works as well as the collector, and nobody who lets his or her fond gaze linger over the works with the full emotion of the collector. The people in the museums guard the work, but do not hold it in their arms. They are external to the work, and do not form an intimate connection with it. Works of art in museums at times enjoy the great vainglory of being seen by hundreds and thousands of people, but as soon as they are dismounted from their exhibitions and returned to storage, they are seen by nobody, and are miserably alone. Although these works may encounter countless spectators and the superficial contact of countless strangers, they are separated from all these people by an impassable chasm. They swing between vainglory and solitude. The works of the collector, although they are shown to few people, are not lonely. On the contrary, they proudly hold all the passion and all the life of the collector.

And the collector? We can do no better than finish with another phrase of Benjamin's - and offer it to the Taikang Art Collection Exhibition in the National Art Museum of China:

"O bliss of the collector, bliss of the man of leisure!"

Wang Min'an
Philosopher
Professor, Beijing Foreign Studies University

收藏十年、赞助十年

唐昕

艺术生态的产生围绕的是艺术本身的属性和价值：学术价值和商业价值。生态格局构成围绕艺术大致可以归结为两大部分：其一，围绕"艺术创作"包括艺术家、批评（含媒体）、展览、美术馆；其二，围绕"艺术市场"包括画廊、拍卖、基金会、收藏。这两部分的核心则分别是：想法和钱。想法和钱如果能实现完美的结合，艺术社会化进程会大大加快，反之则会产生阻碍。

与国际成熟的当代艺术生态相比，在国内，当代艺术为人所知还只是这几年因价格高涨引起的，随之逐渐加入、参与进来的社会因素越来越多，局面越来越复杂，艺术生态的构成因素基本形成，但因位置和分工尚未明了，格局尚未清楚显现。这中间，围绕"想法"的部分发生较早，参与的人都是艺术界的行内人，相对成熟；围绕"钱"的部分则显得青涩很多，特别是从其他行业跨界参与进来的部分，多处于本能的对钱本身有认识，缺乏对艺术属性的基本认知，钱花得不够专业，或者根本花错地方的也大有人在。

收藏是对有意义物品的选择、收集和保藏的行为，其历史可能与人类文明历史一样久远，只是发展到今天我们谈的是有专业要求的收藏，与之相关的包括学术、文化意义、市场交易与公共收藏的关系等等许多方面，其核心是学术价值与市场体系。文化意义是指收藏行为最终留存和保护的是人类发展中一段段的文明史、文化史，这是公共收藏的初衷与最终目的。

在这个生态圈里，泰康人寿对当代艺术的参与是全方位的：想法＋钱。泰康空间是这个金融体制内的非金融部分——一个专业艺术机构，把泰康的钱与艺术创造有机地连在了一起。我们努力为泰康未来的美术馆做着多方面的准备和铺垫，首先是购买艺术品，建设泰康人寿体系化的艺术品收藏；同时以严谨的学术态度对艺术做持久的研究；一如既往地支持、赞助国内实验性的艺术探索。这几部分工作中，收藏是所有工作的最终目标。研究可以让我们保持理性，保持与流行观点的距离；持续有定位和方向的赞助，提供给自己特别好的观察和讨论的机会，让我们能看得更多更近，看到别人不容易看到的内容，对收藏提供非常有效的帮助。这些工作光有钱或者光有想法都是办不到的，它需要二者结合，也使二者更加有效地获得关于价值的判断。

摸爬滚打十年我们得到了一个关于泰康收藏的故事。

结缘

十年前的2001年，当代艺术在国内只是艺术圈内的事，社会上根本没人知道，偶尔看到、听说到的人只觉得它像个怪物，并不愿接触，更别说介入了。在圈内，人人充满热情和想法，每天想的除了艺术还是艺术，此外最多的渴望就是展览。但是全北京几乎完全没有可以提供给当代艺术做展览的场地，也根本找不到钱做个简单的宣传品。泰康与当代艺术结缘就在那段时期。

2001年春天，我策划的当代艺术展《中国人世纪肖像》一切就绪即将启程去德国展出，由于组织过程非常不容易，就想把已经成型的展览出去前找个地方在北京展一下。跟泰康的董事长陈东升先生相识多年，研究经济的他因为创办嘉德，早已在内心深处把艺术与社会发展联系在一起，对另类的当代艺术也有很理性的判断。对于我想要个展览场地和印个小册子的赞助要求，他毫不犹豫地答应了。这个展览参展的艺术家有方力钧、李大鹏、杨少斌和岳敏君，这是他们在国内最早的联展。开幕式当天，400平方米的泰康十一层多功能厅挤满了衣着奇异的、简朴得略显破旧的、邋里邋遢的艺术圈形形色色几百人，与第一次接待他们的现代化的、精致的白领环境形成强烈的反差，也让在这儿上班的很多人感到不舒服，不习惯。不过这次展览让艺术圈初识泰康，随后两年内泰康又赞助了另外几个我策划的展览，于是这里就被大家当成了一个点儿，成了北京城不足十个展览当代艺术的"固定"地点之一。

泰康顶层空间成立

有了这几次合作，2003年"非典"之后，我和陈董商量把这个多功能厅变成长期展厅，于是诞生了泰康顶层空间，我也被"收编"了。空间隶属于泰康人寿公益事业室，为公司回馈社会又增加了一种方式，"空间"的概念也首次成了国内命名艺术场所或机构的称呼，并且从形象上代表了这个地点较强的学术性。与此同时，以当代艺术活动与展示为核心的798艺术区正在迅速成长，里面还有一段佳话。

798一片蒸蒸日上的建设景象与北京城市改造的拆迁声相遇，798的去与留成了热议的话题。2004年3月，时任北京市政协委员的陈东升先生在政协会议上递交了呼吁保护798的提案，并在会上面向市长、市委书记和众委员发表演说，历陈北京的悠久文化历史和现代文化形象的重要性，列举西方发达城市中如巴黎左岸、纽约soho在城市现代文化形象建设中发挥的重要作用，热情洋溢地展望798的未来——把它打造成为北京的文化地标。精彩的演说，热烈的掌声，深深地打动了市政府领导，冯小刚等很多委员会后在陈董的带领下参观了798，亲身领略到了这里独特的魅力。深谙文化与社会发展关系的陈董，也切实地了解国内当代艺术的活力，他的提案和发言对市委领导的决策产生了关键作用，挽救了798的命运。自此，798也常常出现他邀约朋友共访的身影。

从长安街到798

泰康顶层空间初创，公司和领导对我并没有明确的要求，两年中可以随性地策划展览，热情和精力得到有效释放，从前举办展览的渴望缓解了许多，渐渐增加的却是更多的疑问：做这么多展览的目的是什么？泰康花这么多钱做展览干什么？泰康能得到什么？回馈社会这种缥缈的说辞能让空间在企业内部存在多久？798越来越多的专业机构有更好的条件做我们办不了的展览，泰康顶层空间继续存在的意义是什么？几个问题习惯性地跳了出来：泰康人寿要什么？有什么？能付出什么？我们这个公司内部最小的部门，能给公司什么呢？

这几个问题最好回答的是后面两个：它有钱，能出钱。它要什么呢？投资、产品、慈善、回馈社会、美术馆，都可能是公司对艺术的长期需求、愿望。在这个庞大的金融企业里除了陈董没人愿意看什么当代艺术展，每次展览都让其他想在这儿开会的部门牢骚满腹。原因很简单：展期一个月，每天看不见人来参观，他们开会也不能用。展出的内容常常也让他们无法接受：这些东西是不是有失公司体统？客户看见了对公司怎么看？他们态度真诚，担心此事对公司前程有影响，情感真切。有时，有人利用当天展览关闭后的时间在里面开会，便先要对作品进行一番处理：拿桌布把作品盖起来。或许他们真的很难面对这些"乌七八糟"的东西，更不知道他们内心怎么看我：一个成天跟污七八糟的东西和人搅在一起的人。有时，他们到高层领导那里告状，对于公司里一个只花钱不挣钱的人，尽管高层也不甚理解我存在的必要性，也不喜欢展览的东西，但因为对陈董的远见卓识深信不疑，他们都坚决服从陈董的安排，耐心平衡每次的矛盾。所以尽管不怎么受欢迎，在公司楼上办展览的日子我也没觉得太为难。

了解陈东升先生的人都知道，他坚信经济发展后文化的繁荣。他喜欢艺术，喜欢美术馆，经常利用在国外出差的机会带同去的员工参观美术馆。对于有些国外著名美术馆就像纽约MOMA现代艺术博物馆，最初是由民间力量建造的非常推崇，流露出对于大文化能力、大气魄的赞佩。他常说，泰康未来要建造自己的美术馆，话语中充满对泰康未来发展的憧憬和强烈的社会责任。由于常常与在京的使馆人员交往，有几次到欧洲办展览，我对西方艺术的社会化程度，对西方企业与艺术的关系，特别是大企业或金融企业的艺术收藏也略有了解。以陈董的气魄，建立泰康未来的美术馆是他的梦想，这应该就是泰康人寿想要的。

虽然没有正式的会议或成文的工作目标报告，"为了泰康未来的美术馆而努力"还是成了泰康顶层空间明确的长期工作目标，建立有意义的收藏也就成为首要任务。2005年我有了一个同事，虽然公司只跟他签了临时工作合同，但毕竟这个部门不再是我一个人跑单帮了。

如果说2006年到2008年当代艺术价格短时间暴涨让人记忆犹新，那之前的几年画廊和展览机构的飞快发展也恍如转瞬之间。正在我们寻找方向的时候，仅两三年的时间798就成了北京的当代艺术中心，规模巨大而且非常专业。各种具有国际水准的、专业而漂亮的、高大宽阔的展厅，和不知哪儿来的大量资金，打造出一个个宏伟制作的、极其国际化的展览。与它们相比，远在长安街畔的泰康顶层空间看起来"偏僻"、孤单，物理空间也完全不专业，不再被人想起，我们有点落伍了，有即将被人抛弃的危险。

北京的画廊数量猛增，竞争日趋激烈，对空间的硬件、资金、专业化要求越来越高。如果仅仅帮公司买东西，泰康顶层空间展览怎么办？明确了与公司的关系，有了长期工作方向，新的问题又出现了：好像我们光是作为一个企业的艺术品收藏部是不够的。习惯性的问题又跳了出来：泰康顶层空间要什么？有什么？能付出什么？

2006年年底我们搬到了798，藏身在一个安静的角落，展厅、办公全部面积只有100平方米，但是泰康顶层空间步入了新阶段。不是因为迁到798，而是因为我们找到了自己的定位，有了自己的空间理念——鼓舞与激励：鼓舞艺术实验精神；激励年轻艺术家实验探索。这个定位使我们找到了自己在艺术界的努力方向，隶属于金融企业的同时，自身也是独立的，是一个研究、支持实验艺术的专业机构。与其他机构的区别有二：其一，我们有一个明确的服务对象，泰康是我们的服务主体；其二，我们是以支持赞助而非交易为目的的非营利机构。这一年我们为公司买到了很多件好东西，孟禄丁、张群的《在新时代——亚当夏娃的启示》、肖鲁的《对话》等等。

买什么、展什么

对当代艺术我还算熟悉，这么多年对于艺术家和他们的作品还算清楚，但是给公司买东西跟给个人买东西不一样。公司有钱，但也不能见好的都要，或像私人藏家那样凭个人兴趣喜欢什么买什么，然后在一次次偶然的积累中再进行整理。那么多艺术家，每个人又有多个不同阶段，买谁的？买谁的什么？他们共同构成的收藏整体上是个什么？

我认为的当代艺术是80年代以来的实验艺术，艺术家感性的抒发，理性的复苏，艺术向本体的回归，艺术媒介实验的多元发展，一步步向西或向东的矛盾与徘徊，走到今天举世瞩目，与国内其他文化、经济、政治方面的步履是吻合的。这应该就是当代艺术的时代精神。哪些艺术家、哪些作品最能体现这些精神，代表每一步艺术的实验呢？建立以当代艺术发展为核心的收藏，宏观和具体的问题层出不穷，也带着我们越来越靠近了方向。此时，当代艺术市场从无到有到价格暴涨，快得超过了所有人的预料，势头非常猛烈，前一年100万嫌贵的东西，这时200万也不一定能买到了。收藏的市场因素眨眼之间又给我们提出了全新的课题——投资。

这个事儿对我们来说太陌生了，简单理解就是赚钱。当时形势一片大好，买什么都赚钱，只是东西涨得快慢不一样。不过，价格涨的情况跟我们对作品好坏的判断并不完全一致。谁能摸得着市场的脉，预计市场的涨落？谁知道买东西的人凭什么买什么不买什么？再说眼下的市场已经疯了，行情一天一个样，揣摩或者跟随市场简直太不靠谱了。

尽管身在798一个僻静的角落，每天还是能接触到很多形形色色社会上希望参与艺术的人，每天都遇到充满热情兴奋地计划或盘算着怎么下手或投资开画廊的人，每月似乎都有新的媒体创刊，众多新老媒体里除了计算拍卖作品几年几十倍的回报率，就是市场排行榜。多么不靠谱的事天天都在上演：谁谁被什么人包了，一年挣几百万；谁谁在机场两个小时说服煤老板在之后的半年内投资几千万开画廊，买东西；有钱的砸钱，花钱的烧钱，新鲜事奇怪事不胜枚举。艺术圈的人们随着财富的变化更是飞快地拉开了彼此心理的距离，不管是早已成名还是从不被知晓，不管是艺术家还是策展人或批评家，与谁为伴与谁为伍市场和行情说了算。人人胸中燃烧着欲望，但圈子里最多的还是跟艺术天天搅在一起却在市场之外的人，我们也在其中。我们常常在发现好东西的时候去拍卖一搏并不太参与一级市场交易，也就是说因为我们的定位是非营利性质，不以销售为目的，几乎完全不能帮艺术家赚钱，这对空间自己很有杀伤力，而且我们自己也赚不到钱。

价格的暴涨树立了无数的艺术家品牌，市场的红火更引来资本的介入，到2006年，798里满眼看到的都是钱的影子，各画廊、空间展览的状况已非昔日可比。到处都是大牌艺术家，到处都是高投入的制作，画册越来越厚、越来越精美，每周展览的开幕短信多得看不过来，投入百万的大展览一个接着一个，个个开幕式高朋满座名人云集。小小角落里的泰康顶层空间完全被沸腾的798吞噬了，狭小的场地，有限的展览经费，再也无法获得关注。与其他新进入但大手笔、大气魄、快动作的资本相比，泰康人寿的表现让艺术界备感失望，多少熟悉的艺术家跟我说："快让陈老板拿钱呀！"慢慢地人们的兴趣和信心转向了别处。最有说服力和号召力的就剩下钱了，虽然我们是自己出钱给人办展览，但这样的条件和境况，让我们甚至不好意思邀请有名气的艺术家合作，后来只好把目光转向年轻新人身上，以"新摄影、新绘画"作为空间短期的关注话题，举办了许多小型个展，吸引了跟资本尚无缘分的许多年轻艺术家。

虽然境况相当局促，但是我们没有忘记持续关注和支持当代艺术的实验探索，按照空间理念我们依然努力坚持对实验性创作给予力所能及的支持，并且把收藏遇到的问题和市场引发的思考也加入到日常展览的策划中。2006年我们启动了"一件作品"系列，项目是这样设定的：展览邀请一位成熟艺术家，再由他自行邀请另外一位成熟艺术家，两个人共同合作完成一件作品。项目旨在探讨成熟艺术家共同关心的话题，在市场强烈的干扰下成熟艺术家是否可能继续实验，以及具有条件的艺术家集体创作的可能性。到2007年底这个系列完成了三次项目：H+Y洪浩+颜磊，Z+C+S郑国谷+陈再炎+孙庆麟，L+C刘韡+陈浩语(秦思源)。在日日如节日的纷繁中，尽管规模不大，花钱不多，三个项目还是吸引了很多和我们一样关心实验的专业人士的注意，这让我们深感欣慰。

迁址草场地

2008年的金融风暴席卷世界，中国当代艺术市场的火热像经历了一场龙卷风，一夜之间变冷清了，又像被谁按了紧急制动按钮，瞬间停了下来。市场像个加速器，钱是动力源，钱不动，加速器也不转了。突然没有了加速器的艺术降落回自己的轨道上，大起大落之后无力地摇摇晃晃。也许是没有被之前的繁荣眷顾，饱受冷落，厌倦了798的摩肩接踵沸沸扬扬，重新调整了空间的定位之后，我选择了草场地的红房子。陈董亲自察看了这里的环境状况，对我们的新选择给予肯定。在2009年艺术界的一片寂静中，我们乔迁了，更名为泰康空间。

在798的两年半，重新调整的不光是空间定位，还有对价值的重新认识。市场教会我们区分不同的价值内涵来判断投资的长期短期；对国际战后以及经典艺术品市场的研究和参照，让我们明白要深挖更核心的价值支撑，以历史的眼光来考量身边的人和事以及泰康的收藏。于是我们把泰康收藏关注的历史阶段向前延伸，收藏有了更宏观的规划，空间理念也随之从原来的"鼓舞与激励"升级为"追溯与激励"，除了继续鼓励支持当代实验创造，更要追溯历史，了解它得以产生的更远的渊源。所以说，在798我们的收获是极大的。

泰康收藏和泰康空间的发展像两条线，既是平行的又是相互作用的。有了更清晰的认识，在草场地新空间开幕首展，——2009年10月我们同时举办了《泰康收藏摘要》和《51平方1#：赵赵》两个展览，正式向大家展示了泰康收藏的体系定位和泰康空间的新理念。

几年来公司对我们放手管理，给予充分自由，同时也在冷静观察和注视我们的每一步。多年的交流让公司逐步清楚和接受了我们的思考，除了收藏和空间理念，我们还做了更多长远的宏观规划，虽然没有听到领导的任何表态，信任仍然在无声中不断增进。几年来越来越多的公司高层对泰康空间的设置表示理解和认可，公司陆续给我们部门扩大人事编制，到2010年泰康空间团队搭建起来，编制增加到六人。我们按照专业美术馆的职能设计泰康空间的岗位职责，设置了收藏、策划、展览、宣传、行政五个分工，如果将来真能发展成美术馆，现在的每个岗位就是那时的一个个部门。空间的日常展览按照新的理念分为两个方向：对艺术过往的追溯，是针对成熟艺术家的再研究；对艺术未来走向的追踪，继续鼓励支持年轻艺术家的实验创作。艺术家是作品的创作者，是历史的书写者，我们锁定"人"——艺术家作为我们追踪的目标，展览、项目、研究、收藏都会以人为核心，从个案开始。以严谨的学术态度，以项目和展览的方式呈现我们的研究成果，再以这些研究和成果辅助收藏的判断，这就是我们目前的工作形态。同时，除了被收藏，艺术品也为公司的宣传、礼品等提供了更多服务，多年的同行让艺术正步入泰康人寿的企业文化，成为公司传统的一部分。

机构收藏

在艺术生态系统中收藏越来越重要，公共收藏、机构收藏、私人收藏连接起艺术与社会资源。目前国内的收藏多以投资为目的，充分利用艺术品特有的价值属性，这无可厚非。收藏本来就是资本的游戏，说白了收藏的就是价值，收对了就拥有真正的价值，不赚钱才怪呢；收不对可能拥有一时的伪价值或短期价值，不及时脱手，投资可能化为乌有。明确以赚钱为目的的收藏大多是短期的，因为需要变现。以中长期投资为目的的收藏需要巨大的资金实力，一般是大藏家和机构收藏者所为。投资收藏期间本业发展好的会持续收藏，不需要把藏品全部转化为资金投入到本业的再发展中，他们中随着收藏规模的不断增大，加上社会需要，政府支持，很有可能最终演变为民间美术馆，国外很多美术馆就是这么形成的。

泰康人寿属于机构收藏者，虽然明确未来要做美术馆，并不以中长期投资为目的，但从金融的角度说确实也还是中长期投资行为。如何让财富价值最大化？什么样的构成可以实现价值最大化？这里面真正的、持久的价值支撑是什么？不知道公司领导会不会想这些问题，但是从我们的角度是会追问的。为了实现未来的美术馆梦想，在没有理想的政策机制时，如何能让收藏走得更远，成长得更稳健，远到、大到足以成立美术馆的那一天呢？答案是收藏必须是赚钱的，赚多少与能走多远基本成正比关系，所以找到真正的价值支撑，构建最合理的配置，让单件作品间价值实现相互支撑进而构建规模价值。我们的做法是让收藏体系化，构建完整的文化景观，因为这样的构建是无法替代的。

依据美术史的发展，依据社会历史的变迁对文化艺术的影响，2008年泰康收藏有了自己的体系定位，即建立1942年以来的美术史意义的收藏，分为三个阶段，包括1942-1976、1976至今和青年专项部分（指向未来）。

美术馆

国内的艺术品收藏并不是新事物，有着悠久的历史，但从更文明更进步的现代收藏与社会的关系角度看，我们从未有过艺术的社会化过程，封建社会中艺术品从来都只属于少数人。19世纪中叶深受西方思想影响的社会改革人士，把博物馆视为倡导推广新文化的重要手段，开始建议兴建博物馆。之后，第一个以艺术珍品为主的博物馆始于1925年故宫博物院的正式成立和对社会开放，而第一个国家美术馆则是1936年在南京成立的国立美术陈列馆。

进入21世纪，博物馆、美术馆的发展进入一个新的阶段，特别是私人财富的快速增加，民间私营美术馆纷纷涌现，但是命运各有不同。不同的民间美术馆的背后都有一份热情、一份热爱、数目不菲的资金投入，也不排除一时的头脑发热，但不是所有美术馆都以收藏为基础，多数是先挂牌，有了美术馆的名声再以美术馆的名义做收藏，以获取更多的让利。但是由于对美术馆的投入和如何运作准备不足，持续的大量日常花费往往让他们始料不及，远远超过在收藏上获得的优惠，加上收藏的实际投入，很快便无力支撑了。更何况其中还有一些以美术馆的名义，只以收货为目的，并准备随时变现赚钱，这样的美术馆只是徒有虚名，根本算不上美术馆。

专业美术馆是以收藏为基础建立的，收藏有方向设定，或按历史，或按类别，或按地域等等。美术馆针对藏品进行深入的学术研究，按研究梳理出线索，据此策划陈列展出。在拥有和保藏巨大价值的同时，每个日常环节都需要大量资金来维护，美术馆是个真正烧钱的地方。再加上现阶段政府方面还缺少完善的鼓励和扶持政策，缺乏相关的法律法规的保护，所以在建美术馆之前必须做好多方面的充分准备，才不至于伤及可贵的热情和那份热爱，让投入的资金有去无回。

泰康人寿董事长陈东升先生的梦想是拥有泰康自己的美术馆，这也是泰康空间奋斗的方向。按照现阶段收藏体系的定位，我们希望未来观众可以通过美术馆藏品看到中国1942年以来的美术发展，和它与社会不同阶段文化变化的关系。它将是一段历史、一段文化和文明史，守护这样的财富，守护的是一份极大的社会责任。与艺术相伴的这十年，正是泰康人寿快速壮大稳步发展的十年，到今天，泰康人寿在陈东升先生的率领下，已经成为国内前五大寿险公司，保户数量、员工数量和资产规模都是实力雄厚的，相信未来泰康一定有办法、有能力、有实力以专业的、高水准的美术馆回馈社会，报偿时代。

从一个独立策展人，到今天以泰康人寿收藏部负责人和泰康空间艺术总监的身份回忆这十年，从我个人，到泰康人寿，到泰康空间，看时代在变，社会在变，艺术在变，收藏在变，泰康收藏在成长，泰康空间在成长。十年的坚持，十年的积累，泰康支持或赞助了艺术展览和活动数十个，参与的艺术家超过200位，单是用于展览活动的经费便逾千万，在付出的同时我们获得了艺术界一定的肯定，收获了更多自信，公司有了很多重要藏品。作为一个策展人，我感谢泰康人寿对艺术的慷慨支持；作为泰康人寿的员工，感谢陈东升先生以及邱希淳先生等其他领导给予我这么大的信任！感谢身边诸位伙伴毫无怨言的辛苦付出！祝愿泰康收藏继续，对艺术的支持继续！祝愿泰康美术馆的梦想早日实现！

2011.5.24 于北京

唐昕
泰康人寿保险股份有限公司 收藏部负责人
泰康空间 艺术总监 策展人

Ten Years of Collecting, Ten Years of Sponsorship

By Tang Xin

The ecology of art is produced around the properties and values of art itself: its academic and its commercial values. The ecological pattern constituted around art can generally be attributed to two major sectors: the first surrounding 'artistic creation', including artists, criticism (and media), exhibitions and museums; the second around the 'art market', including galleries, auctions, foundations and collections. The cores of these two sectors are ideas and money. If ideas and money can realize a perfect combination, then the process of the socialization of art can be very much accelerated, and if not, obstacles may occur.

Compared to the mature international ecology of contemporary art, the social factors that have come into contemporary art in China have, because of the well-known steep rise in prices over the last few years, gradually increased, and the situation is becoming gradually more complex. The factors that constitute the artistic ecology have basically been formed, but because its position and division of labor is not yet well understood, they do not yet appear clearly. The 'ideas' sector appeared fairly early. Involved in it were the professionals of the art world, and it is relatively mature. In the 'money' sector, a lot of sentiment appeared, in particular among those that crossed boundaries from other professions to become involved. Many of them were very instinctive. They had a good understanding of money as such, but lacked the basic knowledge about the attributes of art, and spent money in an insufficiently professional way. Many people at least in some instances fundamentally misspent it.

Collecting is the activity of choosing, gathering and safely storing meaningful works, and its history is perhaps as old as the history of human civilization. However, what we are talking about today is collecting with a professional view, which includes the relevant academic and cultural significance, the market transactions and relations with public collections, as well as many other aspects, the core of which is academic value and the market system. By cultural significance is meant that what the activity of collecting ultimately preserves and protects is the history of civilization and the history of culture in the various periods of human development. This is the original and the ultimate aim of public collections.

Within this ecological circle, Taikang Life's participation is holistic, that is, based on ideas plus money. Taikang Space is a non-financial part within this financial system. It is a professional art organization that connects Taikang's money with artistic creation organically. We strive in many ways to prepare the ground for the future Taikang Museum of Art, primarily by purchasing works of art and by establishing a systematice art collection for Taikang

Life. At the same time, we maintain sustained research in art applying a stringently academic attitude. As always, we support and fund experimental artistic exploration in China. Collecting is the ultimate goal of all these various aspects of our work. Research enables us to preserve our rationality, and to keep our distance from popular opinon. Sustaining the orientation and direction of our sponsorship provides us with a particularly good opportunity for observation and discussion, allowing us to see more things closer up, and to see contents that others cannot easily see, and it provides us with particularly effective assistance towards research. This work cannot be achieved if one only has money or if one only has ideas. It requires the combination of both, and also allows both together to reach a value judgment more effectively.

After ten years of striving we have managed to arrive at a story about the Taikang Collection.

First bonding

Ten years ago in 2001, contemporary art in China was something that only concerned people in artistic circles. In society as a whole, basically nobody knew about it, and people who by chance saw it or heard about it just thought it looked freakish and wanted nothing to do with it, let alone to get involved with it. Within contemporary art circles, people were full of enthusiasm and ideas, and thought of nothing else all day long - except that what they wanted most of all was an exhibition. However, in the whole of Beijing, there was hardly any space at all that could be used for an exhibition of contemporary art, and it was basically impossible to find money even to make simple promotions. The first bonding of Taikang with contemporary art occurred in that very period.

In the autumn of 2001, an exhibition of contemporary art that I had curated, Millennium Portrait of China, was all ready to be sent to Germany to be shown there. Because the organizational process was very difficult, I wanted to find somewhere in Beijing to show the Exhibition, which was already complete, before it went to Germany. I had known the CEO of Taikang, Mr. Chen Dongsheng, for many years. He had studied economics, and earlier, when he founded Guardian Auctions, he had linked art and social development in his heart and mind, and also had a very rational assessment of alternative kinds of contemporary art. At my request for sponsorship support for an exhibition space and for printing a small catalogue, he promised it without hesitation. Among the artists who took part in this Exhibition were Fang Lijun, Li Dapeng, Yang Shaobin and Yue Minjun, and it was the earliest exhibition in China in which they participated together. On the day of the opening, 400 square meters of the Taikang tenth floor multi-function hall was packed with hundreds of people of various kinds from within the art-world. They were dressed unusually, some of them so simply that they verged on shabbiness, and others more chaotically, forming a strong contrast to the modernized, immaculate, white-collar environment that was receiving them for the first time. This novel situation also caused the people who were working there some awkwardness. However, that Exhibition introduced the artistic circles to Taikang for the first time, and within two years Taikang sponsored two more exhibitions that I curated. Accordingly, this space became known by everybody as a hotspot, and it became one of the 'regular' exhibition spaces in the city of Beijing , where there were a few spaces then.

The Establishment of Taikang Top Space

After the SARS epidemic in 2003, when we had worked together several times, Mr. Chen and I discussed turning this multi-function hall into a permanent exhibition space. Thus Taikang Top Space was born, and I myself was also incorporated. The Space would belong under Taikang Life's Public Welfare Office, and the Company embraced this new way of giving something back to society. The concept of 'space' also, for the first time in China, became the name of an artistic forum or organization. In terms of image, Taikang Space represented the comparatively strong academic character of this location. By this time, the arts precinct 798 was rapidly growing as a centre for contemporary art activities and exhibitions, and here there is another good story.

When the wonderful structural landscape of 798 was linked with the news of the forced demolitions in the renewal of Beijing city, the question of whether 798 would go or stay became a hotly debated topic. In March 2004, Mr. Chen Dongsheng, who was a Committee Member of the Beijing Municipal Political Consultative Conference Committee, raised the case for the urgent preservation of 798 at a Committee meeting, and in a speech directed to the City Mayor, the City Committee

Secretary and the Committee Members as a whole, set out the importance of the image of Beijing's long cultural history and the city's modern culture. He referred to the important promotional use of, among other examples, the Left Bank in Paris and the SoHo precinct in New York in establishing the modern cultural image of advanced Western cities, and said that he fervently looked towards the future of 798 as a landmark in the culture of Beijing. His brilliant speech, and the enthusiastic applause that greeted it, profoundly moved the leaders of the City Government, and Feng Xiaogang and many other Committee Members after the meeting visited 798 under the guidance of Director Chen, so that they could personally experience the unique charm of this place. Mr. Chen, well-versed in the relationship between culture and the development of society, also genuinely understood the vitality of contemporary art in China. His suggestion and speech had a key function for the decisions from leaders of the City Government to rescuing the fate of 798. From then on, friends invited by him were also frequently seen around 798.

From Chang'an Avenue to 798

When Taikang Top Space was first opened, the Company and its leader made no specific demands of me. For two years, I could curate the exhibitions I wanted. My enthusiasm and energy found an effective release, and my previous desire to hold exhibitions to a great degree found an outlet. On the other hand, there were a growing number of questions: what was the purpose of holding so many exhibitions? What was the purpose of Taikang spending so much money on them? What could Taikang achieve? How long could the lofty expression of 'giving something back to society' allow the Space to exist within the enterprise? If more and more professional organizations at 798 could hold exhibitions under better conditions than we could manage, where was the sense in the continued existence of Taikang Top Space? A few habitual questions leaped forth: what did Taikang Life want? What did it have? What could it offer? We were the smallest part of this Company. What could we offer the Company?

The easiest answers to these questions were the two following ones: the Company had the money and could spend it. What did it want? Investment, products, charity, giving something back to society, an art museum… all these might be the Company's long-term needs and wishes for art. In this huge financial enterprise, there was nobody except Director Chen who was willing to look at any contemporary art. Every time there was an exhibition it made the other departments who would rather be holding conferences grumble and complain. The reason was simple. During the month that any given exhibition lasted, there were no visitors promotions. and the Space could not even be used to hold meetings. Even more frequently, the content exhibited was inaccessible to the other staff. Did these things not affect the decorum of the Company? What would the clients who saw them think about the Company? Their attitude was sincere. Worrying about whether this sort of thing would influence the Company's prospects was a valid emotion. Sometimes there were people who used the time after the exhibition closed to hold meetings in it, and they first had to deal with the artworks. They spread tablecloths over them. Maybe they really found it difficult to face messy chaotic things. Moreover did not know in their inner selves how to regard me: someone who spent all day in the company of messy things and people. At times, they reported back to the top leaders about this person who only knew how to spend the Company's money, and not how to make money for the Company. Although top management did not understand the necessity for my existence, and also disliked the things in the exhibitions, because of their unshakable faith in Director Chen's long-term vision, they were all determined to go along with his arrangements, and to patiently balance the contradictions every time. Thus, although the exhibitions were not all that popular, the days of holding exhibitions upstairs at the Company did not feel too hard.

As anybody who understands Mr. Chen Dongsheng knows, he firmly believes that economic development is followed by cultural flourishing. He likes art, and he likes museums of art, and when he is travelling abroad on business, he often takes the people he is travelling with to visit museums of art. He has the greatest respect for some famous foreign museums of art that were originally founded by non-governmental forces, such as the Museum of Modern Art in New York, and he shows great admiration for the enormous cultural ability and boldness of vision that truly powerful enterprises can wield. He often says that Taikang will found its own museum of art in the future, and his words are filled with vision and a strong sense of social responsibility in the future development of Taikang. As I am often in contact with people from the foreign embassies in Beijing, and several times have been to Europe to hold exhibitions, I have acquired some understanding of the degree to which Western art has become a part of society, and of the relations between art and

Western corporations, especially the collection of art by large enterprises and financial corporations. Judging by President Chen's boldness of vision, his dream is to found the future Taikang Museum of Art. This is what Taikang Life wanted.

Although there had been no formal meetings, nor any report in writing of the working goals, 'striving for Taikang's future museum of art' had nevertheless become the clear long-term working goal of Taikang Top Space, and establishing a significant collection was our first and foremost task. In 2005 I acquired a colleague, and although the Company only signed a temporary work agreement with him, from then on, our department was no longer managed just by myself.

If the explosive inflation in prices for contemporary art over the short period from 2006 to 2008 is still fresh in people's mind, then the development of galleries and exhibition organisations had also flown ahead during the preceding few years in what seemed like a flash. Just when we were looking for our direction, 798 became, in the space of two or three years, the centre of contemporary art in Beijing, on a huge scale and also in a highly professional way. Various amply spacious exhibition halls of an international standard, professional and attractive, and great amounts of funding, wherever it came from, created magnificent, extremely internationalized exhibitions. Compared to these, Taikang Top Space, situated far away by the side of Chang'an Avenue, seemed remote and isolated. The physical space was altogether unprofessional, people no longer thought about us, we seemed behind the times, and there was a risk of being abandoned.

The number of galleries in Beijing grew in a frenzy, the competition became fiercer by the day, and the demands of the hardware of the spaces, of the funding and of the professionalism became higher and higher. If it was only buying works for the Company, what should be done about Taikang Top Space? When the relationship with the Company had been clarified, when we had a long-term working direction, new problems appeared: we seemed to have become just the artworks-collecting department of an enterprise. It was not enough. Habitual questions arose again: what did Taikang Top Space want? What did we have? What could we deliver?

At the end of 2006, we moved to 798 and sheltered there in a quiet corner. The total floor area of the exhibition space and the office was one hundred square meters, but Taikang Top Space entered a new era, not because we had moved to 798, but because we had found our orientation, and our own spatial concept: encouragement and incentive. We encouraged the experimental spirit in art, and we provided incentives for young artists to experiment and explore. This orientation allowed us to find our own direction in which to strive in the world of art, and while we belonged to a financial enterprise, we ourselves were also independent. We were a professional organisation that researched and supported experimental art. There were two differences from other organisations. First, we had a clear object of service, Taikang Life being the main body that we served. Second, we were an organisation that used sponsorship rather than trade, that is, we were a non-profit organisation with objectives of sponsorship, not of commerce. In that year, we bought many works for the Company, including Meng Luding and Zhang Qun's In the New Age - The Enlightenment of Adam and Eve and Xiao Lu's Dialogue.

Buy Something, Exhibit It

I consider myself familiar with contemporary art, and having spent so many years with artists and their works, I consider that I know them well, but buying something for the Company is not the same as buying something for an individual. The Company has money, but it cannot desire to acquire everything that seems good, and unlike a private individual, it cannot buy everything it likes on the basis of personal interest, and then gradually organise what has been randomly accumulated. Among so many artists, each with his or her various periods, whose works should one buy, and which works? What kind of thing was the overall Collection that was made up collectively by them?

What I consider contemporary art is experimental art from the 1980s on. In the emotional expression by the artists and the recovery of rationalism, the artists have returned to the essentials, and the pluralistic development of artistic media, the step by step contradictions or hesitations towards West or East, have progressed until today, when they attract the attention of the world, in perfect step with other cultural, economic and political developments in China: this is the spirit of the era of contemporary art. Which artists and which artworks are best able to embody this spirit, and to represent the experiment of each step? In founding a collection with the development of contemporary art as its core, there are endless big-picture and specific questions that also bring us closer and closer to our direction.

At that time, the market went from non-existence to existence to an explosion in value, and it must soon surpass anybody's expectations. The momentum was violent, and things that could be bought for a million yuan renminbi one year earlier could at that time not necessarily be purchased for two million. In a moment, the market factors in collecting had raised a completely new subject for us, namely that of investing.

This was very foreign to us. In simple terms, it was about earning money. At the time, everything was propitious, whatever you bought made money. It was just that the rate of appreciation varied from work to work. Nevertheless, the particulars of the increase in prices were not quite the same as our judgment of the quality of the works. Who could gauge the pulse of the market and predict its rise and fall? Who knew on what basis buyers were buying some things and not others? When the market before you had already gone crazy, and prices were different every day, it was really too hard to figure out or follow the market.

Although our physical presence was in a remote corner of 798, there were still opportunities every day to connect with of people of all sides of society, who were hoping to have something to do with art. Each day we met people who were enthusiastically and excitedly planning or calculating how to get started or to invest in opening art galleries. New publications seemed to be founded every month, with plenty of new and old media that, in addition to calculating the rate of return for auctioned works over so many years, were simply the rating charts of the market. So many odd things were played out every day. Who had been rolled by whom, who had made so many millions in a year, who had persuaded a coal boss over two hours at the airport to invest tens of millions of dollars in opening a gallery and buying works in the next six months. The ones who had money were throwing it around, and the ones who were spending money were burning it. There were fresh and curious stories too numerous to mention. People in art circles even more swiftly put mental distance between one another according to their changes in fortune. Regardless of whether they had early become famous or had never become known, regardless of whether they were artists or curators or critics, the money and the prices had the last say in who became whose partner, and with whom one formed a team. Desire burned in people's breasts, yet within art circles, most were still involved with art on a daily basis and stood outside the market, as did we. When we discovered something good, we often went to auctions to have a try, but we did not get too involved with the primary market transactions at all. In other words, because our orientation was of a not-for-profit character, and we did not have re-sale as our aim, we could hardly help artists make money at all, which was lethal to the Space itself, and also meant that we could make no money ourselves.

The soaring prices established the brand names of countless artists, and the red hot market attracted even more investors to enter. By 2006, the shadow of money had spread all over 798. The circumstances of exhibitions in each gallery and space were changed beyond recognition from previous times. Everywhere there were big-brand artists and high-input productions. Catalogues became thicker and thicker and more and more exquisite, and sms messages about exhibition openings every week were so numerous that one could not get round to reading all of them. Big exhibitions representing million-dollar investments followed one after another, and distinguished celebrities attended every opening ceremony. Taikang Top Space in its tiny corner was swallowed up completely by the raging 798, and the cramped exhibition space and limited exhibition expense account could no longer generate any attention. Compare with the other capital there, recently entered but generous, enthusiastic and fast-moving, Taikang Life's presentation produced a feeling of disappointment in the artists, and many artists I knew well said to me: "Let your boss Mr. Chen pay some money soon!" Slowly people's interest and confidence turned elsewhere. The most persuasive force and the most appealing one left was money. Although we ourselves funded exhibitions for people, these conditions and this situation made us feel embarrassed to invite famous artists to work with us, and later all we could do was to turn to young new artists, in the short term taking "New Photography, New Painting" as the headline topic of the Space, and holding many small-scale individual exhibitions, attracting many young artists who had not yet connected with capital.

Although conditions were fairly constrained, we had not forgotten to continuously pay attention to, and provide support for, experimental explorations in contemporary art, and according to the conception of the Space, we still worked hard to maintain the provision of as much support as we could to experimental creation, and to make allowance for the problems encountered in collecting and the reflections generated by the market into the everyday curating work for our exhibitions. In 2006 we set in motion the "One Work" series. This project was set as follows: for the exhibition, one mature artist would be invited, and this artist would invite another mature artist, and together they would create a work. The project was aimed at exploring whether or not the mature artists could, subject to the intense interference of the market, continue to experiment with topics that the artists both cared about, and at exploring the possibility of the conditional collective creation by the artists. By the end of 2007, three projects had been completed in this series: H+Y:Hong Hao+Yan Lei, Z+S+C:Zheng Guogu+Sun Qinglin+Chen Zaiyan, L+C:Liu Wei+Chen Haoyu (Qin Siyuan). Although their scale was not large, and the amount of money spent not enormous, in the buzz of days that passed like festivals, the three projects still attracted the attention of many professionals who, as we did, followed experimental art, which allowed us to feel very pleased.

Moving to Caochangdi

In 2008, the storm of the Great Financial Crisis swept the world. The heat of the market for Chinese contemporary art seemed struck by a storm and became cold overnight, as if someone had hit the emergency brake button and brought it to a halt in an instant. The market is like a booster engine with money being its source of power. If the money doesn't move, the booster engine stops turning. When there was suddenly no booster engine, art fell back into its own tracks, staggering along listlessly after its great rise and fall. Perhaps it was because we were not blessed by former glory, but, suffering from cold, we tired of the jostling and the hubbub of 798, and, having adjusted the orientation of the Space afresh, I chose the red buildings of Caochangdi. President Chen personally inspected the conditions of this environment, and affirmed our new choice. In the quietude of the art world in 2009, we moved and changed our name to Taikang Space.

After the two and a half years in 798, we readjusted not only the orientation of the Space. We also gained a new understanding of value. The market had taught us to distinguish various kinds of value content, so that we could decide on long-and short-term investment. Research in and reference to the international post-War and classical artwork market allowed us to understand that we must ferret out the more fundamental values to support, measuring the people and things around us - and the Taikang Collection - according to the light of history. Accordingly, we extended the historical period in Taikang's sights. Once the Collection acquired a wider program, the concept of the Space accordingly rose from "encourage and support" to "trace back and support". Apart from continuing to encourage and support contemporary experimental creation, we wanted to trace back history, and to understand the deeper sources of what it could produce. Therefore, our harvest from 798 may be said to have been very significant.

The Taikang Collection and the Taikang Space seem to have developed along two lines, both parallel and serving an interactive purpose. We now had a clearer understanding, and for our opening show in the new Space in Caochangdi, we simultaneously held the two Exhibitions A Selection of Taikang Collection and 51 Square Meters, thus formally showing everybody the systemic orientation and new concept of Taikang Space.

For several years, the Company has relaxed its management of us and given us full freedom, and at the same time it is impassively inspecting and paying attention to our every step. Many years of interaction has gradually allowed the Company to become clear about and accept our considerations, and in addition to the collecting and the concept of the Space, we have made more long-term macroscopic programs. Although we have not heard any expression from the leadership on this, confidence is continuously growing in the silence. At the higher levels of the Company, there have for several years been more and more people who have expressed their understanding and recognition of Taikang Space, and the Company has progressively increased the staffing in our Department. By 2010, the Taikang Space team had been built up and increased to six people. We have designed the job responsibilities of Taikang Space according to the functions of a professional art museum, setting up the five labour divisions of collecting, curating, exhibiting, public relations and administration. If we do develop to the art museum stage in the future, each current post will then become a separate department. The everyday exhibitions of the Space are divided into two directions according to the new conception. One pursues the past of art by researching mature artists afresh. The other tracks the future direction of art, and continues to encourage and support the experimental creations of young artists. Artists by creating their works also write history. We lock in 'people' - the artists serve as the objects of our tracking. Exhibitions, projects, research, collecting all begin as individual cases with people at their core. With a rigorous attitude to research, and in the format of exhibitions and projects, we present the fruits of our research, and then we again use the results this research to assist in our judgments about collecting. This is our way of operating at present. At the same time, as well as being collected, the works of art also serve purposes in the public relations of the Company, as gifts and so on. Many years of travelling together allows art to enter the corporate culture of Taikang Life, and to become part of the Company tradition.

Institutional Collecting

In the ecological system of art, collecting is becoming more and more important, and public collections, institutional collections and private collections link art with the resources of society. At present in China, collecting mostly serves the purpose of investment, and makes full use of the special value attributes of works of art. There is nothing wrong in that. Collecting is in itself a game of capital, and frankly, what is collected is the value of the artwork. If the collector gets it right, then there is real value, and it is only if the collector does not make money that it is considered strange. If the collector gets it wrong, the work may possess for a while a specious value or a short-lived value, and if the work is not sold in time, the investment may come to naught. Most collecting that is carried out for the clear purpose of making money is short-term, for any profit needs to be realised. Collecting for medium- to long-term purposes requires great funding power, and usually only great collectors and institutional collections can manage it. If the business develops well in the period of investing in collecting, it will continue to collect. It does not need to convert the collected works into capital to invest back into re-development of the business itself. As the scale of the collection increases constantly, added to which there are the factors of the requirements of society and of governmental support, some collections may very well ultimately become private - sector or non-governmental museums of art. There are many art museums abroad that were formed in just this way.

Taikang Life is an institutional collector. Although it is clear that we want to become a museum of art in the future, we do not at all have medium- to long-term investment as our primary goal. However, from the financial point of view, our activities are indeed indistinguishable from medium- to long-term investing. How can we maximize the monetary value? What kind of structure can help realize the maximizing of value? What is the true, lasting value support here? I do not know whether the leaders of the Company think about these questions, but we examine these questions closely. To realize the dream of the future museum of art at a time when the policy mechanisms is no good, how can we make the Collection go further, grow more robust, far enough and big enough to reach the day when it can form a museum of art? The answer is that the Collection must make money. Basically, what it can earn is directly proportional to how far it will go, so in finding a true support for the value, in structuring the most rational allocation, in allowing the value realization among the individual works of art to be mutually supportive so as to structure values of scale, our way of doing things is to allow the Collection to become systematic, and to construct a complete cultural landscape, for we consider this kind of structure indispensible.

In accordance with the development of the history of fine art, and with the influence of the vicissitudes of social history on art, the Taikang Collection acquired its own systemic orientation in 2008, namely as a collection about the meaning of the history of fine arts founded in 1942, divided into three periods including 1942 - 1976, 1976 to the present, and the Special Youth Section (towards the future).

The Museum of Art

The collecting of works of art in China is not at all a new thing. It has a long history, but we have never had the process of a true socialisation of art, in the relationship between a more civilised, more progressive modern collection with society. In feudal society, works of art always only belonged to a small minority of people. In the middle period of the nineteenth century, social reformers who had received the deep influence of Western thinking, began to regard museums as an important device in promoting and disseminating new culture, and began to suggest their construction. The first museum to focus on art treasures was the Palace Museum formally established and opened to the public in 1925. However, the first national Museum was the National Art Gallery founded in 1936 in Nanjing.

Entering the twenty-first century, the development of museums and art museums has entered a new period. In particular, it is the rapid increase in private wealth that has allowed the proliferation of non-governmental museums, but their fate varies. Behind the various non-governmental museums, there is always a portion of enthusiasm, a portion of devotion, as well as a considerable amount of funds that have been poured into them - and let us not rule out a moment of hotheadedness. However, not all these museums are based on collections. Most of them first announce their brand-name, and then, when they are known as art museums, they use this prestige to collect works to achieve even more profit sharing. Yet, because the investment in the museums and their operation are insufficiently prepared, the great amount of money required for the daily expenses of continued operation often causes them to fall short of their expectations, far surpassing the value of the preferential treatment they receive in collecting. In addition, there is the actual investment in collecting, so that very soon, they lack the strength to carry on. Moreover, some of them use the prestige of being a museum of art solely for the purpose of receiving artworks and preparing to realize them at the first opportunity to make money. This kind of art museum perhaps only has the name temporarily daubed on it, and cannot be considered a real museum of art at all.

A professional museum of art is founded on the basis of a collection, and the collection will have some set direction, whether based on history, genre, geographical area, or whatever. The museum of art will undertake a deep academic study of the works collected. According to this research it will sift through the clues, and on this basis arrange and exhibit the works. At the same time as great value is held and preserved, every ordinary relevant area requires a great amount of funding to maintain. A museum of art is a real money-burner. Yet again, at present there is a lack of healthy encouragement and of supportive government policies, and a lack of relevant protective laws and regulations. Therefore, before one founds a museum of art, one must make many thorough preparations to avoid harming the precious enthusiasm - that 'portion of devotion' - and avoid the irrevocable loss of invested funds.

The dream of Taikang Life's CEO, Mr. Chen Dongsheng, is for Taikang to have its own museum of art, and this is the direction also of Taikang Space's striving. According to the current orientation of the system of collection, we hope that the public in the future will be able to see in the collected works, the development of Chinese fine art since 1942, and its relationship with the cultural changes in society in various periods. It will be a history, and a history of culture and civilisation. Guarding such wealth is an enormous social responsibility, and Taikang definitely has the way and the means, the ability and the power to give something back to society with this professional, high-standard museum of art, and thus to reward the era.

Remembering these ten years, from being an independent curator to achieving the status of being responsible for the Collection department of Taikang Life, and Artistic Director of Taikang Space, from being an individual to joining Taikang Life, then to directing Taikang Space, I have watched the times changing and society changing, art changing, collecting changing, the Taikang Collection growing and Taikang Space growing. In ten years of persistence and ten years of accumulation, Taikang has supported or sponsored scores of art exhibitions and activities. More than two hundred artists have taken part. More than ten million yuan renminbi has been spent on exhibition activities alone. In paying this out, we have achieved some recognition and more self-confidence in the world of art, and the Company now holds many important works in its collection. As a curator, I thank Taikang Life for its generous support of art. As an employee of Taikang Life, I thank Mr. Chen Dongsheng and the other leaders especially Mr. Qiu Xichun for having such confidence in me. I thank all the colleagues by my side, who have readily given their hard work. I wish that the Taikang Collection will continue, and that its support of art will continue. I hope that the dream of the Taikang Museum of Art will be realised at an early date.

24 May 2011, Beijing

Tang Xin
Head of Collection, Taikang Life Insurance Co., Ltd.
Director & Curator of Taikang Space

革命与启蒙

跨越1942年至1989年，涵盖了从中国革命时代到上世纪80年代文化艺术启蒙时期40余年间美术史上的8件经典之作。这里面既有艺术家针对中国革命和新中国建立后的历史巨变所做的忠实于历史的、饱含激情的创作；也有对中国的艺术实践与理论多元化及人文主义有着启蒙作用的重要作品。这些作品既是表现艺术家代表性艺术语言的巅峰之作，具有极高的艺术研究价值，也是见证历史发展轨迹的珍贵文献。泰康人寿以对历史负责任的态度收藏并保存这些作品，旨在为1942年以来的中国现当代历史与艺术研究提供第一手资料，同时积极地通过展览回馈社会，使更多的社会公众看到、了解这些作品。

Revolution and Enlightenment

The years over 1942 until 1989 are covered by eight classical works in the art history of the forty - odd years from the Chinese revolutionary era to the period of cultural and artistic enlightenment of the 1980s. In this period there were not only the passionate, historically faithful artworks created by artists in response to the great historical changes of the Chinese Revolution and of the period after the foundation of the new China, but also important works that served the purpose of enlightenment with regard to artistic experimentation, theoretical pluralism and humanism in China. These works not only show the representative peak of the artistic language of the artists, but also have high value for art research and are important documents that provide evidence of the trajectory of the development of history. Taikang Life has collected and preserved these works in an attitude of responsibility to history, as providing firsthand materials for contemporary Chinese history and research in art since 1942. At the same time, Taikang Life has also positively given back to society through exhibitions, allowing even more members of the public to see and understand these works.

从民国风度到延安精神
——摄影大师吴印咸的"一张座右铭"

斯然畅畅

1942年,毛泽东在延安窑洞前给120师的干部们作报告,这是中国共产党重要的"整风运动"中的一个事件。为了记录下这历史性的时刻,摄影大师吴印咸拍摄了这张堪称经典的人物肖像作品——《1942年毛泽东在延安窑洞前的报告》。照片中的毛泽东身着粗布灰制服,裤子上打着两块大补丁,脚上穿着土布鞋,艰苦朴素的延安精神在这身行头中体现得淋漓尽致。他站在一个小方凳前,以殷切诚挚的目光注视着广大干部,身体稍向前倾,打着富有表情的手势。虽然只拍了一个人物形象,却使人觉得广大干部就在画面之外,与主席的眼神相互交流,正在全神贯注地听报告。

除了对人物外形特点的细致表现,对最佳神态的敏锐捕捉,这张照片的构图和光影也可圈可点。画面约三分之一的上部,是当时共产党人办公和居住的窑洞,分割建筑物与作报告空场的是略向右上方倾斜的地平线,与地面上平行排列的三个对角线方向的细长人影走向基本一致;而窑洞上一扇凹陷的宽阔窗子和两块矮墩墩的建筑投影,则与这些同样是深色的细线呈垂直关系——它们共同构成一个结实稳定又不失优雅从容的背景框架,十分恰当地衬托出前景中央站立的主席形象。他前倾的身形在这个精心营造的构图中显得生动、潇洒,又充满均衡的庄重感。尤为有趣的细节是画面右侧的小方凳,它的前倾角度与主席几乎完全一致,就像一个压轴的小音符,为整个乐章画上完美的句号。

这张照片与白求恩大夫的照片曾一直挂在吴印咸的房间里。他曾幽默地说:"人家的座右铭是格言,我的座右铭是照片。"而这两张"座右铭",恰是吴老进入延安之后拍摄的最广为人知的照片。如果说,这两张照片中,精湛的摄影技艺来自吴印咸早年在上海的学习与工作经历,那么人道主义的观念和共产主义的理想,则是延安教给吴老的另一笔财富。

在上海:学画、买相机和拍电影

就在拍摄这张照片的同一年,吴印咸加入了中国共产党。1938年9月,在袁牧之的动员下,他从香港抵达上海经武汉到延安,最初只是为了拍摄一部反映延安地区抗战情况的纪录片《延安与八路军》。吴印咸原本打算拍完纪录片便返回武汉,可是,当时他并没有想到,这次多少有些偶然的延安之行,竟然成为他人生的转折点。

吴印咸,字至甫,1900年9月21日出生于江苏省沭阳县。他的父亲是一位清末秀才,毕生以教书为业。尚在父亲创办的县立高等小学读书时,吴印咸便表现出超常的艺术天赋,尤其喜爱绘画、书法、篆刻,深得父亲赏识。1916年高小毕业适逢沭阳水灾,印咸考入半工半读的江苏省立第四工厂。在这家生产棉布和线毯的工厂,他半天学文化知识,半天当织毯工人,还设计出新颖的地毯图案,获得技师的认可和市场的欢迎。1919年,在亲戚和朋友的资助下,他考入上海美术专科学校,开始接受正规的绘画训练。

这时的上海美专,已经突破了初创期传习所性质的教学水平,办学宗旨"由单纯培养图画人才转变为力求改变中国现状,促进艺术振兴,同时也反映了对西方文化艺术吸收融合的基本思想"[1]。课程设置发生重大调整:"一九一六年六月改绘画科为西洋画科,定修业期限为三年,学实技外并重各种原理,添设透视学、美学、美术史,废选科。一九一八年,鉴于各处学校艺术教师之缺乏,设技术师范科,实技手工、图画并重,并注意各种原理。一九二〇年重订西洋画科、国画科、雕塑科、工艺图案科、高等师范科、普通师范科;普通师范科修业期定为一年半,其余各科学程均为三年。"[2]在教学方法上,把"写生"作为西洋画教学规范也是从这里肇始的,陈抱一记述道:"以当时的情形,固未能一步即开始人物写生,但至少感到临画教法大可废除,而代之以写生法为主要的基本课程。"[3]吴印咸入学

---

1 马琳:《周湘与上海早期美术教育》,天津人民美术出版社,2007年5月,第123页。
2 刘海粟:《上海美专十年回顾》,《中日美术》1922年7月20日第1卷第3号。
3 陈抱一:《洋画运动过程略记》,《上海艺术月刊》1942年4月第6期。

后，上海美专的教学已经步入正轨。雄厚的师资力量不仅提供了社会关系和资金支持，也带来综合性人文教育的机会，如20年代曾请梁启超来讲过《美术与人生》《达·芬奇的生平和艺术成就》《论创作精神》等。在这样的学习环境中，吴印咸既通晓了写生造型的技法，又接触到理论文化的熏陶。这些都为他后来的创作奠定了坚实的基础。

然而，在旧货场用三块银元买来的一台美国产的勃朗尼牌旧照相机，改变了吴印咸的学画之路，从此他与拍摄影像结下了终身的缘分。1923年他在江苏老家任教期间，拍了早期摄影作品《晓市》，剪影的人物在城门框出的拱形空间中形成清晰的节奏感，体现出他在光影、构图方面对摄影的探索。1930年拍摄的《力》，也是一个从美学角度探索画面因素的好例子，明暗对比和投影构成的肌理效果，刻画出男人体健美的姿态。1934年的《田螺》还获得了瑞士摄影沙龙荣誉奖。如果说这些作品与他的艺术学习有直接关系，那么几乎同时，吴印咸也对社会现实问题倾注着一个艺术家的关怀和思考。1924年的《饥寒交迫》和1930年的《赌》就是这方面的代表作。当时在照相馆任职的吴印咸结识了左翼进步人士沈西苓、田方、司徒慧敏等人，从此进入左翼电影人的行列。

1935年在夏衍的《风云儿女》中，他第一次担任了电影摄影师。次年又拍摄了袁牧之的《马路天使》，这部影片可谓是中国电影的里程碑："可以说中国电影从《马路天使》起，无论在叙事方式、表演水准、摄影技巧、电影音乐还是在美术设计与制作等方面，开始具有了好莱坞电影模式的民众梦幻般的社会图景。"[4] 1982年的"中国电影五十年回顾展"开幕式上放映了《马路天使》，意大利影评家达西拉奇惊叹不已，他在《团结报》上以显著标题写道："新现实主义诞生于上海。"而在此之前，国际上始终认为"新现实主义"是意大利对世界电影的一大贡献，其实在很大程度上，可以说这就是吴印咸的创作。他借鉴了美国好莱坞商业片的场景调度和蒙太奇手法，以写实的镜头编辑出超现实的空间关系，凸显人物刻画。宫林认为，这部电影"主要的场景关系就是上海的'下之角'贫民窟……每个人生活的空间关系是不明确的，总是在明灭不定的光影中出画入画，遮掩了具体的、实在的空间质感"。[5] 吴印咸在《马路天使》时期已经基本形成了自己的拍摄风格，这种通过精心设计的构图关系来衬托主体人物的拍摄手法，一直体现在延安的纪录片和照片中。

"左翼电影在对过去漠视现实生活、宣传侠道商业电影的反拨中，倡导关注现实，反映社会时代精神的创作，对电影创作产生了积极作用。中国电影的题材得以扩大，清新气息得以出现，真实生活内容得以复现。30年代成为中国现实主义兴盛的第一个高潮时期。"[6] 吴印咸参与了这个现实主义的高潮，更加明确了艺术创作的价值观。1937年应西北电影公司之邀，吴印咸赴太原拍摄影片。由于七七事变爆发，拍摄中断，但留下了这次拍摄的反映战时饥荒的《乞斋果腹》，这是一张纪录片式的静态摄影作品，也可以视为他后来选择留在延安的先兆。

到延安：拍摄纪录片、白求恩和领导人

袁牧之邀请吴印咸来延安拍电影，第一件事却是让他在武汉与荷兰导演伊文思秘密接应，接收伊文思赠送的"埃姆"摄像机和胶片。由于延安地区缺乏摄影设备，而正在拍摄《四万万人民》的伊文思又无法获得进入延安地区的官方许可，所以他想把自己的设备送给中国自己的摄影师，来拍摄延安的纪录片。这可以算是吴印咸第一次执行党组织委派的工作。当黑暗中伊文思匆忙地把东西交给他，并用不熟练的中文低声说"延安，延安"时，吴印咸与伊文思握了握手，便离开了。20年后他们才又见了一次面，终于看清了对方的容貌。司徒兆敦曾说："后来他[指伊文思]和吴印咸见面握手时，我说你们俩是世界上唯一的握过两次手只见过一次面的人。"[7]

了解到延安的条件如此艰苦，吴印咸用自己有限的钱买了三台照相机带到延安。一台是德国"维阿他"135相机，一台是德国"伊可弗莱斯"120双镜头相机，还有一台是专门拍摄4英寸以上照片的木壳照相机，后来因为在延安搞不到专业胶片，改作放大机使用。吴印咸用的就是前两台照相机，在延安和华北抗日前线拍摄了许多珍贵的历史照片，其中包括八路军"自己动手、丰衣足食"的垦荒场面，白求恩大夫冒着火线逼近的危险抢救伤员的珍贵画面，还有毛泽东等领导人在延安的日常工作与生活中的音容笑貌。

1938年，延安电影团成立后，拍摄了第一部纪录片《延安与八路军》。有一次，吴印咸和助手徐肖冰刚刚把摄影机拆开准备修理，便遇上日机空袭。一颗炸弹落在附近，震塌了他们所在的房子一角，吴印咸一下子扑到拆开的机器上，不顾一切用身体挡住掉下来的碎石和瓦砾。飞机还在天空盘旋，吴印咸和徐肖冰从碎石土中爬出来，把拆开的机器零件收拢，然后才躲到墙

4　宫林：《中国电影美术史》，山东美术出版社，2007年6月，第121页。
5　同上，第122页。
6　周星：《中国电影艺术史》，北京大学出版社，2005年2月，第59页。
7　司徒兆敦：《忆尤里斯伊文思二三事》，《记录影视》，1998年第7期，第23页。

角。事后一看，不仅主机完好无损，就连一颗螺丝钉都没有丢失，大家感到非常庆幸。周恩来和谭政得知后特地赶来看望，专门慰问了吴印咸。在这般出生入死的考验中，吴印咸被延安不屈不挠的抗战精神打动，以令人尊崇的敬业精神留在这里。

1942年，吴印咸加入中国共产党。从此，他把自己的生命和中国革命事业紧紧相连，和共产主义事业紧紧相连。在袁牧之离开延安到苏联之后，吴印咸担任电影团的领导工作。由于经济封锁，陕甘宁边区物质供应极度匮乏，电影团的胶片所剩不多，已经无法开展正常的拍摄工作。吴印咸带领同志们开荒种地，当年做到粮食自给有余。他们还用废旧胶片制成纪念章出售，开办照相馆为群众服务，举办各种形式的摄影展览，这样，电影团解决了办公用费和生活开支，还自筹资金盖了六间新房。

对于电影团来说，比解决生活上的困难更为困难的是在几乎不具备开展摄影工作基本条件下，拍摄、制作影片和照片资料。胶片是最珍贵的东西，常常买不到。吴印咸多次告诫同志们并身体力行尽一切可能节约胶片。每拍摄一项活动，他都要仔细观察，反复思考，写出提纲，制订计划，选好角度，精打细算。在南泥湾拍摄《生产和战斗结合起来》时，吴印咸硬是把一千五百英尺胶片用上了一千三百英尺，损废比例降低到最小限度，还做上字幕，用手摇小马达带动扩音器，用留声机放音乐唱片，用小喇叭当话筒播送音乐和解说词。这种全部用土办法搞的"有声电影"，放映的效果竟和真的有声电影不相上下。

胶片拍摄出来了，冲洗、制作的难度更大。"没有自来水，就一担一担地挑来延河水，用明矾澄清后使用。没有拷贝机就用摄影机代替。没有电灯洗印照片，就在窑洞的窗口再开一个小窗孔，用多层黑布遮盖住不使漏光。印制照片时，就用手把印相架推出黑布围绕的小窗外边，利用日光曝光。没有红绿灯，就用纸壳子做成长方形的套子，在纸套中间前后挖两个小圆孔，在上面贴上红绿纸，套在油灯上当红绿灯供冲洗底片和放大照片时使用。没有放大机，吴印咸带着同志们砌了一个平顶而四周没有窗子的小亭子，顶部中央开一个长方形小天窗，在窗口钉上木槽。木槽的大小，是按一只折叠式照相机的大小做的，在照相机的背上，加一个能夹底片的玻璃框子，放大时将相机插入木槽里，使底片向着屋外的天空，就可以利用日光进行曝光了。另做一个木架子，上面放置放大纸，根据放大的要求，上下移动。放大时，小亭子的外面有一个同志观察光线照射的强弱，向里面工作的同志报告，以便正确控制曝光时间。这种原始的古老的'暗房'可能绝此一家。没有洗片机，就将胶片剪成二十尺一段，一段一段地在小木盘里冲洗，全部洗完之后，再接起来。这一切无论在中国电影史上还是世界电影史上都是奇迹！"[8]

这张《1942年毛泽东在延安窑洞前的报告》，就是在这样的历史环境中拍摄出来的。每次听毛主席讲话，为毛主席拍照，吴印咸都深深感到毛主席身上有一种巨大的精神力量。艰苦朴素的延安精神，中国革命领袖的高大与质朴，是这张照片感动人心的灵魂；而在如此艰苦的条件下，吴印咸仍能保持着精益求精的工作态度，从容地发挥摄影师的专业积淀，让艺术语言与主题完美交融相得益彰，不能不说靠的是一段风流激越的民国风度。这同样的风度也体现在毛泽东等开国元勋的举手投足之间，启迪着后来更加伟大的新时代。

激励人心的座右铭

在1974年北京人民美术出版社出版的《革命战争摄影作品选集[抗日战争和解放战争部分]》中，这张照片被命名为《毛主席在延安给八路军作报告》。与目前泰康人寿收藏的这张相比，前景地面上的两个人影被除去了，或许是为了更加突出毛主席的形象。这说明，这件摄影作品可能还有其他副本，而这个删掉人影的版本，也形象地传达了历史上存在过的、一定的价值判断。1993年，由深圳中央文献出版社发行的《吴印咸摄影作品珍藏》中也收录了这张照片，目录中的名字是《艰苦创业——毛泽东给晋绥干部作报告》。在这本画册中，照片完全保留了原样，精心设计的画面构图得以还原。吴老在拍摄领袖肖像时，十分注重构图因素。根据徐肖冰的口述，抗战时期的延安没有"拍伟大领袖时应该仰拍"之类的要求，而吴印咸确实拍过一些毛主席的仰拍镜头[9]，其中最知名的大概可以算是《重庆谈判》，毛主席在登机前摘下帽子挥手致意的形象，后来成为标志着这次战争期间重大转折的经典图像。

当时，毛主席看到这张照片非常喜欢，曾风趣地说"这是最有时代感的照片。"时代感，既是指照片直接反映的粗布衣裤、窑洞门窗等艰苦奋斗精神的写照，也是指这张照片代表的事件——延安整风运动在党内形成的新风气。

抗战爆发后，党内又增加了大批农民和小资产阶级出身的新党员，因此，党内存在着思想不纯、作风不纯的现象。针对这种情况，党中央决定在全党范围内开展一次大规模的整风运动。1942年春运动开始，内容是：反对主观主义以整顿学风，反对宗派主义以整顿党风，反对党八股以整顿文风。方针是："惩前毖后，治病救人"，用"团结－批评－团结"的方式，达到既要弄清思想又要团结同志的目的。方法是："在精读马克思列宁主

8　《百年吴印咸》画册撰文，中国电影出版社，2000年9月。

9　方方：《中国纪录片发展史》，中国戏剧出版社，2003年12月，第114页。

义基本文件基础上，反省自己的工作、思想，实事求是地进行批评与自我批评，具体分析产生错误的原因和克服错误的方法。党的高级干部还着重对党的历史进行了学习、研究和讨论。"这次整风运动，使党的领导机关和干部进一步掌握了马克思列宁主义的普遍真理同中国革命实践相结合的原则，树立了联系群众、调查研究、实事求是的优良作风，并帮助大量非无产阶级出身的新党员转变了思想立场，使全党紧密地团结在以毛泽东为首的党中央周围，为夺取抗日战争的最后胜利和人民民主革命在全国的胜利提供了思想和组织保证。

综合而言，这张照片是一位伟人的精彩瞬间，一次思想学习的真实写照，一个时代的珍贵纪念。摄影师把它作为激励自己为共产主义事业奋斗的座右铭，也把它看成自己艺术上的一件重要作品。它体现了一代摄影大师吴印咸承上启下的艺术成就，也承载着一段党史故事开拓未来的历史佳话。

From the Elegant Manners of the Republic to the Spirit of Yan'an
- A 'Maxim' of Master Photographer Wu Yinxian

By Siran Changchang

In 1942, Mao Zedong gave a speech to the 120th Division's Cadres in front of the Yan'an Caves. This was an event in the Chinese Communist Party's important Rectification Movement. To record this historical moment, the master photographer Wu Yinxian took this photograph, which may be called a classical portrait work, Mao Zedong's 1942 Speech in Front of the Yan'an Caves. In the photograph, Mao Zedong is dressed in clothes of coarse material, with two large patches on his trousers and plain cloth shoes. The harsh and plain spirit of Yan'an is vividly and completely embodied in this outfit. He is standing in front of a small square stool fixing the large crowd of cadres with a look of ardent sincerity, his body leaning slightly forward, his hands making a richly expressive gesture. Although only one figure is in the photograph, it makes one feel the presence of the crowd of cadres who are just out of sight, in mutual communication with the glance of Chairman Mao, and listening to his speech with total attention.

In addition to precisely expressing the characteristics of the figure's outer form and acutely capturing his best spiritual state, the composition and light in this photograph are remarkable. The upper one third of the photograph is occupied by the caves in which the people of the Communist Party worked and lived at the time, and a 'horizon' line, slanting slightly upwards to the right, separates the buildings from the open space where he is making the speech. It basically meets in the same point as the diagonal direction of the three slender silhouette, arranged in parallel lines on the ground, and the wide window of the sunken recess of a cave with the projections of two low buildings present a vertical relationship with the fine lines which are of a similar somberness. Together they form a solid and stable, but not inelegant, background framework that serves as a perfect foil for the figure of the Chairman standing in the centre of the foreground. His forward - leaning posture in this carefully created composition produces a solemn feeling that is vivid, clean and fully balanced. A particularly interesting detail is the small square stool on the right

- hand side of the picture. Its forward - leaning angle is almost identical to that of the Chairman, and it is like a short note that draws a perfect full stop to an entire musical movement.

This photograph and the photograph of Dr. Bethune were hung together in Wu Yinxian's study. Once he said jokingly: "People have a dictum or aphorism as their maxim, my maxims are photographs." These two "maxims" are the most widely known of the photographs that Wu took after he went to Yan'an. If the superb photographic technique of these two photographs was the result of Wu Yinxian's early studies and working experience in Shanghai, his humanist conceptions and communist ideals were another asset, one that Yan'an taught him.

In Shanghai: Art Studies, Buying a Camera, and Making Films

In the same year that these two photographs were taken, Wu Yinxian joined the Chinese Communist Party. In September 1938, mobilized by Yuan Muzhi, he had arrived in Shanghai from Hong Kong and proceeded to Yan'an via Wuhan, originally only to shoot a documentary to reflect the conditions of the resistance fighting, namely Yan'an and the Eighth Route Army. The original plan was to return Wuhan when the documentary was finished, but at the time he had no idea that this rather accidental trip to Yan'an would become a turning - point in his life.

Wu Yinxian, courtesy name Zhifu, was born on 21 September 1900 in Shuyang County, Jiangsu Province. His father was a xiucai scholar of the late Qing Dynasty, and taught for a living. While Wu Yinxian was still in the higher levels of the county primary school founded by his father, he displayed an uncommon artistic gift. In particular, he was fond of painting, calligraphy and seal - carving, and his father was highly appreciative of him. In 1916 his graduation from higher primary school coincided with Shuyang being flooded, and he successfully took an examination to enter the Jiangsu Provincial No.4 Factory, where he combined work and study. In this factory, which manufactured cotton and blankets, he studied cultural learning for half the day and, for the other half, worked as a cotton - weaver. He also designed original patterns for carpets, by which he achieved the recognition of the technical foreman as well as successful sales. In 1919, financially supported by family and friends, he successfully took the entrance examination for the Shanghai Fine Arts Technical College and began to receive a proper training in painting.

Shanghai Arts Tech had at this time already broken through the old conventional educational standards of its first period, and the mission statement of the College was: "To turn from purely cultivating drawing talent to striving to change China's present situation; to promote the revitalization of art, but at the same time to reflect the fundamental thought of taking from, and integrating with Western culture and art".[1] There were great adjustments to the curriculum: "In June 1916 the Painting Department was changed to the Western Painting Department, and the the length of schooling was fixed to three years from then. In addition to the study of the techniques of realism, various principles were stressed, and the following courses were added: perspective, aesthetics and art history, while elective subjects were abolished. In 1918, in view of the shortage of art teachers in the various schools, art teacher training courses were added, practical technical manual skills and drawing received equal emphasis, and equal attention was paid to the various principles." "In 1920, courses in Western painting, Chinese painting, sculpture, craft design, advanced teacher training and general teacher training were added. The duration of the general teacher training course was fixed at one year and a half, and the duration of the other courses was set to three years."[2] In terms of pedagogical method, this was also the beginning of making life drawing the norm in the teaching of Western painting, and Chen Baoyi recalls that: "In the circumstances of that time, it was impossible to begin in one leap to sketch human bodies, but at least we felt the possibility of

---

1 Ma Lin, *Zhou Xiang and Early Art Education in Shanghai*, Tianjin People's Art Press, May 2007, p123.
2 Liu Haisu "Looking Back at Ten Years of Shanghai Fine Arts Technical College", in *Art in China and Japan*, 20th July 1922, vol 1, No 3.

doing away with the teaching methodology of copying the classics, and of replacing it with life drawing as the main basic course."[3] By the time Wu Yinxian had enrolled, Shanghai Technical College had already entered on the right track. The excellent forces of the faculty not only offered social connections and financial support, but also brought the opportunity of an integrated humanist education. For instance, in the 1920s Liang Qichao was invited to come and speak on "Art and Life", "Da Vinci's Life and Artistic Achievements", "On the Creative Spirit" and so on. In this learning environment, Wu Yinxian both got to understand the technique of life drawing and modeling and also came into contact with the influence of theoretical culture. These things provided him with a sound base for his future creative work.

However, when Wu Yinxian spent three silver dollars at a flea market on an old Brownie camera, it changed the direction of his studies, and from then on, his destiny was formed in a lifelong bond with photography. In 1923, while he was teaching in his home town in Jiangsu, he took the early - period photograph *Morning Market (Xiaoshi)*. The silhouette figures within the arched space of the city gate create a clear feeling of rhythm that embodies his photographic explorations with respect to light and composition. *Strength*, taken in 1930, is another good example of exploring the surface from an aesthetic angle, the texture effects of the play of light and shade, and of the composition of the light projection, depict the strong and handsome posture of a male body. *River Snails* (1934) even received the Honor Award at the Swiss Salon of Photography. If these works were directly related to his artistic studies, Wu Yinxian more or less at the same time poured his artist's concern and contemplation into the real problems of society. In this respect, *Suffering Hunger and Cold* (1924) and *Gambling* (1930) are representative works. While working at a photo studio in Shanghai, he got to know left - wing progressives including Shen Xiling, Tian Fang and Situ Huimin, and from then on entered the ranks of the left - wing filmmakers.

In *Children of the Storm (Fengyun Ernü)*, shot in Xiayan in 1935, he became a film photographer for the first time. The following year, he shot Yuan Muzhi's *Street Angel (Malu Tianshi)*. This film may be considered a milestone in Chinese filmmaking: "The beginning of Chinese filmmaking may be dated from *Street Angel*. In terms of narrative format, acting standards, camera technique and soundtrack, and with regard to artistic design, production and so on, it began to have the popular - fantasy kind of social prospects of the Hollywood film model."[4] *Street Angel* was screened at the opening ceremony of Ombre Elettriche, the retrospective on fifty years of Chinese film - making held in 1982 in Torino, Milano and Rome, and Italian film critic Ugo Casiraghi was amazed by it. In the newspaper Unitá, he wrote an article under the significant heading: "Neorealism was born in Shanghai". Before this, it was internationally assumed that neorealism was a major Italian contribution to world cinema. In fact, to a great extent, it can be said to have been created by Wu Yinxian. He learned from the scene scheduling and montage techniques of Hollywood commercial films, and by editing in realistic shots produced super - realistic spatial relationships to highlight the characterization of human figures. Gong Lin is of the opinion that this film's "main setting is the north Shanghai slum of the Lower Corner [Xiazhijiao]… relations of everybody's living spacewere undefined, but generally flickered in and out in the light and shade, obscuring the specific, actual spatial texture."[5] Wu Yinxian had already basically established his filming style by the time of *Street Angel*. This filming device, which through carefully designed compositional relationships matched the main characters, was consistently manifested in the Yan'an documentary films and photographs.

The left - wing films, in their backlash against the commercial films that previously disregarded real life and favoured martial arts, instead promoted work that

---

3   Chen Baoyi "Jottings on the Process of the Western Painting Movement", in *Shanghai Arts Monthly*, April 1942, No 6.
4   Gong Lin, *History of Chinese Film Art*, Shandong Arts Press, June 2007, p121.
5   Idem, p122.

paid attention to real life, reflected the social spirit of the age, and played a positive role in the production of films. With their efforts, Chinese films had broadened their subject matter, a fresh new spirit had appeared, and real-life content reproduced. The 1930s became the first golden age of the flourishing of Chinese realism."[6] Wu Yinxian took part in this wave of realism, and became even clearer about his values in artistic creation. In 1937, by the invitation of the Northwest Film Company, Wu Yinxian travelled to Taiyuan to film. When the July 7 (Marco Polo Bridge) Incident blew up, filming was interrupted, but there remained from this round of filming the film *Begging and Starving to Feed Their Families*, which reflected wartime starvation. This was a documentary-style work of still shots, and can be seen as an omen of his later choosing to stay on in Yan'an.

Arrival in Yan'an: Documentary Films and Photographing Bethune and the Leaders

When Yuan Muzhi invited Wu Yinxian to come to Yan'an to shoot a film, he first had him secretly collude with the Dutch documentary film director Joris Ivens, and to receive the Bell&Howell Eyemo film camera that Ivens was donating, along with some film. Because the Yan'an area lacked film-making equipment, and there was no way that Ivens, who was shooting *The 400 Million People (Siwanwan renmin)*, could get official permission to enter the Yan'an area, Ivens thought that he would give his equipment to China's own master film photographer to use in filming a documentary on Yan'an. This may be considered the first time that Wu Yinxian undertook a task under the instruction of the Party Organizational Committee. When Ivens, under the cover of darkness, hurriedly passed him the equipment, and said softly in broken Chinese: "Yan'an, Yan'an", Wu Yinxian shook hands with him and left. They only met again after twenty years, finally seeing each other's faces clearly. Situ Zhaodun once said: "Later when he [Ivens] and Wu Yinxian met again and shook hands, I said: 'You are the only people in the world who have shaken hands twice but only seen each other's faces once'." [7]

Understanding how hard conditions were in Yan'an, Wu Yinxian used his own limited funds to buy three camers to take to Yan'an. One was a German Welta 135, one was a twin-lens Zeiss Ikon Ikoflex 120, and one was a wooden camera specially for taking photographs larger than four inches. Afterwards, because he couldn't get professional film in Yan'an, he used it as a converted enlarger. Wu Yinxian used the first two cameras to shoot many precious historical photographs of the front in the War of Resistance in Yan'an and Huabei, including many scenes of the Eighth Route Army reclaiming the wasteland and practising 'do your own work, you'll have clothing and food', precious images of Dr. Bethune risking the dangers of the firing zone to rescue the wounded, and also the voices, faces and smiling manner of Mao Zedong and other leaders in their daily work and life at Yan'an.

In 1938, after the foundation of the Yan'an Film Team, it shot its first documentary, Yan'an and the Eighth Route Army. Once Wu Yinxian and his assistant Xu Xiaobing had just opened the camera for repairs when they were subjected to a Japanese air raid. A bomb dropped nearby and demolished a corner of the house where they happened to be. Wu Yinxian risked his own life to protect the camera parts from the falling rubble by throwing himself onto the machine. While the bombers were circling above them, Wu Yinxian and Xu Xiaobing climbed out of the rubble, gathered up the bits and pieces of the opened camera, and only then hid again in the nook of a wall. When they looked afterwards, not only were all the main parts of the camera safe and sound, but not even one screw was missing, and everybody felt very lucky. When Zhou Enlai and Tan Zheng heard about it, they expressly hurried over to visit them and particularly expressed their solicitude for Wu Yinxian. In this test of life and death, Wu Yinxian was moved by the inflexible morale of resistance of Yan'an, and stayed on in an admirable spirit of professionalism.

In 1942, Wu Yinxian joined the Chinese Communist Party. From this moment on, he linked his own life closely with the revolutionary enterprise of China, and also with the Communist enterprise. After Yuan Muzhi left Yan'an for the Soviet Union, Wu Yinxian took up the work of leading the film group. Because of the economic

---

6 Zhou Xing: *History of Chinese Film Art*, Beijing University Press, February 2005, p59.
7 Situ Zhaodun: "A Couple of Memories of Joris Ivens", in *Documentaries*, 1998, No 7, P23

blockade, the supply of material to Shaanxi, Gansu and Ningxia was very short. As the film unit had little film left, it was already impossible to carry on the normal filming work. Wu Yinxian led his comrades in opening up the wasteland and planting the soil, and that year they had enough grain for themselves and a little left over. They used up the discarded old film to make souvenir badges to sell, and opened a photographic studio for the masses, where they held various kinds of photographic exhibitions. In this way the film unit solved the problems of office and living expenses, and themselves financed the building of six houses.

For the film unit, what was even harder than solving the difficulties of living was how to film, and how to produce the materials for films and photographs. Celluloid was the most precious thing, and was often not possible to buy it. Wu Yinxian often warned his comrades, and personally did everything possible, to save film. Every time they filmed an activity, he insisted on first scrutinizing it and weighing it up, writing outlines, settling on plans, choosing angles, and paying close attention to the budget. When filming *Uniting Production with Warfare* in Nanniwan, Wu Yinxian obstinately used 1300 feet out of 1500 feet of film, with the wastage reduced to the lowest minimum possible, and also added titles and used an amplifier driven by a small hand - activated motor, using a gramophone to play music records, and a small speaker as a microphone to broadcast music and announcements. The effect of screening this kind of 'sound movies' produced exclusively by improvised methods was comparable to that of films with real sound.

Once a film was shot, the difficulties involved in developing it and editing it were even greater. "There was no running water, only the water of the Yan River carried up bucket by bucket and clarified with alum before we could use it. We had no copying machine, so we used a camera instead. There was no electrical lamp by which to develop the film, so we opened up a small window in the windows of a cave and used multiple layers of black cloth to cover it so that no light could enter. When developing pictures, we pushed the photo stand inbetween the black cloth and the small window and exposed the photo with natural light. There were no red or green lamps, so we used bits of cardboard to make rectangular sheaths and made two small holes around the middle of the sheaths and stuck green or red paper on top, then put them over the oil lamps to serve as red and green lamps used in developing negatives and enlarging photographs. There was no enlarger, so Wu Yinxian took his comrades and erected a small flat - topped and windowless pavilion, cut a small rectangular window out of the roof, and nailed wooden grooves onto the window. The size of the wooden grooves was made to fit the size of a folding camera, and on the back of the camera, they added a glass frame that could hold a negative. When they had to enlarge something, they would insert the camera into the grooves, turning the negative outwards to face the sky, and thus use the sunlight to carry out the exposure. They also made a wooden framework and installed enlarging paper on top of it, moving it up or down according to the needs of the enlargement. When they were doing the actual enlarging, a comrade would judge the brightness of the rays of sunlight outside the pavilion and report to the comrades working inside the pavilion, so that they could correctly control the time of exposure. The original form of the ancient 'dark - room' was perhaps just the only one of its kind. There was no machine to develop negatives, so they took the film and cut it into twenty foot pieces and developed the pieces one by one in a small wooden vat. After finishing the developing, they would join them together again. This was a miracle, both in the history of Chinese film - making and in the history of world film - making."[8]

The photograph Mao Zedong's Speech in Front of the Yan'an Caves 1942 was made under these historical conditions. Every time he listened to Mao Zedong giving a speech, and photographed him, Wu Yinxian always deeply felt that Mao Zedong had about his person a great spiritual force. The tough and simple Yan'an spirit, with the greatnesss and simplicity of China's revolutionary leaders, is the soul of this moving photograph; however, under these tough conditions, Wu Yinxian still maintained the excellence of his attitude to his work, as he calmly developed the professional accumulation of a master photographer,

---

8 Essay in the Exhibition catalogue: "Wu Yinxian Centenary", Chinese Film Press, September 2000.

perfecting the blending of artistic language and subject matter in a way that complemented both, in what must be acknowledged as a romantic agitation of Republican elegance. A similar elegance can be found in the gestures of the founding fathers of the Nation, inspiring the following even greater period of the new China.

Inspiring Maxims

In *Selected Photographic Works of the Revolutionary Wars (the Anti-Japanese War of Resistance and the War of Liberation)* published in 1974 by the Beijing People's Fine Arts Publishing House this photograph is called "Chairman Mao Addresses the Eighth Route Army". Compared to the work in the present collection, two human shadows on the ground in the foreground have been removed, perhaps so as to let Chairman Mao's figure stand out even more. This makes it clear that there may even be other copies in existence, yet this version where the human shadows have been deleted also figuratively purveys a judgment that existed historically, and has a certain value in that sense too. In 1993, this photograph was also included in *Treasury of Photographic Works* by Wu Yinxian, published by Shenzhen Central Documents Press. In the index, the title is given as "Working Hard - Mao Zedong Addresses the Jin-Sui Cadres". In this catalogue, the photograph has fully retained its original appearance, and the carefully composed composition was changed back to the original. When Wu photographed the leaders, he was totally aware of compositional factors. According to Xu Xiaobing's oral testimony, during the War of Resistance at Yan'an, there was no demand for anything of the nature of 'using low-angle shot to foreground the leaders' greatness'. In fact, Wu Yinxian did make some low-angle photographs of Chairman Mao,[9] the best - known of which is probably *Chongqing Negotiations*, of Chairman Mao taking his cap off and waving hands before boarding the plane, which later became the classical image signifying the great turning point in this period of the war.

When he saw it at the time, Chairman Mao liked the photograph very much, and said humorously: "This is the photograph with the greatest sense of the era." The 'sense of the era' is both the direct reflection in this photograph of the clothes and trousers of rough cloth, the 'windows' of the caves and other indications of the spirit of tough struggle, and also the event represented by this photograph - the new atmosphere of the Yan'an Rectification Movement formed within the Party.

After the War of Resistance erupted, the Party greatly increased the number of members of peasant and petit - bourgeois origin. Accordingly, thinking and practices that were not pure began to exist within the Party. In response to this situation, the Party Central Committee decided start a large - scale Rectification Movement covering the entire Party. The Movement began in the Spring of 1942, and its contents was: oppose subjectivity in order to rectify study practices; oppose factionalism in order to rectify Party practices; oppose stereotyped party jargon in order to rectify cultural practices. The policy was to "punish the past in order to secure the future, and to cure the illness to save the man", by means of "solidarity - criticism - solidarity", so as to achieve the goal of clarifying thoughts as well as uniting comrades The method was: to reflect, on the basis of a careful reading the fundamental texts of Marxism - Leninism, on one's own work, thinking and actions, so as to find the truth, and thus carry out criticism and self - criticism, specifically analyzing the causes that produce error and the methods of overcoming errors. The high cadres of the Party were also to focus on carrying out study, research and discussion of the history of the Party. This Rectification Movement enabled the cadres and the leading institutions of the Party to get a better grip on the principles uniting the general truth of Marxism - Leninism with China's revolutionary practice, and established the excellent practices of connecting with the masses, of investigative research and of seeking the truth in actual facts. It helped a great number of new Party members of non - proletariat origin to transform

---

9 Fangfang, *History of the Development of Chinese Documentary Films*, China Theatre Press, December 2003, p114.

their thinking position, and made the whole Party join in tight solidarity around the Party Central Committee headed by Mao Zedong, so as to achieve the ultimate victory in the War of Resistance against the Japanese and the People's democratic revolution under the ideological and organizational guarantees offered by national victory.

In summary, this photograph is the brilliant moment of a great man, a genuine depiction of ideological study, and a precious memory of an era. The master photographer made of it a maxim that spurred him on to struggle for the Communist cause, and also regarded it as an important work in his own art. It embodies the nexus of artistic achievements of the master photographer of his generation Wu Yinxian, and also conveys the story of a period of Party history that ushers in the historical epic of its future.

吴印咸
Wu Yinxian

艰苦创业
Thriryig the Enterprise by Hard Working
银盐相纸
Gelatin Silver Print
34.5×50cm, 1942

吴作人《捷报》
与第一次文代会

吴雪杉

1949年4月23日午夜南京解放，第二天消息传到北平，人们在街头争相抢购传阅报纸"号外"。画家吴作人携妻女到东单路口亲眼目睹这一景象，并在《解放南京号外》一画中把它记录下来[1]。画家仿佛把观看者带回到那一年的4月24日，让观看者站在长安街东单路口东北角向西边远眺，近前九人围观报纸"号外"，远处市民们三五成群欢呼雀跃。远处地平线上是东长安街牌楼，虽然已于1954年拆除，在当时的北平却是人们耳熟能详的标志性建筑。近处蓝衣青年手中的报纸上写明"号外"，下面隐约可见"人民日报"，报纸内容没有标注出来，但作品名字"解放南京号外"已经解释得很清楚。

然而，"解放南京号外"这个说明性标题要到1962年才正式出现，首见于《吴作人画集》[2]。这件作品在1960年出版的《吴作人作品小辑》里名为"捷报"[3]，1950年《中华全国文学艺术工作者代表大会美术作品选集》里出现时也以"捷报"为题[4]。《中华全国文学艺术工作者代表大会美术作品选集》收录的作品都是1949年7月2日开幕的第一届全国美展参展作品，这就确定了作品完成时间应该在1949年4月底（南京解放）至6月底（举办美展）之间，当时起名为"捷报"（这个名字沿用了13年），而捷报内容对当时人来说则似乎是不言自明的。

从《捷报》变更为《解放南京号外》大约是时代背景转换的结果。1949年7月2日这件作品第一次面对北平观众时，最大的"捷报"就是人民解放军攻克南京，这一胜利极富象征意义，不仅意味着"国民党统治的灭亡"，还预示了"人民民主革命即将取得完全的胜利"[5]。北平在获悉南京解放的消息的当天（4月24日）就举行了大规模游行欢庆活动，"祝捷"活动至少持续了两天，4月26日的《人民日报》专门对此进行了报道（"北平各界人民游行祝捷，加紧生产学习扩大胜利，把热情的狂欢转为积极的工作"）[6]。北平观众想必对数月之前欢欣鼓舞围观"号外"的景象记忆犹新，而吴作人对此亦有足够预期，否则不会仅仅点明"号外"以及模糊不清的"人民日报"。在他看来，这六个字已经足够唤起人们的回忆和印象。13年后的1962年，新中国建设大潮捷报频传，单以"捷报"为题已经无法为观看者提供确切的记忆坐标，将作品题目改为更具描述性的《解放南京号外》也就顺理成章。

但与"解放南京号外"比较起来，"捷报"隐含着一种价值判断，表达出作者以及作品对人民军队辉煌胜利的认同。回到这件作品初创时的1949年，以"捷报"为题具有双重含义，既象征解放南京这一胜利喜讯，又代指传来胜利消息的"报纸"（号外）。在解放战争时期，"号外"往往意味着"捷报"，"有时候，报纸还没印完，捷报又传来了，于是一张《号外》迅速地诞生了；有时一天内要出两期《号外》。当时人们用'捷报如同雪花飘'这句话来形容《号外》之多。"[7]南京解放后，街头抢购、围观"号外"的景象不仅是历史事实，也是由来传达胜利喜悦的艺术手法。在扬州刊行的《人民报》也运用了这一手法。1949年4月25日的《人民报》"号外"上刊载"南京解放捷报传来后的街头速写"

---

1 萧曼、霍大寿：《吴作人》，人民美术出版社，1988年，第221页。
2 吴作人：《吴作人画集》，人民美术出版社，1962年，图20。
3 吴作人：《吴作人作品小辑》，上海人民美术出版社，1960年，图1。
4 中华全国文学艺术工作者代表大会宣传处编：《中华全国文学艺术工作者代表大会艺术展览会美术作品选集》，新华书店，1950年，第24、25页。
5 新华社社论：《庆祝南京解放》，1949年4月24日，转引自南京市档案馆编：《南京解放：1949.4.23》，中国档案出版社，2009年，第602页。
6 "北平人民昨日继续狂欢庆祝南京、太原的解放"，见【本报讯】《北平各界人民游行祝捷，加紧生产学习扩大胜利，把热情的狂欢转为积极的工作》，《人民日报》1949年4月26日，第3版。
7 晓白：《解放战争时期的〈号外〉》，《新闻战线》1961年第2期，第3页。

四幅，其中一幅就是描绘前有市民围观报纸、后有小贩叫卖"号外"的景象[8]。其创作思路和吴作人非常相近，这种情景对于今天来说十分陌生，而在1949年却是当时人共有的经验。

《捷报》是对当下一则重大政治事件的即时回应，这在此前吴作人的艺术创作中极为少见。1949年以前，吴作人几乎没有把自己所处时代的重大社会、政治事件作为绘画题材。当然这并不意味着吴作人远离现实，他也曾创作过带有现实主义色彩的《和平神下的战舰》《空袭下的母亲》，针对某些社会现象和现实问题展开批判，但这类作品数量不多，也没有直接针对某个政治事件[9]。吴作人他真正热爱的可能还是人体肖像、静物风景。南京解放固然令他振奋，但也未见得更甚于1945年9月的抗战胜利。1949年1月发生在吴作人身边的北平解放似乎也没有激发起他创作的灵感。吴作人以南京解放为题进行创作，或者别有怀抱。

无独有偶，徐悲鸿也创作了一件关于南京解放的作品，名为《在世界和平大会听到南京解放的消息》。南京解放时徐悲鸿正出席第一届世界和平大会，这次大会于1949年4月20日至25日在巴黎和布拉格两地同时举行，共有来自72个国家的2000多名代表参加（中国代表团去的是布拉格，法国当时没有和中国共产党领导的政权建立外交关系，不允许中国代表团入境）。24日，消息传到布拉格时，由会议主席当众宣布南京解放，"大会全场立刻爆发了十五分钟的狂热欢呼。中国代表团44人欢欣鼓舞，高声歌唱。各国代表挽着中国代表的手臂游行起来。大会高唱'自由中国万岁'歌。中国代表团团长郭沫若宣称，'中国人民的胜利是整个和平阵营的胜利'"[10]。徐悲鸿作为代表团成员中的一员，其时想必也在高声歌唱，振臂欢呼。徐悲鸿回国后以此为契机创作了水墨画《在世界和平大会听到南京解放的消息》。和吴作人一样，徐悲鸿对他同时代发生的政治事件也缺乏创作热情，为此曾饱受诟病。而和《捷报》相同的是，《在世界和平大会听到南京解放的消息》也是第一届全国美展的参展作品。

在1949年4月到6月，吴作人和徐悲鸿同时选取了一个他们此前并不十分热衷的主题：一个刚刚发生的政治事件。他们几乎同时认为，南京解放是个需要去刻画的对象。激发起他们"现实"关怀的大背景只能是政治权力的更迭，而促使他们对南京解放做出快速反应的则是中国共产党治下第一次文代会的召开以及第一次全国美展的举办。

吴作人《捷报》和徐悲鸿《在世界和平大会听到南京解放的消息》都于1949年7月参加第一届全国美展。这个20世纪下半叶中国最重要的美术展览当时名为"中华全国文学艺术工作者代表大会美术展览会"。从这个名字也可以看出，展览目的是为了配合中华全国文学艺术工作者代表大会（即第一次文代会）。大会于1949年7月2日召开，由郭沫若、茅盾、周扬等42人组成的筹备委员会发起，至19日闭幕。毛泽东在7月6日到会场向代表致意，告诉代表们："你们开的这样的大会是很好的大会，是革命需要的大会，是全国人民所希望的大会。因为你们都是人民所需要的人，你们是人民的文学家，人民的艺术家、或者是人民的文学艺术工作的组织者。你们对于革命有好处，对于人民有好处。"[11] 朱德代表中共中央致辞，周恩来作长篇政治报告，此外还有郭沫若《为建设新中国的人民文艺而奋斗》、茅盾《在反动派压迫下斗争和发展的革命文艺》，以及周扬《新的人民的文艺》等报告，这些报告总结了1942年《在延安文艺座谈会上的讲话》发表以来文艺工作的经验与成就，明确了新形势下文艺工作的新方向和新任务，选举产生中国全国文学艺术工作者联合会全国委员会（俗称"文联"），以及中国文联下属的各个协会及领导机构（包括"美协"）。

中华全国文学艺术工作者代表大会的召开标志着毛泽东在延安确立的文艺政策正式成为新中国的文艺发展方向，因而具有重要意义。同期举办的《中华全国文学艺术工作者代表大会美术展览》则在美术领域展示了这一重大"转向"，参展所有作品都在说明、注解或表征《在延安文艺座谈会上的讲话》。这对于来自解放区的画家自然不成问题，但对那些来自国统区的画家就提出了考验：他们应该提交什么样的作品？

从国统区画家们提交"中华全国文学艺术工作者代表大会美术展览会"的作品来看，相当一部分创作于1949年上半年。除吴作人和徐悲鸿之外，还有董希文的《北平解放》、宗其香的《修复永定河铁桥》、黄均的《庆祝五一劳动节》等作品。他们在距离展览开幕前不久（大概只有两三个月的时间）赶制出这些作品，显然是为了迎接新时代的到来以及新时代带有准官方性质的美术"大展"。中华全国文学艺术工作者代表大会的召开虽然是1949年7月，筹备工作却始于年初。郭沫若在当年3月22日华北文化艺术工作委员会、华北文艺工作者协会举办的文化界茶话会上提议发起，很快就推举出理事并产生筹委会。5月1日，筹委会通过《大会代表资格与产生办法》；6月27日，郭沫若就大会的方针和任务发表谈话；而到7月2日，中华全国文学艺术

---

8 金建陵：《南京解放的"号外"报》，《档案与建设》2009年4期，第28、29页。
9 关于吴作人的艺术活动，见萧曼、霍大寿：《吴作人》，人民美术出版社，1988年，第382-412页。
10 【新华社北平二十四日电】《巴黎布拉格和平大会热狂欢庆南京解放》，《人民日报》1949年4月25日，第1版。
11 中华全国文学艺术工作者代表大会宣传处编：《中华全国文学艺术工作者代表大会纪念文集》，新华书店，1950年，第3页。

工作者代表大会就正式开幕了。可以说,从3月开始,整个北京(当时的北平)文艺界都为筹备会议而奔波操劳,而那些最著名的美术家们却在忙着搞创作,意图自然一目了然。

吴作人是中华全国文学艺术工作者代表大会的参与者。他是平津代表第二团的团委,大会美术组委员。吴作人还是艺术展览委员会委员(艺术展览委员会有主任1人,委员9人),兼任艺术展览委员会布置组的组长。展览的布置工作大约都由他来负责。在会后成立的中华全国美术工作者协会里,吴作人是全国委员会委员,同时也是常务委员会成员。从这一系列职衔可以看出,吴作人从一开始就介入文代会的组织工作,更是"中华全国文学艺术工作者代表大会美术展览"的主要策划者之一。他对自己在这个展览中应该展出什么作品,自会深思熟虑。

强调"解放区"与"国统区"的差异,是因为这是1949年时审视艺术家身份的独特"眼光"。当时所有"文学艺术工作者"都被分成两种:或者来自解放区,或者来自国统区。周恩来《在中华全国文学艺术工作者代表大会上的政治报告》里提到来自解放区的代表和来自前国民党统治区的代表,在报告末尾再把他们团结为"从老解放区来的与从新解放区来的两部分文艺军队的会师"[12]。应邀出席文代会的代表分10个代表团共计824人(实际报到人数为650人),他们当然来自全国各地,但又可以笼统地划分为三个部分:部队、解放区和国统区,前两者实际上是一回事。甚至在代表团的划分上也体现出这一点,吴作人和徐悲鸿所在的平津地区分为两个代表团,"平津第一代表团"基本上是原本来自解放区的文艺工作者,而"平津第二代表团"则主要是原先属于"国统区"平津的艺术家。徐悲鸿、吴作人、董希文、叶浅予、齐白石等人都分配在"平津第二代表团"。

"中华全国文学艺术工作者代表大会美术展览会"的参展作品也被认为来自这两个地方,展览图册前言明确指出了这一点:"其中一部分是解放区的美术工作者的作品,反映了中国人民伟大的解放事业和辉煌的社会建设;另一部分是当时留在国民党统治区的美术工作者的作品,描绘的是当时在国民党反动统治下的社会动态及人民的生活斗争。"[13]按照这种说法,来自国统区的画家就应该描绘国民党的反动统治以及人民对反动统治的斗争。然而,生活在国统区而又长于油画创作的艺术家们大多没有这方面的创作实践,他们只能重起炉灶,和来自解放区的画家一样去"反映中国人民伟大的解放事业和辉煌的社会建设",描绘他们刚刚接触到的新社会和新现象。

在这次文代会上,叶浅予代表国统区美术工作者作"国统区的进步美术运动"专题发言,他承认"由于客观的限制,我们常常不接近群众,也缺乏实际生活的深入体验,在创作上,也只能达到写实主义和自然主义的水平,有的甚至中了欧美没落的资本主义近代艺术的毒,钻进了形式主义的牛角尖,爬不出来。"但他同样展望了现在和未来:"今天,我们完全有了彻底改造自己,放手发挥工作能力的种种有利条件。我们应该很好地学习和贯彻毛主席的文艺方针,和工农群众紧密地结合起来,从工作中学习,以求得进步。并且要在发展生产,发展文化,建设新中国这个目标下,献出我们的力量。"[14]

吴作人对于自己的国统区画家身份有充分自觉。他在1949年撰写的《"七七"以来国统区的油画》里"总结国统区的油画"时说:"过去我们从事油画工作的,仅仅知道在风格上的争论,而没有想到我们是应该为谁服务的。"而对未来的艺术创作方向,吴作人也已坚定了信念:"如今国统区不久就要全部解放了,我们不再受束缚了,我们应该和曾与我们被反动统治者隔绝了好多年的解放区的美术工作同志们在一块,去接近工农兵而为他们服务,在毛泽东的旗帜下进行建设新中国的伟大使命中,在油画上,贡献我们最大的力量。"[15]

1949年是吴作人艺术创作转向的关键时刻,他选择南京解放为题材,为第一次文代会和全国美展献上属于他的"捷报"。如果套用《中华全国文学艺术工作者代表大会美术展览会美术作品选集》"编辑例言"的表述,《捷报》(《解放南京号外》)就是画家对"新中国的诞生的献礼"[16]。这件作品标志着吴作人向毛泽东文艺方向迈进的第一步,也昭示着吴作人面对时代洪流时的立场与选择,而这显然是那一代艺术家共同面对的问题。

---

12 中华全国文学艺术工作者代表大会宣传处编:《中华全国文学艺术工作者代表大会纪念文集》,新华书店,1950年,第27、33页。
13 中华全国文学艺术工作者代表大会宣传处编:《中华全国文学艺术工作者代表大会艺术展览会美术作品选集》,新华书店,1950年,第7页。
14 中华全国文学艺术工作者代表大会宣传处编:《中华全国文学艺术工作者代表大会纪念文集》,新华书店,1950年,第286页。
15 吴作人:《吴作人文选》,安徽美术出版社,1988年,第26、27页。
16 中华全国文学艺术工作者代表大会宣传处编:《中华全国文学艺术工作者代表大会艺术展览会美术作品选集》,新华书店,1950年,第7页。

Wu Zuoren's *Victory!* and the First Cultural Committee Conference

By Wu Xueshan

Nanjing was liberated at midnight on the 23rd of April 1949. Next day, the news reached Beiping, and people competed on the street corners to buy and read the extra edition of the newspapers. The painter Wu Zuoren took his wife and daughter to the intersection of Dongdan Lu for them to see this scene with their own eyes, and recorded it in his painting *Extra Edition on the Liberation of Nanjing*.[1] The artist seems to take the spectator back to the 24th of April of that year, and lets the spectator stand on the northeast corner of the Dongdan Lu intersection with Chang'an Avenue, looking west into the distance, with nine people in the foreground standing in a circle reading the extra edition. In the distance, citizens form groups of three to five joyously excited people. On the distant horizon is the *pailou* on East Chang'an Avenue. Although it was demolished already in 1954, it was nevertheless an iconic building vividly familiar to people in Beiping at the time. In the foreground, the newspaper in the hands of a young man in blue clothes is inscribed: 'extra edition' (*haowai*), and below that we can just make out 'People's Daily' (*Renmin Ribao*). The contents of the newspaper has not been spelled out, however the title of the work, *Extra Edition on the Liberation of Nanjing*, has already made it very clear.

However, the explanatory title *Extra Edition on the Liberation of Nanjing* only appeared formally in 1962, and was first seen in *Collected Paintings by Wu Zuoren*.[2] In the *Selected Paintings by Wu Zuoren* published in 1960, this work is titled: *Victory! (Jiebao)*,[3] as it is also in *Selected Artworks by Literary and Artistic Workers of the Chinese National Representative Assembly*, when it appeared in 1950.[4] The works in this publication were all exhibited in the National Fine Arts Exhibition that opened on 2 July 1949, which confirms that the time of completion for the painting must fall between late April 1949

---

1 Xiao Man, Huo Dashou: *Wu Zuoren*, People's Art Press, 1988, p221.
2 Wu Zuoren, *Collected Paintings by Wu Zuoren*, People's Art Press, 1962, Fig20.
3 Wu Zuoren, *Selected Paintings by Wu Zuoren*, Shanghai People's Art Press, 1960, Fig1.
4 Propaganda Office of the China National Cultural Workers Committee Conference (ed): *Selected Works of Art of the Fine Arts Exhibition of the China National Cultural Workers Committee Conference*, Xinhua Bookstoretore, 1950, pp24 - 5.

(the Liberation of Nanjing) and late June 1949 (in preparation for the fine arts exhibition), and the content of the victory of the title (which has been used for as long as 13 years) seems to have required no explanation for people at the time.

The change of title from *Victory!* to *Extra Edition on the Liberation of Nanjing* is probably the result of the transformation of the background of the period. When this work first faced the Beiping public on 2 July 1949, the biggest 'victorious news' was the successful taking of Nanjing by the People's Liberation Army. This victory was very rich in symbolism. It signified not only the 'extinction of Kuomintang rule', but also presaged that "the People's democratic revolution would seize complete victory".[5] On 24 April 1949, the day that Beiping had news of the liberation of Nanjing, large-scale festivities were held in the form of demonstrations and marches, and the activities in celebration of the victory were continued for at least two days. The *People's Daily* of 26 April carried a report specifically on this ("People of all kinds demonstrate to celebrate victory, step up production and study to expand victory, turning enthusiastic revelry to positive work").[6] Spectators in Beiping would certainly remember the scene from a few months ago of people rapturously gathering around to read the extra edition as if it were new, and Wu Zuoren was sufficiently prescient of this, or he would not have just high-lighted 'Extra Edition' and the rather indistinct 'People's Daily'. In his view these six characters would be sufficient for people to recall both the memory and the impression. Thirteen years later in 1962, when there was plenty of victorious news in the great wave of reconstruction in the new China, simply to use 'Victory!' as a title would no longer offer the spectators a precise basis for recollection, so he changed the title to the more descriptive *Extra Edition on the Liberation of Nanjing*, which was also just logical.

Yet, in comparison to 'Extra Edition on the Liberation of Nanjing', 'Victory!' contains a value judgment, expressing the creator's and the work's acceptance of the People's Army glorious victory. Returning to 1949, the year when this work was freshly created, *Victory!* contained a double meaning. It signified the joyous news of the liberation of Nanjing, and also the extra edition newspaper that carried that news. During the War of Liberation, 'extra edition' often meant 'news of victory'. "Sometimes, news of a victory would be reported before the newspaper was fully printed, and an extra edition would be born. Sometimes, two extra editions might appear in a day. At the time, people would use the saying 'reports of victory are blowing in the wind like snowflakes'. This expression would often be used of extra editions.[7] After the liberation of Nanjing, the scene of people competing to buy the extra edition, and of forming circles to read it, is not only a historical fact. It is also an artistic device to convey the euphoria of victory. The *People's Paper (Renminbao)* at Yangzhou also used this means. In the extra edition of 25 April 1949, the *People's Paper* carried four "Sketches of the streets after the news of the liberation of Nanjing broke". One of the sketches shows just this scene of people gathering in a group to read the extra edition in the foreground, and a paperboy selling the extra edition.[8] The creative idea is very close to Wu Zuoren's, and although it seems quite strange to us today, for people living in 1949 it was a shared experience.

Victory! was an immediate response to a great political event of the time. This was very rare in Wu Zuoren's

---

5   Xinhua Editorial: "Congratulations on the Liberation of Nanjing", 24 April 1949, a reference from *The Liberation of Nanjing: 23 April 1949*, edited by the Nanjing Archives, China Archives Press, 2009, p602.

6   "People of Beiping continue to revel yesterday to celebrate the liberation of Nanjing and Taiyuan", *People's Daily* report: "People of all kinds demonstrate to celebrate victory, step up production and study to expand victory, turning enthusiastic revelry to positive work", *People's Daily* 26 April 1949, 3rd edition.

7   Xiao Bai, "Extra Editions at the Time of the War of Liberation", *The News Frontline*, 1961 No 2, p3.

8   Jin Jianling, "The Extra Edition on the Liberation of Nanjing", *Archives and Construction*, Vol 4, 2009, pp28 - 9.

previous work. Before 1949, Wu Zuoren almost never used the great social and political events of his own era for the subject matter of his paintings. Of course this does not mean that Wu Zuoren was remote from reality. He had created *Battleship under the Spirit of Peace* and *Mother During Air-Raid*, both in a realistic vein and critically aimed at certain social phenomena and real problems, but the number of such works was quite low, and also did not refer to any particular political event.[9] What Wu Zuoren really cared about was possibly just painting human figures, portraits and still-life scenes. The liberation of Nanjing certainly affected him strongly, yet it does not seem intrinsically greater than the victory in the War of Resistance in September 1945. The liberation of Beiping that took place in January 1949 with Wu Zuoren present also does not seem to have aroused his creative inspiration. Possibly, there were other concerns at work in Wu Zuoren's selection of the liberation of Nanjing for his subject matter.

He was not alone, in that Xu Beihong also created a work about the liberation of Nanjing, called *Hearing the News about the Liberation of Nanjing at the World Peace Conference*. When Nanjing was liberated, Xu Beihong happened to be attending the First World Peace Conference, which was held from 20 to 25 April 1949 in Paris and Prague, with more than two thousand representatives attending from seventy-two countries. The Chinese representatives attended in Prague, as France had not yet established diplomatic relations with Communist-ruled China, and would not allow the Chinese delegation to enter France. On the 24th, when the news was conveyed to Prague, and the liberation of Nanjing was publicly announced by the Chair of the Conference, "the whole Conference erupted in fifteen minutes of wild celebration. The forty-four members of the Chinese delegation were ecstatic and sang in loud voices. The delegations of the other countries joined arms with the Chinese representatives and began to march in demonstration. The Conference loudly sang "Long Live Free China". The Leader of the Chinese delegation, Guo Moruo, announced that: "The victory of the Chinese people is the victory of the whole peace camp."[10] Xu Beihong was a member of the delegation. At the time, he too must have been shouting and singing and waving his arms. After he returned to China, he used it as a pretext to create the ink-and-wash painting *Hearing the News about the Liberation of Nanjing at the World Peace Conference*. Like Wu Zuoren, Xu Beihong had lacked creative enthusiasm towards the political events of his own time, and had been criticized for the very same reason. Like *Victory!*, the work *Hearing the News about the Liberation of Nanjing at the World Peace Conference* was exhibited in the First Chinese National Fine Arts Exhibition.

From April to June 1949, Wu Zuoren and Xu Beihong both chose a subject that neither had previously shown much affinity for: a political incident that had just taken place. At about the same time, they thought that the liberation of Nanjing was a subject that needed painting. The only possible larger background for the stimulation of their 'realistic' concern was the change in political power, and what spurred them on to produce a swift reaction to the liberation of Nanjing was the call to the first Cultural Committee Conference under the rule of the Chinese Communist Party, and the holding of the first Chinese National Fine Arts Exhibition.

Wu Zuoren's *Victory!* and Xu Beihong's *Hearing the News about the Liberation of Nanjing at the World Peace Conference* were both shown in the first nation-wide arts exhibition in July 1949. This was the most important fine arts exhibition in the second half of the twentieth century, and was called at the time: "China National Cultural Workers Committee Conference Fine Arts Exhibition". It can also be seen from this name that the purpose of the exhibition was to accompany the China National Cultural Workers Committee Conference (Wendaihui, 文代会). The Conference was convened on 2 July 1949, with the Preparatory Committee made up of forty-two members including Guo Moruo, Mao Dun

---

9   On Wu Zuoren's artistic activities, see Xiao Man, Huo Dashou: *Wu Zuoren*, People's Art Press, 1988, pp382 - 412.
10 Xinhua News Agency cable, Beiping, 24 April 1949: "Paris and Prague Peace Conference Greets the Liberation of Nanjing with Frenzied Joy." *People's Daily*, 25 April 1949, 1st edition.

and Zhou Yang, and was concluded on 19 July 1949. Mao Zedong gave his views to the representatives at the Conference on 6 July, telling them: "This kind of conference that you are holding is a very good conference, it is a conference that the Revolution needs, it is a conference that the people of the whole of China hope for. For you are all men and women that the People needs. You are the literary writers of the People. , the artists of the people, or the organizers of the literary and artistic work of the People. You are good for the Revolution. You are good for the People."[11] Zhu De spoke as representative for the CCP Central Committee, Zhou Enlai made a long political announcement, and furthermore, there were Guo Moruo's "The Struggle to Construct the People's Literature and Art in the New China", Mao Dun's "The Struggle and Development of Revolutionary Literature under the Oppression of the Reactionaries", Zhou Yang's "New People's Literature and Art" and other reports. These reports summarized the experiences and achievements since the "Yan'an Talks on Literature and Art" were published in 1942, specified the new direction and new responsibilities of literary and artistic work under the new circumstances, and elected to give birth to the National Committee of the China Federation of Literary and Art Workers (popularly called: "Wenlian" and the various societies and leading organizations under the Federation including the China Artists Association "Meixie").

The convening of the China National Cultural Workers Committee Conference signaled that the literary and artistic policies established by Mao Zedong in Yan'an formally had become the direction of development of literature and art in the new China, so it had an important significance. The China National Cultural Workers Committee Conference Fine Arts Exhibition that was held over the same period demonstrated this great paradigm shift in the area of fine arts. All the participating works were illustrating, explaining or manifesting the Yan'an Talks on Literature and Art. Naturally, this presented no problem to the artists who came from the liberated areas, but it was a test for the artists from the Kuomintang-ruled areas: what kind of works should they present?

Judging by the works submitted to the Chinese National Literary and Artistic Workers Representative Conference Fine Arts Exhibition by the artists from the Kuomintang-ruled areas, a considerable portion of them were created in the first half of 1949. Apart from Wu Zuoren and Xu Beihong, there were also Dong Xiwen's *The Liberation of Beiping*, Zong Qixiang's *Restoring the Yongding River Iron Bridge*, Huang Jun's *Celebrating the May Day, Workers' Holiday* and other works. They hurriedly created these works close to the opening of the Exhibition (they only had about two or three months' time), and the works were clearly made to welcome the arrival of the new age and the "grand exhibition" that the new age endowed with an official character. Although the China National Cultural Workers Committee Conference was convened in July 1949, the preparatory work commenced in the beginning of the year. On 22 March of that year, Guo Moruo at the cultural circles' tea reception held by the North China Committee on Cultural and Artistic Work and the North China Literary and Artistic Workers Association, suggested that a manager should be elected and a preparatory committee formed very soon. On 1 May 1949, the Preparatory Committee announced the "Qualifications of Conference Representatives and Selecting Methods". On 27 June, Guo Moruo published a talk on the policy and duties of the Conference. By 2 July, the China National Cultural Workers Committee was formally opened. It may be said that from March, the whole of the literary and artistic world of Beijing (then Beiping) was frantically working for the preparatory meeting, and those most famous artists were busy creating works, with a goal that may be seen at a glance.

Wu Zuoren participated in the China National Cultural Workers Committee Conference. He was on the Committee for the Pingjin Second Delegation and the

---

11 China National Cultural Workers Committee Conference Propaganda Office (ed): *Selection of Commemorative Documents of the China National Cultural Workers Committee Conference*, Xinhua Bookstoretore, 1950, p3.

Conference Fine Arts Organisational Committee. Wu Zuoren was a member of the Committee for the Fine Arts Exhibition (the Fine Arts Exhibition Committee had a Chair and nine members), and also filled the post of Group Leader of the Installation Group of the Art Exhibition Committee. The installation activity of the Exhibition was almost entirely his responsibility. In the China Artists Association formed after the Conference, Wu Zuoren was on the National Committee, and at the same time was on the Standing Committee. From this series of duties, it may be seen that Wu Zuoren from the very beginning entered the organizational work of the Cultural Committee Conference, and, moreover, that he was one of the main curators of the China National Cultural Workers Committee Conference Fine Arts Exhibition. He would have given deep thought and mature reflection to which work he should contribute to this Exhibition.

The emphasis on the distinction between the liberated areas and the Kuomintang-ruled areas is due to the particular 'eyes' with which the status of artists were scrutinized in 1949. At the time, all 'Literary and Artistic Workers' were divided into two kinds: they might come from the liberated areas or from the Kuomintang-ruled areas. Zhou Enlai in his "Political Report on the China National Cultural Workers Committee Representative Conference" mentions representatives who come from the liberated areas and representatives who come from the areas formerly ruled by the Kuomintang, and at the end of the report joins them together as the "joint forces of the two parts of the literature and art army, coming from the old liberated areas and the newly liberated areas".[12] The participating representatives of the Cultural Committee Conference were divided into ten representative groups numbering 824 people altogether (the actual reported figure was 650 people). Naturally, they came from all over the country, but they can nevertheless generally be divided into three parts: army, liberated areas and Kuomintang-ruled areas, with the first two being in practice the same thing. In the division of the representative groups, the above distinction also appeared, namely that the Pingjin area to which Wu Zuoren and Xu Beihong belonged was divided into two groups of representatives. No 1 Group of Pingjin Representatives was basically composed of the literary and artistic workers who came from the liberated areas, and No.2 Group of Pingjin Representatives were mainly the artists who originally belonged with the Kuomintang-ruled areas. Xu Beihong, Wu Zuoren, Dong Xiwen, Ye Jianyu, Qi Baishi and others were all allocated to the No.2 Group of Pingjin Representatives.

The works shown in the China National Cultural Workers Committee Conference Fine Arts Exhibition were also considered to derive from these two places, and this point was clearly pointed out in the preface to the catalogue: "These are partly the works of the fine-arts workers of the liberated areas, and reflect the great liberation enterprise and glorious social construction of the Chinese people; another part are the works of the fine-art workers who at the time stayed in the Kuomintang-ruled areas, and what they portray is the state of society and the life struggle of the people under the reactionary rule of the Kuomintang."[13] According to this way of putting it, the artists who came from the Kuomintang-ruled areas should portray the reactionary rule of the Kuomintang and the struggle of the people against reactionary rule. However, the artists who lived in the Kuomintang-ruled areas and who were strong in oil painting, mostly had no creative practice in this direction. They could only start afresh and, like the artists from the liberated areas, "reflect the great liberation enterprise and glorious social construction of the Chinese people", and portray the new society and new phenomena with which they had only just come into contact.

---

12 China National Cultural Workers Committee Conference Propaganda Office (ed): *Selection of Commemorative Documents of the China National Cultural Workers Committee Conference*, Xinhua Bookstoretore, 1950, pp27, 33.

13 Propaganda Office for the China National Cultural Workers Committee Conference (ed): *Selected Works of Art of the Fine Arts Exhibition of the China National Cultural Workers Committee Conference*, Xinhua Bookstoretore, 1950, p7.

At this Cultural Committee Conference, Ye Qianyu, representing the art workers of the Kuomintang-ruled areas, in the special statement on "The Progressive Art Movement in the Kuomintang-ruled Areas", admitted that "because of the objective limitations, we often were not close to the masses, and were lacking in deep experience of actual life. In our creations, we could also only reach the level of Realism and Naturalism, and some of us caught the poison of the decadent capitalist Modern Art of Europe and America, falling into the horns of Formalism and being unable to crawl out of it." Yet he looked forward to the present and the future: "Today, with various favourable conditions, we are totally able to thoroughly remake ourselves, and to get working to develop the various useful conditions of our working ability. We must study well and well put into practice Mao Zedong's literary and artistic policy, and closely join with the masses of workers and peasants, to learn from labor in order to achieve progress. Besides, we mustoffer up our energy to develop production, develop culture and construct a new China.[14]

Wu Zuoren was fully aware of his status as an artist of the Kuomintang-ruled areas. When "summarizing the oil paintings of the Kuomintang-ruled areas" in the article *Oil Painting in the Kuomintang-ruled Areas Since the 'July 7th'* written by him in 1949, he says: "In the past, we who were engaged in oil painting work, only knew how to bicker about styles, and we had no idea that we should serve anybody." As for the direction of artistic creation in the future, Wu Zuoren had already settled on an article of faith: "As things stand now, it cannot be long before the Kuomintang-ruled areas are completely liberated We shall no longer be shackled. We should join with our comrade art workers in the liberated areas, who were separated from us by reactionary rule for many years, and get close to the workers, peasants and soldiers and serve them, and, in the construction, under the banner of Mao Zedong, of the great destiny of the new China, we should offer our greatest energies in oil painting."[15]

1949 was a key moment in the transformation of Wu Zuoren's artistic creation. He chose the liberation of Nanjing for his subject matter, and for the first Cultural Committee Conference, as well as for the National Art Exhibition, presented his *Victory!* In the expression used in the Editor's Foreword in *Selected Works of Art of the Fine Arts Exhibition of the China National Cultural Workers Committee Conference*, the work *Victory! (Extra Edition on the Liberation of Nanjing)* was the artist's "present for the birth of the new China".[16] This work signified Wu Zuoren's first step in the path of Mao Zedong's direction in literature and art, and also announced his own standpoint and choice in the face of the great trend of the era - a question that the artists of that era obviously faced in common.

---

14 Propaganda Office for the China National Cultural Workers Committee Conference (ed): *Selection of Commemorative Documents of the China National Cultural Workers Committee Conference*, Xinhua Bookstoretore, 1950, p286.

15 Wu Zuoren: *Selected Writings by Wu Zuoren*, Anhui Arts Press, 1988, pp26 - 27.

16 Propaganda Office for the China National Cultural Workers Committee Conference (ed): *Selected Works of Art of the Fine Arts Exhibition of the China National Cultural Workers Committee Conference*, Xinhua Bookstore, 1950, p7.

2

吴作人
Wu Zuoren
解放南京号外
Extra Edition on the Liberation of Nanjing
布面油彩
Oil on Canvas
89 × 116cm, 1949

从"流民"到"人民":
为表现新中国
而努力的一种
——试析蒋兆和
《中国人民从此站立起来了》
的重新发现

蒋岳红

画作《中国人民从此站立起来了》,高283厘米,宽132厘米,水墨设色,高丽纸,镜心装裱。画幅靠近左边沿处,竖写题识和落款:中国人民从此站立起来了中华人民共和国诞生之日 一九四九年十月一日 兆和,名字下白底红色阳文"兆龢"钤印。

此幅亦被简称为《人民图》的作品,在创作尺幅上,也是画家本人仅次于《流民图》(高200厘米,宽2700厘米)的一幅画。更有意味的是,这幅因为拍卖而进入公众视野,被称之为画家于《流民图》之外又一幅代表作的《人民图》,却是一直被卷在由画家的夫人萧琼外书"旧纸"的一卷旧纸当中,直到2004年因为画家百年诞辰纪念的缘故,子女在重新整理遗物而意外发现的一张装裱保护都很完好的"新"作品。之所以"新",是因为在此之前,他们谁也不曾看见过,也不曾听父母提起过这件作品。所以,这幅作品首次可考的亮相和著录是《蒋兆和百年诞辰作品集》(第30页,中国文联出版社,2004年)。与《流民图》被动被迫消失近十年后仅留半卷重新回到艺术家手中相比,这幅《人民图》在十八年后的"丢失"之后重新以艺术家代表作及与共和国同龄的作品而为人所知,显露出的似乎是艺术家对其作品的一种回避和退隐,是艺术家本人看似主动的自藏选择——他不曾和子女以及60年代受教于他的学生提起过,也不曾将其收入过生前出版的画集和作品选——那么这幅作品的重新发现,究竟会给我们一些关于艺术家本人的创作经历,关于新中国美术的创作和接受以及评价一些怎样的提示呢?

这件水墨设色纸本的《人民图》,是可以被称之为"中国现代人物画"的作品。之所以不被称做肖像画,是因为所用于创作的材料和工具;而之所以会被称之为"现代人物画",则与创作的方式——"能用中国画笔加入外国法内,为中外特见"(齐白石语),画面中皴擦和渲染技法的运用事实上已经脱离或者也可以说是不囿于传统笔墨语言形式本身具备的特质,而纯为艺术家刻画形象所用,完成以明暗造型的目的。他用写生的方式完成的是现时现世"人民"形象的创作:占据画面半幅尺寸高的一男一女是着意刻画的主体形象——男的戴蓝色带檐软帽,身着带扣翻领的白色衬衫,连体背带的蓝色工装裤,脚上是黑褐色皮鞋,右手在上,左手在下,双手紧握旗杆;女的则头裹白手巾,侧襟小立领的浅褐色上衣,黑色的裤子,裤脚挽起,脚穿黑色的布鞋,左手扶握住旗杆,右手拿着镰刀。两人中,男性身体呈向画面左前方迈步的动势,稍稍挡在双脚分开静立的女性之前,头稍左转,与女性一样稍抬头望向画面的右前方。近四分之三画面上方的空间里,是醒目的迎风飘扬向画面右方的红色五星红旗和男女主体形象。画面下方四分之一处的天际线处是振臂高呼和高举手中工具锤子、斧头、铁锹或农具钉耙、镰刀雀跃的人群,构成了画面后景,与主体人物形象形成一横一竖的呼应,画面平衡稳定之余也造成一种挺拔向上的态势。在主体人物形象的脚下，仅占画面下方八分之一位置的是呈小圆弧形的前景地面，环绕穿插其间的是五只白鸽子，在丰富了画面空间层次感的同时，也作为主体形象的基座完成着作品纪念碑式的整体构图形式。五只彼此呼应的白鸽，在形式上是在竖线的前景人物、横线的后景人群和红颜色的旗面、黑色的地面之外，增添画面灵动的点。画面偏暖的色调及仰视的视角在突出人物形象的高大和纪念碑性的同时也传达给观者以秋高气爽的感受——这是十月，一个收割庄稼，收获的时节，正意合着中华人民共和国成立的胜利果实和其诞生所蕴含的期待和生机。

《人民图》题识中的文字信息除了画者的落款和钤印之外，也对我们解读画作的象征意义给出了明示，画作若干符号和代码的运用中隐藏的象征也因着如此的题识而成为新中国美术作品中显见的象征。比如五星红旗作为国旗，象征的是中华人民共和国，手握红旗以及红旗下欢呼雀跃的都是新政权的拥护者——中国人民，其能指是画中的工人和农民形象。当画面中出现明确的代表工农阶级的形象时，他们是手握红旗的代表者，工人阶级的能指是男性，而农民的能指则一定是女性。男性工人对于代表政权的国旗的双手把握，以及稍居前位，则提示出工人阶级居于领导者的地位。女性农民握住国旗的左手意味着作为工人阶级的同盟对其领导权和新政权的认同和扶助。她手中的镰刀，挽起的裤腿和袖子，以及代表工农群像的人群手中举起的工具和农具，在凸显作为中国人民的农民或工人身份之外，还会让人联想到工农作为生产者，因其对生产工具的占有而成为站起来的生产的主人。白鸽的所指是和平，在画作里，或许可以标示着对战争结束，祥和太平的期冀。"因为此时的我们的革命工作还没有完结，人民解放战争和人民革命运动还在向前发展，我们还要继续努力。"〔毛泽东1949年9月21日在全国政协会议第一届全体会议上发表的讲话〕

如果说艺术家将新中国的开国盛事凝缩在了一个纪念碑性的视觉形象中，那么画家的题识也是这一凝缩的体现。细究起来，"中国人民从此站立起来了"，"中华人民共和国诞生之日"和"一九四九年十月一日"传达出来的是艺术家个人作为接受者的"民"而非政见传达者在新中国诞生成立之时的感同身受。比如"中国人民从此站立起来了"事实上是艺术家个人主观自觉的一个理解，因为毛泽东1949年讲话中的原话是"中国人从此站起来了"，而不是"中国人民从此站立起来了"——讲话原文是"诸位代表先生们，我们有一个共同的感觉，这就是我们的工作将写在人类的历史上，它将表明：占人类总数四分之一的中国人从此站立起来了。中国人从来就是一个伟大的勇敢的勤劳的民族，只是在近代落伍了。"原话强调的是民族立场，是所有中国人的立场，"我们的民族将再也不是一个被人欺负的民族了，我们已经站起来了。"〔毛泽东讲话〕而郑振铎于1949年10月10日出版的《文艺报》上发表直接以引文"中国人从此站立起来了"

为题的诗歌："……中国人像一个钢的巨人似的，雄健地站立着面向着红光亮亮的太阳，'中国人从此站立起来了。'"也佐证了毛泽东的原话是"中国人"而不是"中国人民"从此站立起来了。显然，画家蒋兆和作于开国游行大典当日的作品，他对于此前9月21日的讲话的意会是源于他自己可能都不一定自觉的"人民"的立场。在此幅作品重现时的2004年，"中国人民从此站立起来了"已经"以讹传讹"地成为了熟知的常识，这大概也是画家本人当年所预料不到的。据蒋兆和的女儿回忆，画家的画作经常会拿出来，展开挂在家里的墙壁上，并经常不时地更换，但是在她的印象里，从来不曾有看到过这幅画作的记忆。此外，这幅画作也是目前所知的画家作品中最早出现鸽子形象的一幅，而鸽子也是此后画家画作里经常出现的形象。画家生前喜爱鸽子，并在家专门饲养鸽子供写生之用，逝世之后的墓碑上也以对鸽作为个人形象的象征。这样看来，画家本人不可能不记得自己这一幅作于新中国开国之日的作品。那么，是因为画家本人会在画作装裱完成之后很快发现，或是经人提醒后意识到他的些许"偏差"而将此幅画作卷藏而不示人的吗？

蒋兆和的子女于2004年曾就此画向还健在的裱画工刘金涛询问此画时，刘师傅不记得裱过这张画作了，或许说即使曾经裱过也没有印象了。由此，我们至少可以知道这张画在创作完成的年代里，并不像《流民图》那样具有吸引力和影响力，甚至也不如此后画家完成的一系列画作那样广为认知和获得好评，比如1950年的《鸭绿江边》，1951年的《领到土地证》，1953年儿童节的《把学习成绩告诉志愿军叔叔》，1954年的《小孩与鸽子》和《给爷爷读报》以及1955年的《毛主席和少年儿童》。那么，这一幅《中国人民从此站起来了》与同时期其他画家的代表作，如获得1950年文化部颁发的新年画创作奖金的作品，包括李琦的《农民和拖拉机》，古一舟的《劳动换来光荣》，安林的《毛主席大阅兵》，以及张仃的《新中国的儿童》，包括与画家此后完成的一系列画作相比，《人民图》作为视觉文本所没有显现的东西是哪些？或者，我们也可以说，是画家努力表现新中国的时候"漏掉"的是什么？比如儿童，是新中国的希望，是美好的未来，是革命建设后继有人的象征；比如毛主席，是人民的救星，是代言人，是知心人，是领头人，是人群中的核心人物，作为国家领袖，他就是新中国的能指之一；再比如军人，是国土疆域的守护者，是国威的象征；还比如虽然画家在《人民图》中所努力刻画完成的是一个工农的阶级形象，但是新中国需要的是工业化，是农业现代化，是拖拉机而不是镰刀。

而在蒋兆和同于1949年创作的一幅立轴、水墨设色纸本的《努力生产》〔也作《男女农人》〕〔125×165厘米〕中，画面右边沿竖写题识：努力生产丰收支前新生中国工农联盟各党各派团结一致中苏友好世界和平 广州解放之日 兆和，名字下是同样的"兆龢"钤印。广州解放之日是1949年10月14日。显然，画中的女性农民形象与《人民图》中的女性农民形象是同一女模特，而男性农民形象与《人民图》的男性工人形象似也应是同一模特。据画家的女儿指认，应是后来还一直与蒋家相熟的裱画工刘焕章，以他为模特的形象还出现在题作于晋中解放之日的画作《还乡》(1949)中。我们也会看到，无论是男工人还是男农人的形象，都明显有些偏瘦，甚至在现今收藏于捷克国立博物馆的《男女农人》中，男农人的内衣上还有刻意画出的破洞，而且这一细节显然是画家刻意设计的。由此上种种，我们也可以发现1949年蒋兆和在为表现新中国而努力时所立足的是画家眼见的现实，无论是人物的情态，还是所谓对于小农经济生活的梦寐以求，都是历经磨难之后的新中国的现实。画家为表现新中国的努力显而易见，但是，新中国视觉文化建构中所需要看到的却是未来生活的远景而非画家所眼见的现实情境。所以，当我们重新来看画家作于1949年的《中国人民从此站立起来了》，就像留意那些已经在画面中显现的事物一样，来留意这些被省略（有意或无意地）的符号和代码时，或许才能够更加合乎情理地了解到视觉文本——画作本身所透露出来的画家没能在新中国成立之初的画坛出场并隐藏于旧纸卷中的内情。

的确，对于身处这一时期的画家而言，他们经历新旧中国的变化，"为表现新中国而努力"所表明的既是党和国家的立场，也是他们自身所主动选择的唯一立场。他们需要面临的是新时代的新课题：如何才能够变旧题材画新主题，弃旧形象立新形象，改旧形式造新形式？究竟是哪些题材、哪些事物才是可以用来表现新中国的新题材、新事物？如何去描写和把握？这是一个需要身处其时的画家不断去揣摩和把握的过程。艺术家的个人叙事与国家叙事和集体叙事之间的互动是一个始终值得我们去关注和仔细审视的环节。

这一幅蒋兆和画作《中国人民从此站立起来了》的"失而复得"是一个有谜面却没有谜底的个案，但是它的遭遇或许对于新中国美术史的书写会是一个提示——如何去将那些谜面中隐于不言、细入无间的草蛇灰线一并清理出来留存？或许我们能够由此接触到一个细节更为丰富生动的视觉故事。

2011.5

From Refugees to The People: An Effort to Represent the New China

- An Analysis of the Re - Discovery of Jiang Zhaohe's *From Now On, the Chinese People Has Stood Up*

By Jiang Yuehong

The painting *From Now On, the Chinese People Has Stood Up*, 283 x 132 cm, ink and color, Korea paper, frame-mounted, with a vertical inscription near its left border reading: '*From Now On, the Chinese People Has Stood Up*. The day the Chinese People's Republic was born, 1 October 1949, Zhaohe' and under the name, the imprint of a positive relief seal in red ink on white base reading 'Zhao He'.

In terms of its size, this painting, which is also known by the shorter name of **The People**, is second only to *Refugees* (200 x 2700 cm) in this painter's oeuvre. Even more interestingly, this painting, which entered the public eye because of the auction, and which has been called the artist's second representative work (after *Refugees*), had all along been kept in the artist's house, rolled up in a bundle of old papers labelled 'Old Papers' by his wife Xiao Qiong, until 2004, when his children, re-sorting his estate for the centenary commemoration of the artist's birth, unexpectedly discovered a 'new work' that had been well-protected in its mounting. 'New' because none of them had seen it before, and because they had never heard their parents mention it. Therefore, the first time that this work was reliably presented and recorded was in the *Centenary Collection of Jiang Zhaohe's Works*, China Wenlian Press, 2004, at page 30. Compared to *Refugees*, which returned to the hands of the artist, half of it missing, after having gone missing for almost a decade, *The People*, after eighteen years of being 'lost', and becoming known again as a representative work by the artist - and one that is exactly the same age as the People's Republic - seems to reveal some evasion of and retreat from his work by the artist. It appears that the artist actively chose to keep it to himself. He never mentioned it to his children, nor to the students he taught in the 1960s. Nor did he include it in the collections and selections of his work published during his lifetime. What exactly then can the rediscovery of this work tell us about the creative experiences of the artist himself, and about the creation and reception - and appraisal - of fine arts in the new China?

This ink-and-color work on paper may be classed as a Chinese 'modern work depicting human figures'. The reason it has not been classed as a portrait is because of the materials and tools used in making it. The reason it may be called a 'modern work depicting human figures' has to do with the format of its creation. "The ability to use a Chinese brush within the foreign method, is a special sight in China and abroad." (Qi Baishi). The use of texture-strokes, rubbing technique and layered texturing techniques in the painting are in fact already departures, from, or, in another word, not exclusively belonging to the language and forms of traditional brush-and-ink, and solely serving the artist's needs in portraying figures and creating desired effects of light and shade. What the artist has achieved by using his realistic format is the creation of an image of 'the People' of the present day and age. The focus is on the main subject of a man and a woman who occupy about half the height of the painting. The man is wearing a blue soft cap with a brim, a button-and-collar white shirt, blue overalls and brown leather shoes, and is tightly gripping a flag - pole with his right hand above his left. The woman wears a white kerchief on her head, a small-collar light brown lapel jacket, black rolled-up trousers, and black cloth shoes. Her left hand is wrapped around the flagpole, and her right holds a sickle. Of the two, the male body presents the movement gesture of a step forwards and towards the left-hand foreground of the painting, slightly masking the female who stands still with her legs slightly separated. His head is turned slightly to the left, and, like the woman, he slightly raises his head to look towards the right foreground of the painting. About the upper three quarters of the painting is occupied by a striking Five-star Red Flag blown by the wind in the direction of the right foreground, and by the main figures of the man and woman. The horizon in the lower quarter is a background composed of a delighted crowd of workers shouting approval and brandishing hammers, axes, shovels, and agricultural tools such as *dingba rakes and sickles*. In balancing correspondence with the verticality of the main figures, this horizontal element, apart from balancing and stabilizing the painting also produces an upward trend. At the foot of the image of the main figures, occupying a position of only one eighth of the painting, the ground presents a curved foreground with five doves inserted sporadically here and there. These enrich the feeling of layering in the painting, and at the same time serve as a base for the main figures, completing the painting's monumental overall structural form. Formally, the five coordinated doves add a vivid point to the vertical main figures and the horizontal crowd in the background, as well as to the red flag and the black earth. The rather warm palette of the painting and the upward-looking sightline emphasize the height and monumentality of the human figures, and at the same time convey to the spectator a sensation of clear crisp autumn weather. This is October, a time for reaping and harvesting, corresponding in meaning with the triumphal fruits of the founding of the People's Republic of China, and the expectations and vitality contained in its birth.

The written information in the inscription of **The People** gives us the details and the seal of the artist, but also clarifies for us the interpretation of the symbolic significance of the painting. The symbols hidden in the various signs and codes in the painting also become, in accordance with the inscription, the obvious symbols in the art of the new China. For instance, the Five-star Red Flag as the national flag symbolizes the Chinese People's Republic, and those who support the Flag, as well as those who shout in delight under it, are those who uphold the new governmental authority, namely the Chinese people, which can refer to the figures of workers and the peasants in the painting. When images clearly representing the class of workers and peasants appear in the painting, as the figures holding up the Red Flag here, the working class may be represented by the male, and the peasants are definitely represented by the female. The male worker's two-handed grip on the national flag, which represents governmental authority, and his slightly anterior position, reminds us of the leadership position of the workers as a class. The female peasant's left-handed grip on the flag signifies her alliance to the leading authority of the working class and her acceptance of and support for the new governmental authority. The sickle in her hand, her rolled up trousers and sleeves, and the raised tools and agricultural implements in the hands of the crowd representing the masses of workers and peasants, apart from foregrounding their identities as the Chinese people, the workers and peasants, also remind us that they are the producers, and masters of production who have stood up because they have taken possession of the tools of production. The white doves mean peace, and in this painting they may indicate the end of war, and the hope for peace and security. "As our revolutionary work is not yet completed, the People's Liberation War and at the moment the People's Revolutionary Movement are still developing and moving forward, and we must continue to work hard." (Mao Zedong's speech at the first Plenary Session of the National Committee of the Chinese People's Political Consultative Conference, 21 September 1949).

If the artist has condensed the great founding event of the new China into a monumental visual form, his inscription is also a manifestation of this condensation. A close examination reveals that what "*From Now On, the Chinese People Has Stood Up*", "The Day the Chinese People's Republic Was Born", and "1 October 1949" convey is the empathy of the individual artist as belonging, at the time of the birth and founding of the new China, to the receiving 'people', rather than being a political communicator. For instance, "*From Now On, the Chinese People Has Stood Up*" is in fact an individual, subjective and spontaneous understanding by the artist, for what Mao Zedong originally said in his Speech in 1949 was: "From now on, the Chinese have stood up", and not "*From Now On, the Chinese People Has Stood Up*". The original text of the Speech was: "Representatives! We share a feeling, which is that our work will be written into the history of mankind. It will proclaim: 'The Chinese, who make up one quarter of the total of mankind, have now stood up! The Chinese have always been a nation of great versatility and industry, who have only in recent times fallen behind.'" The original words stress the position of the ethnic nation, that is, the position of all the Chinese: "Our nation will no longer be a nation that is bullied by others. We have already stood up." (Mao Zedong's Speech). Zheng Zhenduo's poem published in *Literature and Art News* on 10 October 1949 under a title that directly quoted: "From Now On, the Chinese Have Stood Up", and which included the lines: "…The Chinese are like a steel colossus, standing vigorously and facing the bright red sun, 'From now on, the Chinese have stood up', provides further evidence that Mao Zedong's original words were "the Chinese have" and not "the Chinese People has" stood up. Obviously, the artist Jiang Zhaohe, in making his work for the day of the grand celebration parade for the founding of the Nation, may have relied, possibly without thinking about it, on his own position as being "of the People", for his interpretation of the meaning of the speech held on 21 September. When this work reappeared in 2004, "*From Now On, the Chinese People Has Stood Up*" had already 'erroneously' become general knowledge, which was something the artist would perhaps have been unable to foresee back then. According to the recollection of Jiang Zhaohe's daughter, the works painted by the artist were normally taken out and hung on the walls of the family home, and were regularly exchanged, but she had no recollection of ever having seen this painting. Besides, this painting, among the works by the artist known today, is also the earliest in which the image of doves appear. Images of doves and pigeons often appeared in the artist's later works. During his life he was fond of pigeons. He kept live pigeons at home specially for the purpose of drawing them, and he made a pair of pigeons as a visual symbol of himself on his gravestone for after his death. From this point of view, the artist himself could not have forgotten this work of his made for the founding day of the new China. Was it, then, because the artist himself discovered his little "deviation" very soon after the framing of the work, or was it after people drew his attention to it, that he realized it and therefore hid his work and never showed it to anybody?

When Jiang Zhaohe's children asked Liu Jintao, the worker who had mounted most of Jiang's work and is still living and in good health, about this painting, Master Liu did not remember and had no impression of ever having mounted this painting. From this, we can know at the very least that in the year when this painting was completed, it did not have the attractive or influential force of *Refugees*, and even that he did not receive for it the wide recognition and good appraisal of the series of paintings that he produced later, such as *By the Yalu River* (1950), *Receiving the Land Certificate* (1951), *Telling Uncle Volunteer about the School Results* (1953, Children's Day), *Child and Pigeon* (1954), *Reading the Newspaper for Grandpa* (also 1954) and *Chairman Mao with Young Children* (1955). What then was absent from the visual text offered by *From Now On, the Chinese People Has Stood Up* (or *The People*), as compared with other representative works painted by artists of that period, such as the works that won the 1950 New Year Scholarships Issued by the Ministry of Culture for the Creation of Paintings, including Li Qi's *Farmers and Tractor*, Gu Yizhou's *Labour for Glory*, An Lin's *Chairman Mao Reviews the Troops*, and Zhang Ding's *Children Of the New China*, as well as Jiang Zhaohe's own later series of works. Or, let's put the question in another way: what was missing when the artist was striving to represent the new China. Children, for instance, were the hope of the new China, its wonderful future, a symbol that there would continue to be people after the Revolution had been established. As another example, Chairman Mao was the saviour of the People, their spokesman, the one who understood them. He was the Chief, the central person in the crowd, the Leader of the nation, and one of the possible references to the new China. Again, there was the army, the protectors of the borders of the nation, the symbols of its prestige. Yet again, although what the artist was striving to depict and complete in *The People* was a class image of workers and peasants, what the new China needed was industrialization and the modernization of agriculture. It needed tractors, not sickles.

In a vertical scroll that Jiang Zhaohe also created in 1949, *Working Hard on Production*, also known as *Male and Female Peasant* (ink-and-color on paper, 165 x 125 cm), there is a vertical inscription along the right hand border of the painting: "Working hard to produce a bumper crop to support the front; the alliance of workers and peasants of the new-born China in solidarity with all parties and factions join in Sino-Soviet friendship and world peace. The day of Guangzhou's liberation. Zhaohe". Under the name there is a similar seal 'Zhaohe'. Guangzhou was liberated on 14 October 1949. The model for the image of the female peasant in the painting is the same as for the female peasant in *The People*. The model for the male peasant seems to be the same as for the male worker in *The People*. According to information provided by the artist's daughter, this male model was probably Liu Huanzhang, who worked mounting artworks, and who later remained on familiar terms with the Jiang family. Images modeled on him also appear in the work titled *Returning Home* (1949), painted on the day of the liberation of Jinzhong. We can see that he clearly looks rather underfed, both in the image of the male worker, and in that of the male peasant. The undershirt of the male peasant in *Male and Female Peasant* (now in the Czech National Museum (Národní Muzeum) collection) even has a tatty hole in it, and clearly this detail was deliberately planned and painted by the artist. From these various pieces of evidence, we can see that in 1949, when Jiang Zhaohe was striving to portray the new China, his basis was the reality that he saw with his own eyes. Whether it was the mood of the human figures, or the so-called dreams regarding the economic life of the petty peasantry, this was the reality of a new China that had gone through suffering and hardship. The efforts of the artist in depicting the new China are plain to see. However, what had to be seen in the construction of the visual culture of the new China was the distant vision of a future life, and not the real situation as seen by the artist with his own eyes. Therefore, when we look again at the artist's 1949 painting *From Now On, the Chinese People Has Stood Up*, it is perhaps only when we notice, in addition to those things that appear in the painting, the signs and codes that have (consciously or unconsciously) been omitted that we are able to understand the visual text in a rational way - and the reason provided by the painting why it could not appear in the art forum of the first period of the founding of the new China, as well as the inner reason why it was hidden in a roll of old papers.

The artists who lived in that period experienced the change from the old to the new China. "Working hard to display the new China" was the position both of the Party and of the nation, and also the only position that the artists themselves had voluntarily chosen. What they needed to face was the new task a new age. In which ways could they change the old subject matter and paint new themes, discard old images and establish new ones, and change old forms and produce new ones? Exactly which subjects and which things could be used to represent the new subject matter and the new things of the new

China? How were they to describe and grasp them? This was a process that artists living in those times constantly needed to fathom out and grasp. The interaction of the narrative of the individual artists with the narrative of the nation and the collective narrative is a nexus that is at all times worthy of attention and consideration.

The losing and finding of this painting by Jiang Zhaohe, *From Now On, the Chinese People Has Stood Up* is a case that appears to be but is not actually a riddle, yet its story may serve as a pointer in the writing of the history of the new China: how do we trace those faint clues that are silently hidden in the seamless shells of apparent riddles and solve them so they may be preserved? Perhaps we can in this way arrive at a visual story whose details are even richer and more vivid.

May 2011

蒋兆和

Jiang Zhaohe

中国人民从此站立起来了

From Now On, the Chinese People has Stood Up

设色纸本

Ink and Color on Paper

283×132cm, 1949

靳尚谊与毛主席肖像画

姜 鹏

一

1950年的夏天，中央美术学院组织学生深入铁路系统体验生活，绘画系一年级学生靳尚谊所在的这一组被分到了浦镇机车厂[1]。此行是与"创作课"相配合的教学环节，这时的美院正在用"老解放区新教育经验"调整课程设置，以实现"反映生活，特别是反映工农兵生活"的艺术取向。其现实动力则是毛泽东1942年在延安文艺座谈会上"文艺为工农兵服务"的主张，随着1949年中共夺取政权，而由政党意志上升为国家政策。于是，这所蔡元培倡导下，肇建于1918年的中国历史上首家国立美术教育学府，除了被重新命名，还要迎接更为深刻的改变。

此时，浦镇铁路工厂里的靳尚谊与同学，正与工人们作息一处，学习劳动技能之余，也为他们画些画儿。高年级学生、身为组长的靳之林将担纲一幅油画，靳尚谊也跃跃欲试，便加入其中，他虽然从未学过油画，但素描基础很好，两人合作，最终完成任务。靳尚谊非常兴奋，这是他平生第一次画油画，所画的便是毛主席标准像。

基本可以断定，这幅领袖像将被安置在浦镇工厂某处重要的公共空间，这种做法随着新中国的到来，开始在全国范围内变得司空见惯。但在此之前，因为中共政权一直作为地方割据势力存在，从瑞金到延安，无论是现存最早的——1933年红色中华出版社《革命画集》中毛泽东肖像素描，还是发行量最大的——1942年王式廓迎合了工农兵审美趣味的套色木刻《毛主席像》，都只能在其控制地区内流行。我们即便将视野由"毛泽东画像"扩大为"毛泽东图像"，考察诸如1941年王朝闻制作、装饰于中央党校礼堂，象征着毛泽东在党内已确立绝对权威的头像浮雕及其衍生品——毛主席像章；宣示政权合法性的、由山东抗日根据地1944年首发的毛泽东肖像邮票以及1945年华东解放区发行的毛泽东肖像纸币，其情况也依然如此。尽管那张由斯诺拍摄于1936年的《毛泽东在陕北》经典照片，曾搭乘着《西行漫记》穿越封锁，通往了黄土高原之外的世界，但毛泽东像的合法地位在全国范围内的真正确立，是它取代天安门上蒋介石像的位置，亮相开国大典的那一刻。

靳尚谊亲历了开国大典，在第二年的"红五月"运动中还以此为题材进行了创作。16岁的少年有的是真诚与热情，却无法预见新国家的未来，甚至关于他自己的未来。在浦镇机车厂首次画油画的靳尚谊，也仅仅"只知道有油画，很喜欢油画"而已，没有想过将来一定要学习这门艺术，更不曾想到将与之相伴一生，走过艰难而漫长的道路。

二

16年后，文化大革命开始了。已经在中央美院完成了本科、研究生、油画训练班学业的靳尚谊正执教于油画系第一工作室。次年，"毛主席肖像画学习班"在这里举办，靳尚谊是教员之一，第一期27名学生全部为工农兵学员，来自北京及外省市的厂矿、机关和部队，这些业余画家以构图简单、色彩单一的宣传画见长，美院的培训也仅仅有限地提高了他们的素描水平。即便如此，于全国数量巨大的美术工作者而言，也殊为难得了，事实上，全国范围内的领袖像绘制狂潮正由更加业余的画家队伍掀起、推动，专业画家们则被剥夺了画画的权利。1970年，靳尚谊被下放，开始一边劳动一边搞运动。

这种错位的荒唐性很快暴露，却以更荒唐的方式进行补救：1972年全国美展筹备，以工农兵和红卫兵为绝对主体的参展者，大多处理不好作品中的毛泽东形象，美术主管部门不得不召集专业画家组成"改画组"，将所有画得不好的主席像修改一遍，

---

[1] 本文史实基本依据靳尚谊口述、曹文汉撰文《我的油画之路——靳尚谊回忆录》，吉林美术出版社，2000年；以及靳尚谊、范迪安主编《靳尚谊全记录：自述、自选、自评》，江苏美术出版社，2009年。

工作量极大。靳尚谊任组长,又因高超的肖像画技巧而专门负责修改领袖头像。

领袖像的重要性,早在靳尚谊的本科学习中便凸显出来,他们当时的培养目标是美术普及工作者,不学油画,也不学国画,基础课是素描、水彩、线描、勾勒,创作课就是"连年宣",但即便如此,仍有过三张油画作业——头像、半身像、领袖像——着眼于毕业后绘制领袖像的现实需要。

靳尚谊的本科课程表正是新中国成立初期"新年画运动"在学院教育中的表现。在这场依据新的历史条件,"升级"延安艺术传统的运动中,涌现了不计其数的领袖题材新年画,其审美趣味贴近大众,而在构图上,又将大众"贴近"慈祥亲切的领袖,在这些作品中,毛泽东所代表的个人、政党以及新国家,与人民之间的甜蜜溢于言表。而后,旨在为中共执政地位提供合法依据的历史画创作展开了,图像化的毛泽东革命履历是这场历史画述中最重要的篇章。接受任务的画家满怀崇敬,投入了创作,而官方也回馈他们以相对独立的思考空间,艺术规律获得尊重,所以,我们才能看到领袖的背影出现在《延河边上》。

"美术创作的宽松局面及其与意识形态的需要之间的平衡,随着毛泽东重提阶级和阶级斗争的问题而结束。"[2] 待到"文革",领袖像的创作已经完全意识形态化——画脸用纯红色,阴影用焦褐色,浅暗的橘黄色画高光,其他部分的肌肤也一概以红色或别的暖色调处理。蓝、绿、灰等冷色应尽可能地避免。颜料挤到调色板上后调制时须按一定的秩序。毛泽东的脸应该分为三个相等的面,着色时须遵守专门为此制定的一张"色饱和度顺序表"。脸部尤其要注意光洁细润,不能见任何笔触的痕迹。要让它放光,显示出神采奕奕,容光焕发……[3]

这一"红光亮"模式是包括靳尚谊在内的所有画家不能逾越的。

三

纵然被模式所羁绊,创作于1966年的《毛主席全身像》却还是流露出了靳尚谊的肖像画理想。

此作只画毛泽东一人,无情节,亦无背景,以暖色烘托。领袖站立,左臂自然下垂,右臂微屈,手略攥握,着中山装,蹬皮鞋,仪态庄严而温和。虽然画毛泽东的作品无以数计,但曾为他写生的只有尹瘦石和沈逸千二人,所以领袖题材的图像来源主要是照片与影像,收集资料便成了创作的第一步骤。在靳尚谊的领袖题材作品中,有些形象来源明确,比如1966年为国际展览公司赴阿尔巴尼亚展览而作的订件画《毛主席在庐山》,就可与吕厚民的同名摄影作品基本对应上;有些则是依靠画家的理解,在照片或纪录片中提取形象,再逐步酝酿、设计、成熟起来。关于这幅《毛主席全身像》,我们没有找到能与之完全吻合的图像资料,比对历史照片,大致可推定,画中毛泽东约处在60年代"文革"前夕。

靳尚谊认为:"肖像画中的形象,应酷似所要表现的人物。但要求貌似只是一方面,人物的个性及其精神状态必须鲜明而生动,两者缺一不可。肖像画在描绘人物酷似这一方面,是较容易做到的,但是如忽视性格、精神状态的鲜明表现,往往就不能成为肖像画,而停留于一般的习作。""构图的选择要非常简练有力,因为肖像画的构图比较单纯,整个画面要严格符合造型美的要求。应尽量避免不美的形体、难处理的动作和杂乱无章的背景。动作和背景的处理,要紧密地配合,不能有一点妨碍形象的地方,艺术语言既要简练、朴素,又要有表现力。"[4]《毛主席全身像》符合以上两个观点,观者在被领袖力量感染的同时,也会因朴素的构图而获得一丝于躁动年代中久违的平静。

这平静源自靳尚谊的思考与坚持。当"全国上下都在搞政治性的重大创作,他却能清醒地用五年甚至十年的时间画习作头像"[5]。今天留存下来的几幅作于1967年的毛主席素描像,是《毛主席全身像》这些同期创作的基础,也代表了靳尚谊在艺术道路上的清醒追求。

四

在《毛主席全身像》之前,1960年与伍必端合作的《我们的朋友遍天下》,1961年的《毛主席在十二月会议上》以及1964年抒写"踏遍青山人未老"词意的《长征》,是靳尚谊领袖题材创作的代表。而需要特别关注的是《毛主席在十二月会议上》。

1961年,中共建党40周年,筹备揭幕的中国革命博物馆向很多画家委托了历史画订件,靳尚谊也在受约之列,他的题目是1947年解放军转战陕北之际召开的中央工作会议,即"十二月

2　邹跃进:《毛泽东时代美术》,湖南美术出版社,2005年,第11页。

3　杨昊成:《毛泽东图像研究》,南京师范大学博士论文,2005年,第76页。

4　靳尚谊:《创作〈毛主席在十二月会议上〉的体会》,《美术》1961年第6期。
　　转引自靳尚谊口述、曹文汉撰文《我的油画之路——靳尚谊回忆录》,吉林美术出版社,2000年,第53-54页。

5　《中国油画家全集·靳尚谊》,四川美术出版社,2005年。

会议"。画家选择了毛主席报告《目前形势和我们的任务》这一核心场面,开始草图创意,但却一直不尽理想。最后,一张正面举手向前推的人物设计在各种光线、各种角度的动作构思之中脱颖而出,因为它既是主席作报告时个人特有的手势,又吻合了"曙光就在前面,我们应当努力"的报告精神,仿佛这一推,便推出了一片曙光,便将中国推进了新的时代。其他画家也都认为很好,并建议靳尚谊不要再画其他人,最终,这件作品成为了一个肖像画的历史画,经由《美术》《解放军画报》的介绍,加之中央新闻电影制片厂将其作为"七一"专题片的重要镜头,影响很大。

而在靳尚谊本人看来,这次创作经历具有很大的偶然性,选择人物肖像表现主题的偶然,一如他于1949年秋天进入国立北平艺专并在此度过一生之偶然。可是,就是这样的偶然却使他坚定了追求"个性与精神状态"和"构图"理想美的愿望,引导了他后来的艺术走向,多年后,他于肖像画的有意而为,正是从毛泽东肖像的无意而为出发的,一路摸索向前。

五

"毛泽东形象的制造是毛泽东时代美术(1942-1976)中最重要的篇章,这不仅表现在数量与质量上,而且更为重要的还表现在它与毛泽东时代的社会政治、文化和思想之间有一种深刻的互动和需要的关系。"[6]承载着复杂的社会动力、政治诉求与意识形态需要的毛泽东肖像要由画家们来完成,这个任务对他们来讲,过于沉重了,然而却是时代的宿命。

"文革"中被下放的靳尚谊曾几度被召回,也都是因为绘制领袖像的缘故。一次是为山西平型关纪念馆画历史画《延安时期的毛主席和林彪》,后来林彪出事,纪念馆被封,画也不知去向;一次是与赵域按照当时的"革命路线"临摹改造董希文的《开国大典》;一次则是为全国美展合作毛泽东在天安门金水桥接见红卫兵的《要把无产阶级文化大革命进行到底》。再加之大量的毛主席头像、全身像、标准像,靳尚谊的眼睛终于在不知不觉中发生了色彩失调,写生用色也近乎"红光亮",而无法使用冷色。长期的劳累终于将其身体拖垮,1972年,他开始病休。

平生第一次尝试油画,所画便是毛主席像;
对他的艺术走向产生了重要影响的创作,也是毛主席像;
"文革"中,让他色彩感失调的还是毛主席头像、全身像、标准像……

1976年,42岁的靳尚谊在河北邢台一条大街的路口,画了一幅18米高的毛主席像,这是他一生中最大尺幅的作品。对于刚从病痛中康复不久的画家而言,更令人欣慰的是,他的眼睛逐步恢复了正常,失调的色彩感回到了"文革"前的状态,"红光亮"的视觉结束了,"红光亮"的岁月也将结束,而中国美术对毛泽东形象的构建运动也即将转向前所未有的解构。

---

[6] 邹跃进:《毛泽东时代美术》,第一部分,湖南美术出版社,2005年。

Jin Shangyi and the Portrait of Chairman Mao

By Jiang Peng

I

In the summer of 1950, the Central Academy of Fine Arts organized for the students to go deep into the railway system to experience life personally. The group including first-year student Jin Shangyi of the Drawing Department was sent to the Puzhen Locomotive Works.[1] This trip was an educational component that went with the 'creative courses'. The Academy at this time was using the 'new experiences of the old liberated areas' to adjust the course curricula, adopting the artistic orientation of 'reflecting life, in particular reflecting the life of the workers, the peasants and the army'. The real driving force behind this was Mao Zedong's advocacy in the 1942 Yan'an Talks on Literature and Art: "literature and art serving the workers, peasants and army". After the Chinese Communist Party seized power in 1949, this Party Resolution rose to become national policy. Accordingly, the National Fine Arts Training Institution, the first in the history of China, which had originally been advocated by Cai Yuanpei and founded in 1918, had not only to change its name but also to accept even more far-reaching changes.

At this time, Jin Shangyi and his fellow students were sharing work and rest with the workers in the Puzhen Railway Works. As well as learning the skills and abilities of manual labor, they also made some paintings for them. The advanced student who served as a group leader, Jin Zhilin, was to provide an oil painting, and Jin Shangyi was also eager to try, so he joined them. Although he had not studied oil painting, his basic drawing skills were good, and the two collaborated and finally completed the task. Jin Shangyi was very excited, as this was the first time in his life that he had painted an oil painting, a standard portrait of Chairman Mao.

Basically we can conclude that this leader's portrait was installed in some important public area of the Puzhen Railway Works. In the wake of the arrival of the new China, this practice was becoming common on a national scale. Previously, it was only current within the Communist-controlled areas, because the Chinese Communist government existed only as local separatist forces from Ruijin to Yan'an. The earliest extant portraits were sketches of Mao Zedong in *Collected Revolutionary Pictures*, Red China Press 1933, and the most circulated were the *Portraits of Chairman Mao*, colored woodcuts

---

1 The historical facts of this article are based on Jin Shangyi: *The Experience of Creating: Chairman Mao At the December Conference*, in *Art Monthly*, 1961, No 6. Quoted in Jin Shangyi (oral) and Cao Wenhan: *The Road of My Oil Painting - Jin Shangyi's Memoirs*, Jilin Arts Press, 2000; and Jin Shangyi and Fan Di'an (ed): *Complete Records of Jin Shangyi: Narrated by Himself, Selected by Himself, Assessed by Himself*, Jiangsu Arts Press, 2009.

by Wang Shikuo catering to the aesthetic tastes of workers, peasants and the army. Even if we widen our scope from 'pictures of Mao Zedong' to 'images of Mao Zedong' and examine for instance the relief head that was produced by Wang Chaowen and installed to decorate the assembly hall of the Central Party School, symbolizing the confirmation of Mao Zedong's absolute authority within the Party, and its derivative products, such as Chairman Mao badges, the postage stamps with Mao's portrait proclaiming the legitimacy of the government and first issued in the Shandong Anti-Japanese Base Area, and the paper money featuring Mao Zedong's portrait issued in 1945 by the East China Liberated Area, this geographical limitation still applies. Although the classic photograph *Mao Zedong in Northern Shaanxi*, taken in 1936 by Snow, crossed the blockade in *Red Star over China* and gained access to the world outside the loess plateau, the legality of Mao Zedong's portrait on a national scale was only really confirmed at the moment of the ceremony of the public founding of the nation, when it took over the position of Jiang Jieshi's (Chiang Kaishek's) portrait over Tian'anmen.

Jin Shangyi was present at the ceremony for the founding of the nation, and in the year after, during the Red May Movement, he used it for creative purposes. The sixteen-year old youth was partly just sincere and enthusiastic. He had no way of foreseeing the future of the new nation, or even his own future. The Jin Shangyi who, at the Puzhen Railway Works, made an oil painting for the first time, also "only knew that there was such a thing as oil painting, and that he liked it". He had no idea that we would study this subject in the future, let alone that it would accompany him on a hard and long road throughout his life.

II

Sixteen years later, the Cultural Revolution began. Jin Shangyi, who had academically already completed the undergraduate course, graduate course, and oil painting training at the Central Academy of Fine Arts, was teaching at the No.1 Workshop in the Oil Painting Department. The following year, the 'Mao Zedong Portrait Class' was founded there, and Jin Shangyi was one of its teachers. In the first session there were twenty-seven students, all workers, peasants or soldiers from factories, mines, offices and units in Beijing and from cities in other provinces. The forte of these amateur artists was making propaganda posters in simple compositions and single colors, and the academic training raised the standard of their sketching only to a very limited degree. Even so, in terms of the great number of art workers in the whole of China, this was an especially rare opportunity. In fact, the national craze for making portraits of the leaders was launched and promoted by the amateur artist teams, and the professional artists were stripped of their right to paint. In 1970, Jin Shangyi was sent down into the countryside and began to labor and to take part in political movements.

The absurdity of this dislocation was soon exposed, but it was remedied in an even more absurd way: in the preparation for the National Art Exhibition of 1972, the participants in the Exhibition, who were absolutely made up of workers, peasants, soldiers and Red Guards, were mostly incapable of properly dealing with the images of Mao Zedong to be exhibited, and the department in charge of fine arts saw no other way but to convene the professional artists in a 'picture-editing group' to edit the badly-made portraits of Mao Zedong. The workload was huge. Jin Shangyi headed the group, and because of his superior portraiture skills took especial responsibility for editing the leaders' head portraits.

The importance of the leaders' portraits had emerged while Jin Shangyi was still taking undergraduate courses. The object of the education of the students at that time was to make them into universal workers. They did not study oil painting or Chinese painting. The basic courses were sketching, water colors, drawing and outlining, and their creative courses were 'comic book, new year pictures and propaganda works [Liannianxuan]'. Even so, there had still been three oil painting homework tasks, namely head portraits, half-torso portraits, and leader's portraits, with an eye to the realistic need to paint leader's portraits after graduation.

Jin Shangyi's undergraduate curriculum was a precise expression of the 'Spring Festival Painting Movement' in academic education during the early period after the founding of the new Nation. In this movement, which relied on the new historical conditions and which stepped up the traditional arts movements of Yan'an, innumerable Spring Festival pictures of the leaders sprang into being. Their aesthetic taste stayed close the masses, and they took for their designs the caring and kind leaders who were so 'close' to the masses. In these works, the sweetness between the People and Mao Zedong, as representing himself, the governing Party and the new China, overflowed beyond verbal description. Later, the creation of historical paintings that relied on the aim of providing legitimacy to the ruling position of the Chinese Communist Party was opened up, and the pictorialization of Mao Zedong's revolutionary record became the most important chapter in this re-telling of history. The painters who accepted this task were full of reverence, and threw themselves into creation. In return they were officially allowed a relative freedom of thinking-space. Artistic standards achieved respect, and only therefore were we able to see the backs of the leaders appear in *By the Banks of the Yan River*.

"The relaxed conditions of creative art and the balance it needed to strike with ideology ended after Mao Zedong again raised the questions of class and class struggle."[2] By the time of the Cultural Revolution, the creation of leader's portraits had already become completely ideologized. Pure red was used for the faces, coke-brown for the shadows, with light orange highlights, other parts of the skin were generally also handled in red or other warm colors. Blue, green, grey and other cold colors should be avoided so far as possible. After squeezing the colors onto the palette for mixing, one should modulate them in a particular order. Mao Zedong's face should be divided into three equal parts, and when applying color, one must observe a 'color saturation sequence table' especially established for this purpose. In painting his face, one had to pay particular attention to its smoothness and fine sheen, and not a single trace of brushwork should be visible. One must let it shine, revealing the radiant glow of his spirit…".[3]

This "Red, Smooth and Luminescent" painting model was a line that all painters including Jin Shangyi were not allowed to cross.

III

Even within the fetters of the model, *Full-length Portrait of Chairman Mao*, created in 1966, reveals Jin Shangyi's ideals in portraiture.

This work depicts Mao Zedong on his own, set off in warm colors without particulars or background. The Leader is standing, his left arm hanging naturally at his side, the right slightly raised, the hand lightly clenched. He is dressed in a zhongshan (Sun Yat-sen) suit and leather shoes, and his manner is solemn but gentle. Although there are countless portraits of Mao Zedong, only two people, Yin Shoushi and Shen Yiqian, have painted him from life, so the material used for portraits of the Leader mainly originates in photographs and film footage, and the first step of creating a portrait was to collect materials. For some of the images in Jin Shangyi's works depicting the Leader, the sources are clear. For instance, the 1966 painting *Chairman Mao at Lu Mountains*, which was commissioned for the International Exhibition Company's touring exhibition to Albania, can be basically matched against the photograph of the same name taken by Lü Houmin. Others have been gradually brooded over, redesigned and matured according to the artist's understanding on the basis of photographs or film stills. As for *Full-length Portrait of Chairman Mao*, we have found no image material that perfectly matches it. Comparing it to the historical photographs, we can probably conclude that the Mao Zedong in the painting belongs to the eve of the 'Cultural Revolution' of the 1960s.

In Jin Shangyi's opinion: "The image in portraits must resemble the person who is being represented. However, the outer resemblance is only one aspect. The subject's character and spiritual condition must be clear and vivid. Both aspects are indispensable. In

---

2 Zou Yuejin: *Fine Arts in the Age of Mao Zedong*, Hunan Fine Arts Publishing House, 2005, p11.
3 Yang Haocheng, "Studies in the Image of Mao Zedong, Nanjing University Doctoral Thesis, 2005, p76.

painting portraits, the aspect of the outer resemblance is relatively easily obtained, but if you neglect the clear expression of character and spiritual condition, it can usually not become a portrait, but remains a mundane exercise." "The choice of composition must be very concise and powerful. Because the composition of portraits is relatively simple, the whole painting must correspond strictly to the demands of good modeling. So far as possible, ugly shapes, movements that are hard to manage, and haphazard backgrounds must be avoided. The management of movements and background must closely match each other. There must be no places that present obstacles. The visual language must be concise and plain, and it must have expressive power."[4] *Full-length Portrait of Chairman Mao* conforms to both those viewpoints. The spectator is infected by the force of the Leader, and at the same time, through the simplicity of the composition, gets - in the midst of a hectic age - a breath of long - gone peace and calm.

This quietness is derived from Jin Shangyi's thinking and his persistence. At a time when "the whole nation was engaged from top to bottom in great political creation, he could soberly spend five or even ten years in practicing his bust portraits."[5] The few extant sketch portraits of Chairman Mao made in 1967 are the basis of *Full-length Portrait of Mao Zedong* and the other creations of this time, and also represent Jin Shangyi's clear-headed pursuit of his artistic path.

IV

Before he made *Full-length Portrait of Chairman Mao*, Jin Shangyi collaborated with Wu Biduan on *We Have Friends All over the World* in 1960, and in 1961 he painted *Chairman Mao at the December Conference*, and also *The Long March* with the inscription "The men who walked the green hills are not yet old." These are Jin Shangyi's representative works that take the Leader as subject. We must pay especial attention to *Chairman Mao at the December Conference*.

In 1961, on the fortieth anniversary of the founding of the Chinese Communist Party, the Chinese Revolutionary Museum, which was preparing to open, commissioned historical works from many artists, and Jin Shangyi also was included among the invitees. His subject was the Central Working Conference on the occasion of the Liberation Army moving the war to Northern Shaanxi in 1947. This Conference was also known as the 'December Conference'. The artist chose the key moment of the Conference, namely Chairman Mao's address "The Present Situation and Our Task." He began the drafts, but continued to find them less than ideal. Finally, the design of the figure facing the front and raising his hand forwards emerged from among the sketches in various lighting and various movement angles, because it was an individual gesture, characteristic of the Chairman when he was making speeches, and it also suited the spirit of the speech: 'Dawn is right in front of us. We must persevere'. It seemed as if, with one push, he'd pushed forward into a new dawn, pushing China into a new age. The other artists all thought it very good too, and suggested that Jin Shangyi should not paint in other people. Ultimately, this work became a painting of the history of a portrait. Through the introduction of *Art Monthly* and *People's Liberation Army Illustrated*, combined with the Central News Film Studio making it an important camera shot in the 'July 1' feature, it enjoyed great influence.

However, in Jin Shangyi's own view, this creative experience had a strong arbitrary element. The choice of subject matter was arbitrary, like the arbitrariness of his having entered the National Beiping Academy of Fine Arts in the autumn of 1949 and spent his life there. And yet, it was exactly this kind of chance element that made him persevere in the pursuit of his idealistic aspiration for 'character and spiritual condition' and 'composition', and which led him in his later artistic direction. Many years later, his conscious making of portraits originated exactly from his unconscious making of Mao Zedong's portraits, feeling his way forward all along.

---

4   Jin Shangyi: "The Experience of Creating: *Chairman Mao at the December Conference*", in *Art Monthly*, 1961, No.6.
    Quoted in Jin Shangyi (oral history) and Cao Wenhan: *The Road of My Oil Painting - Jin Shangyi's Memoirs*, Jilin Arts Press, 2000, pp53 - 4.
5   *Collected Chinese Oil Painters - Jin Shangyi*, Sichuan Arts Press, 2005.

V

"The production of images of Mao Zedong was the most important chapter in the fine arts of the Mao Zedong era (1942-1976). This was not only shown by their quantity and quality, but, even more importantly, was shown in their interactive and necessary relationship with the politics, culture and thinking of society in the Mao Zedong era."[6] The portraits of Mao Zedong required by the complex social dynamics, political demands and ideological needs had to be completed by artists. For the artists, this task was a rather too onerous one, but it was the fate of their times.

Jin Shangyi, 'sent down' during the 'Cultural Revolution', was recalled several times, always for the purpose of producing portraits of the leaders. Once it was to paint a historical painting, *Chairman Mao and Lin Biao in the Yan'an Era*, for the Shanxi Pingxingguan Memorial. Later, when the Lin Biao Incident occurred, the Memorial was closed, and the destiny of the painting is also unknown. Another time it was to copy, with Zhao Yu, *Founding Ceremony of PRC* by Dong Xiwen and to change it according to the 'revolutionary line' of the time. Yet another time it was a collaboration for the National Art Exhibition on *We Must Carry Through the Proletarian Cultural Revolution*, which represented Mao Zedong meeting the Red Guards at Jinshui Bridge on Tian'anmen Square. The workload also included a large number of bust portraits, full-length portraits and standard portraits, and finally Jin Shangyi's eyes imperceptibly developed a color disorder. His use of color in life drawing tended towards the red end of the spectrum, and he was unable to use cold colors. The long-term labor finally wore out his health and in 1972 he began to take time off for his health.

From his first oil painting and throughout his life, he painted portraits of Mao Zedong. The creative work that produced an important influence on his artistic directiosn was also the creation of Mao Zedong portraits. During the 'Cultural Revolution', what caused his sense of color to go off was also head portraits of Mao Zedong, full-length portraits of Mao Zedong, standard portraits of Mao Zedong….

In 1976, at the street corner of a major avenue in Xingtai, Hebei, the 42-year-old Jin Shangyi painted an 18 meter tall portrait of Chairman Mao. This was the largest work of his life. For an artist who had only recently recovered from his illness, what most delighted people was that his eyesight gradually returned to normal, and that his straying sense of color returned to its condition from before the 'Cultural Revolution'. His 'rred-smooth-luminescent vision' ended. The 'red-smooth-luminescent' era was also about to end, and the movement of Chinese fine arts to construct the image of Mao Zedong was about to turn into an unprecedented de-construction.

---

6   Zou Yuejin, *Fine Arts in the Age of Mao Zedong*, Part One, Hunan Fine Arts Publishing House, 2005.

靳尚谊
Jin Shangyi
毛主席全身像
Full-length Portrait of Chairman Mao
布面油画
Oil on Canvas
262 × 137cm, 1966

4

《黄河颂》——新中国美术创作中的奇葩

贾慧明

新中国的官方美术创作，特别是"文革"特殊时期，遵循着严格的创作规则。但陈逸飞的《黄河颂》这幅创作于"文革"期间的油画，无论在形式、内容还是技法方面，都突破了规则的限制，体现了艺术家别出心裁的尝试和创造性。在新中国美术史上，《黄河颂》以其极高的历史价值和艺术价值成为油画创作中的一朵奇葩。

关于《黄河颂》这件作品的创作缘起，陈丹青在2004年第5期《艺术世界》上发表了一篇名为《向上海美专致敬——回忆上世纪70年代沪上油画精英》的文章，回忆了当时的情况："1971年，我已经是一介知青，从赣南山沟流窜回沪，立即得知上海滩头条'油画新闻'：根据1969年创作的钢琴协奏曲《黄河》，由张春桥、姚文元主政的'上海市革命委员会'重点组织创作同名油画系列，严国基画第一乐章'黄河船夫曲'，陈逸飞画第二乐章'黄河颂'，夏葆元画第四乐章'黄河愤'……"[1]

陈逸飞时任上海油画雕塑创作室油画组的负责人。当时的官方美术创作大多来自上级指示，作为一项政治任务，这其中会有诸多因素的限制，并不容艺术家凸显个性，自由发挥。"文革"期间的文艺创作，为了达到政治宣传的目的，其至还出现了"三突出"、"两结合"、"高大全"、"红光亮"等指导艺术创作的基本原则。在这样的氛围中，出现的美术作品大都风格统一，高度程式化。《黄河颂》这幅绘画就诞生在那个年代，取材于脍炙人口的歌曲《黄河大合唱》。然而，这种以歌曲为命题的美术创作在当时并不常见。这就意味着，绘画的形式和内容要受到歌词和旋律两个方面的制约。一方面，作品表达的内容要符合歌词中描绘的情景，与此同时，绘画的风格和主题上也要传神地表达出旋律的情感基调。

关于《黄河颂》的歌词，是1938年诗人光未然与抗敌演剧三队一行，在黄河壶口附近渡河西进延安，他目睹了黄河奔腾不息，尤其是在壶口排山倒海、一泻千里的博大气势，以及黄河船夫们与狂风恶浪搏斗的壮观情景，灵感突发，不久即写成了《黄河颂》组诗[2]：

朋友！
黄河以它英雄的气魄，
出现在亚洲的原野；
它表现出我们民族的精神：
伟大而又坚强！

这里，
我们向着黄河，
唱出我们的赞歌：

我站在高山之巅，
望黄河滚滚，
奔向东南。
金涛澎湃，
掀起万丈狂澜；
浊流宛转，
结成九曲连环；
从昆仑山下，
奔向黄海之边；
把中原大地
劈成南北两面。

啊，黄河！
你是中华民族的摇篮！
五千年的古国文化，
从你这发源；

---

1 曹庆晖：《"既英雄又浪漫"——陈逸飞〈黄河颂〉的故事及特色分析》，《收藏》2007年第5期。
2 郭青剑：《黄河岸边颂黄河——大型文艺演出〈黄河颂〉侧记》，《中国艺术报》2005年8月19日，第4版。

多少英雄的故事，
在你的身边扮演！

啊，黄河！
你是伟大坚强，
像一个巨人
出现在亚洲平原之上，
用你那英雄的体魄
筑成我们民族的屏障。

啊，黄河！
你一泻万丈，
浩浩荡荡，
向南北两岸
伸出千万条铁的臂膀。
我们民族的伟大精神，
将要在你的哺育下
发扬滋长！
我们祖国的英雄儿女，
将要学习你的榜样，
像你一样的伟大坚强！
像你一样的伟大坚强！

艺术家需要根据歌词"造景"，画面的布局与《黄河颂》的歌词描述基本一致。背景由三部分构成：左侧蜿蜒在崇山峻岭中的万里长城，右侧沟壑纵横的黄土高原，中间为主景观——黄河壶口瀑布倾泻而下的激流。中央的黄河将画面纵向分割成三部分却并不突兀，而是过渡自然，画面浑然一体。为表现黄河的雄浑气势和惊心动魄的力量，陈逸飞在创作期间，亲自去黄河沿岸写生，画了许多速写。但画中表现的并非实景，而是经过了艺术家的精巧构思和艺术加工。如此众多而宏大的景物在画面中显得整体而和谐，这不仅体现了艺术家的构图能力，也体现了艺术家对色调的掌控和利用块面造型的概括力。在画法上，前景强调素描，体现了苏联画派的特点；而远景强调色彩的丰富性，在色彩和笔触的处理上有印象派的特点。前景的素描带来的坚实感，也是坚定政治立场的象征，远景的丰富色彩是内心浪漫情怀的流露。

但是，歌词中并没有提供具体的人物形象，如何选取人物，就成为创作中的难点。陈逸飞后来回忆说：《黄河颂》最初的构想，是画一个羊倌，扎着羊肚子头巾，扛着镢头，仰天高唱信天游。反复思量后，发觉这种表现方式几乎是在诠释《黄河大合唱》的歌词，便毅然舍弃，转而改成一个红军战士，站在山巅，笑傲山河。从这一记叙可以看出，画中人物从羊倌到红军战士的转变，画家是经过谨慎考虑过的。联系《黄河大合唱》的主旨来看，这首歌曲表达的是中华民族在艰难岁月中不屈的精神和反抗斗志，以及积极抗日保家卫国的满腔热情和必胜信念。从这个角度上说，选取红军战士这个角色更贴切，因为这个形象更具有时代特色并包含着更多的历史信息。"红军不怕远征难，万水千山只等闲"，此画正是要赞颂这种革命乐观主义精神。此外，对人物的表现也寄予了艺术家的个人情怀，小战士灿烂的笑容，使画面弥漫着浪漫主义情怀。在当时的政治高压下，陈逸飞能把强烈的个人情怀融合进来，表达青春和生命意识，将政治主题和个人情感相结合，在程式化的人物造型中注入个人情感，不能不说是一个大胆的尝试。

值得注意的是，"文革"期间的绘画，将领袖或英雄人物置于大山大水的背景中的构图模式比较常见，如当时的代表性宣传画刘春华的《毛主席去安源》，但将一个普通的战士置于这样的场景并不多见。《黄河颂》中的歌词写道："我们祖国的英雄儿女／将要学习你的榜样／像你一样的伟大坚强！"歌曲中歌颂的对象是拟人化的黄河，实际上，黄河是喻体，本体应是中华民族历史长河中的无数英雄人物。在绘画中，陈逸飞利用图像将本体显现出来，将英雄人物处理成一名红军战士，作为民族精神的象征和学习的楷模。这里的英雄人物是按照理想模式塑造的，并不是现实中存在的真实人物，因此这幅作品是具有象征意味的，而非现实主义作品。黄河、长城、红军战士等均是象征着中华民族精神的特殊意象。同时，黄河中的小船也具有象征意味，在激流中前进的小船暗含着对黄河船夫的歌颂，与《黄河大合唱》的歌词相符，并与画面主体人物的精神相呼应。《黄河颂》中的红军战士不是普通的个体，而是经艺术家理想化处理后的典型人物和英雄形象，呈现出一种纪念碑式的永恒感，像一座历史丰碑屹立在高耸的山崖，与背景具有象征意义的黄河、长城等景物相呼应，代表了中华民族的精神和魂魄。而要达到这一效果，不仅需要过硬的写实技巧，也离不开画面的构图经营、光影等诸多因素。

画中的人物被安排在最佳视觉位置，即画面的黄金分割点上。人物所在的前景被东方斜照过来的光照亮，这暗示着画面表现的是早上太阳初升的情景。远景的天空、大地、山河还是一片混沌，与前景的清晰和明亮形成了鲜明对比，使得画面层次分明，主体突出。前景中的人物立于眩目的岩石之上，好像从画面的底部升腾而起。而人物身后一行掠江而过的大雁，给画面增添了动感和生趣。从构图的角度来看，从西北向东南飞行的大雁恰好填补了画面右侧的空白，并具有向右的动势，达到了平衡画面的视觉效果。另外，画面上的主体人物是红军战士，而红军的长征又与大雁的远飞相呼应。大雁在中国文化中也具有象征意味，有大展宏图、鸿鹄之志等含义。此画运用了中国传统绘画中借物咏怀的手法，将大雁作为英姿勃发的小战士内心情绪的外在显现。此外，这幅绘画中还蕴含着对未来的憧憬和向往：早上太阳初升的情景，给人带来无限希望；大雁朝向东方，指向画面之外，与小战士的目光一致，暗含着对未来的向往；同时，小战士的位置处于长城城墙之外，这种地理上的跨越同样隐喻着放弃保守，展望未来，跨进新时代之意。从构图上看，人物的头部和钢枪的刺刀都高于地平线，脚踩高山之巅，大雁在脚下飞过，这种极度夸张的顶天立地式构图，高度赞扬了人的力量，同时又有高瞻远瞩、展望未来的寓意，从而使得画面的思想得到升华，将题目中的"颂"字表现得淋漓尽致。陈丹青曾描述过看到这幅画的感觉："做人就要做这样的人。"王式廓创作于1972—1973年间的《转战陕北》，与《黄河颂》属于同一时期，在构图上和人物的处理上亦有异曲同工之妙。《转战陕北》描绘的是毛主席站在黄土高原上，高瞻远瞩，指挥战斗的情景。画中的毛主席站在地势的最高点，并处于画面的黄金分割位置，头顶高于地平线，俯瞰远方。比较两幅绘画发现，《黄河颂》赋予画中的士兵以伟人的高度和胸襟气概，这充分体现了艺术家的英雄主义和浪漫主义情怀。

"文革"期间流行的图像多以领袖以及当时的先进人物或英雄事迹为题材。毛泽东关于文艺创作中"革命的现实主义与革命的浪漫主义"相结合的谈话被推广到美术创作中来，被认为是"最好的"创作方法而备受推崇。在《黄河颂》中，陈逸飞在塑造红军战士这个人物时，还注意通过细节赋予其英雄主义和浪漫主义的气息。在谈到创作时，陈逸飞说："我在红军战士肩挎的步枪枪眼里，画了一小团红布，形同一朵盛开的鲜艳的小花，还在他的脚下，画上一行斜飞南行的大雁。我自以为很美，既英雄又浪漫。"对于人物的表现，画家不是简单地按照"三突出"原则进行矫揉造作的塑造，而是巧妙地利用自然光影效果进行渲染，使得人物形象鲜明突出，达到一种既舞台化又合情合理的艺术效果。光影和明暗拉开了近景和远景之间的距离，也使得画面呈现出较强的层次感和立体化效果，克服了"文革"宣传画中平面而僵硬的模式。

陈逸飞对于人物形象的塑造，可以看出他早年受到美术训练的深刻影响。陈丹青在追忆陈逸飞时谈道："他们这一代人，跟建国以后的第一批油画家不同，他们是'文革'后起来的一代，都有一种革命的现实主义和浪漫主义。陈逸飞的成名作《黄河颂》，折射了苏联现实主义的影响。"[3] 陈逸飞1965年毕业于上海美术专科学校，在校期间曾受到苏联美术教学体系的训练。陈逸飞的老师俞云阶早年毕业于中央大学徐悲鸿门下，50年代中期进入中央美术学院苏联专家马克西莫夫油画训练班学习。这个班的素描教学非常强调"结构"、色彩教学，尤其关注"外光"，创作教学则特别致力调动学生对个体生活经验和情感的概括与把握。结合《黄河颂》来看，这几块主干内容经由俞云阶都传导给了陈逸飞，并被其消化和吸收了[4]。据说陈逸飞在创作红军战士这个人物形象时，曾仔细研究过苏联的油画印刷品，画面内容是列宁检阅军队，一排排战士手握步枪。然而，这幅画的独特之处在于，它并不是完全按照苏联画派的画法进行表现的，只是在前景人物的处理上体现了这种画法。远景的天空和大地并没有呈现通常的固有色，色彩的丰富性和笔触感却有着明显的印象主义倾向，这是在当时现实主义潮流下做出的超越历史的大胆尝试。陈逸飞在当时苏联画派占据主导地位的官方美术创作中突破规则的限制，表现出独特的风格，这其中有着复杂的原因。结合当时的社会文化环境来看，这从一方面反映了"海派"绘画的精神传承。"海派"绘画历来注重吸取外来文化，兼收并蓄，具有鲜明的时代感，敢于变革，敢于融合西画之长。"海派"绘画在风格上注重色彩的表现力，作品常具有象征意味。陈逸飞的《黄河颂》在精神气质上体现出鲜明的"海派"绘画的特点。

对于"黄河"图像的表现，在新中国美术史上不乏先例。关山月在1959年的作品《江山如此多娇》，同样是一项政治任务，同样是巨幅绘画，画中也出现了黄河和长城，画中对河川的表现采取的是传统中国画的"三远"构图。而陈逸飞的《黄河颂》是按照西画惯用的焦点透视法表现"黄河"的，这样的构图更利于表现壶口瀑布倾泻而出的张力。同时，图中黄河之水的原点在人物的一侧，并低于人物的头顶，好像从人物本身生发出来，使得画面中的战士具有一种气吞山河的气势和喝令三山五岳开道的豪情壮志。

在"文革"特殊时期对美术创作施以条条框框的束缚之下，陈逸飞的《黄河颂》突破了这些限制，不论在技法还是观念方面都体现了当时油画创作的最高水准，甚至超越了那个时代，成为新中国美术史上熠熠生辉的一笔。这件融合着当时的政治激情和英雄主义情结的应时之作，也是逸飞先生自己认为最得意的作品。遗憾的是，这幅作品在当时未能及时展出或发表，直到"文革"结束后的1977年全军美展上才得以正式亮相。这其中的原因现有几种说法，有认为是"同行相嫉，他'文革'时的力作几乎全部被上海的官展所否决，又被北方官展贬视为'海派'"[5]，也有认为是"这种所谓'印象主义'倾向正是该画当时被尘封的'罪名'"[6]。无论如何，拂去历史的滚滚尘埃，当面对这幅历经周折而重见天日的珍贵作品，我们唯有惊叹、赞美，以及对已故艺术家陈逸飞先生的深深敬意。

3　蒯乐昊：《陈丹青追忆陈逸飞："没有人能够替代他"》，《书摘》2006年第1期。

4　曹庆晖：《"既英雄又浪漫"——陈逸飞〈黄河颂〉的故事及特色分析》，《收藏》2007年第5期。

5　陈丹青：《退步集续篇》之《回想陈逸飞》，南宁：广西师范大学出版社，第68页。

6　曹庆晖：《"既英雄又浪漫"——陈逸飞〈黄河颂〉的故事及特色分析》，《收藏》2007年第5期。

Eulogy of the Yellow River – A Wonder in the Artistic Creation of the New China

By Jia Huiming

The official creation of art in the new China, especially during the exceptional era of the Cultural Revolution, followed strict creative rules. However, Chen Yifei's *Eulogy of the Yellow River*, despite being an oil painting of the Cultural Revolution era, broke free of the limitations of these rules with respect to form, content and technique, and manifested the artist's original experiments and creativity. In the history of the art of the new China, *Eulogy of the Yellow River*, with its extremely high historical and artistic value, became a wonder among oil paintings.

As for the creative origin of *Eulogy of the Yellow River*, Chen Danqing in *Art World*, 2004, No.5, published an article called "Tribute to the Shanghai Training School of Fine Arts - Remembering the Oil Painting Elite in Shanghai in the 1970s", in which he recalled the conditions of that time: "In 1971, I was just an ordinary educated youth fleeing back to Shanghai from the Gannan Valley, and, immediately found out the Shanghaitan "top news about oil painting", based on the *Yellow River* Piano Concerto composed in 1969, the Shanghai City Revolutionary Committee stressed the organization of the creation of an oil painting series of the same name, and that Yan Guoji had painted the First Movement, 'Song of the Yellow River Boatman', Chen Yifei had composed the Second Movement, '*Eulogy of the Yellow River*', and Xia Baoyuan had painted the Fourth Movement, 'Yellow River Anger'.[1]

Chen Yifei was responsible for the Oil Painting Group of the Shanghai Oil Painting and Sculpture Studio. The official artistic creative work at the time was mainly directed from above. It was a political task that might contain many factors and restrictions, and it was not easy at all for an artist to show individuality, or to develop freely. In artistic creation at the time of the Cultural Revolution, to achieve the aims of political propaganda,

---

1 Cao Qinghui, "Both Heroic and Romantic - The Story of Chen Yifei's *Eulogy of the Yellow River* and an Analysis of its Characteristics", in *Collection*, 2007 No.5.

there even appeared some basic principles to direct artistic creation, such as 'The Three Things That Must Stand Out', 'Uniting the Two', 'Tall, Big, Complete' and 'The Use of Red-Smooth-Luminescent visual'. In this atmosphere, the style of the works of art that appeared was largely unified, and formulaic to a high degree. The painting *Eulogy of the Yellow River* was born in this era, and took its subject matter from the popular song *Yellow River Cantata*. However, the kind of artistic creation that takes its title from a song was not at all common at the time. It meant that the form and the content of the painting had to be restricted by the two aspects of the lyrics and the melody of the song. On the one hand, the content expressed by the work had to correspond to the mood portrayed in the lyrics, and at the same time the style and subject matter of the painting had to vividly express the emotional keynote of the melody.

The lyrics of *Eulogy of the Yellow River* are a stanza composed in 1938 by the poet Guang Weiran when he crossed the Yellow River near Hukou westwards to Yan'an. He gazed at the Yellow River rushing on without rest, and at the great momentum of its especially earthshaking, thousand-miles-in-one-crash quality at Hukou, and the spectacular scene of the Yellow River boatmen fighting the wild wind and waves. He had a flash of inspiration and wrote the poem cycle *Eulogy of the Yellow River*.[2]

Friend!
The Yellow River with its heroic spirit
Rises in the distant wilds of Asia;
It displays the spirit of our race:
Great but also strong!

Here
Facing the Yellow River,
We sing our song of praise:

I stand on the peak of the tall mountain,
Gazing at the Yellow River rolling, rolling,
Rushing to the southeast.
Golden waves surge and swell,
Raising a thousand feet of wild billows;
Turbidly flowing as if rolling,
It forms nine winding links;
Down from the Kunlun Mountains,
Rushing to the Yellow Sea's edge;
Splitting the great Middle Plateau
Into two faces, north and south.

Oh, Yellow River!
You are the cradle of the Chinese race,
Five thousand years of ancient culture
Flow from you, its source!
How many stories of heroes
Were played out on your banks!

Oh, Yellow River!
You are great and strong,
Like a giant,
You appear above the plain of Asia,
And with that heroic physique of yours
Construct the bulwark of our race.

Oh, Yellow River!
You flow ten miles at a leap,
Mighty, mighty,
Against both banks north and south,
You stretch ten thousand arms.
The great spirit of our race
Will develop and grow
In your embrace!
Heroic sons and daughters of our ancestral land,
Will learn from your example,
And be great and strong like you!
Great and strong like you!

The artist had to 'recreate the scene', making the composition in the painting basically identical to what the lyrics described. The background is composed of three parts. On the left hand side is the Great Wall, winding its ten thousand *li* along the steep ridges of high mountains. On the right hand side are the up-and-down gullies of the loess plateau, and in the middle is the main scene: the

---

2 Guo Qingjian, "Hymning the Yellow River on the Cliff-banks of the Yellow River-Side: Notes to a Large - Scale Literary / Artistic Performance of *Eulogy of the Yellow River*", in *China Art Report*, 19 August 2005, 4th edition.

rushing flow of the crashing rapids of the Yellow River at Hukou. The Yellow River in the centre divides the painting into three parts, which is not unexpected, but forms a natural transition, so that the painting is seamlessly unified. To express the vigorous momentum and stirring force of the Yellow River, Chen Yifei, when he was creating the painting, personally went to the banks of the Yellow River to draw it from life, making many sketches of it. But what is expressed in the painting is not at all a realistic scene, but has passed through the ingenious ideas and artistic value-adding of the artist. That so many great features appear unified and harmonious in the painting, does not only manifest the compositional skill of the artist, but also his mastery of color gradation and the summarizing power in his use of block-face modeling. As for his painting method, the foreground emphasizes the sketching feel, embodying the characteristics of the Soviet School, while the distance emphasizes the richness of the colors. His handling of colors and brushstrokes has Impressionist characteristics. The solid feel of the depiction of the foreground also symbolizes a firm political stance, while the richness of the colors of the background comes from the outpouring of a romantic heart.

However, the lyrics of the song made no mention of a specific human figure, it thus became a hard part of the creative process to choose such a figure. Chen Yifei later recalled: "My first scheme for *Eulogy of the Yellow River* was to paint a shepherd wearing a cloth turban and carrying a hoe, raising his head and singing 'Xintian You'. After considering the matter, I sensed that this expressive format was almost an interpretation of the *Yellow River Cantata*, and I firmly rejected the shepherd. I switched instead to a Red Army soldier standing on a peak and smiling proudly at the mountains and the river." From this narrative it can be seen that the artist had carefully considered the matter before he changed the shepherd into a Red Army soldier. As for the connection between the main subject and the *Yellow River Cantata*, this song expressed the inflexible spirit of the Chinese people through the years of hardship and their will to keep up the resistance fight, as well as the positive enthusiasm and confidence in victory in defending home and country against the Japanese. From this angle, choosing to use a Red Army soldier was more apt, for this image had more of the character of that period and contained more historical information. The Red Army fears no hardship of distant expeditions, and shrugs off ten thousand rivers and a thousand mountains" - this painting was intended precisely to praise this spirit of revolutionary optimism. Besides, the representation of the human figure endowed some individual emotion. The young soldier's dazzling smile filled the painting with the emotions of romanticism. Under the high pressure of politics at the time, Chen Yifei could blend in powerful individual emotion to express youth and the awareness of life, combining the political subject with individual emotions, in what must be called a brave experiment.

It is worth noting that in paintings made during the time of the Cultural Revolution, the model of placing leaders or heroes against the background of great mountains or great rivers was fairly common, as in the propaganda painting, representative of the era, by Liu Chunhua, *Chairman Mao Goes to Anyuan*. To place a common soldier in this kind of context, however, was not common at all. The lyrics of the *Eulogy of the Yellow River* run: "Heroic sons and daughters of our ancestral land, Will learn from your example, And be great and strong like you!" The object of praise in this song is the personified Yellow River, but in fact the Yellow River is a metaphor for the countless heroes in the long river of Chinese national history. While painting, Chen Yifei used this image to express the fundamentals. He managed a heroic human figure and turned it into a Red Army soldier, so that it could serve as a symbol of the national spirit and as a role model to learn from. The heroic figure here was formed according to an ideal model and definitely not any actual person existing in the real China. Therefore this painting has a symbolic flavour, and is not a realist painting. The Yellow River, the Great Wall, the Red Army soldier and so on, are, equally, special images symbolizing the spirit of the Chinese nation. At the same time, the little boat that progresses in the Yellow River has symbolic value as it suggests the eulogy of the Yellow River boatmen eulogy, which corresponds to the lyrics of *Yellow River Cantata*, and to the spirit of the main figure in the painting *Eulogy of the Yellow River*. The Red Army soldier in *Eulogy of the Yellow River* is not an ordinary individual, but is a typical human figure and a heroic image. He has been idealized by the artist and presents a feeling of monumental eternity, like a historical monument placed on a steep mountain cliff. The soldier corresponds to the symbolic scenery with the Yellow River and Great Wall in the background, representing the spirit and soul of the Chinese people. To achieve this effect, what is required is not just strong realistic skill. One cannot do without management of the composition, light and shade and many other factors.

The human figure in the painting has been placed in the optimal visual position, in the golden section point. He is obliquely lit up by light shining from the East, suggesting that an early morning scene is represented. The sky, earth, mountains and river in the distance are still indistinct, making a clear contrast to the clarity and light of the foreground, causing the picture to assume several layers of lighting, and the main subject to stand out. The figure in the foreground is standing on a dazzling cliff and seems to spring up from the lower part of the picture, and behind the figure, a row of wild geese are sweeping across the river, adding a sense of movement and joy of life. In terms of composition, the wild geese flying in formation from the northwest towards the southeast neatly occupy the space on the right hand side of the picture, and have a momentum towards the right, achieving he visual effect of balancing the picture. Besides, the main figure in the painting is a Red Army soldier, and the Long March of the Red Army corresponds to the distant flight of the wild geese. In Chinese culture, wild geese have symbolic meaning, implying grand plans, swan-like aspirations and so on. The painting uses the device of 'using things to express feelings' of Chinese traditional painting, serving as an external expression of the internal emotion of the heroically enthusiastic little soldier. Further, this painting suggests a longing for the future. The early morning scene at sunrise gives people an unbounded hope. The wild geese are heading east, that is, beyond the painting, following the gaze of the little soldier, hinting at a yearning for the future. At the same time, the geographical overstepping of the little soldier's position outside the ramparts of the Great Wall is similarly a metaphor for the notion of throwing off conservatism, looking to the future and stepping into a new age. Also, the head of the human figure and the tip of his bayonet are both higher than the horizon, his feet are treading on the peak of a high mountain, and the wild geese are flying below his feet. This kind of exaggerated 'head in the clouds and feet on the ground' composition to a high degree glorifies the strength of the man, and at the same time implies 'standing tall and seeing far' and looking to the future. Accordingly, it sublimates the ideas in the picture, giving vivid expression to the word 'eulogy' (*song*, 'song of praise, paean, praise') of the title. Chen Danqing has expressed his feeling on seeing this painting: "If you're a man, you should be this kind of man." In *Moving the War to Northern Shaanxi*, created by Wang Shikuo in 1972-1973, that is, in a similar period to that of *Eulogy of the Yellow River*, the composition and the handling of the human figure is of a similar wonderful skill applied to a different theme. *Moving the War to Northern Shaanxi* depicts Chairman Mao standing on the loess plateau, standing tall and seeing far, in a scene of commanding a battle. Chairman Mao stands on the highest point of the topography, also in the golden section position in the picture, his head above the horizon, looking down into the distance. Comparing the two paintings, we discover that *Eulogy of the Yellow River* endows the soldier in the picture with the height, mind and spirit of a great man. This fully manifests the artist's feelings of heroism and romanticism.

The popular images of the Cultural Revolution period mostly take leaders, advanced people of the time and heroic deeds for their subject matter. Mao Zedong's talks on the combination of "Revolutionary Realism and Revolutionary Romanticism" in the creation of literature and art were promoted in the creation of fine arts, and were reverently considered to be the 'best' creative method. When Chen Yifei was modeling the figure of the Red Army soldier for *Eulogy of the Yellow River*, he was also attentive to endowing it, through its various details, with a breath of heroism and romanticism. In talking about the creation, Chen Yifei said: "In the mouth of the barrel of the shoulder - held rifle of the Red Army soldier, I painted a small ball of red cloth, similar in form to a small bright flower in bloom, and at his feet, I added an oblique flight of southbound wild geese. I personally think it is beautiful, both heroic and romantic." As for the representation of the human figure, the artist did not proceed to shape it artificially by simply complying with the principle of 'The Three Things That Must Stand Out', but ingeniously used the natural effects of light and shade to achieve a color-gradation that makes the image of the human figure stand out freshly and achieve an artistic effect that is both staged and reasonable. The lighting and shading open up the distance between the foreground and the distance, and allow the picture to present a rather strong layered feel and three-dimensional effect, overcoming the flatness and rigidity of the Cultural Revolution propaganda painting model.

In Chen Yifei's modeling of human figures, one can see the deep influence of his early arts training. Chen Danqing says in retrospect of Chen Yifei: "The people of that generation were different from the first generation of oil painting artists after the founding of the Nation. They emerged after the 'Cultural Revolution', and there was a kind of Revolutionary Realism and Romanticism about them. Chen Yifei's *Eulogy of the Yellow River* refracts the influence of Soviet Realism."[3] Chen Yifei graduated in 1965 from the Shanghai Training School of Fine Arts. While at the School, he received the Soviet system of fine arts training. Chen Yifei's teacher Yu Yunjie graduated in his youth from the National Central University as a student of Xu Beihong's. In the mid-1950s, he entered as a student in the Soviet expert Maximov's oil painting training class at the Central Academy of Fine Arts. The drawing education in this class especially emphasized 'structure' and the color education, and paid especial attention to 'plein-air light', while the creative training was particularly devoted to mobilizing the student's experiences of individual life and the summarization and mastery of emotions. From the point of view of the integration of *Eulogy of the Yellow River*, these core components were all transmitted to Chen Yifei, and digested and absorbed by him.[4] It is said that while Chen Yifei was creating the figure of the Red Army soldier, he carefully studied prints of Soviet oil paintings, and the content of the picture is based on a military review by Lenin, which features ranks and ranks of soldiers holding rifles. However, the uniqueness of this painting lies in its not altogether relying on the painting method of the Soviet School for its expression. This painting method is only embodied in the management of the human figure in the foreground. The sky and the landscape in the distance present no kind of common color. The richness of the palette and the feeling of the brushstrokes show a clear Impressionist tendency, which represents a daring experiment that transcends its historical time, in what was then the Realist mainstream. Chen Yifei broke the limitations of the rules of the official creation of art, where Soviet Realism occupied the leading position, by representing a unique style. There were complex reasons for this. In view of the cultural environment in society at that time, in one respect it reflected the spiritual heritage of the painting of the 'Shanghai School'. 'Shanghai School' painting had all along focused on drawing on outside culture in an eclectic way that gave it a clear sense of the times, as well as the courage to renew itself and to blend in the best of Western painting. Stylistically, the painting of the 'Shanghai School' focused on color and expressive power, and the paintings often had a symbolic meaning. Chen Yifei's *Eulogy of the Yellow River* in its spiritual disposition embodied clear characteristics of the 'Shanghai School' of painting.

As for the representation of the image of the Yellow River, there is no lack of precedent for that in the history of fine arts in the new China. Guan Shanyue's 1959 work This Land So Rich in Beauty, was also a political assignment, also a large painting, and also featured the Yellow River and the Great Wall. For the representation of the River he used the traditional Chinese painting 'three distances' method of composition. Chen Yifei's *Eulogy of the Yellow River*, however, represents the Yellow River by means of the standard vanishing point perspective of Western painting, and this kind of composition is better suited to representing the tension of the crashing falls at Hukou. At the same time, the vanishing point of the water in the Yellow River of the picture is to one side of the human figure, and lower

---

3 Kuai Lehao, "Chen Danqing Remembers Chen Yifei: 'None Can Replace Him'", published in *Digest of Books*, 2006, No.1.

4 Cao Qinghui: "Both Heroic and Romantic - The Story of Chen Yifei's *Eulogy of the Yellow River* and an Analysis of Its Characteristics, in *Collection*, 2007, No.5.

than the crown of his head, and it seems to issue forth from the man himself, giving the soldier in the picture a gargantuan momentum and a grandeur of sentiment and aspiration that bids the mountains clear the way.

Within the constraints imposed by the strict rules applied to artistic creation during the unusual period of the Cultural Revolution, Chen Yifei's *Eulogy of the Yellow River* broke through these limitations and manifested, both technically and in terms of conception, the highest standard of creativity in oil painting at the time. He even transcended that era and became a shining brush in the art history of the new China. This work, which blends the political enthusiasm of the time and romanticist feelings in response to the age, also is the work that Mr. Yifei himself was most satisfied with. It is regrettable that the work could not be immediately exhibited or published, and it was only in 1977, after the Cultural Revolution, that it was given its formal debut at the National Army Art Exhibition. There are various current explanations of the reasons for this neglect. Some say that it was due to peer envy, and that Chen Yifei's masterpiece of the Cultural Revolution era was almost completely rejected by exhibitions in Shanghai, as well as being despised as being of the 'Shanghai School' by the northern official exhibitions.[5] Others think that "This so-called Impressionist tendency was the 'crime' that covered that painting in dust."[6] Be this as it may, when we wipe away the dust and grime of history and face this precious painting that has been through setbacks before appearing again, we can only sigh in admiration, praise its beauty, and express our deep respect to the deceased artist Chen Yifei.

---

5 Chen Danqing: "Remembering Chen Yifei" in *Stepping Back - Collected Articles*, Nanning, Guangxi Normal University Press, p 68.
6 Cao Qinghui, "Both Heroic and Romantic - The Story of Chen Yifei's *Eulogy of the Yellow River* and an Analysis of its Characteristics", in *Collection*, 2007, No.5.

陈逸飞
Chen Yifei
黄河颂
Eulogy of the Yellow River
布面油画
Oil on Canvas
143.5×297cm, 1972

解读吴冠中
《北国风光》画稿

王瑀

吴冠中的油画壁画稿《北国风光》在2009年首次现身嘉德秋拍之时，便引起了多方关注。一时间，"红色经典"、"油画"、"李瑞环同志捐赠"等类似的关键词见诸各种相关报道，而此作在后来拍出的天价，更成为坊间所津津乐道的话题。显然，这件作品已经"被赋予了艺术之外的更深内涵"[1]。

事实上，《北国风光》并不能称得上是吴冠中最具代表性的油画作品，真正引起我们注意的是这件作品创作的时代——1979年。了解吴冠中艺术的人都知道，正是在这一时期前后，他发表了大量阐述其有关"抽象美"、"形式美"、"油画民族化"等艺术思想的文章，并且引发了美术界的大讨论。如若将《北国风光》还原到这样一个历史环境中去解读，那么我们将会对该作产生新的理解与认识，而非如目前这样仅仅关注到作品本体之外的问题。

一、《北国风光》的画面

根据作者的回忆，《北国风光》是1979年为完成首都机场装饰工程任务所创作的装饰壁画画稿[2]。为求顺利通过审查，吴冠中根据毛泽东《沁园春·雪》中"山舞银蛇，原驰蜡象"两句的意象绘制了这件作品。

从本作画面的构成上来看，前景为几株平冠苍松，与后方高高雄起的雪山共同组成了画面的主景。雪山上逶迤的长城将画面的近景、中景与远景串联起来，不仅密切了画面各部分间的联系，也增加了画面的动感，使观者有"舞"的感受。画家在描绘时，通过明暗的变化勾勒出群峰的阴阳向背。在主峰的阴面脚下，作者以寥寥数笔勾勒出一片林海，林海之后还有一列火车正在驶出远方的群山，驰骋于雪原之间。主峰的阳面连接着不远处的另一座峰峦，在那座峰峦的深处，建立了一座高坝。高坝又蜿蜒到主峰的背后，引导观者的视线环绕主峰并向更远的群山背景投射过去。远处连绵的群山，虽是用寥寥数笔勾出，但依然很有层次感，营造了"千里冰封"的意境。总体上来看，整个画面的布局围绕前景主峰展开，四周的配景与主峰产生环绕形的呼应关系，而配景彼此之间也通过林海、火车、水坝等保持着虚虚实实的内在联系。可以说，无论是那简单数笔画就的长城，还是环抱主峰的远山，都体现出画家在经营构图时的良苦用心。所以连吴冠中自己也会说这画稿"是尽了全力的，所以其实不再是'稿'，已体现了巨幅作品的最终效果"[3]。

关于油画画面的构图问题，吴冠中有着自己独到的认识。他曾在晚年总结过在创作实践中得出的一条经验："画面上面积愈大的部分，在整体效果中其作用愈大。"[4]而这种作用过大，就会压制画面中景和远景的丰富展现，造成画面"大而空"的问题。从眼前的这张《北国风光》中我们可以发现，画家当时便已经注意到这样一个画面矛盾，并"设法移花接木另觅配偶"[5]以使中景和近景"引人入胜"。

追溯吴冠中这种对于经营画面位置的观念，源自他学生时代临摹大量中国山水画的经历。画家在晚年谈论油画风景画与中国山水画关系时回忆起这段经历，认为正如当时其师所论的那样，犹如中国山水画讲求"起承转合"并以"起"为最难，油画中的"起"——画面前景也是构图时最难处理的部分。吴冠中用自己学习中国画的经历来解构油画构图中的主次关系，这本身也是他对于"油画民族化"问题的实际阐释，而《北国风光》

---

1 孙国胜：《爱心的传递——记吴冠中〈北国风光〉》，《嘉德通讯》2009年第5期，第133页。
2 吴冠中：《旧画重提》，转引自《嘉德通讯》2009年第5期，第132页。
3 同上。
4 吴冠中：《邂逅江湖——油画风景与中国山水画合影》，载《吴冠中文集·艺术散论》，上海：文汇出版社，1998年。
5 同上。

便是这一阐释的极佳注脚。仅从构图来看，在《北国风光》中所采用的环抱式结构无疑是一种非常巧妙的处理方式。这种画面结构既可以凸显主景，又可以让中景和远景的丰富层次得以充分地展示，同时增加了画面的动势，烘托出壮阔的气魄。我们认为，这种构图方式不仅缓和了画面中前中后景之间的矛盾，更重要的是非常适合该作作为装饰壁画的特殊性——作为装饰壁画，无疑需要更宏大的气魄和更广阔的视角，而环抱式的构图显然正好可以满足这样的需求——即便最终放大成六米见方的壁画原作，也不会破坏这件画稿中所营造的氛围。

色彩是另外一个烘托画面氛围的重要手段。在这件《北国风光》中，我们发现，尽管描绘的是冬景，但画家有意使用了掺有红色、黄色笔触的暖色调，充分利用色彩间相互作用的关系来丰富画面，柔和观者的视觉感受。值得注意的还有在远山的处理上也并非一般油画所惯用的虚化轮廓的处理技法，而是较为明确地交代了每一座峰峦的结构。这些都使得从整体视觉效果上来看，本作能给人以晴冬的和暖而并非严寒的料峭。如此处理画面，不仅丰富了远景的层次，也似乎暗合了本作所谓"红色经典"的背景。

可以说，无论从画面的构成还是色调的把握上，吴冠中都始终在刻意缓和画面内在的冲突，力求在尺幅间充分体现画面的丰富性，并把握形式上的美感。而这种在当时仍可谓是探索的创作方式，在吴冠中后来的文章中得到了提炼、总结与伸张，从这个角度来看，《北国风光》是颇具标本意义的。

二、《北国风光》——非写生的风景画

从《北国风光》的名字来看，显然是一件风景作品。然而，值得注意的是，它并非一件实景写生风景画。不过更有趣的是，若将这件作品问世前后吴冠中的其他油画风景作品参校一遍，便会发现本作中的山峦苍松其实是各有来源的。

在画家创作于1977年的油画《井冈山》中，我们可以发现《北国风光》的身影。这件作品的构图颇具新意，前景的松柏被置于画面的视平线以下，似乎在有意弱化其前景的地位——事实上，井冈山的松柏正是最负盛名的景观，也是吴冠中较为热衷描绘的题材之一，而在这里画家则着意要描绘处于背景位置的山峦——尽管一眼看去犹如平涂，但仔细品味便会发现背景内在的丰富性。画家使用放纵的笔触来勾勒每一段山势，其间的来龙去脉隐约若现，条缕分明。同时，每下一笔的笔触中间也都包含了丰富的颜色——尽管色相的差别并不明显，但整体的色彩效果足可以使观者得以区分出大致的山面走向，以此配合

笔触体现出山峦的结构。这种自由而又不失章法的描绘无疑大大增加了背景的丰富性与可赏性，提高了背景在整个画面中的地位。在这种处理方法上，《北国风光》便与《井冈山》非常类似，可被认为是画家此期探索画面前后景均衡努力的连续，由此也可得知画家是在对实景写生的过程中逐渐摸索和凝练成这种表现技巧的，在创作装饰壁画稿时凭借之前的经验进行画面处理。

在《井冈山》中，吴冠中描绘了两棵松树。这种平冠松树是井冈松的造型特点之一，其弧度柔缓的树冠和遒劲有力的枝杈，是画家较为热衷描绘的对象之一。事实上，画家并非仅仅热爱描绘井冈松，他曾经讲述过去泰山寻访五大夫松的经历[6]，可见对于描绘松树的爱好。1977年，吴冠中创作了一幅名为《重比泰山》的油画作品。这件作品与《井冈山》相比正好相反，画家着力强调了主景——泰山松树，对之进行了深入的刻画。尽管在构图用意上与《井冈山》和《北国风光》都不尽相同，但仅从松树形象的刻画上来看，我们还是可以发现这棵泰山松与《北国风光》前景中群松的关系——画家所使用的都是略有弧度的厚重笔触同向皴擦，以概括出树冠的走势——只是在后者中，这种笔触更为洒脱和随意。从此我们可以看出《北国风光》中的群松从形式和技法上也都有着写实积累的渊源。

长城的形象是《北国风光》中的又一重要元素，可谓是画面中"转"的部分。画中的长城，寥寥数笔便成就了蜿蜒之势。与背景和松树的情况相似，在1978年吴冠中创作的两件《长城》水粉稿中，我们都能看见与《北国风光》里气势相近，在功能上串联起画面前后景的、舞动的简笔长城形象。

综上所述，无论是从画面的条理结构，抑或是画面中重要的组成元素来看，我们都能在吴冠中创作《北国风光》稿本之前不久的作品中找到可资参考的来源。我们并不认为这些早先的作品是吴冠中为创作《北国风光》壁画而有意搜集的材料，但是这幅并非写生的《北国风光》，确实大量调集了画家胸中长期积累的写生素材，通过不同的组合与夸张，按照画家的构图意愿集合在一起，成就了现在的画面，可谓是"搜尽奇峰打草稿"。

三、两本《北国风光》

我们眼前的这张《北国风光》只是尺幅不大的画稿。据吴冠中回忆，他是"移植了自己早先作过的一幅《北国风光》，改变了画幅的比例及部分内容"[7]来创作了这件作品。2007年，在香港佳士得春季拍卖会上出现的另一件同名作品引起了我们的兴

---

[6] 吴冠中：《风筝不断线——创作笔记》，载《吴冠中文集·艺术散论》，文汇出版社，1998年。
[7] 吴冠中：《旧画重提》，转引自《嘉德通讯》2009年第5期，第132页。

趣。这件作品据信创作于1973年[8]，被认为即是吴冠中后来创作机场壁画时所取法的那件早年作品[9]。那么，吴冠中究竟做了怎样的改动呢？我们不妨将这两件作品作一个比较便可知晓。

我们还是从主景开始。尽管两作的主景都包含松树和雪山，但创作时间更早的佳士得本中的松树显然要工致得多，情况类似的还有主峰上盘绕的长城，不仅描绘仔细，动感也不如后来稿本中的那般激烈。对于主峰的刻画，佳士得本更显细腻，以至于有些琐碎——过多地切割出山峰细部的阴阳面——使得主峰的整体气势未得伸张。而佳士得本中与主峰相连的山峦，其阴阳面的对比又不够强烈，直接导致了该本在画面纵深性的观感上不如稿本强烈。在两本中主峰的背面脚下，同样都是林海雪原、列车奔驰的景象，但佳士得本依旧显得拘谨，不似稿本那般简练。而且仔细比较两作对于这一部分视平线高度的处理，也可看出作者的细腻用心——佳士得本此部分的视平线显然是高于稿本的，这便使得稿本中的景物显得更为"深远"，而这一点正是通过比较两作的远景部分亦能得出的结论——稿本中天际线以上的部分要大于佳士得本，这明显使得稿本的视角更为平缓开阔，而佳士得本则显得高耸陡峭。我们认为这种差别的产生，除了包含吴冠中为了适应壁画作为大型装饰的特殊观赏需要外，也是如前所述所作的对于缓和画面矛盾的探索——在佳士得本中，前景抢占了太过重要的画面位置。在佳士得本中，画家也没有精心刻画远山的层次关系，这更使得前景跃然画面——显然，在创作佳士得本时，作者应当还未对画面前后景关系的矛盾产生浓烈的注意，还是如绝大多数油画家那样重视主景，当画家后来意识到画面前后景之间存在矛盾时，便趁着改动的机会着意加以缓和——绘画思想的深入与问题的发现与解决便是画家做出改动的原因。比较发生在两本《北国风光》之间的这一变化，正好说明了吴冠中70年代油画创作钻研过程中的收获。

顺便值得一提的是，我们猜测两本之间这种在构图上的差别可能还从一个侧面反映出画家在1973年创作《北国风光》时并未如后来创作稿本时那样上升到"山舞银蛇，原驰蜡象"的诗意境界，也许仅仅是为了描绘心中的北国雪景而已。而且，从形式关联上来看，画家笔下这种雪山景象的来源也极可能与他早年写生玉龙雪山的大量绘画有关——事实上，《北国风光》中的雪山、松树等也许与真正的北国并没有什么切实关系，仅仅如前所述是以画家的思想为中心重新组合写生素材而已，不过这已是另外值得探讨的问题，恐怕只有画家本人才知道真相吧。

四、余论

我们解读《北国风光》到这一步，已经可以清晰地在画家的艺术生命历程中得到它的坐标。然而，于画家自我的艺术生命之外，在当时的历史社会背景此一更大的参照系中释读这件作品也是值得我们关切的。

诚如前文所论，1979年，在画家的艺术生涯中有着非比寻常的重要意义，而同样是在1979年，中国的改革春风正在渐渐吹遍九州大地。经历了拨乱反正的重要历史时期后，曾经高度集中统一的社会结构正在渐渐发生变化，人们的视野在拓展，思想在沸腾，沉寂已久的美术界也迎来了绚烂的春天，多元的时代。可以说，七八十年代之交首都机场壁画工程的完工，应当在近三十年的中国美术史上有着极为重要的发端意义，象征着当局对于艺术创作"百花齐放"的默许。其中最有名的事件莫过于那件引起了热烈反响，由中央美术学院袁运生教授主创的泼水节题材壁画。一些画家借助这次政府工程的机遇，展示自己对于新时代的期望以及对于中国美术前进方向的思索。与袁运生的壁画一样，尽管画家并没有直言，但是吴冠中的《北国风光》在不经意间也扮演着同样的角色，尽管表现的是主旋律的题材，但是表现形式是同类题材绘画中从未见过的，在画家的创作中尽管是先有了创作主题，但是在具体的绘画过程中，依然是形式至上主义的。这种不经意的角色扮演，究其原因，正是来自画家长久以来对于所谓"写实主义"绘画的经意诟病，来自画家同时开始的对于绘画形式美的追求与探索。当这样一件充满形式美的作品被允许登上首都机场这样的大雅之堂时，它所产生的价值与意义显然已经超越了美的边界，显示了时代对于这种创作观的肯定与尊重。

然而，若从创作任务的角度考虑，画家此刻的这种不经意似乎又是经意的。吴冠中一生创作的任务绘画比较少，除了这件《北国风光》外，我们已知的作品还有他在1974年应北京饭店要求参与创作的《长江万里图》长卷。比较这两件相隔时间并不久的作品，我们可以清晰地发现其中的差别。《长江万里图》相对于《北国风光》来说显然是较为具象的，当然其中有两次任务的不同之处，例如《长江万里图》的创作经过了专门的写生，而《北国风光》更多则是集合了画家胸中的意象，尽管如此，我们还是能够感受到这种差别所反映出的历史环境的改善和创作气氛的松动——1979年这一生机勃勃的时代在画家的两件任务创作之间画上了淡淡的红线。

8　数据来源：http://www.ionly.com.cn/nbo/auction/ZuoPin.aspx?id=49405
9　http://news.artxun.com/youhua-1077-5383145.shtml

可以说，尽管《北国风光》在艺术成就上并非吴冠中油画的杰出之作，无论是画家本人还是热爱画家艺术的人们都未曾给予这件作品以艺术上的过多推崇，但是经过我们的解读发现，若将《北国风光》作为个案进行研究，竟是完全可以反映吴冠中对于油画构图、写生创作等问题的认识与变化的，而且，在大历史的环境下，这件作品也显示出了画家在新时代下创作心态的变化，默默反映出时代对于吴冠中绘画创作潜移默化的影响。从这些角度来说，这件不大的画稿无疑具有最朴素而历史的意义。

Interpreting Wu Guanzhong's Sketch *Northern Landscape*

By Wang Yu

When Wu Guanzhong's oil paint mural sketch *Northern Landscape* appeared for the first time at the 2009 Guardian Autumn Auction, it attracted much attention from various quarters. There was a time when phrases such as "Red Classic", "Oil Painting", "a donation from Comrade Li Ruihuan" were seen in various related reports, but the astronomical price that this work later attracted at auction became an even more popular topic. Clearly, this work had already been "endowed with an even deeper significance beyond the artistic."[1]

In fact, *Northern Landscape* cannot be called a representative oil painting by Wu Guanzhong. What really attracts our notice is the period in which this work was created: 1979. Everybody who understands Wu Guanzhong's art knows that it is exactly around this period that he published a great number of articles on his thinking on art, including "Abstract Beauty", "Formalist Beauty", "Nationalism in Oil Painting", and moreover that this generated a huge discussion in the world of art. If we return *Northern Landscape* to this historical environment in order to interpret it, we may produce a new understanding of, and knowledge about, this work, rather than just paying attention to questions external to the work itself, as we do now.

I : *Northern Landscape* as a Painting

According to the recollections of its creator, *Northern Landscape* was a sketch made in 1979 for the mural decoration that was to complete the work of the Beijing Capital Airport project.[2] To ensure a smooth approval process, Wu Guanzhong composed this work in the spirit of, and in reference to, two lines in Mao Zedong's *To the Tune of Qin Yuan Chun: Snow*: "Mountains dance - silver snakes, the plateau gallops - wax elephants".

In the surface structure of this work, the foreground is occupied by several flat-topped pines, which, along with the grand, tall snow-clad mountains behind them make up the main view of the painting. Along the ridges of the snow-clad mountains, the winding Great Wall links the foreground and the middle ground with the background, not only knitting the various parts of the painting closely together, but also

---

1 Sun Guosheng: "The Transmission of Love - On Wu Guanzhong's *Northern Landscape*", in *Guardian Communications*, 2009, No.5, p 133.
2 Wu Guanzhong: "Revisiting an Old Painting", *Guardian Communications*, 2009, Issue No.5, p132.

increasing the sense of movement in the painting, giving the spectator an impression that it is 'dancing'. When the artist was composing the work, he outlined the sunny and shady sides of the mountain ranges through changes in the opposition of light and shade. At the foot of the shady side of the main mountain peak, the painter with a few brushstrokes has outlined a wooded landscape, and behind the woodlands there is also a train rushing through the distant mountains, galloping between the snowy flats. On the sunny side of the main mountain, there is another set of peaks and ridges in the middle distance, deep within which he has positioned a dam. The dam also winds its way behind the main peak, making the spectator's gaze lose itself in the distance between the main peak and the background of the mountain ranges even further away. The continuous mountains in the distance, despite being outlined in a few brushstrokes, have a clearly layered feel, creating a notion-realm of "a thousand miles all locked in ice". Overall, the entire layout of the surface of the painting opens up around the main peak in the foreground, and the subsidiary scenes on all sides produce a reciprocal relationship surrounding the main peak, as well as building intangible external relations between each other through the wooded forest, the train and the dam. One can say that regardless of whether one looks at the Great Wall achieved in a few simple strokes, or at the distant mountains that embrace the main peak, they embody the care and thought that the artist has put into managing the composition. Thus even Wu Guanzhong may say that this sketch "is made with all my powers, so it is in fact no longer a 'sketch', but rather it already embodies the ultimate effect of a giant work."[3]

Wu Guanzhong has his own unique understanding of the question of the composition of the surface of an oil painting. Once in his later years, he said: "The greater the surface area occupied, the greater the overall effect."[4] But if this principle is taken too far, it may suppress the richness displayed by the middle ground and the background, creating the problem of an effect of 'vast but empty' in the painting surface. From the *Northern Landscape* that is before us, we can see that the artist at the time was already alert to this kind of paradox in the surface composition, and "grafting a flower onto another tree, and finding another spouse" to make the middle distance and the background fascinating.[5]

Tracing back Wu Guanzhong's conception of managing positioning in the painting surface, we find it comes from his experience of large-scale copying of Chinese *shanshui* paintings while he was a student. In his later years, when the artist discussed the connections between oil landscapes and Chinese *shanshui* landscapes, he recalled this experience, and was of the opinion, just as his teachers had said at the time, that Chinese *shanshui* painting emphasized 'begin, carry, turn, unite' (*qi, cheng, zhuan, he*) and that the hardest part of this was the beginning. The 'beginning' of oil painting, that is, the foreground of a painting, was also the hardest part of the composition to handle. Wu Guanzhong used his own experience in studying Chinese painting to deconstruct the sequential relations in the composition of oil paintings. This in itself is his actual explanation of the problem of 'nationalism in oil painting', yet *Northern Landscape* is the finest footnote to this explanation. Just looking at the composition, the embracing structure used in *Northern Landscape* is undoubtedly an exceptionally clever format in which to manage things. This kind of surface composition can both highlight the main scene, and let the rich layering of the middle ground and background achieve a full display, and at the same time add to the aspect of movement in the surface of the painting, and by contrast highlight a magnificent boldness. We think that this kind of compositional format not only mitigates the contradictions between fore-, middle and background in the surface of the painting, but even more importantly, that it is particularly suitable to the special character of that work as a decorative mural. As a decorative mural, it no doubt needs an even greater boldness and an even more magnificent perspective, and the embracing composition clearly

---

3 Ibidem.

4 Wu Guanzhong : "Encountering Rivers and Lakes - A Group Portrait of Oil Landscapes and Shanshui Landscapes in Chinese painting", in *Selected Writings by Wu Guanzhong: Essays on Art*, Shanghai Wenhui Press, 1998.

5 Ibidem.

is just right for meeting those requirements. That is, even being ultimately enlarged to the original mural size of six meters squared cannot spoil the atmosphere created in this sketch.

The color range is another important device by which the ambience of the surface is enhanced. In this work, we discover that, although a winter landscape is depicted, the painter has deliberately used a warm palette of mixed red and yellow strokes, and made full use of the connections of interaction between colors to enrich the surface, and soften the visual feeling experienced by the spectator. Also worth noticing is the technique of virtual contours, which is not at all common in oil painting, used here to manage the distant mountains, and which nevertheless accounts with relative clarity for the structure of each mountain range. All of this enables the work, just by its overall visual effect, to give spectators the warmth of a sunny winter rather than the chill of a severe one. Treating the surface composition in this way not only adds richness to the layering of the distant scene, but also happens to coincide, it seems, with this work's so-called 'red classic' background.

It may be said that both in the composition of the surface and in the mastery of the color scheme, Wu Guanzhong has deliberately softened the internal clashes of the painting throughout, and done his best to fully embody the richness of the painting and master its formal aesthetics on this small surface. This creative format, which might at the time still be called exploratory, was later refined, summarized and extended in Wu Guanzhong's writings. From this angle, *Northern Landscape* rather has the meaning of a specimen.

II : *Northern Landscape*
- a Landscape Paining Not Drawn From Life

Judging by its name, *Northern Landscape* is evidently a landscape painting. However, it is worth noticing that it is not the sketch of an actual scene. But, even more interestingly, if one were to compare other oil landscapes by Wu Guanzhong from about the time when *Northern Landscape* was put before the public with this one, one might discover that the mountains and the pine trees in this work have separate origins.

In the oil painting *Jinggang Mountain* (oil on board, 1977, 50 x 71 cm), created in 1977, we discover shades of *Northern Landscape*. The composition of this work features a novel notion. The pine trees in the foreground are placed below the sightline, in what seems a deliberate weakening of the position of the foreground - in actuality, the pine trees of *Jinggang Mountain* are its most celebrated view, as well as being one of Wu Guanzhong's favourite subjects, but here the artist deliberately sets out to depict the positioning of the mountain ranges in the background - although they seem at first glance to be spread out flatly, a closer inspection reveals the richness of the background. The artist uses indulgent brushstrokes to outline each mountain feature, and how the mountains appear, indistinctly snaking in and out, their repeated lines clear. At the same time, every brushstroke is rich in color - although the variations in color are subtle, the overall effect of the palette is sufficient to allow the spectator to distinguish the general directions in the mountain landscape, thus coordinating the structure of the mountain ranges embodied in the brushstrokes. This depiction, free but without losing the art of composition, without a doubt greatly increases the richness and beauty of the background, and raise the position of the background in the overall layout. In this method of managing the layout, *Northern Landscape* is very similar to *Jinggang Mountain*, and it may be considered a continuation of the artist's striving during this period to explore the balance between foreground and background in the layout of the painting. Thus we can also know that the artists was gradually finding his way to and consolidating this expressive technique, and that at the time when he was making this sketch for the decorative mural he was relying on previous experiences to manage the layout of the surface of the painting.

In *Jinggang Mountain*, Wu Guanzhong depicted two pine trees. These flat-topped pines are one of the characteristics of the modeling of *Jinggang Mountain*. Their gently curved crowns and vigorous His predilection for depicting pine trees is evident. In 1977, Wu Guanzhong created an oil painting called *Heavier Than Mount Tai* (*Heavier Than Mount Tai*, oil on canvas, 1977, 202 x 226 cm, Chinese National Museum collection). This work is the opposite of *Jinggang Mountain* in that the artist has emphasized the main theme with all his might, namely a pine tree on Mount Tai, and carried out a deeper depiction of it. Although there are deliberate structural differences between this painting and *Jinggang Mountain* and *Northern Landscape*, we can nevertheless, purely in terms of the formation of the formal image of the pine tree, discover a relationship between this pine tree and the multitude of pines in the foreground of *Northern Landscape*. In both cases, the artist has used thick, slightly curved brushstrokes similar to the texture-strokes of ink-and-wash to summarize the trend of the tree-crowns - it is just that in the latter, the brush-strokes are even more free and easy. Hereby we can see that the trees in *Northern Landscape*, from the point of view of form and technique, also have their origin in a realistic accumulation.

The formal image of the Great Wall is another important element in *Northern Landscape*. It may be considered the 'turn' part of the layout. In the painting, the Great Wall achieves a winding trend in a few brushstrokes. Similar to the situation of the background and the pine trees are the images of the Great Wall that we see in Wu Guanzhong's two 1978 gouache paintings of the *Great Wall* are close to the manner of the Great Wall in *Northern Landscape*.

As narrated above, regardless of whether we look at the structural layout of the painting or the major component elements of the painting, we find in Wu Guanzhong's works that closely precede the sketch for *Northern Landscape*, informative sources of reference. We do not think that these earlier works were deliberately made by Wu Guanzhong to gather material for the decorative mural *Northern Landscape*, but in fact they do assemble realistic materials that were accumulated over a long period in the mind of the artist, and which, after going through a process of combination and exaggeration, were brought together according to the structural desires of the artist to achieve the paintings we have now, and which might be called "seeking out interesting mountains and making sketches of them".

III : Two Versions of *Northern Landscape*

The *Northern Landscape* before us is merely a sketch of limited size. According to Wu Guanzhong's recollections, he transplanted his own earlier work *Northern Landscape*, changing the proportions and part of the content to create the mural.[6] At Christie's 2007 Spring Auction in Hong Kong, another work of the same name appeared and aroused our interest. It is said to have been created in 1973[7] and is believed to be the "earlier work" referred to by Wu Guanzhong as his source for the airport mural.[8] If so, exactly how did he change the earlier work? Let us compare the two works and find out.

Let us begin with the main scene. Although this is in both works made up of pine trees and snow-clad mountains, the pine trees in the earlier work ("the Christie's version") are clearly more meticulously worked out. The same applies to the Great Wall, which winds around the main mountain: not only is it depicted in detail, but the feeling of movement is inferior to the intensity of the later sketch. As for the characterization of the main mountain, the Christie's version is more delicate, verging on the trifling in its excessive chiseling out of the detailed shady and sunny sides, penning in the grandeur of the overall figure of the main mountain. The mountain ranges that are linked to the main mountain in the Christie's version are insufficiently strong in their opposition of sun and shade, which results directly in insufficient strength in terms of the depth of viewing experience of that version compared to the sketch. In both versions, the back of the foothills of the main mountain feature a scenery of woodlands, snowfields and a speeding train, but the Christie's version still seems cautious, unlike the concision of the sketch. Besides, when we carefully compare the handling of the sightlines in this part of both two works, we can see the exquisite efforts of the artist. The sightline in this part of the Christie's version is clearly higher than that of the sketch, which makes the scenery

---

6 Wu Guanzhong: "Revisiting Old Paintings", quoted in *Guardian Communications*, 2009, No.5, p132.
7 Digital source: http://www.ionly.com.cn/nbo/auction/ZuoPin.aspx?id=49405
8 http://news.artxun.com/youhua-1077-5383145.shtml

of the sketch seem more "deep and distant", and this point can also be derived from a comparison of the handling of the distance in the two works. In the sketch, the part above the horizon line is relatively greater than it is in the Christie's version, which clearly makes the viewing angles of the sketch flat and open, while they are steep and towering in the Christie's version. Apart from Wu Guanzhong's meeting the special viewing demands of the mural as a large-scale decoration, we also think, as explained earlier, that the differences were produced in the exploration of how to mitigate the contradictions within the painting surface. In the Christie's version, the foreground occupies an excessively important part of the layout of the painting. Also in this version, the artist has not meticulously characterized the layered relationship of the distant mountains, which causes the foreground to stand out even more vividly in the painting. Clearly, when he was creating the Christie's version, the creator must not yet have become fully aware of the contradictions in the relations between fore- and background in the painting surface, and like most oil painters he also focused on the foreground . When he later became aware of the existence of these contradictions, he seized the opportunity of changing them and deliberately made them more gentle. The reason the artist changed them was to deepen his thinking in painting, and to discover and solve problems. The comparison between the two works with regard to this change, explains the achievements of the process of detailed research on Wu Guanzhong's oil painting creations of the 1970s.

It is worth mentioning in passing that we guess that the compositional differences between the two works indirectly reflect that the artist had not yet, to the degree that he had at the time of the later sketch, risen to the realm of the poetic notion of "Mountains dance - silver snakes, the plateau gallops - wax elephants" when he painted the *Northern Landscape* of 1973, and it is perhaps simply that he was painting the northern snowy scenery in his heart. Besides, in terms of formal relationships, the origin of these snowy landscapes from the brush of the artist is very possibly connected with his numerous early paintings of the *Jade Dragon snow mountain*. In fact, the snow-clad mountains, pine trees and so on in *Northern Landscape* possibly have no genuine connection with any actual *northern landscape*, but are simply, as explained above, a re-combination of realistic materials centered on the artist's thinking. This is already another question for consideration, one about which we're afraid perhaps only the artist himself knew the truth.

IV : Epilogue

Having reached this step in our interpretation of *Northern Landscape*, we can clearly discern the coordinate of the work in the painter's life of art. However, apart from the artist's own artistic life, it is also worth our interpreting this work paying attention to the wider frame of reference of the historical social background of that period.

As stated previously in this article, 1979 carried an unparalleled significance in the artistic career of the artist. It was also in 1979 that the spring wind of reform was gradually sweeping across China. After going through the important historical period of restoring order from chaos, the social structures that had to a high degree been centralized and unified gradually began to change. People's field of vision became wider, thinking was fermenting and bubbling, and the art world, long silent, also welcomed in the age of glorious spring and pluralism. At what may be called the crossroads of the 1970s and the 1980s, the completion of the project of the Capital Airport mural should be considered to have had the significance of an extremely important starting shot for the history of the fine arts of the last thirty years in China, symbolizing the acquiescence of the "May the Hundred Flowers Bloom" towards the arts by the authority. The most famous incident of the time was one that aroused unsurpassed reverberation, the Water Splashing Festival mural by Professor Yuan Yunsheng of the Central Academy of Fine Arts. Some artists took the opportunity of this government project to display their own expectations of the new age, and ideas on the way forward for Chinese fine arts. Like the mural by Yuan Yunsheng, although the artist did not directly say so, Wu Guanzhong's *Northern Landscape* inadvertently played a similar role. Although the expressed subject matter was mainstream, its expressive form had not been seen before in paintings of subject matter of the kind. Although the creative theme already existed in the artist's creative work, in the specific process of painting it, it was still a kind of Formal

Suprematism. In tracing the reason for the inadvertent playing of this role, one may find it precisely in the artist's longstanding deliberate criticism of so-called Realist painting, deriving from the artist's beginning to pursue and explore Formalist beauty in painting at the same time. When a work as brimful of Formalist beauty as this one was approved for installation in a hall as grand as that of the Capital Airport, the value and significance produced by it has clearly already transcended the limits of beauty. It reveals the affirmation and respect of the age towards this kind of view of creation.

However, considered from the angle of a creative assignment, the artist's inadvertence at this moment almost seems advertent. Commissioned paintings occupy a relatively sparse number of creative artwork in Wu Guanzhong's life. Apart from *Northern Landscape*, we also know *Ten Thousand Miles of the Yangtze River (Changjiang Wanli Tu)* the long scroll painting in which he was invited to participate by the Beijing Hotel in 1974. If we compare these two works, which are not that distantly separated in time, we may discover some clear differences. *Ten Thousand Miles of the Yangtze River* is, in comparison to *Northern Landscape*, clearly more figurative. Of course, there is also a difference between the two in terms of the nature of the assignment. For instance, the creation of *Ten Thousand Miles of the Yangtze River* went through specifically realistic painting from nature, while *Northern Landscape* was, rather, a gathering of the notional images in the artist's mind. Despite this, we can still sense the improvement in historical conditions and the loosening of the creative atmosphere reflected in these differences. The vibrant era of 1979 has painted in a faint red line between these two assignments of the artist.

It can be said that although *Northern Landscape* is hardly an outstanding work among the oil paintings of the artist in terms of its artistic achievement, and neither the artist himself nor people who are enthusiastic about the painter's art have praised this work very highly, yet, through our interpretation, we have discovered that if we carry out case study research of *Northern Landscape*, we really can completely reflect Wu Guanzhong's understanding of and changes to oil painting composition, realistic creations and other questions. Besides, in the greater historical environment, this work also reveals the changing creative attitude of the artist in the new age, silently reflecting the subtle influence of the age on Wu Guanzhong's creation of paintings. From this angle, this small sketch without a doubt contains a modest but historical significance.

吴冠中
Wu Guanzhong
北国风光
Northern Landscape
布面油画
Oil on Canvas,
68 × 179.5cm, 1979

重读《在新时代——亚当夏娃的启示》

秦晓磊

孟禄丁[1]、张群[2]的《在新时代——亚当夏娃的启示》这一作品，创作于1985年，即二人进入中央美术学院油画系学习的第二年，最早为公众所知是1985年5月在中国美术馆，由国际青年中国组织委员会主办的"前进中的中国青年美展"上，随作品送交展览会的还有一份说明文字。作为该美展评委与该作品创作过程见证者的徐冰，谈及此作"从制作、评选到展出一直是一张有争议的作品"[3]。由于作品本身的争议性，在当时仅获得了鼓励奖。然而在经历了'85美术运动洗礼的中国美术界，对于此作品并未遗忘。与其他获奖作品相比，批评界与美术史界对于此作品的关注度反而超越其他作品。高名潞在其论著中，曾多次从该作品画面所具有的理性精神角度，分析其对于'85美术所具有的启蒙性质[4]。杭间认为其是"新具象绘画的萌芽"[5]，殷双喜则认为其是"80年代较早出现的新古典主义油画样式"[6]。批评家们从其各自角度出发，对此绘画做出判断。美术史家则看重其对于后来美术潮流的影响，吕澎、易丹在《中国现代艺术史1979-1989》中谈及此作"是一幅具有象征意味的宣传画，它所起到的鼓动作用是不可忽视的"[7]，邹跃进认为创作者"通过各种象征符号来表达他们的思想和观念，这一点正好开启了后来所有中国现代主义艺术的先河"[8]。今日更有媒体定论云："此作品作为'85运动的先锋作品而载入史册。"[9]

不论是批评家，还是美术史家，都着重于为此作品寻找定位。本文则试图回到作品本身，分析作品的创作过程及作品的最终面貌。据徐冰《他们怎样想？怎样画？》一文中谈及此作品的创作初衷："据他们自己说，画这张画的用意在'破'字，就是想通过作品向人们提出一些问题"，"他们的创作构思是围绕'破'字展开的。起初他们想画一张带有创作性质的人体，以此来打破我国绘画创作领域里这一不应有的局面。至于人体在干什么并非事先考虑成熟的。而亚当、夏娃这一基本形象在下意识思维中的突然出现，促成了他们对'新时代'这一基本主题的选择。"[10]张群、孟禄丁谈及这幅画的创作方法"是从精神素材中创造出来的，它完全以一种理念和主观性为其思索的主线"[11]。由以上材料可知，孟、张二人在创作此作品时是观念先行的，重在表现"破"的概念，具体形式则采用人体。至于亚当和夏娃的形象，是作为瞬间灵感的迸发，从而被表现在画面上的。因而"画什么"这个问题在孟、张这里并不十分重要，

---

1. 孟禄丁，1962年生于河北保定市，祖籍北京通州。1979年考入中央美术学院附属美术学校，1983年进入中央美术学院油画系学习，1987年留校执教于中央美术学院油画系第四画室。1990年就读于德国卡斯鲁赫国立美术学院。1992年移居美国。2006年在北京设立工作室。1993年任教于美国理德学院，1989年成为中国美术家协会会员，1993年作为评委参加"中国油画双年展"（中国美术馆）。1985年获"国际青年美展"鼓励奖，1987年获"中央美术学院双年展"奖，1993年获"中国油画双年展"特别荣誉奖。
2. 张群，1962年生于内蒙古包头市。1979年考入中央美术学院附属美术学校，1983年进入中央美术学院油画系学习，1987年执教于首都师范大学美术系，1988年作为客座艺术家赴加拿大班芙艺术中心（Banff Centre），1990年移民加拿大成为自由艺术家，1991年任加拿大温哥华华人艺术家协会理事。
3. 徐冰：《他们怎样想？怎样画？》，《美术》1985年7期，第29-30页。
4. 高名潞：《关于理性绘画》，《美术》，1986年8期，第42页。高名潞：《85美术运动》，广西师范大学出版社，2007年，第119页。
5. 杭间：《新具象艺术——在现实和内心之间》，吉林美术出版社，1999年5月，第97页。
6. 殷双喜：《80年代后期中国油画的古典意向》，《美术学报》2003年第3期，第35页。
7. 吕澎、易丹：《中国现代艺术史1979-1989》，湖南美术出版社，1992年5月，第111页。
8. 邹跃进：《新中国美术史1949-2002》，湖南美术出版社，2002年11月，第204页。
9. 伟子主编：《美术档案——中国油画》，四川出版社，四川美术出版社，2010年5月，第89-90页。
10. 徐冰：《他们怎样想？怎样画？》，《美术》，1985年第7期，第30页。
11. 张群、孟禄丁：《新时代的启示——〈在新时代〉创作谈》，《美术》1985年第7期，第47页。

重要的是如何去画。那么孟、张二人如何解决"怎么画"的问题？笔者将从其作品最终呈现的面貌入手。

从《在新时代——亚当夏娃的启示》这一作品来看，画面主体为一正一背的男女裸体，尽管将其表现为东方人，然其造型、姿态，皆为欧洲文艺复兴时期亚当与夏娃的典型样式。画画正中为一正面走来的女青年，画面右下角为一半身侧面男子。此外还有大量细节，如时钟、苹果、玻璃碎片等等。其中象征东方的元素皆处于破碎或开放的状态，如打开的大门，破碎的太极盘与佛教造像，女青年周围的玻璃碎片，皆暗合了"破"的概念。

从表现方法上看，其有借鉴超现实主义手法之处，尤以受到超现实主义代表画家达利影响为深。画面的蓝黄对比色调，低矮的地平线，皆为达利画作中常出现的特点。在细节描绘上，如夏娃的脚与山石的融合，桌子掀起的一角，女青年从虚空中走来，破碎的玻璃片，中国式大门与天空的融合，皆可看出超现实主义对此作品的影响。孟禄丁于2009年访谈中坦言："我们选择了超现实主义的表现手法来展示我们的作品，用这种方式表达内容和形式，更自由地释放了我们的思想，从而产生了《在新时代——亚当夏娃的启示》。"[12] 两位创作者采用了超现实主义的手法，然而他们走得并不太远，首先其具体元素的选择尚在当时官方与大众的可接受范围之内。从画面元素的选取上来说，皆为东西方古典元素，太极、佛教造像为典型中国古典文化代表，其破碎的状态可以被解释为封建势力的土崩瓦解。亚当夏娃则是西方艺术中的古典母题，在当时被赋予人性解放的含义[13]。至于占画面主体的裸体形象，在经历了1979年北京国际机场壁画中两个全裸女子形象引发的争议，1980年《美术》杂志第4期发表的几幅西方人体雕塑引起的热议后，《在新时代——亚当夏娃的启示》中的两个裸体形象在当时所具备的话题性应已大大减少。

其次将具体元素抽出单看，皆为写实之作，在当时也算得上中规中矩之作。如位于画面正中央的托苹果盘女青年，除却手势予人以神秘莫测之感外，可说是一位现实中女青年的写生肖像，对于形体和光影的把握和处理显示出画家良好的写实能力，并无任何特殊之处。然而这件作品超出其时代的特点就在于，其将写实元素以一种非现实的方式并置一处，形成一种超现实之感。在具体细节上，如前文所述，也有一定的借用超现实主义手法之处。

回到上文笔者提出的问题：孟、张二人为何采用这样的方式解决"如何画"的问题？为何画作最终以此种面貌呈现？

从作者的经历与教育背景来看，两位创作者皆为60年代初生人，正如他们自己所言："我们与四川为代表的一代青年画家不同，他们懂事的时候是在农村。这段生活使他们建立起特有的生活态度和与人民的直接感情。而我们从附中到大学，接受的东西是书本的，是人类思想的结果。我们的生活就是画室，画室的背景就是重新思考过去和开放政策下改革的新中国。"[14] 两位创作者未曾受过"文革"、上山下乡的洗礼，接触正规美术训练的途径一致，皆为美院附中毕业升入美院油画系学习，受的皆为正统的学院派教育。在1979年美院恢复教学至80年代中期，美院油画系所强调的正是写实的传统与扎实的素描训练，油画系从1984年改为四年全部画室制[15]，此时张群、孟禄丁正是大二学生，分别进入第一工作室和第四工作室。第一工作室十分注重培养学生的造型基础能力，崇尚素描，对于写实绘画传统的把握、严格的造型训练是其主要教学特色[16]；第四工作室强调油画的探索与创新，然而在当时还处于组建状态[17]。不论各工作室的侧重点为何，对于刚刚进入工作室的张、孟二人来说，自其接受正规美术教育以来，即是强调造型基础能力和写实传统的学院派教育。从占画面主体的人体所呈现的雕塑般的坚实感，及光影的微妙变化，皆显示出画家受过良好的素描训练。因而这种具体元素写实的描绘，从二位创作者的美术教育经历来看，正是他们所擅长的。

值得注意的是孟、张二人创作此作品时，皆不过二十多岁的年纪，在艺术理想上，有着当时青年所普遍具有的革新精神，二人在创作谈中说："一切定论对青年来说都是有疑问的。时代的压力迫使我们对以往进行反思。原有的秩序对我们来说越来越不适应。我们不满足于过去，要求进一步开拓、发展。"[18] "我们有自己的知识结构，它决定了我们对世界的思考和追求。"[19] 在2009年的访谈录中，孟禄丁谈道："从附中升到美院，开始有点沉闷，因为课堂教学都是重复的，我们从附中就开始质疑，艺术为什么必

---

12 伟子主编：《美术档案——中国油画》，四川出版社、四川美术出版社，2010年5月，第89-90页。
13 "亚当、夏娃吃禁果的叛逆行动带来了革命，从此由蒙昧状态进入文明，由中性的天人变成人间的恋人，由禁锢的伊甸园来到自由的人世。"
   张群、孟禄丁：《新时代的启示——〈在新时代〉创作谈》，《美术》1985年7期，第47页。
14 徐冰：《他们怎样想？怎样画？》，《美术》1985年第7期，第30页。
15 《中国·中央美术学院油画系第三工作室》，河北美术出版社，1998年，第2页。
16 《中国·中央美术学院油画系第一工作室》，河北美术出版社，1998年，第1-2页。
17 《中国·中央美术学院油画系第四工作室》，河北美术出版社，1998年，第1-8页。
18 张群、孟禄丁：《新时代的启示——〈在新时代〉创作谈》，《美术》1985年第7期，第47页。
19 徐冰：《他们怎样想？怎样画？》，《美术》1985年第7期，第31页。

须是现实主义？为什么必须是客观反映现实？为什么不能表现个人的观念，表现哲学的思考？"[20] 正是这种青年所具备的革新精神，使他们不满足于当时中国美术界的现状，要求有变化，有创新。体现在《在新时代——亚当夏娃的启示》这一作品上，其主要表达的"破"这一概念正是对美术界原有模式的一种反抗与批判，在具体手法上也采用了不同以往的表达方式。

还需注意的是超现实主义流派在中国的引入与介绍。如果不了解超现实主义的表达方式，接受学院派正统训练的两位作者恐怕也想不到可以用这种手法表现自己内心的现实。早在19世纪30年代中期，具有先锋意识的西画社团就已将超现实主义流派介绍进中国[21]，19世纪70年代末80年代初，邵大箴等学者开始了新一轮的西方现代艺术流派的介绍，开始于邵大箴1979年发表于《世界美术》的《西方现代美术流派简介》，此后还有一系列文章，诸如1980年的《现实主义精神与现代派》，1981年的《现代派美术与想象》等，1982年更是出版了在当时极具影响力的《现代派美术浅议》。这些文章及专著中皆有对于超现实主义流派的介绍与评议。对于超现实主义流派的专门讨论则有邵大箴发表于1980年的《美术中的超现实主义》，1982年陈绶祥的《米罗、达利与超现实主义》，这些文章及专著同时选印了代表艺术家的代表作品。正是这些对于超现实主义的艺术观念与绘画作品的引入，为当时青年艺术家的艺术革新提供了可兹借鉴的素材。邵大箴对于超现实主义的艺术观有如此概括："超现实主义认为，用现实主义的方法表现客观的、物质的世界是古典艺术家已经完成了的任务，超现实主义的使命是挖掘新的、未被探讨过的那部分心灵世界，以扩大和开辟艺术表现领域。"[22] 在孟、张二人的创作说明中可看到类似论述："我们发现以往对艺术源泉仅仅确定为一个视觉表象的现实，我们称为'客观'现实。殊不知，大脑的思维也是一种现实，是一种隐性的现实，也有其自身的确定性。艺术家不仅可以以'唯实'的观察，也可以用'唯心'的灵性去感应我们生存其中的世界。"可以说，在作品表达方式与观念上，《在新时代——亚当夏娃的启示》皆受到超现实主义流派的启发。

值得注意的是，当时被一同介绍入中国的西方现代艺术流派，还有诸如未来派、表现主义等，为什么创作者借鉴的是超现实主义手法，而非其他西方现代派的手法？笔者认为原因有二：其一，超现实主义对于细节的真实描绘，与二位接受艺术训练时的经验不谋而合，即创作者本身对于写实技巧的熟练掌握。尽管创作者本身对于艺术为何要客观反映现实有质疑，然而不可否认，描绘现实的写实技法确实是他们所擅长的。其二，超现实主义对于局部真实的描绘，大体上符合当时国内大多数人对于艺术的认知与期望值，在当时的文化氛围中，走得太远未必能被接受。如上文所述，这件作品的独特之处在于将写实元素以一种非现实的方式并置一处，形成一种神秘莫测的超现实之感。此外，借鉴其他西方现代派的手法是否能通过审查，更不得而知。

至于其借鉴超现实主义之处，如前文所述，走得并不太远，这其中不可忽视的是社会整体环境的影响。当时官方及民众对于西方现代诸流派的接受程度有限，在介绍西方现代派艺术的同时学者不得不边介绍边批判，如邵大箴在《现代派美术浅议》一书结尾谈道："我们提倡对一切事物采取分析的态度。对于现代派美术，我们也不应一概肯定或一概否定。"[23]《世界美术》1982年第4期有林源《对外国美术要取分析态度》一文，着重谈到对西方现代派应如何做到批判地接受。那么采用作为西方现代派之一的超现实主义流派的艺术手法，能否被展览会审查方接受，是二位创作者必然考虑过的问题。事隔二十多年后，作者谈及当时参加国际青年画展的兴奋之情："中国美术馆搞青年美展那年，正好是'85国际青年年。那时我是美院油画系二年级学生，从附中升到美院，开始有点沉闷，因为课堂教学都是重复的。在那个年代搞创作、参加大的美展都是很兴奋、很认真的。"[24] 既如此看重此次美展，那么在作品面貌是否能够通过审查上，定是做了一番考量与取舍的。徐冰曾提及他们在展览中对作品的说明："至于现在看到的画面上有些说明性的内容，他们不隐晦地说是为审查时能通过加上去的，如封建大门打开等。"[25] 从在展览说明上作出的解释上，同样能看到画家所做的妥协与让步。孟、张二人在1985年创作的谈中并未提及超现实主义手法的使用。同样参与此展的《渴望和平》一画，在当时被认为受到达利的影响，作者在创作谈中特意对采用的超现实主义手法作解释："有人说我们的画中有很多超现实主义画家达利的因素，我们只能承认是受到了他一定影响，这只是我们在主题性绘画创作中借鉴西方现代派的某些绘画形式的一点探索，因为我们不具备达利当时所处的时代环境。他的那种挖掘新的心灵世界，无意识或潜意识的世界，把现实与梦境结合起来的创作意念，在我们这个时代是得不到社会和人们充分支持和共鸣的。"[26] 此亦可对当时的文化空气和审查制度严格作一例证。

20　伟子主编：《美术档案——中国油画》，四川出版社、四川美术出版社，2010年5月，第89-90页。
21　杜少虎：《独立画家群的"新方位"——民国时期超现实主义美术的引进和传播》，《文艺研究》2009年8期。
22　邵大箴：《西方现代美术流派简介[续]》，《世界美术》1979年第2期，第62页。
23　邵大箴：《现代派美术浅议》，河北美术出版社，1982年10月，第97页。
24　伟子主编：《美术档案——中国油画》，四川出版社、四川美术出版社，2010年5月，第89-90页。
25　徐冰：《他们怎样想？怎样画？》，《美术》，1985年第7期，第30页。
26　王向明、金莉莉：《我们与〈渴望和平〉》，《美术》，1985年第7期，第45页。

通过以上分析，现今被认为作为'85美术运动的开篇之作载入史册的《在新时代——亚当夏娃的启示》这一作品，最终呈现的面貌，实则是——学院派的教育传统，青年所具有的革新精神，西方现代派艺术的引入，依旧严格的审查制度——以上多方力量相互较量后的结果。两位作者采用了极为智慧的手法，结合自身优势，在可利用艺术资源有限而社会环境尚未完全放松限制的条件下，既表达出自身的艺术理想，又在一定程度上获得官方及公众认可。其后的美术发展证明了这两位年轻的艺术家具有超出其时代的眼光。然而这一现象的另一方面，也反映了学院派艺术所具有的折中性。因而'85美术运动虽则开篇于学院，但轰轰烈烈的展开却在、也只能在各地方民间艺术家团体的艺术实践之中。

参考

专著：

邵大箴：《现代派美术浅议》，河北美术出版社，1982年10月。
吕澎、易丹：《中国现代艺术史1979-1989》，湖南美术出版社，1992年5月。
杭间：《新具象艺术——在现实和内心之间》，吉林美术出版社，1999年5月。
《中国·中央美术学院油画系第三工作室》，河北美术出版社，1998年。
《中国·中央美术学院油画系第一工作室》，河北美术出版社，1998年。
《中国·中央美术学院油画系第四工作室》，河北美术出版社，1998年。
邹跃进：《新中国美术史1949-2002》，湖南美术出版社，2002年11月。
高名潞：《85美术运动》，广西师范大学出版社，2007年。
伟子主编：《美术档案——中国油画》，四川出版社、四川美术出版社，2010年5月。

论文：

邵大箴：《西方现代美术流派简介[续]》，《世界美术》1979年第2期。
邵大箴：《美术中的超现实主义》，《文艺研究》1980年第6期。
林源：《对外国美术要取分析态度》，《世界美术》1982年第4期。
陈绶祥：《米罗、达利与超现实主义》，《外国文学》1982年第7期。
徐冰：《他们怎样想？怎样画？》，《美术》，1985年第7期。
张群、孟禄丁：《新时代的启示——〈在新时代〉创作谈》，《美术》1985年第7期。
王向明、金莉莉：《我们与〈渴望和平〉》，《美术》1985年第7期。
高名潞：《关于理性绘画》，《美术》1986年第8期。
殷双喜：《80年代后期中国油画的古典意向》，《美术学报》2003年第3期。
杜少虎：《独立画家群的"新方位"——民国时期超现实主义美术的引进和传播》，《文艺研究》2009年第8期。

Another Look at *In the New Age: the Enlightenment of Adam and Eve*

By Qin Xiaolei

Meng Luding[1] and Zhang Qun's[2] *In the New Age: the Enlightenment of Adam and Eve* was created in 1985, when the two creators were entering the second year of their studies in the Oil Painting Department of the Central Academy of Fine Arts. The painting first became known to the general public when it was shown in the National Art Museum of China Beijing in May 1985, in the "In Progress China Youth Art Exhibition" sponsored by the Chinese Committee of the International Youth Organisation, when there was also an explanatory caption that accompanied the work to the Exhibition. Xu Bing, who was on the Jury Committee for that Exhibition, and a witness to the process of the creation of the work, has said about it that: "All the way from its production to its selection for exhibition, it was a controversial work."[3] Due to the controversy, the work just won "Encouragement Award". However for the art world after '85 Art Movement, it had made a deep impression. On the other hand, the degree of attention that the critics and the art historians paid to this work far surpassed that given to the other prize-winning works. Gao Minglu in his writings has several times analysed its enlightening quality in relation to the

---

1. Meng Luding, born in 1962 in Baoding, Hebei, original residence affiliation Tongzhou, Beijing. Entered the High School of the Central Academy of Fine Arts 1979, and the Oil Painting Department of the Central Academy of Fine Arts in 1983. In 1985 he won the Encouragement Award at the International Youth Exhibition. In 1987 he stayed on at the Academy to teach in the No.4 Workshop of the Chinese Painting Department, Central Academy of Fine Arts. In the same year he won a Prize at the Chinese Academy of Fine Arts Biennial Exhibition. In 1990 travelled to Karlsruhe, Germany, to study at the Staatliche Akademie der Bildenden Künste Karlsruhe. He emigrated to the USA in 1992 and taught at Reed College in 1993 and also was recognised in that year for his Outstanding Achievement in Chinese Art. He established a studio in Beijing in 2006.
2. Zhang Qun, born 1962 in Baotou, Inner Mongolia, 1962. Entered the High School of the Central Academy of Fine Arts 1979, and the Oil Painting Department of the Central Academy of Fine Arts in 1983. From 1987 taught at the Capital (Shoudu) Normal University's Fine Arts Department. In 1988 he was Visiting Fellow at the Banff Arts Centre, Canada. In 1990 he emigrated to Canada to become a free artist, and in 1991 he became Director of the Chinese artists Association in Vancouver, Canada.
3. Xu Bing: "What Do They Think? How to Paint?" *Arts Monthly* 1985, No.7, pp29 - 30.
4. Gao Minglu: "On Rationalist Art", *Art Monthly*, 1986, No.8, p42. Gao Minglu: *The 1985 Art Movement*, Guangxi Normal University Press, 2007, p119.
5. Hang Jian: *New Figurative Art - Between Realism and Conscience*, Jilin Arts Press, May 1999, p97.

art of 1985 from the angle of its rationalist spirit.[4] Hang Jian considers it the "germination of New Figurative Painting",[5] and Yin Shuangxi considers it "a relatively early appearance of the New Classicist Oil Painting model of the 1980s".[6] The critics judged this work from their various angles. The art historians attached importance to its influence on the subsequent wave in fine arts. Lü Peng and Yi Dan in their *History of Chinese Modern Art 1979 - 1989* said that this work "is a painting with symbolic significance, and the stimulating function it served cannot be ignored".[7] Zou Yuejin thinks that the creators "expressed their thinking and conceptions through various symbols, and this established a precedent for all subsequent Chinese Modernist art."[8] Today even more media conclude that: "This work will go down in history as an pioneering work of the 1985 Art Movement."[9]

Both critics and art historians focused on positioning this work. This article attempts to return to the work itself, to analyse the process of its creation and its ultimate appearance. According to Xu Bing's comments on the original intention of this work in his article "What Do They Think? How to Paint?": "According to their own words, their intention in painting this painting lay in the word 'breaking'(*po*), that is, through this work they wanted to raise some problems with people", "their creative idea was unpacked around the word 'breaking'. At first they wanted to paint a human body of a creative character to break open a situation that should not be there in the field of our Chinese painting. As for what the human body was doing there, they had given no mature thought to this before creating it. However, the sudden appearance in their subconscious of the basic figures of Adam and Eve inspired them to choose the fundamental theme of the 'New Age'.[10] Zhang Qun and Meng Luding said about their creative method in this work: "it was created from spiritual materials, using a completely ideal subjectivity for the main thread of its line of thinking."[11] We can see from the above material that when Meng and Zhang were creating this work, they started from a concept. The emphasis was on the concept of 'breaking', for which they happened to use the specific form of a human body. As for using the figures of Adam and Eve, it was a momentary burst of inspiration to represent them in the painting. Accordingly, the question of 'what to paint' was not very important to Meng and Zhang here. The important question was how to paint. The present writer will attempt, from the ultimate appearance of this painting, to answer the question of how the two artists solved the question of 'how to paint?'.

Looking at the work *In the New Age - The Enlightenment of Adam and Eve*, the main subject is a respectively frontal and rear view of the naked bodies of a male and a female. Although they are of Eastern appearance, their modeling and attitudes are shown in the manner typical of the era of the European Renaissance. In the middle of the painting a young woman is walking towards us, and in the lower right hand corner there is a seated male figure, seen side - on. In addition there are a great number of details, such as a clock, apples, pieces of broken glass, and so on. The elements that symbolize the East are all in a broken or opening state, such as the open main door, the broken plate with the *taiji* motif and the Buddhist statue, all suggesting the concept of 'breaking'.

Looking at the method of representation, it contains references to Surrealist devices, and shows a particularly deep influence received from the representative Surrealist artist Salvador Dalí. The opposition of blue and yellow tones in the palette of the painting and the low horizon are both characteristics that often appear in Dalí's paintings. In the depiction of the details, and the blending of Eve's feet with the rock she is standing on, and the raising of one corner of table, the walking in thin air of the young woman, the broken pieces of glass and the blending of the Chinese-

---

6 Yin Shuanxi: "The Classical Intention of Chinese Oil Painting in the Latter Part of the 1980s", in *Art Journal* 2003, No.3, p35.

7 Lü Peng and Yi Dan, *History of Chinese Modern Art 1979 - 1989*, Hunan Fine Arts Publishing House, May 1992, p111.

8 Zou Yuejin: *New Chinese Art 1949 - 2002*, Hunan Fine Arts Publishing House, November 2002, p 204.

9 Wei Zi (ed) *Fine Arts Archives - Chinese Oil Painting*, Sichuan Press, Sichuan Arts Press, May 2001, pp89 - 90.

10 Xu Bing: "What Do They Think? How to Paint?" in *Art Monthly*, 1985, No.7 p30.

11 Zhang Qun, Meng Luding: "The Inspiration of the New Age – On Creating In the New Age", in *Art Monthly*, 1985, No. 7, p47.

style gates with the sky, the influence of Surrealism on the work can be seen. In a 2009 interview, Meng Luding said frankly: "We chose the expressive devices of Surrealism to exhibit our work, using this format for both content and form so as to express our thinking more freely, and that's how *In the New Age - The Enlightenment of Adam and Eve* was born."[12] The two creators used the devices of Surrealism, but they did not go too far. Firstly, their choice of specific elements remained within the bounds acceptable officially and to the masses. On their choice of elements, they are all classical whether Eastern or Western. *Taiji* plates and statues are representative of classical Chinese culture, and their fractured state can be interpreted as the collapse and dissolution of feudal forces. Adam and Eve are classical topics of Western art, which have at present been endowed with the implication of human liberation.[13] As for figures of the naked bodies that make up the major subject in the painting, after the controversy aroused by the two completely naked female figures in the murals of the Beijing international airport in 1979 and the lively discussion produced by the publication in the fourth issue for 1980 of the *Art Monthly* magazine of several Western sculptures of human bodies, the value as a topic of conversation of the figures of the two naked bodies in *In the New Age - The Enlightenment of Adam and Eve* was already greatly diminished by this time.

Secondly, looking at the component elements taken one by one as realistic works, they were all considered at the time to be works made according to the rules. For instance, the young woman positioned in the centre of the painting with her tray of apples, apart from the mysterious feeling of her beckoning gesture, can be considered a realistic portrait of a young woman in real life. The mastery and management of modeling and light show the excellent realistic capabilities of the artists, but there is nothing special about her. What sets this work ahead of the characteristics of its era lies in its juxtaposition of realistic elements with a non-realist format, forming a surrealist feeling. As stated before, there are also specific borrowings from the devices of surrealism.

Returning to the question asked before: Why did Meng and Zhang use this kind of method to solve the problem of 'how to paint'? Why is the work ultimately presented in this guise?

As for the experience and educational background of the creators, both were born in the beginning of the 1960s. As they put it themselves: "We are different from this generation of young artists in Sichuan, for instance, in that they grew mature in the village. This period of living establishes in them a particular attitude to life and a direct feeling for the people. But we went straight from high school to university, and the things we encounter are books, the result of the thinking of humanity. Our life is that of artists, and the background of artists is to rethink the past and the new China under the policy of opening up and reformation."[14] Neither of the creators received the baptism of the 'Cultural Revolution' and of being sent to the mountains or the countryside. They both received the same proper course of fine arts training. Both graduated from the High School of the Central Academy of Fine Arts into its Oil Painting Department to study, and there they received a genuine academic education. From the revival of teaching at the Academy in 1979 until the mid-1980s, what the Oil Painting Department of the Academy emphasized was exactly the realist tradition and a solid training in drawing, and from 1984, the Oil Painting Department changed over to being a four-year completely workshop-based system.[15] At this time, Zhang Qun and Meng Luding were second-year students, and entered No.1 Workshop and No.4 Workshop, respectively. No.1 Workshop focused exclusively on

---

12 Wei Zi (ed) Fine Art Archives – Chinese Oil Painting, Sichuan Press, Sichuan Arts Press, May 2010, p89-90.
13 "The disobedience of Adam and Eve eating of the forbidden fruit led to revolution, and from then on they left their benighted state and entered one of civilization; from being neutral humans in Heaven, they became lovers in the world of humans; from the imprisonment of the Garden of Eden, they came to the free world of humanity." From Zhang Qun and Meng Luding.
14 Xu Bing: "What Do They Think? How to Paint?" in *Arts Monthly*, 1985, No. 7, p30.
15 *Chinese Central Academy of Fine Arts No.3 Workshop*, Hebei Arts Press, 1998, p2.

cultivating the students' basic skills in modeling, and stressed sketching. Its main pedagogic character lay in a mastery of the realistic painting tradition and in a strict training in modeling.[16] No.4 Workshop stressed exploration and innovation in oil painting, but was still in formative mode at the time.[17] Regardless of where the special emphasis of each Workshop lay, for Zhang and Meng, who had just entered their Workshops, they had, ever since they began to receive a standard training in fine arts, been receiving an emphasis on their basic modeling ability and an academic training in the realistic tradition. From the sculptural feeling of solidity of the human figures that occupied the subject matter of the painting to the subtle changes in light, it showed that the artists had received an excellent training in draftsmanship. Accordingly, this specific element of realistic drawing was, in terms of the process of their fine arts training, exactly where their forte lay.

It is worth noticing that when Meng and Zhang created this work, both of them were in their twenties. In terms of their artistic ideals, they shared the reforming spirit generally held by the young people at the time. As they talked about the creation process: "Any conclusion about young people is questionable. The pressure of the era forces us to reconsider the past. The order of the status quo is, for us, more and more unsuitable. We are not satisfied with the past, we demand more opening and development."[18] "We have our own thought structure, and it determines our reflection and pursuits in relation to the world."[19] In the record of an interview in 2009, Meng Luding said: "When I graduated from High School to the Academy, I began to feel a bit depressed, because the teaching became repetitive, and those of us who had come up from the High School began to ask why art has to be realistic. Why does it have to reflect reality objectively? Why can it not reflect the conceptions of the individual and reflect philosophical thinking?"[20] It is exactly this kind of revolutionary spirit characteristic of young people that left them unsatisfied with the condition of the world of fine arts in China at the time. They demanded change and renewal. It can be seen in the work *In the New Age - The Enlightenment of Adam and Eve*, and the concept of 'breaking' that is the main thing it expresses is precisely a kind of resistance against and criticism of the existing models of the world of fine arts. In the specific devices employed, they have also used various old expression.

Also, it must be remembered how the Surrealist School entered and was introduced into China. If the two creators had not understood the language of Surrealism, I'm afraid the two creators with their classical academic training would also not have been able to think that they could use this kind of device to express the reality of their own conscience. In the mid-1930s, Western art groups with pioneering ideas were already introducing the Surrealist School into China.[21] In the late 1970s and early 1980s, Shao Dazhen and other scholars began a new cycle of introducing schools of modern Western art, beginning with Shao Dazhen's "Short Introduction to Schools of Modern Art in the West", published in *World Art* in 1979, and after this there was another series of his articles, for instance "The Spirit of Realism and the Modernist School" (1980) and "The School and the Imagination of Modernist Art" (1981). In 1982, he also published *Discussion of the Art of the Modernist School*. These articles and monographs all contained introductions and critiques of Surrealism. As for specialized discussions of the Surrealist School,

---

16 See *Chinese Central Academy of Fine Arts No.1 Workshop*, Hebei Arts Press, 1998, p1 - 2.
17 See *Chinese Central Academy of Fine Arts No.4 Workshop*, Hebei Arts Press, 1998, p1 - 8.
18 Zhang Qun and Meng Luding: Talks about the Creation of 'In the New Age' in *Art Monthly*, 1985, No.7, p47.
19 Xu Bing: "What Do They Think? How to Paint?" in *Art Monthly*, 1985, No. 7, p31.
20 Wei Zi (ed): *Fine Arts Archive - Chinese Oil Painting*, Sichuan Arts Press, May 2010, pp89 - 90.
21 Du Shaohu: "The Independent Artist Collective 'New Direction' - The Introduction and Propagation of Surrealist Art in the Time of the Republic", *Literary Research*, 2009, No.8.

there was Shao Dazhen's *Surrealism in Art*, published in 1980 and Chen Shouxiang's *Miró, Dalí and Surrealism* (1982). These articles and monographs at the same time published representative works by representative Surrealist artists. It was exactly the introduction of these artistic conceptions and paintings of Surrealism that provided valuable reference materials for artistic renewal by the young artists of the time. Shao Dazhen's artistic view of Surrealism can be summarized as follows: "Surrealism holds that using realistic methods to manifest the objective, material world is a task that has already been fulfilled by the classical artists. The mission of Surrealism is to dig out the new, unprobed part of the spirit, so as to broaden and develop the field of artistic expression."[22] In the creative explanation of Meng and Zhang, one can find a similar account: "We discovered that the source of art was previously simply identified as a visual representation of reality, which we call 'objective' reality. However, we little imagined that, the thinking of the brain is a kind of reality, a hidden kind of reality with its own identity. The artist is not limited to a 'realistic-only' observation of the world, but can use a 'mental-only' spirit to respond to the world in which we live." One can say that in the conception and the expression of the work, *In the New Age - The Enlightenment of Adam and Eve*, they both receive the inspiration of Surrealism.

It is worth noticing that there are other directions in Western modern art that were introduced into China at the same time, such as Futurism, Expressionism and so on. Why did the artists refer to the devices of Surrealism and not to the devices of the other schools of Western modern art? The present writer thinks that there are two reasons for this. First, the realistic depiction of details in Surrealism was immediately compatible with the experiences of the two painters during their artistic training, that is, their mature mastery of a realistic technical skill. Although the creators themselves had raised questions about why art had to reflect reality objectively, it was undeniable that the realistic technical skill in depicting reality was in fact their forte. Second, the realistic depiction of details of Surrealism conformed, in general, to the understanding and expectations of art in China at the time. In the cultural atmosphere of that time, going too far would not necessarily have been accepted. As stated earlier, the uniqueness of this work lay in the non-realistic juxtaposition of realistic elements, creating a mysterious feeling of Surrealism. Besides, it was even more impossible to know whether references to the devices of other Western schools of art would have passed inspection.

As for the references to Surrealism, as stated before, they did not go too far. Here, the influence of the social environment as a whole must not be neglected. At the time, the degree of official and popular reception of the various schools of Western modern art was very limited. At the same time as they were introducing Western modern art, scholars had to criticize them on the side. For instance, at the very end of Shao Dazhen's book *Discussion of the Art of the Modernist School*, he stated: "We recommend an attitude of analysis in employing all things. As for Modernist Art, we must also neither affirm everything nor deny everything."[23] In the April 1982 issue of *World Art*, there was an article by Lin Yuan, "We Must Adopt an Analytical Use of Foreign Art", which focused the discussion on how a critical reception should be given to sWestern Modernist art. Could the use of the devices of Surrealism, one of the modern schools of Western art, be accepted by exhibition committees inspection rules? The two artists must have considered this question. Two years later, they talked about their excitement at the time of taking part in the International Youth Exhibition: "The year that the National Art Museum of China held the Youth Exhibition was 1985, the International Year of Youth. At the time I was a second year student in the Oil Painting Department of the Central Academy of Fine Arts. Graduating from the High School to the Academy, I felt a bit bored, because the teaching was all very repetitive. Creating work for and taking part in the Art Exhibition

---

22 Shao Dazhen: "Introduction to the Western Modernist School of Art (Continued)", in *World Art*, 1979, No.2, p62.
23 Shao Dazhen: *Discussion of the Art of the Modernist School*, Hebei Arts Press, October 1982, p97.

was all very exciting, and very serious."²⁴ Since this Exhibition was taken so seriously, considerations and trade - offs would definitely have been made on the question of whether the appearance of the work would pass the inspection or not. Xu Bing has stated about the explanatory note that accompanied the work: "As for some of the explanatory content of what we see now on the canvas, they said quite openly that they added it to pass the inspection, such as 'opening up the gates of feudalism' and so on."²⁵ From the explanation provided for the Exhibition, we can similarly see the compromises and concessions made by the artists. Meng and Zhang artists' talk in 1985, said nothing about using the devices of Surrealism. The Painting *Longing for Peace*, which likewise took part in this Exhibition, was considered at the time to have been influenced by Dalí, and the artist at the creator's talk deliberately explained the use of the devices of Surrealism: "Some people say that in our work there are many elements from the Surrealist artist Salvador Dalí. We can only acknowledge that we have received a certain influence from him. This is just a bit of exploration of the pictorial forms referring to Western Modernism in the creation of the thematic depiction, because we don't live in the environment of the era of Dalí. That excavation that he makes of new spiritual material, the unconscious or subconscious world, the creative concept of uniting reality and dreams, cannot in our age gain the full support and sympathy of society and people."²⁶ This may also serve as an example of the cultural atmosphere and the rigor of the inspection system at the time.

Through the above analysis, the work that is presently considered to be the opening chapter of the 1985 Art Movement and is recorded in history as *In the New Age - The Enlightenment of Adam and Eve* is in fact, in its ultimate guise, the result of the following powers, after their mutual contest: the educational tradition of the Academy; all the reforming spirit of youth and introduction to the art of Western Modernism; and the same old strict inspection system. The two authors have used some extremely clever tricks, along with their own advantages, in restricted conditions where the permissible artistic resources were limited and the social environment could not yet altogether relax, and both expressed their own artistic ideals, and also to a certain degree achieved official and public acceptance. Subsequent developments in art have demonstrated that the two young artists had a vision that transcended their era. However, another aspect of this phenomenon was that it reflects the compromises contained in Academic art. Accordingly, although the 1985 Art Movement began its first chapter within the Academy, the truly imposing opening was indeed present, but only to be found in the artistic practices of the non - official artist collectives of various localities.

---

24 Wei Zi (ed): *Fine Arts Archive – Chinese Oil Painting*, Sichuan Arts Press, May 2010, pp89-90.
25 Xu Bing: "What Do They Think? How to Paint?" in *Art Monthly*, 1985, No.7, p30.
26 Wang Xiangming, Jin Lili: "*Longing for Peace* and Us", in *Art Monthly*, 1985, No.7, p 45.

References

Monographs:

Shao Dazhen: *Discussion of the Art of the Modernist School*, October 1982. Lü Peng, Yi Dan: *History of China's Modern Art 1979 - 1989*, Hunan Fine Arts Publishing House, May 1992. Hang Jian: *New Figurative Art - Between Reality and Conscience*, Jilin Arts Press, May 1999. *Chinese Central Academy of Fine Arts Oil Painting Department No.3 Workshop*, Hebei Arts Press, 1998, Chinese Central Academy of Fine Arts Oil Painting Department No.1 Workshop, Hebei Arts Press, 1998; *Chinese Central Academy of Fine Arts Oil Painting Department No.4 Workshop*, Hebei Arts Press, 1998; Zou Yuejin, *New Chinese Art History 1949 - 2002*, Hunan Fine Arts Publishing House, November 2002. Gao Minglu: *The 1985 Art Movement*, Guangxi Normal University Press, 2007; Wei Zi (ed): *Fine Art Archives - Chinese Oil Painting*, Sichuan Press, Sichuan Arts Press, May 2010.

Articles and Essays:

Shao Dazhen: "Introduction to the Schools of Western Modernist Art(continued), in *World Art*, 1979, No2. Shao Dazhen : "Surrealism in Art", *Literary Research*, 1980, No.6; Lin Yuan: "We Must Take an Analytical Attitude to Foreign Art", *World Art*, 1982, No.4; Chen Shouxiang: "Miró, Dalí and Surrealism", in *Foreign Literature*, 1982, No.7; Xu Bing: "What Do They Think? How to Make Art?" in *Art Monthly*, 1985, No.7. Zhang Qun, Meng Luding: "The Inspiration of the New Age - Creators' Talk on *In the New Age*", in *Art Monthly*, 1985, No.7. Wang Xiangming, Jin Lili: "*Longing for Peace* and Us", in *Art Monthly* 1985, No.7; Gao Minglu: "On Rationalist Art" in *Art Monthly*, 1986, No.8; Yin Shuangxi: "The Classical Intention of Chinese Oil Painting in the Latter Half of the 1980s", *Art Journal*, 2003, No.3; Du Shaohu: "The Independent Artists' Collective 'New Direction' - The Introduction and Propagation of Surrealist Art in the Republican Era", in *Literary Research*, 2009, No.8.

孟禄丁、张群

Meng Luding, Zhang Qun

在新时代 – 亚当夏娃的启示

In the New Age - The Enlightenment of Adam and Eve

布面油画

Oil on Canvas

196 × 164cm, 1985

聚焦与定格
——再论《对话》

胡晓岚

1989年2月5日，农历大年三十，中国美术馆"中国现代艺术展"开幕约两小时后，当时26岁的女艺术家肖鲁向自己的装置作品《对话》连开两枪。两声枪响立刻成为国内外媒体关注的焦点，《对话》从此成为'89"中国现代艺术展"的标志。

装置作品《对话》的主体是两个铝合金电话亭。当年由杭州市电信局免费提供材料并安装。电话亭的正面玻璃上覆盖了两大张照片，展示一男一女各自打电话的背影。两座电话亭中间由一个镜面连接。镜前的白色台子上放置一红色电话座机，话筒垂下。两座电话亭相对的侧面一分为二，一半镶镜面，一半镶照片。镜面与照片交错相对。作品的镜面部分由红色粗线条分割开来。电话亭外贴有三张小招贴。据肖鲁《关于1989年在中国美术馆枪击作品〈对话〉的说明》，作品《对话》产生于她作为浙江美术学院油画系1988年毕业生的毕业创作，受到老师郑胜天与胡振宇的指导。之后在老师宋建明对作品"破一破"的建议下产生了用枪的想法却未能实施，直至1989年"现代艺术大展"两次枪击之后作品《对话》才得以完成[1]。

以上叙述似乎显得过于冷静。让我们试着回到当时"现代艺术大展"的火热现场。开幕式当天，孵蛋、洗脚、卖对虾、撒避孕套等等各色事件你未唱罢我登场，"这时展览现场已经是一片混乱，组委会的人四处'灭火'，WR小组的朱雁光被驱逐出场。朱雁光高叫：'我自己会走！'各种离奇的突发情况此伏彼起，WR的三个白衣人被人带进办公室以后，高名潞及时冲过去救援，公安人员也很紧张，蒙着白衣服也挺恐怖的，不知道衣服里有什么，命他们赶快把衣服扒了，朱雁光衣服脱到一半警察问：'你们是谁，哪儿来的？'他大喊一声：'大同游击队！''砰——砰——！'就在这个时候，枪声响起。中国第一次现代艺术大展彻底陷入混乱。"[2]

枪击事件使唐宋和肖鲁被公安机关逮捕，并导致了大展期间中国美术馆第一次闭馆。世界四大通讯社美联社、路透社、法新社和共同社都立刻报道了该消息。《纽约时报》《时代周刊》《基督教科学箴言报》《曼谷邮报》香港《申报》以及欧洲的大报都报道了肖鲁的枪击行为。国内的所有报纸和媒体也都追踪报道了这个消息，并且把《对话》和打枪行为描述为"中国现代艺术展"的头条新闻。在新闻传播方面，迄今为止，还没有任何中国当代艺术作品像肖鲁的这件作品那样产生强烈的新闻冲击[3]。

最初曾有大展负责人对于枪击行为表示非常愤慨，也有负责人向媒体表示枪击是对画展严肃性的破坏，声明概不负责[4]。但是后来，作为大展主要负责人的高名潞和筹展人的栗宪庭都对枪击《对话》做出了很高的评价。栗宪庭认为这是一个"事件艺术"，"承杜尚以小便池揶揄社会审美习惯的艺术智性，标志了中国前卫艺术在艺术观念上向智慧方向的拓展"，并且成为了"新潮美术的谢幕礼"[5]。而高名潞则认为："有许多当初不知道的事情，今天看来，都增强了肖鲁枪击《对话》的逻辑性和合理性。这件作品可以称之为中国当代美术史上最有影响的装置与行为相结合的作品，也是中国当代美术史上最为重要的标志性作品之一。由于它的重要

---

1 肖鲁：《关于1989年在中国美术馆枪击作品〈对话〉的说明（修订稿）》，艺术数据网http://www.art-here.net/html/av/7431.html 2004年2月2日于杭州下满觉陇初稿（2004年4月23日刊登于"美术同盟"网站）；2004年6月30日修改于北京呼家楼（2004年10月，刊登于《艺术家茶座》总第二辑，山东人民出版社），2005年7月25日再次修改于北京呼家楼（2005年5月，刊登于《天涯》杂志，海南省报刊发行局发行）；2005年10月19日再次修改于北京呼家楼（2005年10月21日，刊登于"美术同盟"网站）；2007年8月2日再次修改于北京东营艺术区。
2 蒯乐昊：《20年前现代艺术"七宗罪"》，《南方人物周刊》2009年第11期，第62-66页。
3 高名潞：《一声枪响——半生对话：对肖鲁作品〈对话〉的解读》，《嘉德通讯》2006年第3期，第98-101页。
4 唐宋：《关于1989年2月5日〈枪击〉事件的简要陈述》，艺术数据网http://www.art-here.net／html／av／7380.html，1989年2月27日。
5 栗宪庭：《两声枪响：新潮美术的谢幕礼 附：唐宋、肖鲁作品点评》，《重要的不是艺术》，江苏美术出版社，2000年8月，第255页。

性,几乎每一本中文和外文的中国当代美术史书都介绍了这件作品"[6]。大展之后,枪击《对话》的录像和照片曾参加1990年在美国纽约举办的"1950年代到1980年全球观念艺术展"(the Point of Origin: Global Conceptualism)和1998年"蜕变与突破:全球华人新艺术展"(Inside Out: New Chinese Art)等重要展览。从枪击行为中对射击目标——作品《对话》的瞄准聚焦,到媒体对于事件报道的聚焦,直至最后《对话》被定格为'89"中国现代艺术展"的标志。这一枪击行为的开始与结果无疑与当时能够产生激烈震动的社会背景与特定语境有关。

中国艺术中对于现代艺术的追求早在20世纪上半叶就出现了,如倡导西方现代美术的社团决澜社和林风眠、庞薰琹等从事现代艺术实验的艺术家。到了70年代末80年代初,从上海的"十二人画展"到北京的"星星美展"继续借鉴现代艺术。后者与"伤痕美术"以不同方式对"文革"时期的革命现实主义进行反拨。而'85新潮美术则是对现代梦的奋力追逐。

80年代延续了革命的模式,是"中国现代艺术批评形成并最有活力的时期"。批评家常常基于启蒙主义的立场,作出宏观判断。1985年以前,《1844年哲学经济学手稿》对于异化、人道主义和人性论的讨论起到了不可忽视的作用。1985-1989年,"文革"问题逐渐淡化,人们开始思考为什么会出现"文革"。现代和传统的问题凸显出来。1985年出现文化热,表现出全盘西化的倾向,最后以纪录片《河殇》的集体观点为代表。媒体与出版界发挥了重要作用。各种西方现代哲学与文艺的书籍翻译出版,既有尼采、萨特、海德格尔等人的著作,也有克莱夫·贝尔和贡布里希的理论。讨论的模式一时间变得复杂起来,各种理论在文化热中相互混杂,从存在主义、生命哲学、现代主义、分析哲学到中国的老、庄、禅。

躁动的文化热正是新潮艺术家初期艺术反叛的文化背景。许多老照片记录了当时的盛况,这些年轻人戴着黑框眼镜,穿着老棉袄、中山装、背心、裤衩、解放鞋,蹲在一起讨论尼采、弗洛伊德、蒙克与毕加索,交换欣赏画册和作品幻灯[7]。各地美术团体如"厦门达达"、"浙江池社"、"北方群体"、"西南艺术研究群体"等等雨后春笋般纷纷涌现,八仙过海各显神通[8]。'85新潮美术运用西方的方法和语言来回答西方文化的问题,最后发展成为了现代而现代。现代像魔鬼一样鞭催艺术家创新,除了疲于奔命还得生搬硬套迅速翻新[9]。艺术家努力用视觉的方式表现哲学思想,在艺术语言上进行各种探索,无论是野兽派、立体派、表现主义,还是抽象艺术、达达主义以及装置、行为等等形式,"将西方整个现代艺术重新进行了一次演习"。

'85新潮美术作为艺术运动实际上是80年代整个社会文化潮流的一部分。各种先锋实践与语言实验不仅出现在艺术界,还表现在文学界的先锋文学和先锋诗歌、电影界的探索电影、音乐界的先锋音乐等各个方面。"20世纪80年代是一个政治上走向开放,而商业化压力尚未到来的空白时期。这一时期为孕育理想主义热情、激发各种乌托邦幻想设置了最理想的温床。"[10]那个"短暂、脆弱却颇具特质、令人心动的年代"[11],充满了梦想与激情,焦灼与躁动。人们在疯狂中寻找希望,纯粹又没有方向。肖鲁给高名潞的信中曾说:"激情是那个年代留给我最珍贵的纪念。"[12]

新潮美术在1987年开始走下坡路,至'89"中国现代艺术展"成为新潮美术的谢幕礼。提出"中国现代艺术展"的最初动议是在1986年的珠海会议。之后经过黄山会议,到大展开幕已经是三年以后了[13]。前卫艺术第一次大规模进入中国美术馆展出,集体公开亮相。在筹展人栗宪庭的眼里,由于大展变成了"缺乏前卫性指导思想"和"预见性把握"的回顾展,因此将展览的意义放在其社会性上,企图制造有别于以往的"新鲜和刺激"。而两声枪响所产生的强烈效果立刻使得其他艺术家的出格行为都变得黯然失色。枪声准确把握了"被压抑过久以后希望宣泄的"时代心态,成为集体焦灼情绪的爆发口[14]。

---

6 高名潞:《一声枪响——半生对话:对肖鲁作品〈对话〉的解读》,《嘉德通讯》2006年第3期,第98-101页。
7 《'85新潮 中国当代艺术"考古"》,中国先锋艺术家联盟 http://blog.sina.com.cn/wincome77,2008年7月4日,来源:《外滩画报》。
8 具体情况见黄燎原:《关于'89艺术大展上"七个行为"的对话》,http://www.ionly.com.cn/nbo/zhanlan/showAtt_358.html,来源:东方视觉网站。
9 尹吉男:《现代 现代》,《独自叩门》,生活·读书·新知 三联书店,2002年8月,第253页。
10 费大为:《'85新潮,一次出轨的瞬间》,《'85新潮 中国第一次当代艺术运动》,上海人民出版社,2007年。
11 查建英:《写在前面》,《八十年代》,生活·读书·新知三联书店,2006年5月,第3页。
12 肖鲁:《就"'89现代艺术大展"枪击作品〈对话〉给高名潞的信》中的第4封信,艺术数据网 http://www.art-here.net/html/av/7375.html,2004年3月23日写于杭州下满觉陇。
13 相关具体情况可参见2009年第3期《当代艺术与投资》,其中刊登了《中国现代艺术二十年》纪念回顾专题,专题的呈现重点为一种口述的历史,采访了'89大展主要组织者与部分参展艺术家。
14 相关具体情况参见栗宪庭:《关于〈枪击事件〉与部分当事人的访谈录与再解读》,艺术数据网 http://www.art-here.net/html/av/7372.html 2004年春初稿,2005年10月3日改毕,来源:Tom专稿。

1989年注定是不平凡的一年，有人将枪声与1989年的政治事件联系起来。'89大展确实引起了全世界媒体的关注。枪击第二天，美国《时代周刊》的封面标题就是"孵蛋、枪击、避孕套"。政治与性一直是媒体敏感的话题。"枪杆子里出政权"，枪与暴力、国家政权的天然联系使其自身具有政治隐喻，何况枪击发生在代表国家意识形态的国家美术馆，发生在明令禁止枪支流通的社会主义的中国。前卫与主流，越界与禁忌，国外媒体自然地对于枪击事件作出政治性解读。

枪击在装置作品《对话》上留下了小小的弹孔与裂纹，其引发的轰动与新闻性使得作品《对话》定格为标志与符号，亦折射出转型期与敏感期的特定政治、社会与文化语境，成为历史物证与遗迹。

尽管新潮美术在发生、发展的过程当中会出现这样或那样的问题而受到当时评论家的批评，但是如果立足于当下，对中国当代艺术的发展历程进行反思，新潮美术的反叛姿态和对自由与理想的追求依然具有闪光的精神力量。新潮美术和'89中国现代艺术展在美术史上的地位与价值将无法回避。那么，《对话》作为标志性作品，也是当代艺术史书写过程中无法回避的作品。

历史常常交织了必然性与偶然性。从肖鲁自己对于作品《对话》创作前后的回忆中，可以发现《对话》自诞生直至枪击之后最终得以完成的整个过程中存在很多偶然性。肖鲁在1988年进行毕业创作时就产生过枪击作品的想法，并曾向浙江省射击队的沙勇借枪，由于沙勇临时与她联系不上而没有实施。如果枪击早在那时完成，就远不会有后来的轰动效应了。如果肖鲁没有高干背景，没有在北京的社会关系，那么将连枪支本身都无法获得。如果'89大展在筹展过程中就展场问题与农展馆达成协商，那么枪击就不会在中国美术馆发生，事件的新闻性也会相应减弱。另外，在肖鲁的叙述中，我们可以发现从创作者的主观意图来说，肖鲁枪击作品的目的在于个人情感，是她对情感阴影与困扰的告别。她并没有过多考虑到法律后果、社会影响及作为独立事件的意义[15]。反观艺术史，艺术作品的出现往往充满偶然性。然而，尽管在肖鲁个人的叙述中，枪击作品的目的是出于个人情感，但恰恰是这种情感的困扰，无处诉说的压抑状态与当时特定时代集体心理的压抑状态相符合。肖鲁借助枪击行为完成情感宣泄的宿命与当时社会中焦灼情绪一触即发的紧迫状态正好对接，因此作品产生的必然性自然凸显了。正是个人心态与时代心态的契合，造成了枪声所具有的集体性与社会性。

近观作品《对话》会进一步发现其中蕴含的一系列悖论。悖论似乎一开始就存在了，就创作目的而言，作品《对话》是纯粹个人情感的表达和无法言说的个体感情的释放，而从其引发的结果来看却具有强烈的新闻性与社会性。很长一段时间以来，或许正由于其社会性的遮蔽，人们对于作品本身的创作目的并不十分关注。

装置作品《对话》取材于现成品——电话亭。电话亭作为80年代都市环境所特有的公共设施，本应是透明的，虽然其作为一个相对独立的空间存在。而在《对话》中，两个电话亭被转换为密闭的黑房间，尽管两个电话亭的正面各有一男一女打电话的背影，但是背影本身的背景也是黑色的。对话往往在双方开诚布公的前提下最为有效，黑色中的对话也许正暗示了沟通的隔离。此外，两座电话亭之间由一个镜面连接，但是镜面上同时出现了红色粗线条将镜面分割。不现实的联系与实际的隔离同时并存。

从表面上看，装置《对话》展示了正在打电话的一男一女，似乎是他们两人在通电话。以往的阐释大都认为两座电话亭之间悬置的话筒暗示了男性与女性之间对话的无效，不过，从现实层面来说，人们似乎相对较少从一个公共电话给另一个公共电话打电话。那么如此看来，我们是否也可以将作品阐释为两人原本没有相互对话的意愿，而是各有谈话对象？那么中间话筒空置的电话座机或许可以进一步解读为对话对象的缺席，或至少是一种暂时的缺席。

此外，枪作为一种武器意味着破坏力与杀伤力，枪击直接且有效。无论是"枪杆子里出政权"还是"党指挥枪"，枪象征着国家机器或者国家政治。"向反动派打响了第一枪"，一声枪响常常成为对被奴役、被压抑状态的突破。从装置作品《对话》所反映的状态来看，对话首先依靠电话进行，并非采用一种直接面对面的方式，那么，作者对于作品本身的射击是否可以解读为对直接对话的渴望？或者，更进一步地，可以将肖鲁的枪声作为对国家政权的挑衅？在特定历史时期，枪声是否还可以解读为对自由对话的无限向往？

时隔这么多年，仅从作品自身所蕴含的一系列悖论出发，《对话》仍然具有被进一步解读的空间。作品一旦诞生就同时获得了无限阐释的可能，正如王尔德在《道连·格雷的画像》的序言中所说的，艺术之镜反映出的是观者本身而不是生活。无论是发生在作品与观众之间的对话，还是两性之间、传统与现代之间的对话，虽然常常出现错位与隔离，但是对话的渴望与努力会始终存在。我们，作为观众，与已被聚焦并定格成为标志性作品的《对话》之间所进行的对话同时包含两性之间、传统与现代之间、作品与艺术史之间多重对话的可能性。

2011年5月15日于望京

15　相关具体内容请参见肖鲁与栗宪庭与高名潞的通信，关于枪击事件的说明及补充说明以及栗宪庭对于肖鲁的访谈。

Focus and Freeze – Revisiting *Dialogue*

By Hu Xiaolan

On 5 February 1989, on the traditional Chinese New Year's Eve, about two hours after the China / Avantgarde Exhibition at the National Art Museum of China Beijing opened, the female artist Xiao Lu, who was 26 at the time, fired two shots in quick succession at her own installation work *Dialogue*. The sound of these two gunshots immediately became a focus of attention for media in and outside of China, and *Dialogue* from then on became the emblem of the 1989 China / Avantgarde Exhibition.

The main body of the installation *Dialogue* was two aluminium alloy telephone booths. The Hangzhou Telecommunications Bureau had provided the materials for these and assembled them free of charge. The front glass panels of the telephone booths were covered by two large photographs that represented a man and a woman seen from behind, both engaged separately in telephone conversation. A mirror connected the two telephone booths. On a white table in front of the mirror, a red telephone was placed with the receiver hanging down. The two inward-facing sides of the telephone booths were divided into two, and were inlaid, half with mirrors, half with photographs. The mirrors and the photographs were staggered and faced each other. The mirror in the middle of the work was quartered by thick red lines. On the outside of the telephone booths there were three small posters. According to Xiao Lu in her "Explanation of the work *Dialogue* shot with a gun at the 1989 China / Avantgarde Exhibition at the National Art Museum of China Beijing", *Dialogue* was born as her 1988 graduation work in the Oil Painting Department of the Zhejiang Academy of Fine Arts, and was created under the guidance of her teachers Zheng Shengtian and Hu Zhenyu. Later, the suggestion from another teacher, Song Jianming, that she "break" the work a little produced the idea of using a gun, although it could not be put into practice at the time, so that the work *Dialogue* only achieved completion after the two gunshots at the 1989 China / Avantgarde Exhibition.[1]

This account appears rather dispassionate. Let us try to return to the flagrant scene of the China / Avantgarde Exhibition at that time. On the day of the opening ceremony, there were various incidents, including ones involving incubating eggs, washing feet, selling prawns and scattering condoms, all in rapid and chaotic succession: "At this time the scene of the Exhibition was already one chaotic mess, the members of the organizing committee were already 'putting out fires' in all directions, and Zhu Yanguang of the WR Group was ejected from the Exhibition area, shouting loudly: "I know how to walk on my own!" Various bizarre emergency situations were arising all around. When three

---

1 Xiao Lu: "Explanation of the work *Dialogue* attacked with gunfire at the 1989 China / Avantgarde Exhibition at the National Art Museum of China Beijing (revised edition)" at the arts website: first draft: 2 February 2004 at Lower Manjuelong, Hangzhou, published on the tomarts.cn website on 23 April 2004; revised at Hujialou, Beijing 30 June 2004 (published in *Teahouse for Artists*) Second general series in October 2004, Shandong People's Press); revised again 25 July 2005 at Hujialou, Beijing (published in May 2005 in *Tianya* (Horizon) Magazine, Hainan Province Newspapers and Publications Bureau); revised again 19 October 2005 in Hujialou, Beijing (published on the tomarts.cn website 21 October 2005); again revised 2 August 2007 in Dongying Arts Precinct, Beijing.

white-clad people of the WR Group were taken into the office, Gao Minglu rushed to the rescue. The security people were also very jumpy, and it was indeed rather terrifying that there were these people concealed in white garments. Who knew what was inside those garments? They were ordered to remove the white material, and Zhu Yanguang had half pulled off the clothes when a policeman asked: "Who are you? Where are you from?" He bellowed "Datong guerillas! " "Bang… bang…" The sound of gunfire reverberated at this very moment, and China's first big exhibition of modernist art descended completely into chaos.[2]

The gunshot incident resulted in Tang Song and Xiao Lu being arrested by Public Security, and it led to the first temporary closure of the National Art Museum of China. The four great international news agencies, Associate Press, Reuters, Agence France-Presse and Kyodo News all immediately reported this news item. *The New York Times, Times Magazine, Christian Science Monitor*, the *Bangkok Post*, the Hong Kong *Shun Pao* and the major European newspapers all reported on Xiao Lu's gunshot performance. All newspapers and media in China pursued and reported it, and described *Dialogue* and the gun performance art as the top story associated with the China / Avantgarde Exhibition. From the angle of news dissemination, even now there has never been another Chinese contemporary artwork that has generated such a startling news media assault as this work of Xiao Lu's.[3]

Initially, some of the organizers of the Exhibition expressed great indignation at the gunshot performance. Some organizers told the media that the shooting incident was seriously damaging to the Exhibition, and stated that they took no responsibility for it.[4] Later, however, the Principal Curator of the Exhibition, Gao Minglu, and the Preparatory Organizer, Li Xianting, both rated the shooting of *Dialogue* very highly. Li Xianting considered this an example of Happening Art: "Carrying on the artistic intellect of Duchamp's use of a urinal to ridicule the aesthetic sensibilities of society, it marks an expansion of the artistic conceptions of Chinese avantgarde art in an intellectual direction."[5] Gao Minglu on the other hand thought that: "There were many things that were unknown at first, but which, when we look at them today, all increase the logical and reasonable character of Xiao Lu's shooting of *Dialogue*. This work can be considered the most influential combination of installation and performance art in the history of Chinese contemporary art, and is also one of its most important emblematic works. Because of its importance, almost every Chinese and foreign-language book on the history of Chinese contemporary art has introduced it."[6] After the Exhibition, the video and the photographs of the shooting of *Dialogue* took part in the *Global Conceptualism: Point of Origin, 1950s - 1980s* Exhibition held in New York in 1999 and in *Inside Out: New Chinese Art* held in 1998, and in other important exhibitions. From the focused target shooting of the gunshot performance with its focus aimed at the work *Dialogue*, to the focus of the media reports of the Incident, finally *Dialogue* has been frozen as the emblem of 1989 China / Avantgarde Exhibition. The beginning and consequence of the gun-shooting performance unquestionably cannot be viewed independent from the social context and background that were on the verge of tremor.

The pursuit of modernism in Chinese art appeared already in the first half of the twentieth century, in groups such as the Juelan Society, and in the work of Lin Fengmian, Pang Xunqin and other artists who promoted Western modern art and pursued artistic

---

2 Kuai Yuehao: "Seven Deadly Sins of Modern Art, Twenty Years Ago", *Southern People Weekly*, 2009, No.11, pp62 - 6.

3 Gao Minglu: "One Gunshot - Half a Life of *Dialogue*. Interpreting Xiao Lu's Work *Dialogue*." in *Guardian Communications*, No.3, 2006, p. 98 - 101.

4 Tang Song, "Brief Statement on the Shooting Incident on 5 February 1989", Art Data Net 27 February 1989 (http://www.art - here.net / html / av / 7380.html).

5 Li Xianting: "Two Gunshots: the Curtain Call of the New Wave in Art - with a Review of Tang Song and Xiao Lu's Work" in *Art Is Not The Important Thing*, Jiangsu Art Press, 1st edition, August 2000, p255.

6 Gao Minglu, "One Gunshot - Half a Lifetime of *Dialogue*: An Interpretation of Xiao Lu's Work *Dialogue*." in *Guardian Communications*, 2006 No.3, pp98 - 101.

experimentation. By the end of the 1970s and the beginning of the 1980s, from the Twelve Artists Exhibition in Shanghai to the Stars Group exhibitions in Beijing, there were continuous references to modern art. The latter refuted the Revolutionary Realism of the Cultural Revolution period in a format that was different from that of Scar Art. As for the '85 New Wave in art, it strove to pursue the dream of modernity. The revolutionary model was extended in the 1980s, which were "the formative and most vigorous period in Chinese modern art criticism". Critics often took their standpoint in the Enlightenment and produced big-picture judgments. Before 1985, the discussion of alienation, humanism and human nature in Marx's *Economic and Philosophical Manuscripts of 1844* played a considerable role. In the years from 1985 to 1989, the question of the "Cultural Revolution" gradually faded, as people began to wonder how it could have happened. The question of modernity versus tradition arose. In 1985 there was a craze for culture, expressed in a tendency towards whole-sale westernization, and represented finally in the collective view of the documentary *Heshang*, usually translated as *River Elegy*, 1988). The media and the publishing world played important roles. Many kinds of modern Western philosophical and cultural / artistic books were published in translation, from Nietzsche, Sartre and Heidegger's writings to the theories of Clive Bell and Gombrich. The discussion models became more complex for a time, various theories mingling in the craze for culture, from existentialism, philosophy of life, modernism and analytical philosophy to China's own Laozi, Zhuangzi and Chan (Zen) Buddhism.

This restless culture craze was exactly the rebellious cultural background of the early art of the New Wave artists. Many old photographs have recorded the spectacular events of that time, and these young people with their black-framed glasses, their old cotton-padded jackets, Sun Yat-Sen suits, vests, shorts and army sneakers, huddling together to discuss Nietzsche, Freud, Munch and Picasso, in shared appreciation of art books and slides of works.[7] Art collectives in various places, such as Xiamen Dada, Zhejiang Pond Society, Northern Group, Southwest Art Group and so on sprang up like mushrooms after rain, each finding its own style and method, like the Eight Immortals crossing the sea, each showing their unique power.[8] The '85 New Wave art used Western methods and visual language to answer the questions posed by Western culture, and ultimately developed into a 'modern' Modernism. Like a devil, modernity whipped the artists into creating something new. As well as struggling to keep up with the pace, they also had to apply the new things mechanically and rapidly.[9] The artists worked hard to use visual forms to express philosophical thinking, and carried out various explorations using the language of art, whether Fauvist, Cubist, Expressionist or Abstract, or Dadaist, and, using forms such as installation art or performance art, they have put the whole Western modern art into practice anew.

The art of the '85 New Wave as an art movement was in fact part of a cultural trend in society as a whole. Various avantgarde practices and experiments with artistic language appeared not only in the world of art, but were also expressed in various respects in avantgarde literature, through poetry and lyrics in the world of letters, through experimental films in the world of the cinema and, in the world of music, by avantgarde music, and so on. "The 1980s were a blank era, politically tending towards opening, while the pressure of the commercial markets had not yet arrived. This period provided a most ideal hotbed for the gestation of idealistic enthusiasm and the stimulation of various utopian illusions."[10] That "brief,

---

7 "The 'Archaeology' of the '85 New Wave of Chinese Contemporary Art ", the Chinese Avant-garde Artists Alliance http://blog.sina.com.cn/wincome77, 4 July 2008, source: *Bund*.

8 Huang Liaoyuan: "*Dialogue* on the 'Seven Performance Works' of the Great Exhibition of 1989." http://www.ionly.com.cn/nbo/zhanlan/showAtt_358.html,

9 Yin Ji'nan: "Modern Modern" in *Knocking at the Door Alone*, Life · Reading · New Knowledge, Joint Publishing, Beijing, August 2002 (1st edition), p253.

10 Fei Dawei: "The '85 New Wave - a Moment of Going Off the Rails" in The '85 New Wave - China's First Contemporary Art Movement, Shanghai People's Press, 2007.

fragile, but rather characteristic and moving era"[11] was full of dreams and passions, anxiety and restlessness. In the madness, people were seeking hope. It was pure but lacked direction. Xiao Lu once wrote in a letter to Gao Minglu: "Passion was the most precious memory left to me by that era."[12]

The art of the New Wave began to decline from 1987 until its curtain call in the 1989 China / Avantgarde Exhibition. The earliest proposal to hold the China / Avantgarde Exhibition was mooted at the Zhuhai Conference of 1986. The Huangshan Conference followed after that, and three years passed before the opening of the Exhibition.[13] Avantgarde art for the first time entered the National Art Museum of China to be exhibited on a large scale in a collective public appearance. In the eyes of Li Xianting, who prepared the Exhibition, because the Exhibition had turned out to be a retrospective exhibition that "lacked a guiding avantgarde ideology" and "predictability", he placed the significance of the Exhibition in its social significance, and aimed to produce something different from the usual "freshness and stimulation". The strong effect produced by the two gunshots immediately caused the transgressive performance works of other artists to appear dull and colorless. The gunshots precisely captured the mental state of the era, one that longed for catharsis after overlong suppression, and became an explosive outlet for the collective feeling of anxiety.[14]

1989 was foreordained not to be an ordinary year. Some people connected the shooting with the political events of 1989. In fact, the '89 Exhibition did attract the attention of the world media. On the day after the shooting, the front-page headlines of Time Magazine read: "Eggs, Gunshots and Condoms". Politics and sex have always been touchy subjects in the media. "Political power grows out of the barrel of a gun", and the natural connection between guns and violence and the political power of the state makes them a political metaphor in themselves, let alone when the shooting occurs in a national art museum that represents the ideology of the state, in a socialist country that expressly prohibits the circulation of firearms. Avantgarde and mainstream, transgression and taboo. The international media naturally produced a political interpretation of the Shooting Incident.

The shooting left tiny bullet holes and cracks in the installation work *Dialogue*, but the sensation and news value froze the work *Dialogue* into an emblem and a sign, which also refracted the specific political, social and cultural discourse of a period of transformation and sensitivity, and became historical evidence and a historical relic.

Although, in the process of the birth and development of the New Wave art, various problems appeared and received the critical assessment of critics of that period, if we reflect on the developmental progress of Chinese contemporary art from the standpoint of the present, the rebellious attitude of New Wave art and its pursuit of freedom and ideals still preserves a dazzling spiritual force. The position and value in art history of New Wave art and of the 1989 China / Avantgarde Exhibition are unavoidable. As an iconic work, then, *Dialogue* is also unavoidable in the process of writing the history of contemporary art.

History often weaves together necessity with chance. From Xiao Lu's own recollection of the circumstances of her work *Dialogue*, we can see that from the inception of *Dialogue* until after the shooting, many elements of chance must ultimately have featured in the whole

---

11 Zha Jianying: "Foreword", in *The 1980s*, Life · Reading · New Knowledge, Joint Publishing, 1st edition May 2006, p3.
12 Xiao Lu: the fourth letter in *Letters to Gao Minglu about the Shooting of Dialogue at the 1989 China / Avantgarde Exhibition*, Art Data Net, http://www.art-here.net/html/av/7375.html. Written in Lower Manjuelong, Hangzhou, on 23 March 2004.
13 For specific circumstances, see the 3rd issue of Contemporary Art & Investment (2009), which includes "Twenty Years of Chinese Contemporary Art" a commemorative review special that presents the main points in the form of oral history interviews of the main organizers of the Exhibition and some of the participating artists.
14 Li Xianting: "Interviews about the Shooting Incident with Some of the Persons Involved - and a Reinterpretation." Art Data Net http://www.art-here.net/html/av/7372.html. First draft spring 2004, final revision 3 October 2005. Source: Featured article, TOM Online.

process. When Xiao Lu was completing her graduation work in 1988, the idea of shooting the work, and of borrowing a gun from Sha Yong of the Zhejiang Shooting Team, occurred to her. It was only because Sha Yong could not contact her at the time that this was not carried out. If the shooting had been carried out then, it would never have had its later sensational effect. If Xiao Lu were not of high cadre background, and if she had not had her social connections in Beijing, then she would not even have been able to obtain the firearm. If the '89 Exhibition had, in the preparatory process, been able to reach a consensus regarding the exhibition space with the Agricultural Exhibition Hall, the shooting would not have occurred in the National Art Museum of China, and the newsworthiness of the incident would have been correspondingly diminished. Besides, as for the subjective intention of the artist, we can see from Xiao Lu's narrative that her purpose in shooting the work had to do with her personal emotions. It was her farewell to emotional shadows and troubles. She had given no thought whatsoever to the legal consequences, the social impact and the significance of the individual incident as such.[15] When we look back on the history of art, creation of artworks often appears incidental. However, although the purpose of shooting the work came, according to Xiao Lu's personal narrative, from her individual emotions, it was exactly the troubles of these emotions, and the pressured state of having no - one to tell them to, that corresponded to the collective state of psychological pressure of that particular era. By means of the shooting performance, Xiao Lu's fulfilment of her destiny of emotional catharsis linked up precisely with the explosively urgent state of anxious emotion in society at the time, and accordingly, the quality of necessity in the work was naturally highlighted. There was an exact fit between the individual state of mind and the state of mind of society, and this produced the collective and social character of the gunshots.

Looking closely at the work *Dialogue*, we discover a further series of contradictions, which seem to have existed in it from the beginning. As for the motive in creating it, the work *Dialogue* is a pure expression of individual emotion and an ineffable release of private emotions, but in terms of the results it produced, it has an intense newsworthiness and sociality. In the very long term, perhaps exactly because of the masking of its social character, people are not at all that intent on the reasons for creating the work in itself.

The installation work *Dialogue* draws upon a ready-made object, a telephone booth. Telephone booths were a characteristic public facility of the urban environment of the 1980s. In themselves they should be transparent, despite their spatial existence being relatively independent. Yet, in *Dialogue*, two telephone booths have been transformed into sealed black rooms. Although the two telephone booths feature the rear view of, respectively, a man and a woman telephoning, yet the rear view of the rear view itself is black. Dialogue is usually most effective when both parties are frank and open, and maybe the *Dialogue* in the dark is precisely a hint of the severing of communication. Besides, the two telephone booths are connected by a mirror, but at the same time, the surface of the mirror features a thick red line that divides it up. Unrealistic connection and actual segregation co-exist.

Viewed superficially, the installation *Dialogue* shows a man and a woman making a phone call, and it would seem that they are on the telephone to each other. The old explanations generally considered that the dangling receiver between the two telephone booths suggested that Dialogue between men and women was futile, yet, from a realistic point of view, it seems that people rarely ring each other from one public telephone booth to another. If we look at it like this, can we explain the work as two people who originally have no wish for mutual Dialogue, but separately have someone to talk to? If so, perhaps the handset in the middle with the receiver off the hook could be further interpreted as the absence, or at least the temporary absence, of someone with whom to have a dialogue.

---

15 Regarding the specific content please see Xiao Lu's correspondence with Li Xianting and Gao Minglu on the Explanation, the Supplementary Explanation, and Li Xianting's Interview with Xiao Lu on the shooting incident.

Apart from this, the gun as a martial weapon signifies destructive and murderous force, and shooting is direct and effective. In "political authority grows out of the barrel of a gun" as in "the Party controls firearms", the gun symbolizes the machinery of the State, or national politics. "The first shot has been fired against the reactionaries!" The sound of a gunshot often becomes a breakthrough against a state of servitude or oppression. Judging from the state reflected by the installation work *Dialogue*, dialogue primarily relies on a telephone to take place. It does not take a direct face-to-face format. If so, can the creator's attack on her own work itself be interpreted as a longing for direct Dialogue? Or, taking it a step further, can we take Xiao Lu's gunshots as a provocation of the political authority of the State? At a specific time in history, can the sound of gunfire still be interpreted as an unlimited yearning for free dialogue?

After so many years, there is still room for further interpretation of *Dialogue*, purely on the strength of the series of contradictions that are contained in the work in itself. As soon as a work is born, it is endowed with limitless possibilities of interpretation. As Oscar Wilde says in his Preface to *The Picture of Dorian Gray*, "It is the spectator, and not life, that art really mirrors." Whether in dialogues between the work and the spectator, or between the sexes, or between tradition and modernity, dislocations and separations often appear, but the yearning and striving for dialogue will exist at all stages. The dialogue carried on between us as spectators and *Dialogue* as a work that has already been focused and frozen into an icon, simultaneously contains the possibility of multiple dialogue between the two sexes, between tradition and modernity, and between the work itself and art history.

15 May 2011, Wangjing

肖鲁
Xiao Lu
对话
Dialogue
行为 / 装置
Performance / Installation
240 × 270 × 90cm, 1989

多元的格局

这部分收藏包括了从'85新潮至今的24位(组)艺术家的重要作品。这些作品充分地呈现了随着中国日益深入地参与到全球化进程中,中国当代艺术无论是创作的形式、媒介还是理论的在地应用与建构,越来越呈现出多元化的发展格局。从这些作品里我们可以看到"艺术"作为一个概念是如何不断地被拓宽边界的过程以及"艺术"作为一种体制成为被建构、解构与思考的对象。十年来,泰康人寿密切关注中国当代艺术的发展,不仅通过准确的判断建立起了具有美术史意义的当代艺术收藏体系,而且创办泰康空间,深度参与到中国当代艺术的传播与推广中,为中国当代艺术的发展贡献自己的力量。

Pluralistic Patterns

This part of the Collection includes important works by twenty - four artists or combinations of artists from the 1985 New Wave till today. These works fully show how, as China ever - increasingly has taken part in the process of globalization, Chinese contemporary art, no matter in terms of the forms or media of creation, and in the local application and construction of theory, more and more has presented a pattern of globalization in its development. In these works we can see how 'art' as a concept is a process of boundaries being constantly expanded, and how 'art' as a system becomes an object of thinking that is being constructed and deconstructed. For the last ten years, Taikang Life has paid close attention to the development of Chinese contemporary art, not only through establishing, on the basis of precise judgments, a system of collecting contemporary art that makes sense in terms of the history of art, but also by founding Taikang Space and participating deeply in the dissemination and promotion of Chinese contemporary art, thus offering Taikang's forces in the service of the development of Chinese contemporary art.

王广义
凝固的北方极地 25 号

北方是我创作的生命所在，北方极地的场景使我想到人类与自然的原初形态。

"极地"的造型是偶然出现的，最初的试验是《25号》，这是第一幅，虽然我编号是25号。

这种具有上升感的绘画，从外观上来看应带有"斯特拉斯"（德国的一座著名建筑）那样的形态，它腾空而起，崇高壮观，浓荫广复而千枝纷呈，在它的巨大而和谐的一体之中，表现出一种崇高的理念之美，它包含有人本的永恒的协调和健康的情感。在这里，创造者和被创造者所感受到的是静穆与庄严，而决非一般意义的赏心悦目。

王广义，1985

20世纪80年代初王广义曾经是一个标准的文化乌托邦主义者，他曾相信一种健康、理性和强有力的文明可以拯救丧失信仰的文化。他早期的艺术活动"北方艺术群体"和早期作品《凝固的北方极地》系列，都呈现了一种对泛文化追求的热情和幻觉，这种文明的风格表征是：富于秩序，冷峻和简练。

黄专，《视觉政治学：另一个王广义》，2008（节选）

Wang Guangyi
North Pole Amalgamation No.25

The North is where my creative destiny lies. The scenery of the North Pole reminds me of the primordial form of mankind and nature.

The modeling of "Pole" occurred by chance. The earliest experiment was *No.25*. This came first, although I numbered it No.25.

The outer appearance of this kind of painting with its sense of rising has the morphology of the famous architecture of the Strasbourg Cathedral in Germany. It leaps into the sky to a spectacular height, its rich shadow is wide and complex and it has a thousand intricate details. Within its huge but harmonious body, it expresses a beautiful concept of the sublime, and it contains a feeling of the eternal harmony and soundness of humanism. Here, what the creator and the created feel is serenity and solemnity, and by no means just the ordinary delightful feast for the eyes.

Wang Guangyi, 1985

At the beginning of the 1980s, Wang Guangyi was a standard cultural utopianist. He believed that a healthy, rational and forceful civilization could rescue a culture that had lost its beliefs. His early artistic movement "Northern Art Group" and the early *North Pole Amalgamation* series, both presented the passion and illusion of his pursuit of a kind of omni - culture, and the characterization of this kind of civilization was rich in order, gravity and concision.

Huang Zhuan, *Visual Politics: Another Wang Guangyi*, 2008 (Extract)

王广义
Wang Guangyi
凝固的北方极地 25 号
North Pole Amalgamation No.25
布面油画
Oil on Canvas
65×90cm, 1985

余友涵
1985-4

我创作"圆系列"时,是逃避的,觉得社会太吵闹了,我需要找个地方,象牙塔之类的地方躲起来。

余友涵,2009

如果不讨论30年代以上海、广州画家为主要成员的决澜社、中华独立美术协会等现代艺术团体所进行的前卫艺术活动(主要是后期印象主义、立体主义、超现实主义、野兽主义),中国内地的抽象艺术真正生发,是在20世纪80年代西方现代主义潮流进入中国后的历史现象。伴随着80年代中国前卫艺术对传统的以写实主义教育为主的学院派艺术的反省与质疑,抽象主义与抽象艺术也以一种艺术革命的形态进入中国现代艺术的行列。

殷双喜,《长河潜流:1978年以来的中国抽象艺术》,2010(节选)

余友涵早在1981年即开始了《黑与白》、《紫色图腾》等抽象作品的创作,他的作品脱离自然现象,以一些重复出现的圆点、线的走向和色域来表明他对世界的特殊理解。其后的"圆"系列更潇洒自如地表达了他的这种思考,并且还注入了更富概括力的图形。

龚云表,《上海:抽象艺术报告》2005(节选)

Yu Youhan
1985 - 4

When I created the *Round* Series, it was an escape. I felt society was too noisy. I needed to find a place, a place like an ivory tower in which to hide.

Yu Youhan, 2009

If we do not include the avant-garde art movements of the Juelan Society, the Chinese Independent Art Association and other modern art groups of the 1930s, mostly made up of artists from Shanghai and Guangzhou-mostly Post-Impressionists, Cubists, Surrealists and Fauvists, abstract art on the Chinese mainland only really developed as a historical phenomenon after the Western modernist wave entered China in the 1980s. Accompanying the Chinese avant-garde art of the 1980s and the Academist art that reflected on and questioned the tradition that used an education in realism as its core, Abstraction and abstract art also used the morphology of a revolution in art to enter the ranks of Chinese modern art.

Yin Shuangxi, *Long River Undercurrent: Abstract Art in China Since 1978*, 2010 (Extract)

Yu Youhan had begun early on, in 1981, to create abstract works such as *Black and White* and *Purple Totem*. His works broke away from natural phenomena, and used the repeated round dots and the directions of lines and a color gamut to express his particular understanding of the world. The later *Round* series with even greater casual ease expressed this thinking of his, and also poured in graphics of an even richer power of generalization.

Gong Yunbiao, *Shanghai: Report on Abstract Art*, 2005 (Extract)

余友涵
Yu Youhan
1985-4
布上丙烯
Acrylic on Canvas
161.5×114.5cm, 1985

韩磊
陕西，洛川县

我不会去赋予我的照片中的那些小人物以雕塑般的意思，他们司空见惯比比皆是……这正像我当时漫不经心按下快门的状态一样，这些照片作为一种连贯也会呈现漫不经心的面目……但他们之于我的重要性在于，在十多年后，在这些照片里，我不仅被释放了时间的忧郁，我更被那些曾经擦肩而过，然而却永远定格在我胶片上的面孔所感动，似曾相识却感到陌生，他们来自生活中最隐秘的层面。

韩磊，2007

在中国摄影艺术家当中，韩磊是极少数始终坚持以平实、笨拙的摄影技术来呈现心中所念的一个人。他的艺术不是建立在感官的娱乐化，而是筑基在对历史与现实的一种错置，构成个人微观世界与宏观历史的对话。

郑乃铭
《重叠——历史与现实的新思辨图像：读韩磊的摄影艺术》
2007〔节选〕

Han Lei
Luochuan, Shaanxi Province

I will not endow the small human figures in my photographs with the meaning of sculptures. They are common and everywhere…This is just like my state at the time of carelessly pressing the camera shutter. These photographs as a coherent series will present the faces of carelessness… But their importance for me lies in the fact that after more than ten years, in these photographs, I am not only released from the depression of time, but even more that I am moved by these faces who once just passed me by but were fixed eternally on my camera film. They seem to be familiar but feel strange. They come from the most secret layers of life.

Han Lei, 2007

Among photographers in China today, Han Lei is one of a very small number who stick to the plain, clumsy techniques of photography to present what he is thinking. His art is not founded in the gratification of the senses, but is structured in a misallocation of history and reality, forming a dialogue between the microscopic world of the individual and the macroscopic world of history.

Nai-ming Cheng, *Overlap - The New Reflective Image of History and Reality: Reading Han Lei's Photographic Art*, 2007 (Extract)

韩磊
Han Lei
陕西，洛川县
Luochuan, Shaanxi Province
黑白照片，版数：7 / 20
Black and White Photograph, Edition: 7 / 20
1989

叶永青
失眠

绘画是燃起和恢复生命全部权利的一炬烽火，是对生命真实的把握和超越。

叶永青，《西南艺术的自然意识略述》，1986〔节选〕

在这些作品中〔80年代中后期的——编者〕，文明对自然的侵犯和现实对人的伤害，即生命存在的困境以及由此引发的精神冲突主宰了他的创作倾向。于是，在他充满生命气息的画面上，出现了就在他住房背后高耸入云的发电厂大烟囱，出现了他每天都可以撞见的因为某种失落而无所事事的青年，出现了精神的奔逃者，惊惶的兽形面孔和坠落的羽毛不振的鸟类。这些形象对观众来说不再是自在的现实，而是心灵的象征。梦幻情调和悲戚的慨叹渐渐笼罩画面。不过他总是把这种慨叹隐埋在深处，不像许多新潮画家那样直接地、观念化地去表现工业文明和环境压力的反抗，而是更多地去体验生命的孤独，和它与本生状态的距离。自然的背离和社会的奴役共同指向一个深藏的生命意蕴：对自我保存的肯定。

王林，《文人眼底的中国》，1994〔节选〕

Ye Yongqing
Sleepless

Painting is the flame of a torch that sets life on fire and recovers all its rights. It is a true grasping and transcending of life.

Ye Yongqing, *On the Nature Awareness of South-Western Art*, 1986 (Extract)

Among these works [of the mid - to late 1980s - Noted by Editor], the assault of civilization on nature, and the harm inflicted on man by reality, that is, the plight of living existence and the spiritual clashes arising thence dominated their creative direction. Accordingly, in his paintings, full of the breath of life, there appeared just behind the houses in which he lived, the towering smokestacks of power plants, there appeared the youths whom he could come across every day and who because of suffering whatever loss, had nothing to do, and there appeared those running away in spirit, the terrified faces of animals and sluggish birds who had lost their plumage. These images were, for the beholders, no longer reality itself, but symbols of the soul. Dreamy moods and sorrowful sighs gradually occupied the surface of the paintings. However, he usually buried these sighs in some deep place and, unlike many painters of the New Wave, he did not represent his opposition to industrial civilization and environmental pressures in any direct or conceptualized way, but rather manifested the solitude of life, and its distance from the original state. Nature's turning its back and the slavery of society together indicated a deep implication of life: the affirmation of maintaining one's own self.

Wang Lin, *China in the Eyes of a Scholar*, 1994 (Extract)

叶永青
Ye Yongqing
失眠
Sleepless
布面油画
Oil on Canvas
160×200cm, 1988

丁乙
十示 93-1

那时我思考两个问题：一是对流行的表现形式进行突破的问题，另一个是对内心的能量进行转换的问题。突破的可能性就是把艺术做得不像艺术，过滤掉所有的技巧、叙事性和绘画性。在工作中最熟悉的印刷标识"十"形坐标线于是成为我的符号。人们常问我它的含义是什么，其实在我的画里它没有含义。

丁乙，1997

（早期）丁乙利用直尺、胶带和相同符号的机械、重复的绘画方式，加上丙烯光洁、平滑的工业效果，至少在激动人心的91-1号作品以前，他成功地减弱了作品的绘画性。他的工具和他的形式把他的个人情感阻止在作品外面，他的作品里维持着一个有限的、几乎是规则的空间，他的作品还是有效地消除了意义。

1993年丁乙作出了重要的决定，让自己的绘画进入更加自由的状态。他的双手一旦获得解放，他的绘画高峰随之而至。徒手作画使他的画面像丰饶的田野进入盛夏一样，呈现蓬勃茂盛的态势，一派繁荣景象。到1993年6月在威尼斯双年展展出他的三幅黑白作品时，他的高峰期还在延续。这个时期他的作品恰到好处地综合了前一个机械阶段的规范、冷漠和新方法的激情和紧张，饱满有力，既迈开了艺术前进的步伐，又吸引了公众的视线。

萧开愚，《不断走向反面的画家：丁乙》，1997（节选）

Ding Yi
Appearance of Crosses 93-1

At that time I was thinking about two problems. One was the problem of how to break through the popular forms of expression, and the other was the problem of transforming my inner energy. The possibility of breaking through was to make art no longer resemble art, by filtering out all the technical skills, narrative and painterly qualities. The coordinates of the cross-shape [the Chinese character for 'ten', "十"] that is the most familiar printed logo in my work became my symbol. People often ask me what it signifies. In fact, in my paintings it does not signify anything.

Ding Yi, 1997

[In his early period - Editor] Ding Yi used a ruler and adhesive tape and similar symbolic mechanical and repetitive painting formats, and the clean and smooth industrial effect of acrylic at least until the exciting work *No.91-1*, he successfully reduced the painterly quality in his works. His tools and his forms blocked the personal feelings out of his works, his works maintained a limited, almost regulated space, and they rather effectively eliminated meaning.

In 1993 Ding Yi made an important decision to let his paintings enter a freer state. Once both his hands were liberated, the peak of his painting followed. Freehand painting allowed his paintings to enter their midsummer like fertile fields, presenting a rich, lush state, and a booming prospect. By June 1993, when he exhibited his three black and white paintings in the Venice Biennale, his peak was still continuing. In this period, his works showed just the right combination of the regulation and coldness of his previous mechanical period and the passion and tension of his new method. They were full and powerful, both opening the way for art's stepping forward, and attracting the eye of the public.

Xiao Kaiyu, *An Artist Constantly Going towards the Obverse: Ding Yi*, 1997 (Extract)

丁乙
Ding Yi
十示93-1
Appearance of Crosses 93-1
布上丙烯
Acrylic on Canvas
139.5×159.5cm, 1993

张晓刚
血缘系列：陈为民

冷静而又非理性；充满幻想而又保持应有的节制；真实可怖却又令人感到陌生；利用可见的物体，使人的思维跨入不可见的隐秘隧道，呈现出某种神秘的哲理和灰色的幽默——马格利特的这种魅力使我长久地着迷，同时也成为我长期以来对自己艺术的某种价值判断和境界追求。

张晓刚，《我的知己——马格利特》，2000（节选）

无论是"血缘"还是《大家庭》都是一种真正意义上的"个人叙事"，在张晓刚把自己定位成为一位"内心独白型"的艺术家时，营造一个祛神后的"个人世界"就成为当务之急，这是一种由形而上的宗教叙事向经验化的个人叙事的转移，由抽象的生命存在向具体的世俗生活发问的转移，由尊神的卡夫卡向渎神的昆德拉的转移；也是视觉上由象征性表达向意象化描述的转移，由空间性叙事向时间性叙事的转移。

《大家庭》关心的仍然是孤独的个体在历史和集体中的命运，但那些历史化的公共世界不仅构成个人生活的背景，它还是个人命运得以展开的直接母体。这一主题很像加西亚·马尔克斯笔下马贡多的布恩蒂亚家族，虽然它不能像后者那样提供宏大诡谲的历史场景和跌宕起伏的人物命运，但无论涉及的问题和表现手法我们都能找到它们的相通之处：家族性神话原型与突变性的现代命运的交融与冲突，时间和记忆消失造成的巨大的心理恐慌和焦虑，意象性的象征叙事形成的陌生化和距离感。从这个意义上讲，《大家庭》更像是一部视觉化的《百年孤独》，一部有关普通中国人的"日常生活的史诗"。

黄专，《张晓刚：一个现代叙事者的多重世界》，2008（节选）

Zhang Xiaogang
Bloodline Series: Chen Weimin

Calm yet irrational; full of illusion yet maintaining an appropriate restraint; genuinely horrific yet giving people a sense of strangeness; using visible objects, but leading people's thinking into invisible tunnels, presenting some kind of mysterious philosophy and grey humour-this charm of Magritte's long fascinated me, and at the same time became a kind of long-term value judgment on, and realm to pursue in, my own art.

Zhang Xiaogang, *My Close Friend - Magritte*, 2000 (Extract)

Whether it is *Bloodline* Series or *Family*, it is a personal narrative in the true sense. When Zhang Xiaogang established his own orientation as an artist of the 'interior monologue' type, creating a post-God 'personal world' became a top priority. This was the transformation from a metaphysical religious narrative to an empirical individual narrative, from an abstract life existence to asking questions in a specifically secular living, and from a pious Kafka to a blasphemous Kundera. It was also visually a transformation from symbolic expression to image depiction, and from spatial narrative to temporal narrative.

Family was still about the destiny of the solitary individual in history and in the collective, but those historicized shared worlds did not only construct the background to the life of the individual, but were also the direct matrix in which the individual destiny could unfold. This subject is very similar to the Buendía family of Macondo in the writings of Gabriel García Márquez. Although *Family* cannot contribute the grand and bizarre historical scenes and the ups and downs of the human fortunes of the latter, yet regardless of the questions involved and the ways of expressing them, we can still find things that they have in common, such as the blending and clashing of family archetypes with mutated modern destinies, the great psychological panic and anxiety created by the disappearance of time and memory, and the alienation and feeling of distance created by the imagistic symbolic narrative. From this angle, *Family* is more like a visualized *One Hundred Years of Solitude*, as an 'epic of everyday life' about ordinary Chinese people.

Huang Zhuan, *Zhang Xiaogang: The Multiple Worlds of a Modern Narrator*, 2008 (Extract)

张晓刚
Zhang Xiaogang
血缘系列：陈为民
Bloodline Series: Chen Weimin
油彩画布
Oil on Canvas
100.4 × 85cm, 1993

曾梵志
无题

早在1992年左右，在曾梵志的创作中就蕴含着两种风格，一种是表现主义的风格，一种是抽象主义的风格。在90年代当代艺术的上下文关系中，艺术家自主地选择了表现主义的风格。

对于熟悉中国当代绘画的人来说，曾梵志的成功是和他成熟的表现主义风格，对死亡题材的关注密切相关的。在这些作品中，油画语言本身的直接性，绘画的速度感以及年轻生命对死亡、疾病、痛苦的独特关注为他赢得了一片好评。

皮力
《从道德的对抗到创造的对抗
——小析曾梵志1989-2004年的绘画创作》，2006〔节选〕

Zeng Fanzhi
Untitled

Back in 1992 or so, there were two styles implied in Zeng Fanzhi's creative work. One was expressionism, the other was abstraction. Against the context of contemporary art in the 1990s, the artist independently chose the expressionist style.

For people who are familiar with Chinese contemporary painting, Zeng Fanzhi's success is closely associated with his mature expressionist style and with his attention to the subject matter of mortality. In these works, the directness of the language of oil painting as such, the sense of speed in the paintings and the unique concern of a young life with death, disease and suffering, have won him critical acclaim.

Pi Li
From Moral Confrontation to Creative Confrontation
- A Little Analysis of Zeng Fanzhi's Paintings 1989-2004,
2006 (Extract)

曾梵志
Zeng Fanzhi
无题
Untitled
布面油画
Oil on Canvas
150×130cm, 1993

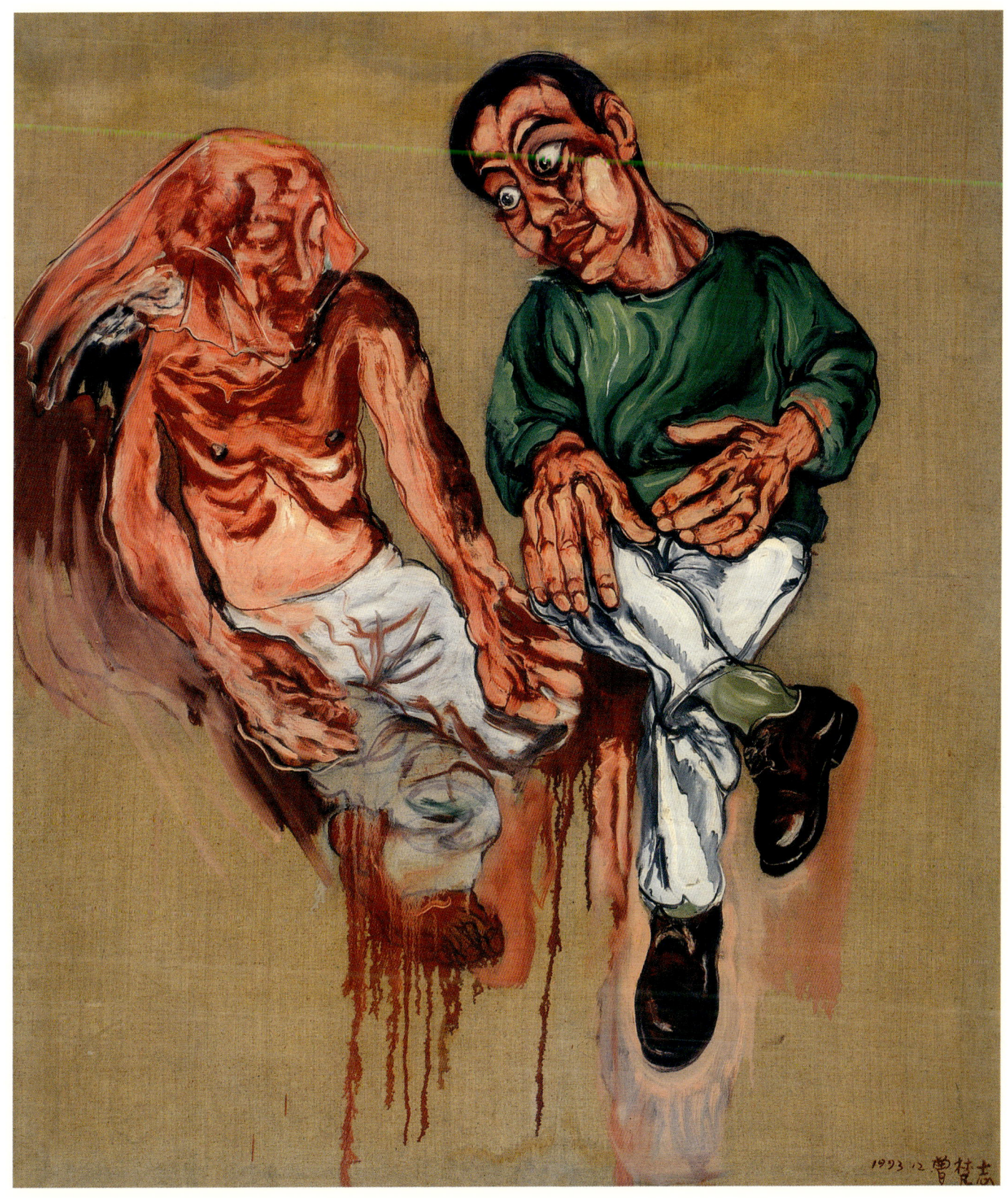

李山
乐园

我的语汇就是我自己。

李山，2009

从《胭脂》以后我想进一步去摆脱人物，从纯粹生命的角度去思考。因为画面一出现人物，又是历史的、文化的等等，很复杂。用纯粹生命本体的东西，更简单，更单纯，所以我要彻底放弃人文的东西。走到今天才发现，无论是毛、鹅还是白脸人，其实也还在束缚我，紧紧地束缚着我，只再摆脱一次，一直向单纯的方向去发展。

《阅读》系列，我是思考人本身，动植物本身，完全抛开以前的。重新开始的是自己最本质的思考。艺术家是我的身份，而我的本质思考完全不是艺术的，是人类的，科学的，各方面的。我没有从艺术本身这样的语言意识和脉络去思考问题，艺术家一生追求突破语言样式，很难，有的艺术家一生都没有找到。我没有走这样的老路！我在思考生命存在的本质性问题：为什么？价值在哪里？

刘淳
《李山访谈录：绘画就是寻找自己内心真实的过程》，2001 [节选]

Li Shan
Paradise

My vocabulary is myself.

Li Shan, 2009

From *Rouge* onward, I thought that I wanted to get rid of human figures and to think from the angle of pure life. For as soon as human figures appear on the canvas, it again becomes historical, cultural and so on, very complex. Using things of pure life itself, it becomes simpler, purer, so I wanted to get completely rid of anything humanistic. It is only after arriving at today that I realize that regardless of whether it is Mao Zedong, geese or the actor in the white mask, they in fact all shackle me, shackle me tightly, and I can only get rid of them again and always go and develop in a pure direction.

In the *Reading* series, I was thinking of mankind in itself, plants and animals as such, and completely put aside everything that had gone before. What I began again from scratch was an essential reflection on myself. Being an artist is my identity, but my essential thinking has nothing to do with art. It is about mankind and science, about various aspects. I do not have the linguistic awareness and context from art itself to go and think about problems. It is very hard for an artist to pursue break-through linguistic patterns, and some artists do not find them in their lifetime. I did not go along this kind of old road! I am thinking about the essential questions of life existence. why? Where is the value?

Liu Chun, *Recorded Conversation with Li Shan: Painting Is a Process of Seeking Your Own Inner Truth*, 2001 (Extract)

李山
Li Shan
乐园
Paradise
布面油画
Oil on Canvas
100×180cm, 1997

张大力
拆·紫禁城

这个符号来自我本人的形象，是我个人形象的抽取，我用这个符号代表我和这个城市进行交流，我想了解这个城市的情况，它的变化，它的结构。我把我的这个行为起名叫"对话"。当然艺术家和城市的交流有很多方式，我之所以采取这种方式，其中一点就是它能很迅速地、很快地将我的作品置于城市的各个角落。

张大力，2000

正如张大力在这个计划的题目揭示的，它们希望记录的并不是作为客观社会观察和美学欣赏对象的城市，而是由艺术家通过自己的主观介入——首先是把他的自画像强加给整个社会——所发起的一场"对话"。

我所做的是从张大力提供给我的400多幅照片中挑选出7幅，用以凸现出一位公共艺术家和一座飞速变化的中国城市在1995至1999年这短短五年里所进行的紧张协商（negotiation）。由于这种协商已经成为当代中国实验艺术中的一个核心问题，通过一个具体个案反思一个更为普遍的艺术史现象。

张大力照片中的第二种建筑"对话"发生在拆迁的废墟与被保护的古代遗迹之间；它们对比鲜明的影像显示了对待传统的两种截然不同的态度。例如图6（《拆·紫禁城》，1998——编者注）的整个画面几乎完全被一座半毁房屋的残墙充满，张大力在墙上喷绘了他的光头形象，然后用斧凿将这个形象挖空。粗糙的缺口仿佛是一道新伤，透过这个缺口人们能够望见远处一个辉煌的、如同海市蜃楼般的影像——紫禁城角楼的金色屋顶。

以极为简洁、平实的方式，这张照片表现了北京在现代，特别是过去十年里所经历的"破坏"与"保护"的双重进程。

巫鸿，《张大力的〈对话〉：与城市交谈》，2000（节选）

Zhang Dali
Demolition: Forbidden City

This symbol comes from my own image. It is abstracted from my own image. I use this symbol to represent the exchange between myself and this city. I want to understand the situation of this city, its changes and its structure. I call this performance of *Dialogue*. Of course, there are many formats of the exchange between the artist and the city. The reasons I have chosen this one include the point that it can very rapidly, very quickly put my works in various corners of the city.

Zhang Dali, 2000

As Zhang Dali reveals in the program of this project, they hope to record not the city as an object of objective social observation or aesthetic enjoyment, but according to the 'dialogue' - primarily, it forces his self-portrait onto the whole of society - that arises from the artist's own subjective intervention.

What I did was to choose seven photographs from the more than four hundred that Zhang Dali gave me, and used them to highlight a public artist's tense negotiation with a rapidly changing Chinese city over a short period of five years from 1995 to 1999. As this kind of negotiation has already become a core topic in Chinese contemporary experimental art, it reflects on an even more general phenomenon of art history through an individual case.

The second kind of 'dialogue' with buildings in Zhang Dali's photographs takes place between the wastelands of the forced demolitions and the preserved ancient relics. The distinct contrast between the images shows two diametrically different attitudes of dealing with tradition. For instance, the overall surface of image No.6 [*Demolition · The Forbidden City* 1998 - Editor's note] is almost completely filled by the ruined wall of a half-destroyed house, and Zhang Dali has sprayed the image of his bald head onto the wall, and then dug this image out with an axe chisel. The rough-edged cavity looks like a fresh wound, and through this hole people can see in the distance a brilliant, mirage-like image of the golden roof of a Forbidden City watch tower.

In an extremely simple and plain way, this photograph represents Beijing in the modern age, in particular the dual process of 'destruction' and 'preservation' experienced in the last ten years.

Wu Hung, *Zhang Dali's Dialogue: Conversations with the City*, 2000 (Extract)

张大力
Zhang Dali
拆·紫禁城
Demolition: Forbidden City
彩扩照片，版数：9／10
Color Photograph, Edition: 9／10
150×100cm, 1998

方力钧
1998.11.15

从生活里，我觉得有很多我们自己都有的，特别讨厌的东西，甩也甩不掉。

我这时发现绘画有一种可能性，这种可能性比其他的文字都更直接，能够直接把生活压缩到很小的一个平面里去，在这里边去感受，去慢慢地体会。

方力钧，1998

方力钧1989年以来一系列作品所创造的"光头泼皮"的形象，即成为一个无聊、泼皮的语符。其一，表情或是嬉笑，或是发呆，或是无表情的背影后脑勺，或是打哈欠之类的无聊表情，就把表情完全无意义化了。而泼皮感的光头加上无意义的表情，就成为一种以无意义——消解现有意义系统的带叛逆、嘲讽意味的形象，也使这种叛逆嘲讽成为自我嘲讽，成为对意义系统的自我逃离的形象。其二，以蓝天、白云、大海这些空阔场景代替了最初人物背景的堵塞处理。作为一种意象，海阔天空实际上表达了一种从内心压力中自我解脱的感觉，既不屈从意识形态，也不采取对抗的方式，这种泼皮式的滑稽、无聊的形象，便成为一种"事不关己"和"不在场"的角色，使自己在内心获得一种海阔天空的感觉。同时，作为一种诗意的对比因素，反衬和加强了泼皮与无意义形象的突出。其三，强调非表现性的无聊与冷漠，突出"不在场"的气氛。其四，色彩始终倾向纯净、鲜亮，保持内心从自我解脱、净化出的愉悦。〔栗宪庭〕

巫鸿主编，《重新解读：中国实验艺术十年（1990-2000）》
澳门出版社，2002，第344页

Fang Lijun
1998.11.15

From living, I feel that there are very many particularly nasty things that we all have ourselves, and that we cannot shake off, try as we may.

At this time, I discovered that there was a possibility in painting, and that this possibility was more direct than any writing, and that it was possible to compress life into the smallest surface, and to feel it in there, and to experience it slowly.

Fang Lijun, 1998

The images in Fang Lijun's series of works created from 1989 on, became a symbol of boredom and loutism. First, their expression is giggling or dazed, the back of the head perhaps backing onto an expressionless background, or yawning as if looking bored, rendering expression completely meaningless. When one adds the feeling of loutism in the bald heads to the meaningless expressions, they become images that signify rebellion and ridicule by dissolving any pre-existing system through meaninglessness, and that also cause this rebellion and ridicule to become a self-ridicule, an image of the self escaping the systems of meaning. Second, the wide open scenery of blue sky, white clouds and ocean have replaced the earliest treatment whereby the background was blocked with human figures. As a notion-image, the wide ocean and empty sky in fact express a feeling of personal liberation of the self from inner oppression. It neither submits to ideology, nor adopts the format of active resistance. These images of loutish comedy and boredom become a kind of role of 'none-of-my-business' and 'non-presence', allowing the self to achieve an inner feeling of 'wide ocean and empty sky'. At the same time, as a contrasting poetic factor, it contrasts and strengthens the prominence of the lout and the meaningless image. Third, it emphasizes the lack of brushstrokes and coldness of the non-expression, highlighting the atmosphere of 'non-presence'. Fourth, the colors tend to be pure and bright throughout, maintaining the inner pleasure from the liberation and purification of the self.

Li Xianting
Edited by Wu Hung
Reinterpretation: A Decade of Experimental Chinese Art (1990-2000)
Macao Press, 2002, P344

方力钧
Fang Lijun
1998.11.15
布面油画
Oil on Canvas
483×121.5cm×5, 1993

刘小东
温床

一般的绘画写生是在可控制的画幅内，面对人物或风景画出同一光线、同一气氛下的客观物象。我选择260×1000cm的大幅画布，铺在地上，面对眼前物象写生，身在其中，无法控制全局，无法在有限的时间内完成同一光线气氛下的物象。我和时间赛跑，中午画的人物，等画他背后的风景时已是傍晚了，拒绝借助摄影的提示，完全置身于每一秒的时间变化的真实世界里。像耕种一样，有泥土，有汗水，有时间错乱。我把颜料直接挤在画布上，直接调色画出眼前具体人物，打破抽象的颜料与具体的人物之间的界限，似是而非。

刘小东，《关于温床》，2006〔节选〕

和传统的现实主义不同，写生不再是对于记忆和手段的训练，而是一个不断接近对象并与之对话的过程。因此，无论是刘小东，还是他所代表的新生代，都不是对于"现实主义"的否定，相反，他的工作应该被看做是对于现实主义的当代意义上的转化。同样，对于写生的重新发现，不是对于摄影和摄像的保守主义的对抗，而是绘画试图在机械复制时代重新召回其特性与意义的一次巨大的努力。如果说"温床"所折射的问题是个体在都市化浪潮中的存在的话，那么艺术家用来实现它的手段和观念则将另一个无法回避的问题抛向了他自己和我们，即"绘画在今天可以干什么？"

以力，《关于温床的几个关键词》，2006〔节选〕

Liu Xiaodong
Hot Bed

Usually painting from life is done within a controllable size, facing the human figure or landscape, and painting an objective physical picture with consistent light and atmosphere. I chose a large canvas of 260x1000cm, laid it on the ground and painted the physical picture before my eyes. Being bodily in it, I could not control the entire surface in any way, and there was no way I could complete the material image in the same light and atmosphere within the limited time. In my race against time, I painted the human figures at noon, and it was already late afternoon when I painted the landscape behind them. As I refused to use the pointers with which photography could assist me, I exposed myself to the temporal changes of every second in the real world. As in farming, there is mud, there is sweat, and there is confusion of time. I squeezed the colors directly onto the canvas, and directly mix ed them to paint the specific figure in front of my eyes, breaking down the abstract borders and speciousness between colors and the specific figure.

Liu Xiaodong, *About Hot Bed*, 2006 (Extract)

Different from traditional realism, painting from life is no longer an exercise in memory and technical devices, but is a process of constant contact and dialogue with the object. Accordingly, neither Liu Xiaodong nor the young generation he represents negate 'realism'. On the contrary, their work should be regarded as a contemporary transformation of realism. In the same way, their rediscovery of drawing from life is not against the conservatism of photography and video, but is the great struggle by painting in the attempt to recall its character and meaning in an age of mechanical reproduction. If the problem that *Hot Bed* refracts is that of individual existence in the wave of urbanization, the means used by the artist to realize his devices and conceptions is to toss himself and us the unavoidable question, namely "what can painting do today?"

Pi Li, *Some Key Words about Hot Bed*, 2006 (Extract)

刘小东
Liu Xiaodong
温床
Hot Bed
布面油画
Oil on Canvas
260×1000cm, 2000-2006

曾浩
2003年11月30日早上9点

一个人会怎么样？其实这种东西并不重要，重要的就是每天重复不断的那种很日常的生活决定你的一生。

曾浩

对于曾浩这个系列的论述，有论者似乎都将关注的焦点集中在艺术家对人与物现实比例的改写，比如冯博一认为正是通过这一点艺术家实现了对商品社会消费的批判。巫鸿则认为曾浩这种微观化的方式所营造的是一个为外部空间及其时间感所指涉的，但又相对独立的典型的内部空间。结合中国的当下现实，他认为曾浩的作品也反映出中国公共空间和私人空间之间的反差，通过对私人空间的主观性、私密性和时间性（标题）甚至是人物的不安全感的表达，从而对混乱而无休止的中国公共空间拆迁形成一种否定的批判。同时艺术家似乎也在暗示由于中国个体个性的长期缺乏，所谓的私密空间的存在也是无法被确保的。

在我看来，它们并非只指向中国的政治经济现实；这种不安全感和失落感的本质来源是艺术家开始洞察出自身被物品所包围、控制，甚至按照物品的节奏来生活的消费社会现实。曾浩的作品很难说是一种意识明确的批判，但是他却能用游离于20世纪90年代中国绘画语言之外的方式，将一个中国城市生活经验的片断呈现在一个全球文化的背景下，而且呈现得如此感性、丰富和精确，以至于当我们凝视这些画面时，感到的是同样强烈的失重感和漂浮感。

皮力，《从摆设到风景：对曾浩作品的再阅读》，2010（节选）

Zeng Hao
9a.m, Nov.30, 2003

What is a single person to do? In fact, these things are not at all important. What is important is that the very ordinary life that is constantly repeated every day decides your entire life.

Zeng Hao

Discussing this series by Zeng Hao, critics seem to concentrate the focus of their attention on the re-writing by the artist of the realistic proportions between humans and things. For instance, Feng Boyi considers that it is just through this point that the artist realizes his criticism of the social consumption of commodities. Wu Hong on the other hand thinks that what is produced by the microscopic format of Zeng Hao refers to a feeling of external space and its time, but is also a relatively independent typical inner space. Synthesizing the current reality of China, he thinks that Zeng Hao's works also reflect the contrasts between public and private space in China. Through the subjectivity and privacy and temporality of private space, (the title) is even an expression of the feeling of insecurity of the human figures, thus forming a kind of negative criticism of the chaotic and never-ending forced demolitions in China's public space. At the same time, the artist seems to be hinting that because of the long-term lack of individuals and individuality in China, the existence of the so-called private space cannot be ensured.

As I see it, they do not only refer to the political and economic realities of China. The source of the essence of this feeling of insecurity and of being lost is the artist's beginning to gain insight in the material objects that surround him, that control him, and even the consumerist social reality that lives according to the rhythm of these material objects. It is very hard to say that Zeng Hao's works are a consciously clear criticism, but he is able to use formats that extend beyond the painting language of the 1990s, and can present a slice of life experienced in a Chinese city against a globalized cultural background, and also present it in a way that is so emotional, rich and accurate that when we gaze at these paintings, we feel a similarly strong feeling of weightlessness and floating.

Pi Li, *From Display to Landscape: A Re-reading of Zeng Hao's Works*, 2010 (Extract)

曾浩

Zeng Hao

2003年11月30日早上9点

9a.m, Nov.30, 2003

布面油画

Oil on Canvas

240×180cm, 2003

蔡国强
天空中的人、鹰与眼睛

《天空中的人、鹰与眼睛：为埃及锡瓦作的风筝计划》是在西撒哈拉的一个边缘小镇锡瓦绿洲举行的，最好地表现了蔡国强社会项目的四大特点：探索在社会情境中的艺术象征的力量；对地方历史和文化的浓厚兴趣并敏锐地运用在项目之中；与当地各阶层人民，从孩子到政府官员的积极合作；对当地社区既有文化上的又有经济上的贡献。"锡瓦艺术计划"是一个以注重环境意识在国际上推动锡瓦文化遗产的组织，邀请蔡国强在当地创作一个临时和以大地为主的作品。锡瓦的历史和原始环境促使艺术家运用风筝作为媒介。正如该作品的标题所示，该项目包括三个象征性的主题："人"代表历史起因的人类；"鹰"代表横跨撒哈拉沙漠在锡瓦接受神谕的亚历山大大帝；"天空中的眼睛"代表人类的梦想。项目中最重要的成分，尽管是非物质的，是在当地民众中所产生的兴奋和600名参与学生的热情。学生们在蔡国强的带领下，参与了风筝的绘画工作，在300只从每年举办国际风筝节的中国潍坊市带来的风筝上绘画。在这片原始的沙漠上空，在锡瓦著名的神庙遗址和古要塞上空，大约40名年龄稍大的学生帮助放飞了这些色彩斑斓、极富想象力的风筝。作为整个项目的结尾，最后用100个风筝进行了一项爆破事件。令蔡国强感动的是，当地由此形成了一个习惯，每年晚秋的时候当地人都会放飞风筝，来纪念他的这一项目。蔡国强本人创作了一系列的火药画，来纪念这一项目。

富井玲子，《天空中的人、鹰与眼睛》，2003（节选）
《蔡国强：我想要相信》
[美] 所罗门 R. 古根汉姆美术馆出版，2008

Cai Guo-Qiang
Man, Eagle and Eye in the Sky

Created at Siwa Oasis, a remote town in the western Sahara, *Man, Eagle, and Eye in the Sky* best exemplifies the four most salient characteristics of Cai's social projects: his exploration of the symbolic power of art in a social context; his profound interest in local history and culture and astute incorporation of them into a project; his active collaboration with the local people at all levels, from children to government officials; and his contribution, both cultural and economic, to the local community. The artist was invited to create an ephemeral land-based work by Siwa Art Project, an organization that promotes Siwa's cultural heritage internationally in an ecologically sensitive manner. Siwa's history and pristine environment inspired the artist to use kites as his medium. As indicated by its title, the project had three emblematic motifs. "Man" signifies humankind as an agent of history. "Eagle" refers to Alexander the Great, who traversed the Sahara Desert to receive an oracle in Siwa. And "eye in the sky" represents humankind's vision. The most significant, though intangible, ingredient of the project was the excitement it generated among the local population and the enthusiastic engagement by over 600 schoolchildren, who participated in the painting workshop led by Cai and painted 300 kites brought from Weifang, China, the city that hosts the annual Weifang International Kite Festival. Some forty older boys helped fly the colorfully and imaginatively painted kites over the pristine desert and over the temple ruins and former strongholds for which Siwa is known. One hundred kites were used in an explosion event as a finale to the whole program. Cai found it gratifying to learn that a new custom has formed there, as people in Siwa have subsequently flown kites every year in late autumn, marking the anniversary of the project. The artist himself memorialized the project by creating a series of gunpowder drawings.

Reiko Tomii, *Man, Eagle, and Eye in the Sky*, 2003 (Extract)
Published in *Cai Guo-Qiang: I Want to Believe*. New York: Guggenheim Museum Publications, 2008.

蔡国强
Cai Guo-Qiang
天空中的人、鹰与眼睛
Man, Eagle and Eye in the Sky
火药、纸
Gunpowder on Paper
230 × 77.5cm × 9, 2004

刘野
阮玲玉

我很早就认为,作为艺术家,一方面是个人化特别重要,还有一个就是艺术应该超越它作为批判工具的功能。艺术的一个重要功能就是帮助你挖掘更深层的情感和神秘感,这点适合任何国家,包括中国。

刘野,2008

长期以来,刘野寻求的是一个超然于现实的个人形象,而现实不仅意味着极权化的政治现实,也意味着任何一种对于个性的侵扰与吞蚀。在面对新生的艺术事态时,他作出的回应是自我反观,剖析个人的艺术之中是否隐含了与风潮共通的病症,其结果是,他察觉到一种向古典作进一步回溯的必要,也就是将自己的那种"轻"与"透明"的风格放置到一个更为悠远的时空里重新掂量。

朱朱,《双重的迷恋》,2007﹝节选﹞

Liu Ye
Ruan Lingyu

I believed very early that for an artist, it was particularly important to be individual, and another thing: art should transcend its function as a critical tool. An important function of art is to help you excavate feelings and a sense of mystery at a deeper level. This applies to any country, including China.

Liu Ye, 2008

For a long time, Liu Ye has been seeking an individual image that transcends reality, and reality does not just mean totalitarian political reality, but also means any kind of interference with and encroachment on individuality. When facing the newly formed conditions of art, his response has been to re-examine himself, dissecting whether his art implies disease shared with the trend. The result is that he has become aware of the necessity of taking a further step back towards the classics, that is, to place that 'lightness' and 'transparence' of his in a more distant time to weigh it again.

Zhu Zhu, *Double Fascination*, 2007 (Extract)

刘野
Liu Ye
阮玲玉
Ruan Lingyu
水彩纸本
Water Color on Paper
100×65cm, 2004

周铁海
伯爵

安慰药并不是针对某一病症的药物,它只是给人以心理安慰的努力。

作品具有以下几个鲜明特征:一、代表人类文明先进主流的西方文化,对人类的生活状态是采取一种药物治疗的方法的,用中国的话说是"治标不治本",最终只能是一种自我安慰,或自我陶醉。二、作品本身在试图解读西方标准、主流文化包括非主流文化的同时,也自认无力摆脱其标准图景,如同一个惊醒的梦中人,不由得成为其世界性大文化的一个陪衬。三、这是东西文化交流中具有标志性意义的现象:一方面,对西方文化的成就充满敬意,试图用西药解救东方病;另一方面,明知该药有副作用,而且不能根治病症,病急乱投医,这正是作者无奈和痛苦的所在。

周铁海,《对"安慰药"和"补品"的解释》,2006 (节选)

Zhou Tiehai
Nobleman

Placebo medicine is not a medicine for any illness at all. It only works in giving people psychological comfort.

The works have the following distinctive characteristics. First, the Western culture that represents the mainstream of mankind's civilized progress has taken a drug therapy approach to the living conditions of humanity. This is expressed in Chinese as zhibiao bu zhiben: it treats the symptoms, not the cause. Ultimately, it can only serve as self-comfort, or narcissism. Second, the works themselves are aiming to interpret Western standards. Mainstream culture at the same time contains non-mainstream cultures that consider themselves unable to get rid of the standard picture, just like someone who is awakened in the middle of a dream. They cannot help becoming sideshows to the big global culture. Third, this is a phenomenon of landmark significance in the cultural exchange of East and West. On the one hand, it is full of respect for the achievements of Western culture, and seeks to use Western medicine to solve Eastern illnesses. On the other hand, it well knows that those medicines have side effects and cannot radically cure diseases. However when the disease is critical, one turns to doctors at random. This is where the artist's helplessness and pain are.

Zhou Tiehai, *Explanation of Placebo and of Tonic*
2006 (Extract)

周铁海
Zhou Tiehai
伯爵
Nobleman
布面油画
Oil on Canvas
140×112cm, 2005

洪浩
我的东西——圆之 2

2001年时，我开始利用实物扫描与计算机合成来执行创作。扫描这种做照片的方法和照相机的拍照是不一样的，首先，它必须有一种触摸，比如把这些东西拿来放在上面已经有了动作，物体与扫描仪是零距离。而照相机与被拍摄者是不能接触的，拍一个人不能摸他不能碰他，必须有距离才能拍照。事实上扫描仪也是有镜头的，但它跟相机的镜头又不大一样，相机的镜头可以视为人眼的延续，也就是说人眼看到的东西也是它看到的，同时这种"看"是一种有距离的"观看"，它是把人眼看到的东西用工具记录下来转化成一种媒介形象。而扫描仪所捕捉的却恰恰相反，它看到的东西正是我们看不到的那一部分，而且是"零距离"地看。另一方面，扫描可以和实物保持一比一的比例关系，输出后作品中的物品尺寸也是原比大小，而且细节是绝对的，面面俱到的，它有着一种强烈的证据感，证据感是一种客观化，这只有是扫描仪能够做到最准确的，它是一种客观的绝对性。而照片必须经过放大，不知道原大是什么。另外，扫描的特点是可以将影像平面化，进行平铺直叙的罗列，这有些像中国古代的拓片所呈现的结果，不像摄影的画面，有虚有实，有远有近。所以我的工作更多地是探讨一种用扫描方法做照片所产生的一种影像美学上的东西或者价值。

洪浩，2011

Hong Hao
My Things About Circle No.2

Since 2001, I have started my art practice that involves scanning of daily objects and computer-based postproduction. I find that making photographs by a scanner is so different from a camera. First of all, it requires touching of the object. When you're putting the object on the scanner, the action of touching is already involved. There's no distance between the object and the scanner, while a camera can never touch the object or a person it is shooting. In fact, there's a hidden lens inside the scanner, but it is very different from the lens in a camera which could be considered extension of human's eye. That is to say, what you see with your eye is what the camera see, both are images in distance. What the camera does is to record what our eyes have seen and transform it into image. However, what a scanner can do is just the opposite, as it sees what we cannot see with our eyes. It keeps no distance to what it captures with the lens. In addition, the image produced by the scanner is of the same proportion, and the details of the object are totally kept. This makes it something like a proof which is absolutely objective. What the scanner does is precise, absolutely objective. An image obtained through camera will finally be produced with the procedure of enlargement, from which we can never learn the original size of the object. What's more, one character of the scanner is that its working process actually is to flatten an object plane. Very straightforward. This is something like what we can see in the Chinese rubbings. It is different from what a camera did, as we still have perspective on the photo obtained through the camera. My practice is more about the exploration of the ascetics or value about the images obtained through scanning.

Hong Hao, 2011

洪浩

Hong Hao

我的东西－圆之2

My Things About Circle No.2

数码照片，版数：2／12

C - print, Edition: 2／12

165×270cm, 2006

刘韡
波浪 No.5

它就是图像,它主观性吸引着我们。在不同时代,绘画有不同的意义。比如,现在我们谈到直接的视觉体验,涉及画画的时候,跟过去还是不同的,还是需要新的方式。我们现在看的东西和看的方式与过去不同。现在我们可以通过电脑看,通过各种媒介看,观看的频率以及方方面面都在改变。所有视觉的东西都在不停改变。更重要的是你看的方式改变的不只是图像,而是内容的附带品。

田霏宇,《刘韡访谈》,2010 [节选]

Liu Wei
Wave No.5

It is an image, one that subjectively attracts us. In various eras, painting has various meanings. For instance, when we speak of 'direct visual experience' now, it is different from the past so long as painting is concerned. We need new formats. The things we look at today and the ways of looking at them are different from those of the past. Now we can look at things using computers, through various media, and the frequency of viewing and all sorts of aspects are changing. All visual things are constantly changing. Even more importantly, what your way of viewing changed is not just the images but also the incidental products of the content.

Philip Tinari, *Interview with Liu Wei*, 2010 (Extract)

刘韡
Liu Wei
波浪 No.5
Wave No.5
布面油画
Oil on Canvas
250×784cm, 2006

洪浩 + 颜磊
泰康计划

《泰康计划》是由洪浩和颜磊合作完成的,作品主要由两部分组成:一部分是一幅3×5.9米的绘画;一部分是三份总值近700万元人民币的人身保险。

这是一件观念艺术作品,洪浩和颜磊采用的不是主客体反映论方法,而是强调符号的深层和多意义的视觉方法论,他们选择了"梵·高"和"泰康"作为两个主要创作元素。西方艺术体制已经成为中国艺术体制建设的一个巨大的参照体系,《泰康计划》针对体制问题,通过作品探讨在这种模式的影响下,中国未来艺术体制建设的问题,提出建立一种非单元化的公共关系和公共制度的主张。

唐昕
《〈泰康计划〉——一个针对体制的公共理想》,2006(节选)

Hong Hao + Yan Lei
Taikang Project

Taikang Project is a compilation between Hong Hao and Yan Lei. This work was comprised of two parts: one 3x5.9 meter painting, and three life insurance policies valued at 7 million Yuan.

This is a conceptual artwork. What Hong Hao and Yan Lei use is not the subjective-objective reflection theory methods, but the visual methodology that emphasizes the deep and multilayered significance of symbols. They chose "Van Gogh" and "Taikang" as the two main creative elements. The western art system has become a giant system of reference for the construction of the Chinese art system. *Taikang Project* is aimed at issues in the system. Through an exploration of the work under the influence of this format, they advocate constructing a non-compartmentalized public system of public relationships for the construction of China's future art system.

Tang Xin, *Taikang Project - Public Idealism Pointing at the System*, 2006 (Extract)

洪浩 + 颜磊
Hong Hao + Yan Lei
泰康计划
Taikang Project
布面油画及保单文件
Oil on Canvas and Three Life Insurance Policies
300×590cm, 2006

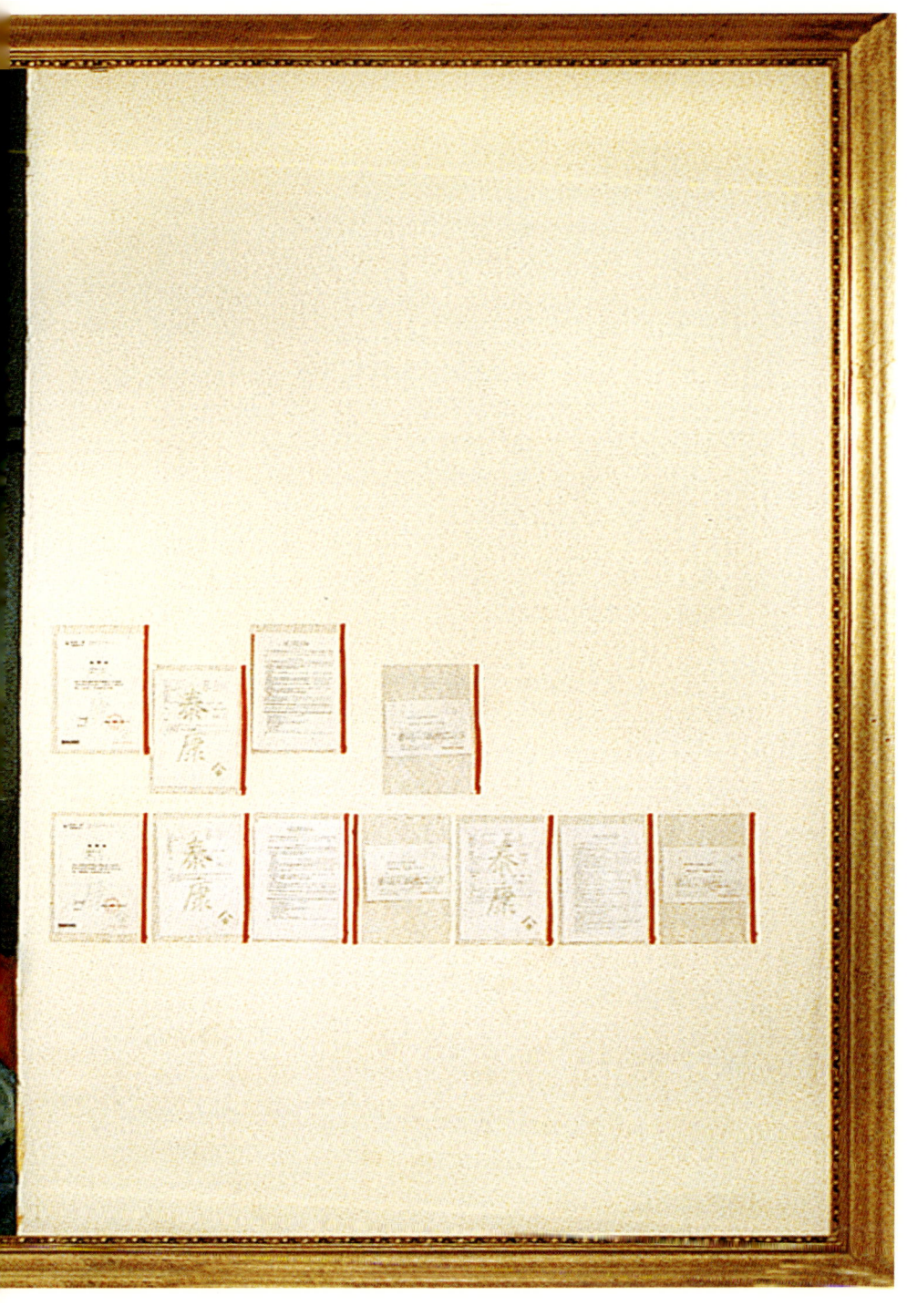

阳江组
鼠牛虎兔龙蛇

书法之外还有书法吗?

阳江组

"阳江组"中的三位艺术家郑国谷、孙庆麟和陈再炎都来自广东阳江,作品充满强烈的地缘性。"阳江"是他们共同的地域、人文和社会文化资源;"书法"是他们共同的针对问题,共同感兴趣的创作方式;"现场"是他们作品的综合呈现形态,共同构成了阳江组创作的三大基本特征。

阳江组对书法的介入是从逃离开始的,要想获得新的可能性必须先脱离传统书法体系,他们回到"书写"和"书写的人"寻根溯源,以回到书法体系形成之前寻找和发现问题。他们带着书写用具——笔、墨和纸,回到了书写的初始境地,把书写的工具和权利交还给了草根民众。在粗砺和生猛的涂抹中,书法的形态被改变,也从生态上被放归自然,回到大众社会。书法的实用性得到复原,它与现实生活的关系也被重新建立起来,底层社会生活透过这种水墨涂鸦被映照得非常生动、准确。

唐昕,《阳江组——将书法和阳江带到现场》,2007(节选)

Yangjiang Group
Rat Ox Tiger Rabbit Dragon Snake

Is There Calligraphy Outside Calligraphy?

Yangjiang Group

The three artists in the Yangjiang Group, Zhen Guogu, Sun Qinglin and Chen Zaiyan all come from Yangjiang in Guangdong, and their works are full of geographical affinity. Yangjiang is their shared area, their humanistic and socio-cultural resource. Calligraphy is the creative format that they share for dealing with problems and their shared area of interest. 'Site' is the combined presentational morphology of their works. Yangjiang, calligraphy and 'site' together are the three great basic characteristics that structure the Yangjiang Group's creative work.

The Yangjiang Group's involvement with calligraphy began with an escape. If they wanted to get at new possibilities they first had to get out of the traditional system of calligraphy, and they returned to writing and people who write to find their roots, to look for and discover the problems before they returned to the formation of calligraphy. They took with them the tools of writing, pen, ink and paper and returned to the primeval conditions of writing, handing over the writing tools and the right to write to the grassroots masses. In the rough and vigorous smearing, the morphology of calligraphy was altered, and also, ecologically, was returned to nature, returned to the society of the masses. The practicality of calligraphy was restituted, and its relationship with reality was also reestablished, and life at the bottom social level was reflected through these ink graffiti with exceptional vigor and accuracy.

Tang Xin, *The Yangjiang Group - Bringing Calligraphy and Yangjiang to the Site*, 2007 (Extract)

阳江组
Yangjiang Group
鼠牛虎兔龙蛇
Rat Ox Tiger Rabbit Dragon Snake
水墨宣纸书画
Ink on Rice Paper
280 × 130cm, 2006

郑国谷
猪脑控制电脑之六十二

《猪脑控制电脑》这一系列绘画的命名源于1999年某个香港朋友的自嘲,这是用文字组合的绘画,它的义字大多数来源于香港的八卦娱乐杂志与花边新闻,被殖民式的中英文结合起来使用非常有趣与幽默,文字简练,容易传播,最早在香港非常流行,近几年中国也开始流行,是一种中西杂交的产物。我把这些文字在电脑上重新设计与组合,令画面形式感非常强与诱人,怪不得收藏家都喜欢收藏它,这是我预期的效果。还有,远看挺抽象的,近看可细细阅读,让人觉得这种杂交过的句子和用词非常"八卦"而又"好玩",就像它的名字《猪脑控制电脑》一样,挺"无厘头"的。

郑国谷,2011

Zheng Guogu
Pig VS Computer No.62

The name of *Pig VS Computer* series originates from the self-mockery of my Hong Kong friend. This is painting combined with writing. Most of its characters come from Hong Kong gossip and entertainment magazines and news. This combination of colonized Chinese and English is very fun and humorous, also simple and easy to transmit. It was very popular in Hong Kong in earlier time and has become popular in China as well in the last several years. It is a product of the combination of China and the west. I re-designed and re-combined these words on my computer and made the form of the picture look very strong and attempting. No wonder the collectors like it and this is what I have expected. Furthermore, it looks rather abstract from afar, but can be read carefully in a close distance, making people think this kind of combined sentences and words very gossip and entertaining, just like its loony-tone name *Pig VS Computer*.

Zheng Guogu, 2011

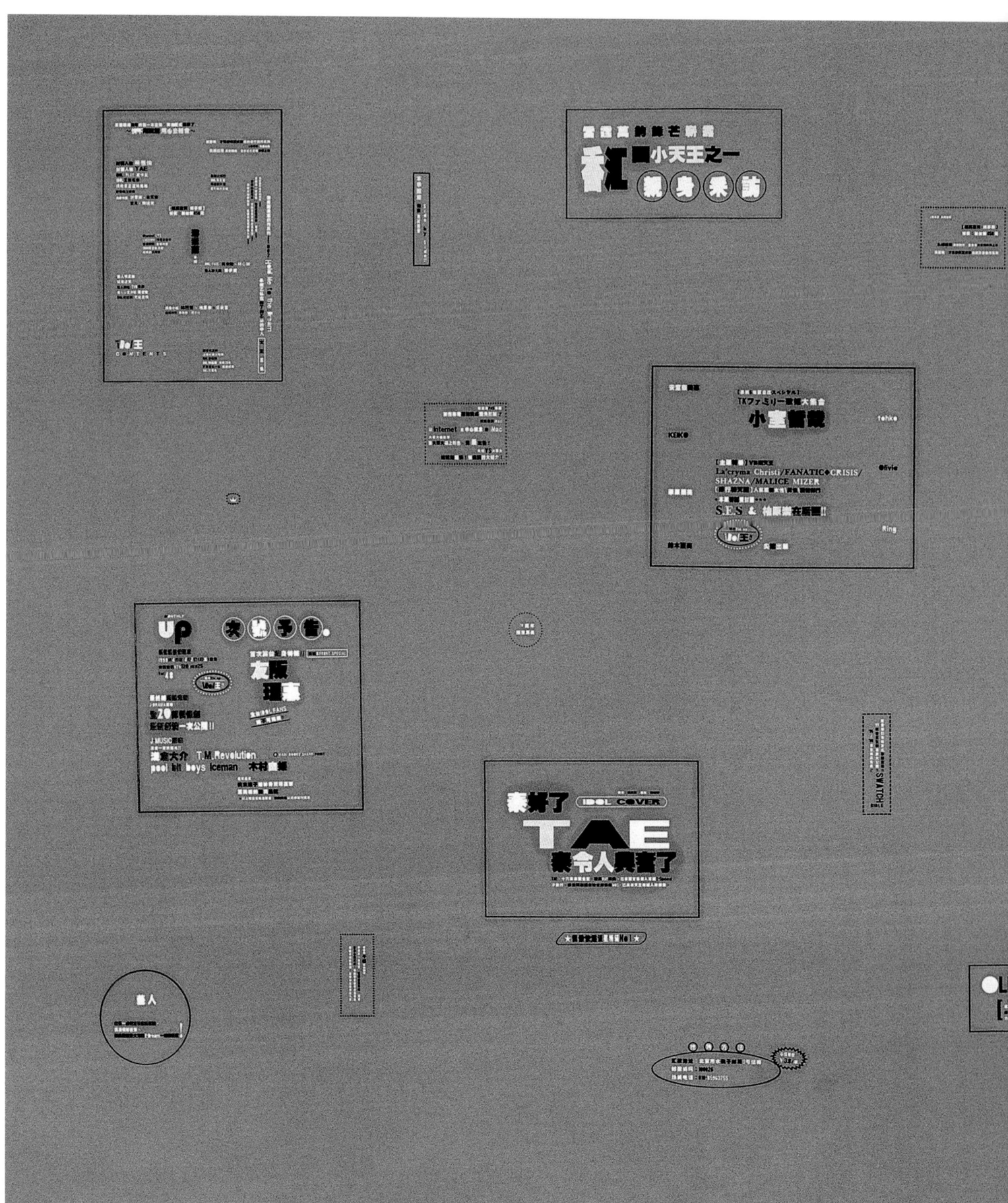

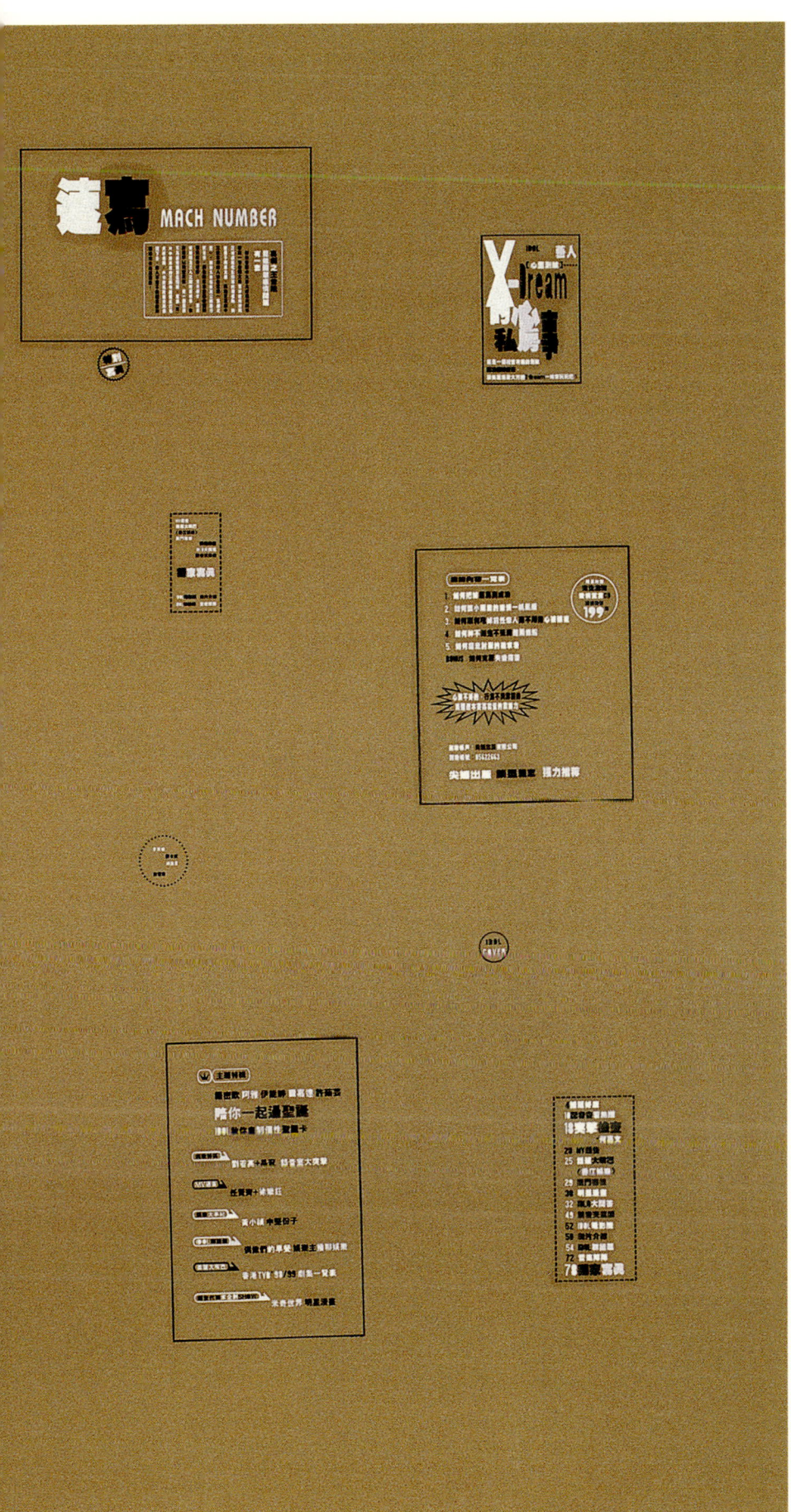

郑国谷

Zheng Guogu

猪脑控制电脑之六十二

Pig VS Computer No.62

布面油画

Oil on Canvas

190×290cm, 2006

黄永砯
五边形计划——从五角大楼到拿破仑堡

这幅水彩草图是为2003年Ostende（比利时）"Beaufort"展览提供的计划，拿破仑垒"Le Fort Napoléon"建于1773-1823年，现在改为博物馆。我当时建议在堡垒内院建造一个缩小的五角大楼。这是从建筑的五边形出发，从一个老帝国——拿破仑堡到一个新帝国——五角大楼，一个同形但变换的帝国。后来这个计划未实现。

黄永砯，2011

黄永砯的风格独一无二，他有自己特殊的表意技术：首先是他频繁使用的"搬运"——将彼时彼地之物搬运到此时此地中来，并进行改装、嫁接和重写。

这些空间和物件，经过了模拟、微缩、组装和嫁接后，在一个新的时空中，在一个新的"现场"，重新获得了自身的意义。

黄永砯的作品，总是将各种意义置于一个空间内彼此竞技，这使得他的作品总不是被一个单一的意义牢牢地捆绑住。意义的复杂性和冲突性，使得任何确定的看上去无可置疑的自然现实——无论是政治的、经济的还是文化的现实——分崩离析。黄永砯以其独一无二的方式不停地保持着艺术批判，这正是黄永砯的意义所在。

汪民安，《黄永砯的"意义"》，2008（节选）

Huang Yong Ping
Pentagon Plan: From C to P

This water-color sketch is a proposal provided for the *Beaufort Triennale* in Oostende, Belgium. Fort Napoleon was constructed during 1773-1823. It is now a museum. At the time I suggested to erect a small-scale model of the Pentagon in the inner courtyard of the fortress. The point of departure for this proposal was the pentagonal shape of the building: from a ruined fortress in an old imperialist country, to the Pentagon in a new-isomorphic but transformed-imperialist country. Ultimately, the proposal was not realized.

Huang Yong Ping, 2011

Huang Yong Ping's style is unique. He has his own expressive technique: first is his frequent use of 'transportation' - he takes objects of some other time and some other place and transports them to this time and this place, as well as modifying them, grafting them and re-writing them.

After being simulated, scaled down, assembled and grafted, these spaces and objects re-acquire a meaning of their own in their new time and space and in their new 'scene'.

Huang Yong Ping's works generally take various meanings and place them in a space where they compete with one another. This leads to his works generally not staying securely bound by a single meaning. The complexity and confrontation of meanings results in the disintegration of any definite, seemingly unquestionable natural reality - whether political, economic or cultural. Huang Yong Ping uses his unique format to constantly preserve his artistic criticism, which is exactly where his meaning resides.

Wang Min'an
The 'Meaning' of Huang Yong Ping
2008 (Extract)

黄永砅
Huang Yong Ping
五边形计划——从五角大楼到拿破仑堡
Pentagon Plan: From C to P
水彩
Watercolors
65.5×76cm, 2007

汪建伟
三岔口

我对事物的看法来自于不同的知识领域，它们之间既提供了相互关联的认识基础，同时又可以形成一种相互"诘难"的思维方式。

我希望通过这种互相交叉、非线型的方法，可以发觉被某种惯常和秩序所遮蔽的潜在事物。由此，艺术有可能被赋予一种新的功能？即它有可能通过改变人们的认识习惯，而获得某种陌生的、有差异的世界。而作为传统的方法，我们只能借助类似于人类学的"异地调查"来获得，而今天，"异"的概念不仅仅是空间的概念，也包含知识与认识方式带来的"异质空间"。

汪建伟，2008

《三岔口》的概念来自于一部同名的中国传统戏曲，对历史文本的重新解读，让我获得一种不同的方法去延续我的工作，同时，通过将历史作为某种时间的维度，如何与今天的社会产生新的关系？在《三岔口》这段戏曲中，我们看到了通过对身体与行为的重新设计，使这个空间充满了互相矛盾的共时性，为了被观看，或者说被他人观看，空间必须保持正常的被观看的条件（亮度、体积……）。但是，在这个被观看的行为中，表演者必须自我认定为是在黑暗中进行，在一种"正常"的空间，身体被分割为双重性，他们必须在对方的指引下决定自己的行为方式，两个事实并列在空间里，一个是在黑暗中的身体如何相互产生反应；另一个是这种反应如何被他人完全地观看。《三岔口》的借喻更多的是来自于关于显现与隐藏，时间的压缩和空间的重叠，而不是它特殊的民族寓义和对传统的崇尚。

汪建伟，《关于"三岔口"》，2007（节选）

Wang Jianwei
Dilemma - Three Way Fork in the Road

My way of looking at things comes from various intellectual domains, between which a cognitive foundation of mutual connections and a thought model of mutual querying are both provided.

Through this intersecting, non-linear method, I hope to be able to discover latent things that are obscured by habit and order. Is it possible to give art a new function by this means? That is, can it, by changing people's cognitive habits, achieve the creation of an unfamiliar world of difference? Traditionally, we can only achieve this by relying on the method of 'off-site investigation' similar to that of anthropology. However, nowadays the concept of 'difference' is not just a spatial concept, but also includes the 'heterogeneous space' that intellect and cognition bring to it.

Wang Jianwei, 2008

The concept of *Dilemma - Three Way Fork in the Road* comes from the traditional Chinese opera of the same name. The reinterpretation of the historical text allowed me to achieve a different method by which to extend my work. At the same time, how does one produce new relations with today's society by making history a temporal dimension? In the opera *Dilemma - Three Way Fork in the Road*, we saw how, by the new design of bodies and actions, the space is filled with contradictory synchronicity. To be observed, or rather, to be observed by others, the space must maintain the normal conditions of being observed (light, volume…), yet, in this action that is being observed, the actors must identify themselves as acting in darkness. In a 'normal' space, the bodies are divided dualistically. Guided by their opponent, they must decide their own format of performance. Two facts are juxtaposed in space: one is how the bodies are to produce reciprocal reactions in the darkness, and the other is how these reactions are to be completely observed by others. The metaphor of *Dilemma - Three Way Fork in the Road* relates mainly to appearance and being hidden, to the compression of time and the overlapping of space, and not to its particular ethnic metaphorical meaning or an upholding of tradition.

Wang Jianwe
About Dilemma - Three Way Fork in the Road
2007 (Extract)

汪建伟
Wang Jianwei
三岔口
Dilemma - Three Way Fork in the Road
激光数码输出
C-print
153×73cm×3, 2007

王兴伟
无题

《无题》完成在《大划船》系列作品之后,形体做了"概念化"的立体简化,用形体的相似性进行联系和"偷换"。例如用方形的电脑和方形的头建立关联,把圆的自行车轮转换成圆球。背景是舞台化的。

王兴伟,2011

通过不断的艺术实践,王兴伟建立了一套庞大、精致而独特的绘画语言体系。其中的每个元素虽然看起来互不联系,但每个元素都是进入艺术家"视觉字典"的重要"词条"。这些并置的元素通过其巨大的力量,以及无法预见的可能性有意地打破了人们惯常的思维与知识逻辑。

风靡于上世纪20年代老上海的漫画和卡通成就了现今的动漫产业。王兴伟在2006至2007年间通过大量的绘画作品逐渐萃取、凝练出卡通漫画在形式上的精华,作品《无题》(2007,120×120cm)正是其中的经典范例之一。在2007至2008年间,王兴伟着力在画布上谱写他"视觉字典"中的"标题字"。《无题》(2007)完美地呈现了艺术家"视觉标题字"的重现与重组。

萧岭,《王兴伟——〈无题〉(2007)》,2011(节选)

Wang Xingwei
Untitled

Untitled was completed after the *Large Rowboat* series of works. In physical shape, it was a 'conceptualized' simplification of three-dimensional space, and the resemblance between physical shapes was used to carry out connected 'substitutions'. For instance, by establishing a connection between a square computer and a square head, and transforming round bicycle wheels into balls. The background was made to resemble a stage.

Wang Xingwei, 2011

Through continous art practice, Wang Xingwei has been building up an exquisitely unique pictorial language in which seemingly disconnected elements - each serving as a conceptual entry from the artist's own 'visual dictionary' - are juxtaposed in order to purposely dismantle the acknowledged logic of thinking and create, by means of their disruptive power, new and unpredictable interpretative possibilities.

Untitled (2007, 120 × 120 cm) is a work resulting from an increasingly extreme formal simplification of the cartoonist trend that, inspired to the Shanghai comic tradition of the Twenties, hallmarks a number of paintings executed by Wang Xingwei between 2006 and 2007. *Untitled* (2007) constitutes a significant example of re-emergence and recombination of one of the artist's favoured 'pictorial headwords' of his 2007-2008's canvases.

Nataline Colonnello
Wang Xingwei - Untitled (2007)
2011(Extract)

王兴伟
Wang Xingwei
无题
Untitled
布面油画
Oil on Canvas
120 × 120cm, 2007

没顶公司
蔓延 C-009

没顶公司 MadeIn 是由徐震在2009年创立于上海的文化有限公司，公司致力于艺术创造、制作、传播、支持以及策划，是一个多功能的复合式文化有限公司。

没顶公司关注已有艺术系统的内部结构，而不仅仅停留在使用经验和个体生存经验上，公司的尝试扩大了原有个体的工作范围，形成了另一种工作方向。

可能针对没顶公司的理解，大都是从身份、商业、生产等几个方面展开，但没顶公司的重点是针对问题研究的不可封闭性，对理解方式的不限制性进行工作，并强调一种能产生事实的态度和方法。关键词是"产生"而非"生产"。

没顶公司

《蔓延》项目是没顶公司从全球的各类漫画中挑选、组合并创造性地开发出的一个独立的艺术项目。这个项目的原则是利用不断出现的全世界的漫画作为材料，使用其中的形象、内容和概念，用各种方式进行再创造。此项目于2009年启动。项目将以绘画，装置、拼贴、动画等各种方式呈现。

没顶公司，"蔓延"系列介绍，2011〔节选〕

MadeIn
C - 009 (Series: Overspread)

MadeIn company was established in 2009 in Shanghai by Xu Zhen. This pluri-disciplinary cultural company is devoted to art creation, production, promotion, support and curation.

MadeIn focuses on the inner structure of the art system, seeking to expand its working field beyond the mere accumulation of experiences or individual subsistence, and opening a new direction.

Although the understanding of MadeIn company is often based on identity issues, commercial and production activities, its objectives reside in probing the extent of research possibilities, developing unlimited interpretations, and emphasizing attitudes and ways of creating realities. MadeIn's central concern is to 'generate' and not to 'produce'.

MadeIn

Spread is an independent art project developed by MadeIn company since 2009. Ideas and elements of cartoons from all over the World are continuously selected and assembled into creative compositions in the form of collages on canvas, installations, paintings, animations, etc.

MadeIn, *Introduction to overspread series*, 2011 (Extract)

没顶公司
MadeIn
蔓延 C-009
C-009 (Series: Overspread)
综合材料
Mixed Materials
135×125cm, 2010

延伸的视界

十三位正在逐渐走向成熟的年轻艺术家通过他们的作品展示了中国当代艺术最具有活力的一面：大胆的实验与突破，对社会与生活更为深入、细节的体验，对艺术本体更加个人化、创造性的探索与开拓，这种清新的气质与鲜活的血液为我们提示了中国当代艺术精彩的未来。泰康人寿出于对中国当代艺术未来发展的远见，十年不断地积极支持、赞助年轻艺术家的创作并为他[她]们提供展览的机会。伴随一拨年轻艺术家走向辉煌，一拨渐渐成熟，新一拨正在涌现，越来越多的人跟随泰康的目光有机会同步了解、发现艺术发展的当代性魅力。

Extended Vision

Thirteen young artists who are gradually achieving maturity, display in their works the most vital aspect of Chinese contemporary art: the brand - new character and fresh blood of these bold experiments and breakthroughs, of these deeper and more detailed experiences of society and life, and of this more individual and original exploration and unpacking of the essence of art, give us notice of the brilliant future of Chinese contemporary art. Taikang Life's point of departure is its long-term view of the future development of Chinese contemporary art, and we have for ten years constantly provided positive support and encouragement to young artists in their creative work, and offered them opportunities to exhibit their work. We accompany one wave of young artists on their path towards glory, as one wave gradually matures, another wells forth, and more and more people, following Taikang's gaze, have the opportunity of at the same time understanding and discovering the contemporary fascination of artistic development.

蔡东东
给予 | 舀

……而他最新的作品《给予》则把摄影自身放在了一个悖论情境中：为了拍摄暗房的内部，暗房必须明亮，但是现实中的暗房——就像这个词的意思一样——却应该是昏暗的。最终，蔡东东只有专门搭建一个用来拍摄的暗房，在这个明亮的暗房中，他布置了大量与摄影有关的细节，这些细节提供了知识，然而知道与看始终是两回事，在这个叫做"现场"的摄影作品中，真正属于摄影的看的"现场"恰恰是缺席的，这就是悖论之所在。

观念摄影不仅仅是挪用、模拟、摆拍、虚拟这些技巧及技术性因素就能支撑得住的，更重要的是艺术家的问题意识与思考方法，以及提问与思考不得不依赖的知识背景，蔡东东的作品证明了这一点。

鲍栋，《摄影的戏剧》，2009〔节选〕

Cai Dongdong
Offer | Scooping Up

…His new work *Offer* puts photography in a paradoxical situation: in order to photograph the interior of a darkroom, the darkroom needs to be bright. However the darkroom in reality - just like the meaning of this word - is supposed to be dark. In the end, Cai Dongdong had no choice but to build a darkroom that is especially for being photographed. In this bright "darkroom", he arranges many details concerning photography. These details provide knowledge, but "knowing" and "looking" are different. In this photography of "Photographer's Working Scene", the real scene for "looking", which is supposed to belong to photographer, is absent. This is where the paradox lies.

Conceptual photography cannot be supported merely by appropriation, imitation, stage photography, fabrication or other technical elements. What's more important is the artist's consciousness of realizing a problem and his way of thinking, as well as the knowledge background that questioning and thinking rely on. The works by Cai Dongdong have proved this point.

Bao Dong, *the Drama of Photography*, 2009 (Extract)

蔡东东
Cai Dongdong
给予
Offer
彩色照片，版数：1／12
C - print, Edition: 1／12
150×208cm, 2009

蔡东东
Cai Dongdong
舀
Scooping Up
彩色照片，版数：1 / 8
C - print, Edition: 1 / 8
150×187cm, 2010

胡向前
蓝旗飘飘 | 向前美术馆

居住在广州的年轻艺术家胡向前在他的创作中开展体验性的、浪漫主义的实践，而且他自己往往充当这个实践中的主角。在他的旧作《蓝旗飘飘》中，这个年轻人居然"异想天开"地去参加村长竞选。这个行为充满了对政治系统所宣扬的公正性的信任和想象，而艺术家被宣布无资格参加竞选和被逐出竞选的结果又让这个游戏的不公正性不言自明。

卢迎华，《偶然的观念主义作品之二——胡向前》，2009（节选）

两个多世纪以来，作为一个神圣的建筑及内在空间，美术馆收集着人类文明艺术的发展。当今美术馆更是社会文化景观中的一个主导性特征，除了价值标准的树立和把持，其权威性带来的一切包括收藏、展示、传播、教育等等都在发挥着它的影响力，拥有绝对的话语权，在被不同领域赋予各种意义的同时，美术馆也披挂上多种伪装。

在作品《向前美术馆》中，艺术家胡向前用自己名字命名的，以身体为建筑的"向前美术馆"，记忆空间收藏着被他个人肯定的许多作品，通过"述说"这种语言描绘的方式展示、传播，挑战的却是当今文化景观中美术馆的价值体系和话语权。

唐昕，2010（节选）

Hu Xiangqian
Flying Blue Flag | Xiangqian Art Museum

The young artist Hu Xiangqian, who lives in Guangzhou, in his works opens up an empirical, romanticist practice, and he himself often appears as the protagonist of this practice. In his old work *Flying Blue Flag*, this young man even fantastically entered an election as candidate for the position of village head. This performance was full of imagination and confidence in the integrity of the propaganda of the political system, but the outcome of the artist being declared ineligible to take part as a candidate in the election and being chased from the election on the other hand made the injustice of this game self-evident.

Carol Yinghua Lu
Accidental Conceptualism Work No.2 - Hu Xiangqian
2009 (Extract)

For more than two centuries, as a sacred building and inner space, museum collects the development of art and culture of human beings. Nowadays, museum has even become a dominant character of the cultural landscape of the society. Apart from the establishment and control of the value standard, museum has an absolute power of discourse and all things that are brought by its authority, such as collection, exhibition, transmission and education, are fully playing their roles. As provided with all sorts of meanings by different fields, museum also puts on many masks.

In the work *Xiangqian Art Museum*, artist Hu Xiangqian creates Xiangqian Art Museum whose name is his own name and whose building is his own body. The space of his memory collects many works that are approved by himself. He demonstrates and transmits these works through the means of linguistic narration. However, what he challenges is the value system and power of discourse of museum in current cultural landscape.

Tang Xin, 2010 (Extract)

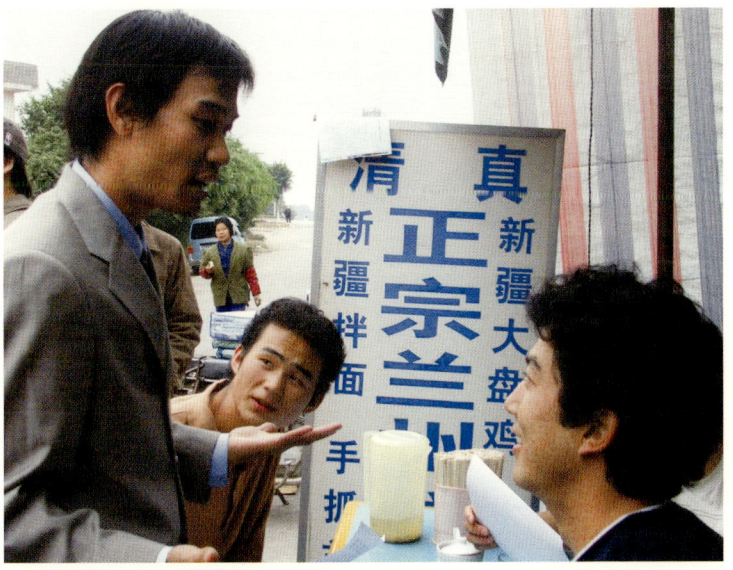

胡向前
Hu Xiangqian
蓝旗飘飘
Flying Blue Flag
行为录像，版数：4 / 5
Performance Video, Edition: 4 / 5
19'13", 2006

胡向前
Hu Xiangqian
向前美术馆
Xiangqian Art Museum
行为录像，版数：1 / 5
Performance Video, Edition: 1 / 5
14'31", 2010

刘窗
无题（舞伴）｜无题（节日）

刘窗善于发掘当下生活中隐藏在日常性情节背面的内容，它昭示着艺术家对于生存权利无声流失的危机感。抛除意义，这些"日常性情节"的正常运转保障着时间的有效，历史的生成，物种的延续；而一旦被追问并质疑，它们便显露出其制度化的本质。

制度能够赋予"剥夺"以合法性的假象，尤其当"剥夺"的过程是以"转化"的方式发生时，那么当事人甚至也可能忽略其存在。……单频录像《无题（舞伴）》则扩大了讨论的范围，视频中两辆同型号的汽车以最低限速并列行驶穿过城市，它们严格遵循刘窗所设定的规则，似乎干扰了路面上的正常秩序，却也没有引发拥堵，更不至于造成交通瘫痪。当观众站在一个通常的角度对视频中的情节做出道德判断的同时，刘窗揭示这种"道德"的实质是多数人对少数人的强权，而法律则是权力制度化的产物。日常生活要求人们必须具备适应规则的耐心，而一旦某种规则被最大范围地认可和接受，它就可能反过来成为限制个体自由的工具，其隐层含义是"凡是不合乎规则的，就是反规则的，也即是恶意的、不合法的、必须被规范的"。它最终形成一种天然的、巨大的道德压力，将生活中诗意的可能性挤压殆尽。

刘窗借由审视和重置日常生活中的微观系统，引发敏感者对于蕴藏在周遭事物中的整个社会系统的反思，并从中寻找到制度的线索。

张夕远，《艺术界》第7期，2011（节选）

Liu Chuang
Untitled (Dancing Partner) | Untitled (the Festival)

Liu Chuang is skilled at unearthing contents hidden beneath the surface of life's quotidian systems, which reveals the artist's sense of crisis about the silent lose of right to live. In doing so, he unmasks these systems as an apparatus that controls the perception of time, ensures the production of history, and protects the perpetuation of the species. And the moment they are questioned or doubted, their institutionalized essence is exposed.

A system can endow "deprivation" with the illusion of legitimacy. When the process of "deprivation" occurs by way of "conversion," even those privy to it may overlook its existence. The single-channel video work *Untitled (Dancing Partner)* (2010) expands the scope of the discussion; in the recording, two cars of the same make and model drive side-by-side through the city at the minimum speed limit (60 km); they strictly follow the regulations set by Liu Chuang, seemingly interfering with the order on the roads, but not to the point of causing congestion, let alone gridlock. While the audience watches from a vantage point far above, making moral judgments about the plot of the video, Liu reveals that the very substance of this "morality" is the power of the majority over the minority, and that the law is a product of the institutionalization of power. Everyday life demands that people have the patience to adapt to the rules; and once a certain rule has been acknowledged and accepted on a great enough scale, it can, conversely, become a tool for the restriction of individual freedoms. The implication is, "Anything that does not conform to the rules is automatically against them, and is thus malicious, illegal, and in need of regulation." This ultimately leads to an enormous inherent moral pressure, one that squeezes out any of life's potential poetry.

By examining and replaying the micro-systems of everyday life, Liu Chuang triggers our sensitivity to them, and makes us reconsider the social system embedded in our surroundings and find the clue of it.

Zhang Xiyuan, *LEAP* No.7, 2011 (Extract)

刘窗
Liu Chuang
无题（舞伴）
Untitled (Dancing Partner)
行为、录像，版数：1 / 3
Performance and Video, Edition: 1 / 3
2010

刘窗
Liu Chuang
无题(节日)
Untitled (the Festival)
行为、录像，5分14秒，版数：1／3
Performance and Video, 05'14", Edition: 1／3
2011

马秋莎
从平渊里4号到天桥北里4号 |
黎明是黄昏的灰烬

出生于80年代的马秋莎是所谓中国幸运一代中的一员。她在国家扩张、发展的时代中接受教育；身为独生子女，她是父母全部精力的焦点，而这同样也是问题所在。在她的录像作品《从平渊里4号到天桥北里4号》中，马秋莎含着藏在舌头上的刀片，讲述了一个充满过度期望和约束的生活故事。刀片的在场让她的故事多了一份犹疑、踌躇的特质。直到录像结束，她把刀片从嘴里拿出来的时候，才揭示出她讲述这个故事经历了何种艰难。

马秋莎讲了一个女孩的故事：她在童年就被发现有绘画天赋，继而成为父母远大抱负的重心。他们坚信她会成为一个成功的艺术家，因此他们做出的所有努力都针对这个目标。最终他们决定她应该出国学习，她也确实那么做了，而回家之后却发现"离开母亲一年，她开始变老了"。

马秋莎说的故事不仅仅是关于自己的，而是关于很多承载了父母期盼的同龄人。……马秋莎告诉我她对出生地北京的变化速度感到不适，她相信这也导致了人们的迅速变化。她的作品试图纪念亲密的时刻，而如果想看到这些诸如亲密的东西，就需要我们减慢速度。当生活疾驰而过的时候，她却平静地请求我们关注。

欧美琳，《表象背后》，2009〔节选〕

Ma Qiusha
From No.4 Pingyuanli to No.4 Tianqiaobeili | Twilight is the Ashes of Dusk

Born in the 1980s, Ma is a member of what is considered to be China's lucky generation. Educated in a time of expansion and development, she is one of the only-children upon whom all their parents' have been focused. In which lies the problem. In her video *From No.4 Pingyuanli to No.4 Tianqiaobeili*, Ma holds the razor blade hidden on her tongue and tells us a story of a life of excessive expectation and discipline. The presence of the blade gives a hesitance and halting quality to her story. It is only at the end of the video that it is revealed with what difficulty she has told it as she takes the razor blade from her mouth.

Ma tells a story of a girl, who, discovered to have a talent for drawing at an early age, becomes the focus of her parent's ambition. They conceive the idea that she should become a successful artist and all their efforts are directed to that goal. Finally they decide she should go abroad to study, which she does, only to find when she comes home that "after a year away my mother had begun to be old."

Ma says her story is not just about her, but about many in her generation who bear the burden of their parents' expectations. ……Ma tells me she is uncomfortable with the speed of change in her native city of Beijing, which she believes makes people change too fast also. Her works seek to memorialize intimate moments, and some like Intimacy require us to slow down if we are to see them at all. As life rushes past, she asks calmly for our attention.

Madeleine O'Dea, *What Lies Beneath*, 2009 (Extract)

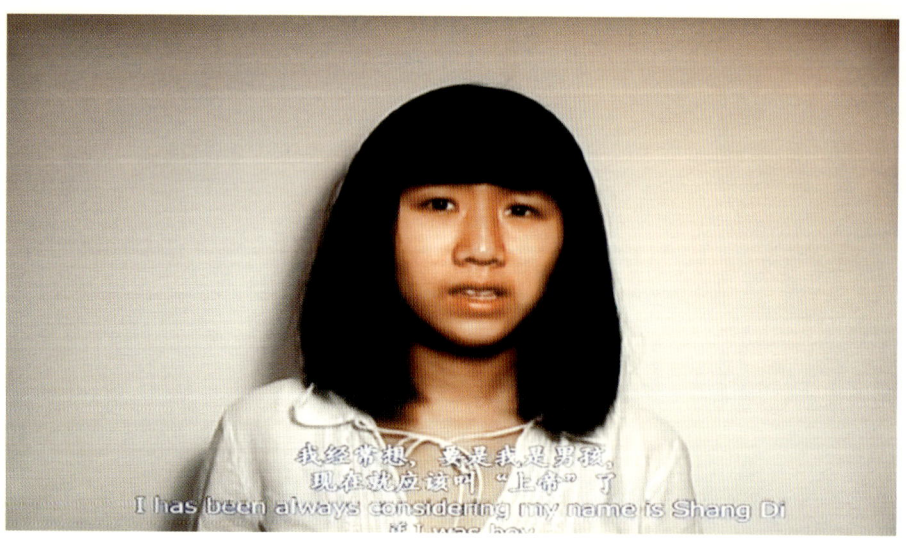
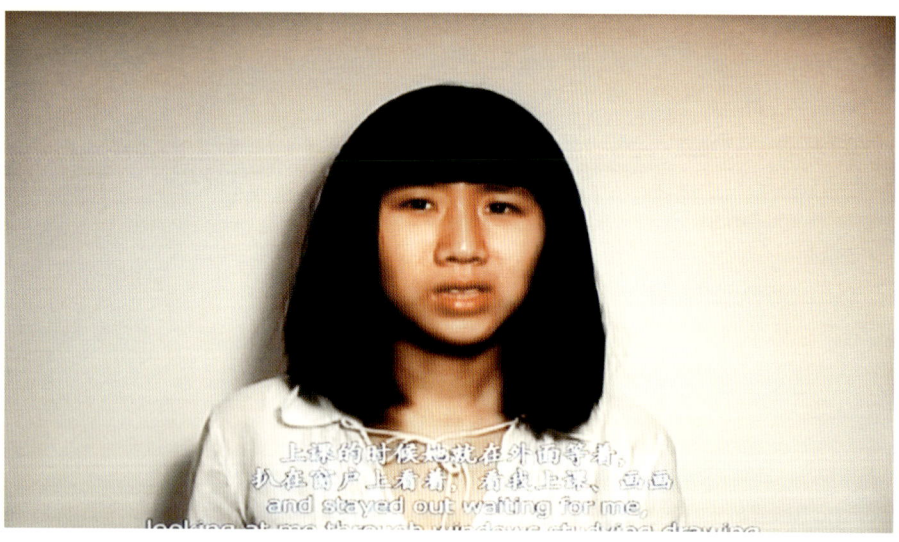

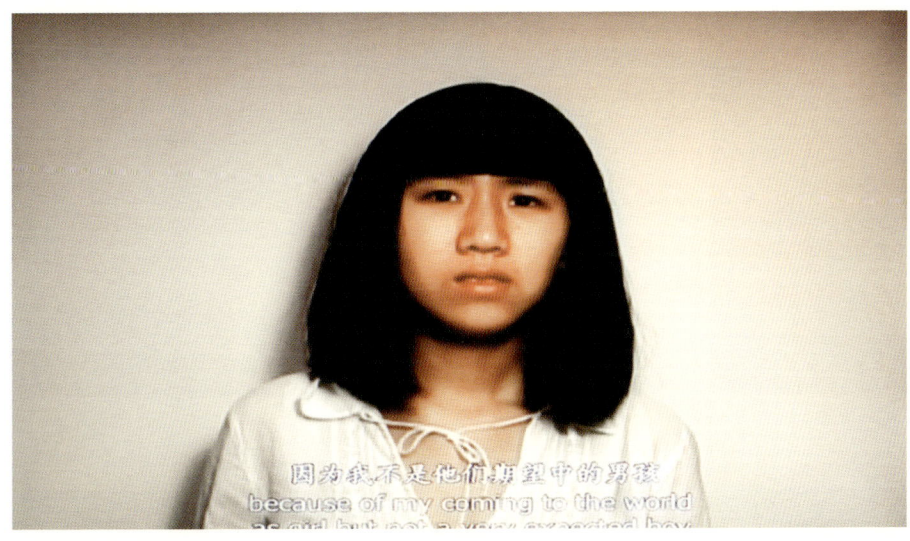

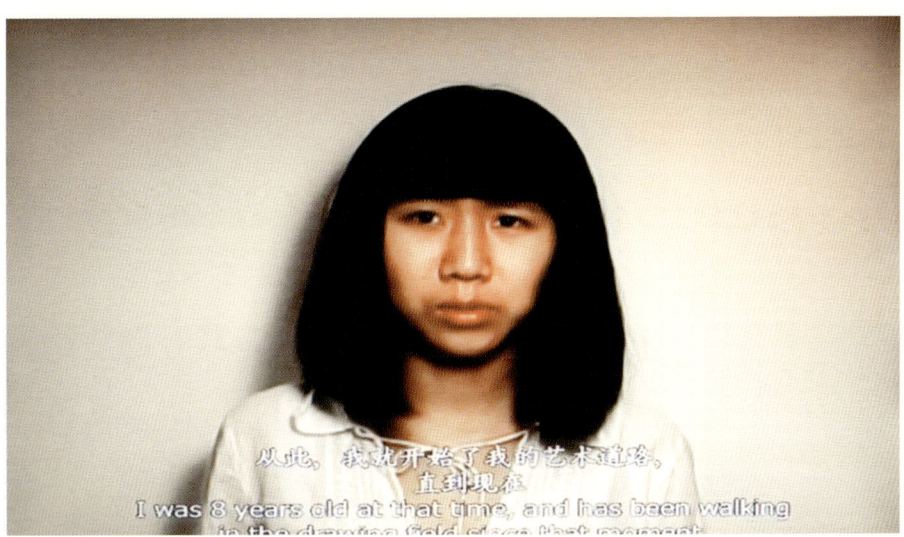

马秋莎
Ma Qiusha
从平渊里4号到天桥北里4号
From No.4 Pingyuanli to No.4 Tianqiaobeili
单频录像，版数：4／6
Single - channel Video, Edition:4／6
07'54", 2007

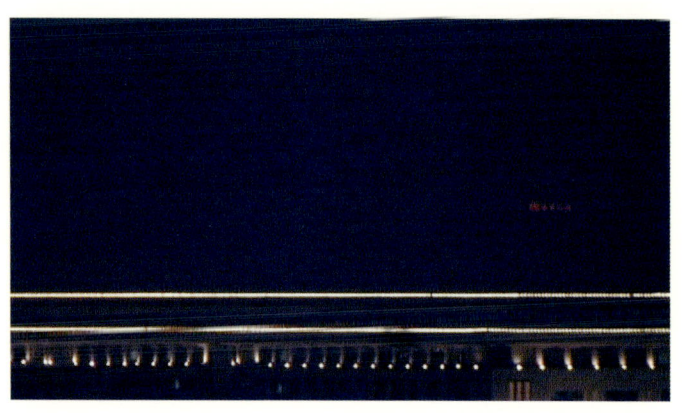

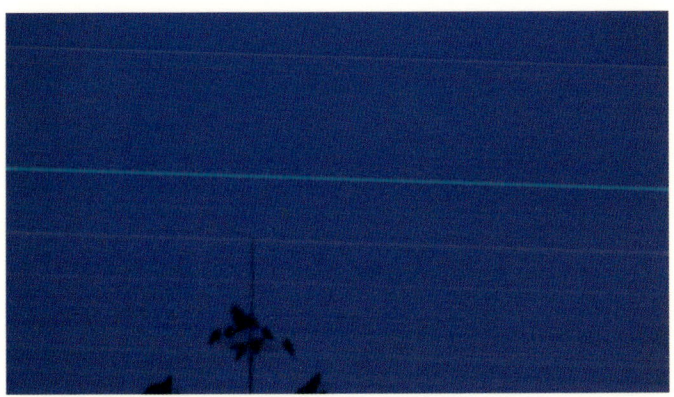

马秋莎
Ma Qiusha
黎明是黄昏的灰烬
Twilight is the Ashes of Dusk
单频录像，版数：1 / 6
Single - channel Video, Edition: 1 / 6
03'15", 2011

裴丽
丢失了些什么？

裴丽的作品《丢失了些什么？》的灵感无疑是来自最原始的冲动，是不可以修改的作品。修改只能降低低声的愤怒，降低作品中所叙述的被苦乐参半的挫折支配着的姿态和狡猾的双关语，也可能会降低流露出的幽默程度。作品中的潜台词和力量掩藏在她在整个空间的墙之间绘制的颓废的花边中。但是，可能作品表达的所有情感只有在第二次参观后才能完全被接收。首先，《丢失了些什么？》是一次催眠的经历，你不得不陷入这个抒情的空间，画在墙之间展开来，作品中融入了艺术家自己的身体和动作。她很坚决也很顽皮，你知道她在玩，在找乐子，但从她的面部表情可以发现她被内心深藏的那份坚定驱使着，一旦释放出来她真实的愤怒、挫折和沮丧，那会是很可怕的。

选择这个题目，"关于主题，"她说，"我觉得在生活中，我丢失了很多东西。面对选择或是牺牲总是很难接受的，但如果你不把它们放在一边，你会变得很压抑，这是更不好的。"《丢失了些什么？》因此是对人们痛苦的阐释。

凯伦·史密斯，《精力充沛的新手》，2009（节选）

Pei Li
Isn't Something Missing?

Isn't Something Missing? undeniably lives for the rawness of those first impulsive elements that inspired Pei Li to create it in the way she did. It is not a work that can be finessed. That would only reduce the undertone of anger, the bittersweet frustration that dictates the gestures and the sly quips at narrative embedded within the work. It would probably diminish the seam of humour it exudes too. The force or subtext of the work is belied by the decadent lacework of inky black and watery grey lines that she paints across the walls of the space in which *Isn't Something Missing?* is projected. But all of these sensations only perhaps find full force on a second viewing. Initially, *Isn't Something Missing?* is a mesmerizing experience, and you can't help but be drawn into the lyrical motion of the painting that spreads across the walls, and which is echoed in the piece in the body and motion of the girl in action, who is none but the artist herself. She has a determined but impish air. You know she's playing, that she's having fun, but from the expressions that cross her face, you also know that she is driven by an internal concealed determination and quiet control such that if released, if made visible the sight of her real anger, frustration or dismay would be formidable indeed.

Of her choice of title as well as theme she says "I feel I have lost so many things in my life. It's always hard to accept that you have to make choices or sacrifices, but if you can't put it aside then you repress it which is worse." *Isn't Something Missing?*, therefore, is an interpretation of the pain that engulfs human existence.

Karen Smith, *The Feisty Freshman*, 2009 (Extract)

裴丽
Pei Li
丢失了些什么？
Isn't Something Missing?
单频录像，版数：1 / 4
Single – channel Video, Edition: 1 / 4
06'45", 2009

苏文祥
再见一个老人 | 五色令人目盲

作品《五色令人目盲》(2009)标志着艺术家创作的新阶段，他将一组宝丽莱600相纸从相机中取出再装回去拍照，从而获得一组已自动曝光、名义上的白色图像。创作过程的本质尽管是分析性的，得出的作品却令人振奋地诗意，而他运用的思路恰恰是这一领域的先行者们——譬如重要的媒体艺术家刘韡、张培力——通常不予采用的方式。这件强有力的作品指向一个智性探索的创作方向，它将谨密的观念推向形式的极端，在定义该事物的同时，重新构筑狭小的中国当代艺术领域中关于同类命题的创作语言。

与此相类，在作品《再见一个老人》(2008)中，艺术家重复打印前政治家华国锋的标准像直到打印机墨水消耗殆尽，试图记录一个政治人物消逝的过程；而在《M100, Y100》(2009年持续进行)中，艺术家每月重复打印一张仅涂有红色墨水的纸张。虽然前者因指涉一名极无争议的国家领导人而含有政治暗示，它的主要作用还在于成为后者观念抽象化的陪衬，使作品脱离历史、记忆以及象征图像所裹挟的强力，取而代之的是一种从技术角度对持续时间的描述。

岳鸿飞，《相机、打印机、电视机和电脑》，2009 (节选)

Su Wenxiang
Goodbye An Old Man | The Oneness of the Five Colors Blind the Eyes

In one landmark piece, *The oneness of the five colors blind the eyes* (2009), a number of sheets of Polaroid film are removed from the camera before a single shot is taken, producing nominally white images of a process of automatic exposure. This process is analytical in spirit, but the resulting work is courageously poetic in a way that its progenitors - critical media artists like Liu Wei and Zhang Peili - would generally avoid. This compelling work points towards a direction of intellectual exploration that pushes rigorous concepts to their formal extremities as a way to both define the matter at stake and reframe the language that circulate around such questions within the narrow field of contemporary art in China.

Similarly, *Goodbye an Old Man* (2008) records the process of the disappearance of former politician Hua Guofeng as the artist repeatedly prints his portrait until there is no ink left, while *M100, Y100* (2009 - ongoing) requires the artist to print a single sheet of paper covered purely with red ink on a monthly basis. Although the former work implicates the political through its allusion to a particularly uncontroversial state leader, it serves largely as a foil for the conceptual abstraction of the latter, giving way to an account of duration as a technical move divorced from the greater forces of history, memory, and symbolic imagery.

Robin Peckham, *Cameras, Printers, TV Sets and Computers*, 2009 (Extract)

苏文祥

Su Wenxiang

再见一个老人

Goodbye An Old Man

相纸、HP Deskjet F388彩色打印机，版数：1／1

Photo Paper and Color Print by HP Deskjet F388, Edition: 1／1

29.7×21cm×87, 2008

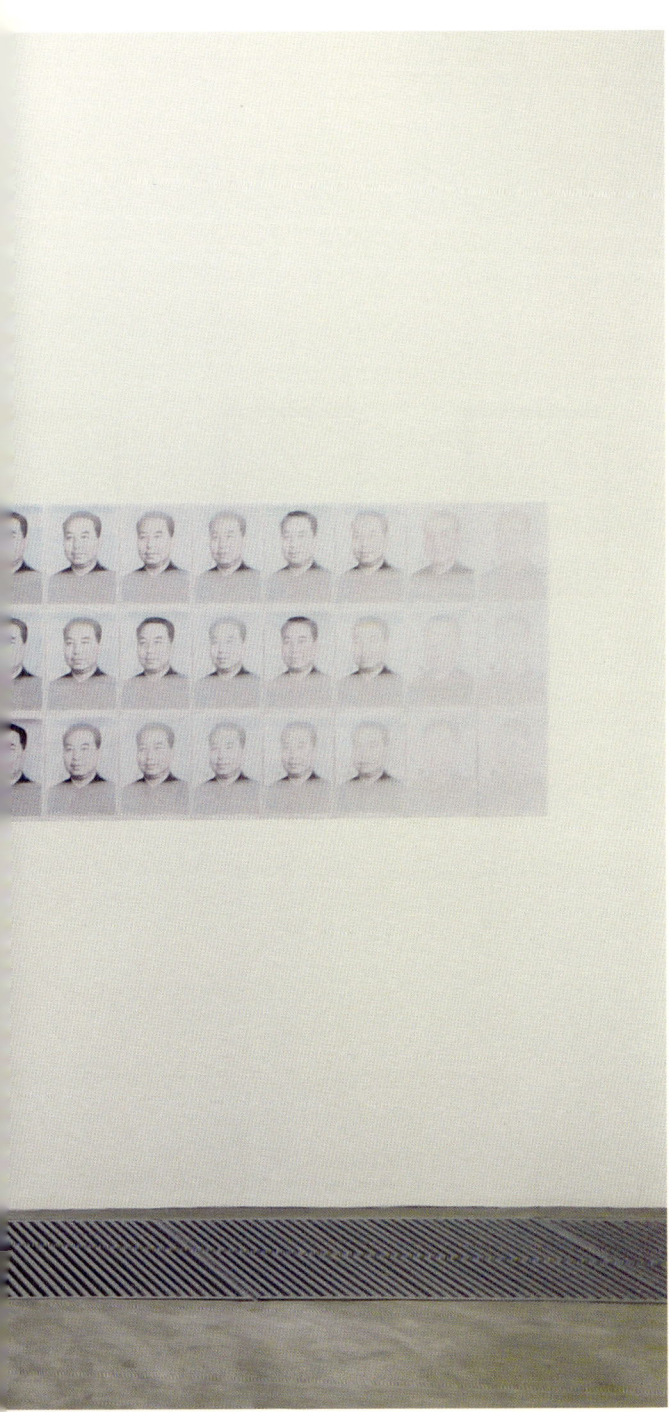

苏文祥

Su Wenxiang

五色令人目盲

The Oneness of the Five Colors Blind the Eyes

宝丽莱600相纸，版数：1／1

Polaroid 600 Photo Papers, Edition: 1／1

8.8×10.8cm×10, 2009

王思顺
多巴胺之巅

进入展厅，观者发现的只是一幅直接在墙面上粗略勾画出来的速写式地图，或者出游路线图。后面的小展厅里不停循环播放着一个短视频。从这个纪录片得知艺术家为此次展览开幕安排了几辆巴士，准备把观众带到环铁一带距离他工作室有段路的某个白雪覆盖的荒郊野外；这一行动据称是去寻找曾在王思顺的一个梦里同样的地理空间背景中现身在他面前的一位仙女。在伴随展览的文本材料中，他把这个梦描述为"多巴胺之巅"，并称该展览应提供给观众一个"弥补现实的美好梦想"。

这不是一个适合展开细读的项目，尽管相对于他的劳动政治学，它看上去确实更易于贴合王思顺将某个设定的行为视做心理状况与文学体裁两者间的裂缝的观念；此处观念的转变很有意思：心理的表现形式为体裁而不是内容。

岳鸿飞，《王思顺和情感乌托邦》，2010（节选）

Wang Sishun
The Top of Dopamine

Entering the gallery space, the viewer finds only a sketchily drafted map or travel itinerary painted directly onto the wall surface. In the small room behind, a short video loops continuously. Through this documentation it emerges that, for the opening of the exhibition, the artist arranged several buses to take visitors to a snowy, barren corner of the Huantie area some distance from his studio; this was purportedly a quest to discover a fairy that appeared to Wang Sishun in a dream against the background of this same geographic space. In the accompanying textual materials, he describes the dream as a "Top of dopamine," claiming that the exhibition should offer to the audience a "wonderful dream that compensates for reality."

The project does not lend itself to close reading, although it does appear to sit more easily with Wang Sishun's conception of a given action as split between psychological state and literary genre than with his politics of labor. The conceptual move is interesting: the presentation of a psychology not as content but as genre.

Robin Peckham
Wang Sishun and Emotional Utopia
2010 (Extract)

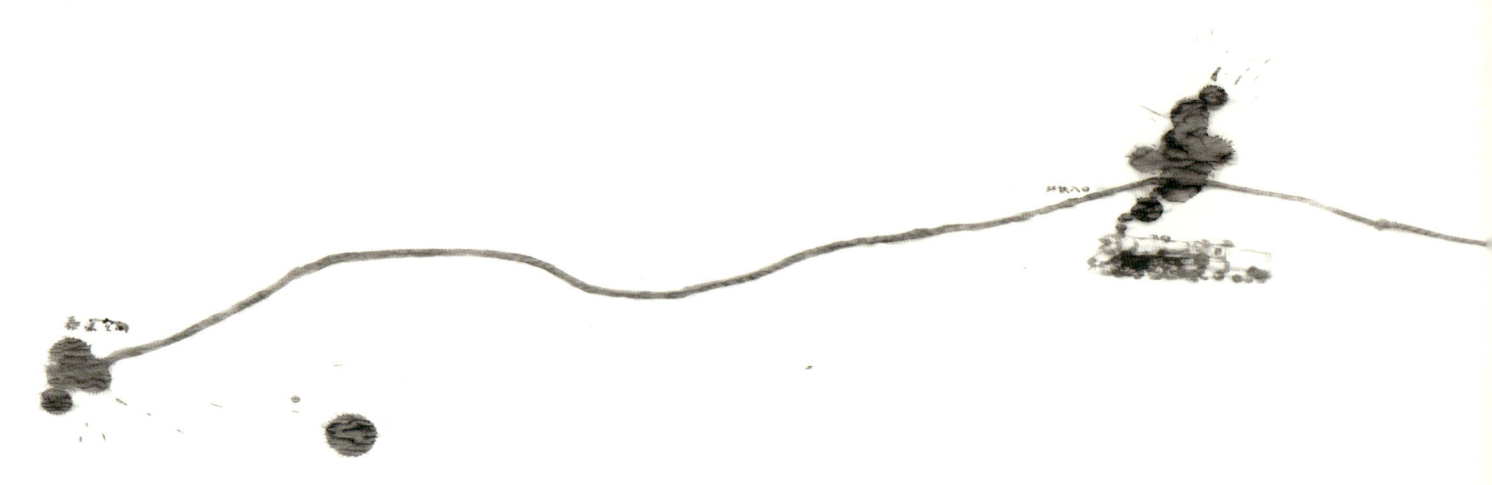

王思顺

Wang Sishun

多巴胺之巅

The Top of Dopamine

硫酸纸,版数:1/1

Acid paper, Edition: 1/1

225×45cm, 2010

行为录像,版数:1/8

Performance and Video, Edition: 1/8

06'38", 2010

王郁洋
图与字 | 说

王郁洋此次个展是51m² 项目系列的最后一个展览，采用了抽象手法，将讯息符码与媒介相结合，试图以一种有意味的方式描述关于自主交流的本体论。

展览的主要视觉组成部分是题为《图与字》(2010)的作品，一组巨幅壁画绘在三面墙上，与之相对，剩下的第四面墙挂着几张镶框的白纸，上面是以打印和印刷的方式出现的字词列表。墙上的绘画看上去很像条形码，但被处理成不规则的黑白色块，未经专门训练的眼睛无法从中读出任何语义信息。至少理论上而言，这是语言和图像之间的自动转译，符码被故意曲解成文学，生成一种图形诗的形式，从而使图像能够传递形式化的，或抽象化的第二图像。作品以这种方式完成了自身的二度"书写"，虽然试图从观念艺术以外的层面来欣赏该作品依旧是个挑战。参展的第二件作品，题为《说》(2010)，通过录音机播放该机器录音时所发出的声音的录音磁带，表达介于媒介和材料双重角色之间的某种张力，作为工具的媒介转向了作为内容的物质实存。

岳鸿飞，《51 m² : 16# 王郁洋》，2011 (节选)

Wang Yuyang
Picture and Character | Speak

This exhibition, the last in the 51m² project space series, adopts the tactics of abstraction, relating signal to medium in an attempt to describe in a meaningful way an ontology of autonomous communication.

The visually dominant component here is the work entitled *Picture and Character* (2010), a massive set of wall paintings on three surfaces paired with typed, printed, and framed lists of words on otherwise blank paper mounted on the fourth wall, left unpainted. The paintings appear similar to barcodes, applied in uneven patches of black and white bars that convey no semantic information to the untrained eye. This is, at least in theory, an automatic translation between language and image that intentionally misconstrues code as literature, generating a form of graphic poetry that, generously speaking, allows one image to convey a second formalized or abstracted image. In this way the work 'writes' itself twice, although appreciation of the work on a level other than the conceptual remains a challenge. The second work included, entitled *Speak* (2010), expresses a certain tension between the dual roles of medium and material by playing back a recording of the sounds of its own recording, moving from the use of media as a tool to the focus on its material existence as content.

Robin Peckham, *51m² #16: Wang Yuyang*, 2011 (Extract)

王郁洋
Wang Yuyang
图与字
Picture and Character
综合媒介，数码输出 80×50 厘米 ×6，版数：1/1
Mixed Media, Photograph 80×50cm×6, Edition: 1/1
2010

王郁洋
Wang Yuyang
说
Speak
装置，磁带、播放器，版数：1/5
Installation, Tape and Speaker, Edition: 1/5
2010

辛云鹏
发电

昏暗空间里的灯是由《古兰经》"99赞"的"99赞美真主的尊名"组成，使用人力发电机点亮这些尊名，也点亮这盏吊灯。

《发电》是大学五年级时做的，当时对制作还是充满乐趣，但这个乐趣没能持续很久，也是有点顾不过来。再说我的伊斯兰家族背景，其实对我影响蛮大的，它与家庭角色越发在我道德层面上起作用，这样我就能比较踏实也愿意相信他人。

辛云鹏，
《51m² 访谈录：16位年轻艺术家》，2011（节选）

Xin Yunpeng
Generate Electricity

The lamp in the dullish space is made up of *99 names* in *Alcoran*. Lightening this lamp with manpower generators also means lightening these names.

I did *Generate Electricity* in my fifth year in college when I still enjoyed the fun of making something, which didn't last for long though. I soon got a tight schedule. I have the Islamic tradition in me. My Islamic background and my family role are something that shapes my moral world so that I do things in a more practical manner and I am willing to believe others.

Xin Yunpeng
51m² Interview: 16 Emerging Chinese Artists, 2011 (Extract)

辛云鹏
Xin Yunpeng

发电
Generate Electricity

装置，手摇发电机、灯管，版数：2 / 3
Installation, Hand – cranked Generator and Tubes, Edition: 2 / 3
90 × 120cm, 2007

徐渠
逆水行舟

……一只橡皮艇，顺着京郊某条常年散发难闻异味的河流，向市区方向一路划行，遇水行舟，遇陆则徒步，途经东风北桥、朝阳公园、亮马桥、燕莎、东直门、雍和宫、积水潭、西海、后海、前海等地，辗转五个多小时后最终在靠近中海时被拦下。这次旅行被拍摄并剪辑成15分钟的单频录像作品出现在展厅中，徐渠将它命名为"逆水行舟"，既是对作品情节的直观描述，也是对作品内容的概念抽取。

徐渠为这件作品设计了一个颇具象征意义的逆流而上的情节，它兼有赫尔佐格式的异想以及在特定社会环境中的节制表达，其实施过程却又显得避重就轻；对情绪化因素和个人经验的控制力赋予作品以冷静的气息。对于那些擅长文本解读的观众来说，这一情节所承载的隐义十分清晰，它指向的是同时存在于政治和文化内部的体制印记。

……在《逆水行舟》中，形式既不作为一种转述观念的语法结构，也非媒介论的产物；它秘而不宣的姿态，正如同画面中出现的市井喧嚣一般令人怀疑，这正是徐渠所抛出的谜题。

张夕远，《逆水行舟》，2011〔节选〕

Xu Qu
Upstream

…One kayak was sailing towards the downtown direction along some river that sends out bad smell throughout the year in the suburb of Beijing. When there was a river or lake, they rowed the kayak; when there was land, they walked. They passed Dongfengbei Qiao, Chaoyang Park, Liangma Qiao, Yan Sha, Dong Zhi Men, Yonghegong Lamasery, Ji Shui Tan, Xi Hai, Hou Hai and Qian Hai, etc; they spent more than five hours and were finally stopped near Zhong Hai. This trip was filmed and edited into a 15-minute single channel video that is shown in the exhibition space. Xu Qu named it *Upstream*, which is not only the direct narration of the content of the work, but also the extraction of the concept.

Xu Qu designed a rather symbolic plot for *Upstream*. It possesses both a Herzog-style caprice and a continent expression in a specific social environment. However, its implementation chose the lighter way; the control of emotional elements and personal experiences provides the work with a calm atmosphere. For the audience who are good at interpreting the text, the hidden meaning carried by this plot is very explicit. What it refers to is the mark of system that exists in the interior of both politics and culture.

…In *Upstream*, form is not the grammatical structure of retailing a concept, nor is it a product of media theory. Its secret gesture is as suspicious as the uproariousness that appears in the picture. This is the conundrum that Xu Qu throws.

Zhang Xiyuan, *Upstream*, 2011 (Extract)

徐渠

Xu Qu

逆水行舟

Upstream

综合媒介，录像，版数：1 / 3

Mixed Media and Video, Edition: 1 / 3

14'58", 2011

路线图

Line map

纸本套色丝网，版数：1 / 5

Silkscreen Print, Edition: 1 / 5

77×108cm, 2011

闫冰
棉被

我喜欢使用比较原始朴素日常的材料来创作，通过一些抽象的形态去触摸自身与周围世界以及记忆的一些深层关系。这些关系是软性的，隐秘的，熟悉而陌生的。

关于《棉被》这件作品，有感于"温暖的凉意"这一体会而作。我用鞣制的非常柔软光滑的牛皮和棉花做成两条棉被，棉被温暖舒服的属性和牛皮的沉重以及它所携带的一个动物过往生命的痕迹，造成了一种表情：痛苦的温和。

闫冰，2011

Yan Bing
Cotton Quilt

I like to use comparatively original, plain and daily materials to make artworks and to touch upon some deep relationships of myself, the surrounding world and the memory. These relationships are soft, secret, familiar yet strange.

The work *Cotton Quilt* was inspired by the feeling of "warm chilliness". I used cotton and very soft and smooth cow leather after the process of tanning to make two cotton quilts. The warm and conformable natures of the cotton quilts, the heaviness of the cow leather and the trace of the past life of an animal carried by it produce a kind of expression: painful gentleness.

Yan Bing, 2011

闫冰
Yan Bing
棉被
Cotton Quilt
装置，牛皮、棉花、木箱，版数：1／1
Installation, Oxide, Cotton and Wooden Case
Edition: 1／1
2009

赵要
每天一次｜他们都笑了

不难看出观念的提出和实施在赵要的创作中的重要性，反复思辨的过程最大限度地控制了作品中的情绪化因素，赋予其以冷静的气质，这在《安静》和《微笑》中尤为突出。从最初对摄影的敏感，到后来不断尝试新的材料和媒介，赵要的形式练习持续深化下去，重复、侵占和填充物是练习的关键词。对重复的陈述在《一万次》《每天一次》等作品中突出而明确地呈现，这种重复性覆盖了时间、动作以及对一种状态的强调；而同样的陈述体现在《窗口》《我爱北京》等作品中时，则更多关照社会的或是政治的议题。侵占的概念在空间里发生效应，在一个陌生的环境中，《来自内部》状如畸变怪物般的外观闯入视觉域，造成异物感和不舒适感。填充物被赵要指定为是人与物空隙的中介，在《它》中，以接近"Mental Sculpture"的面貌出现，放大了日常体验的无差别获取。很难从作品的创作思路、材料或针对物上找寻到他的轨迹，但可以看到的是从2006年前后的摄影发展至今，赵要已经越来越明确地将对形式的探索作为某种恰当言说的出口。

张夕远
《工作坊：赵要》——《当代艺术与投资》No.5
2011（节选）

Zhao Yao
One Time Each Day | They Are All Smiling

It's not difficult to see the importance of raising and implementing a conception in Zhao Yao's creation. The repeated speculation ultimately controls the emotional elements in the work and provides it with a quality of calmness. This is especially outstanding in *Quietness* and *Smile*. From the initial sensitiveness of photography to the consistent attempt of using new materials and media later on, Zhao Yao's form practice has kept on deepening. Repetition, appropriation and stuffing are the key words of his practice. The statement about repetition is clearly presented in *10,000 Times* and *One Time Each Day*, etc. This kind of repetition covers time, action and the emphasis of a kind of status; but when the same statement appears in *Window* and *I Love Beijing*, etc, it cares more about social and political topics. The concept of appropriation does the deed in the space, in a strange environment: in *From the Interior*, a mutated monster intrudes into the vision and produces a feeling of strangeness and discomfort. Stuffing is appointed by Zhao Yao as the medium between people and objects. In *It*, it appears in a look that is similar to Mental Sculpture and enlarges the indiscriminate acquirement of daily experiences. It's hard to find his track from his thought of creation, materials or targets. But we can see clearly that from the photography in 2006 until now, Zhao Yao has more and more taken the exploration of form as the exit of some sort of proper dialogue.

Zhang Xiyuan, *Workshop: Zhao Yao* - No.5 Issue of *Contemporary Art and Investment*, 2011 (Extract)

赵要

Zhao Yao

每天一次

One Time Each Day

装置，布条、水彩笔，版数：1／1

Installation, Cloth Strip and Color pen, Edition: 1／1

2×5000cm, 2009

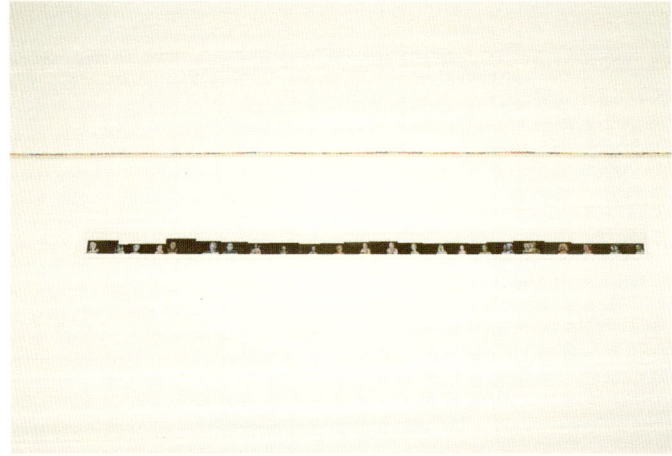

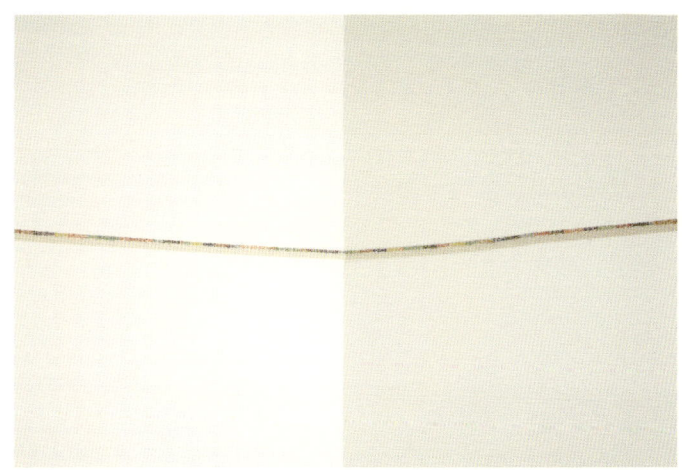

赵要

Zhao Yao

他们都笑了

They Are All Smiling

综合媒介，铅笔，纸币 10 张，版数：1 / 7

Mixed Media, Pencil, 10 Bank Notes, Edition: 1 / 7

2009

赵赵
5113

赵赵的新作品缘自一次搬家过程中的不经意的发现，那是散落在地上的一粒粒鼠粪。通过对它们进行社会／资本主义市场经济眼光的审视以及防腐处理，最后被制作成艺术品。不同于曼佐尼对待粪便的封闭态度，它们是开放并可见的，其中的一粒被精心装置在镜框里，以及剩余的等待可出售的一堆，总共是5113粒。赵赵深谙风水思维对中国人的影响，它们的排列依据中国特有的对数字消费的逻辑被组合成一个独特的编码体系——按照数字的凶吉来确立某颗艺术鼠粪的价格。在此，动物的消耗与生产和人类的对于可持续生产的愿望联系在了一起。此外还有同样由于对于鼠粪这样的坏趣味念念不忘而发展出来的两组绘画作品，虽然它们的形态都忠实于实在的参照物，但最后都变成了具有繁复美学风格的抽象作品。

苏文祥，《51m² : 1#赵赵》，2009（节选）

Zhao Zhao
5113

Zhao Zhao's new series is inspired by an inadvertent discovery of scattered rat droppings on the floor when he was moving. They were incorporated into his work after he examined it through socio-capitalistic market perspective and through anti-corrosion treatment. Unlike Manzoni's containment of excrement, the droppings are open and visible and one of them is carefully framed on the mirror. The rest, including the framed one, totally 5113 pieces, can be sold. Due to the influence of fengshui on the Chinese, the excrement has been combined according to a unique numerical logic - the price of each piece is determined by good luck or bad omen numbers. Here the animal's waste and production are associated with human's desire of sustainable productivity. Moreover, there are two series of paintings that stem from the unchanging interest in rats. Even though the form adheres to the actual object, however, they've eventually become abstract works with complex aesthetic style.

Su Wenxiang, *51m² Project: 1#Zhao Zhao*, 2009 (Extract)

赵赵
Zhao Zhao
5113
综合媒介
Mixed Media
2007

艺术家简介

Artists' Biographies

吴印咸
Wu Yinxian
(1900 – 1994)

吴印咸生于1900年9月21日,1994年9月7日逝世于北京,江苏沭阳县人。中国著名摄影艺术家,曾担任过延安八路军总政治部电影团摄影队长,主持电影团工作,东北电影制片厂技术部长、副厂长、厂长,北京电影学院副院长兼摄影系主任,文化部电影局顾问,中国摄影家协会副主席、名誉主席,中国电影摄影师学会副理事长、名誉主席,全国文学艺术联合会委员。

吴印咸先生与世纪同龄,他是中国革命史上许多重大事件的参与者和纪录者。他用手中的摄影机和照相机,站在时代和历史的潮流中,忠实地记录着中国民主革命、社会主义革命和建设、改革开放的风云际会。在长达70年的摄影艺术生涯中,拍摄了数万张黑白和彩色照片;拍摄了7部故事片和5部纪录片,曾获得全国电影"百花奖"的"最佳摄影奖";编著了20多本摄影艺术专著;举办了近20次个人摄影展览。

主要展览

1935	上海青年会展出作品56幅
1961	北京中国美术馆展出作品,后在七个省市巡回展出
1985	《吴印咸摄影六十年作品展》北京中国美术馆展出,展出作品310幅,后在二十余个省、市、地区巡回展出
1988	美国纽约国际摄影中心(I.C.P)展出作品43幅,展览名为《新中国诞生地——延安》
	法国阿尔勒艺术城第十九届国际摄影节,展出作品81幅
	上海第二届国际摄影展《吴印咸摄影回顾展》,展出作品121幅
1989	《吴印咸摄影回顾展》在新疆乌鲁木齐展出
1991	中国人民抗日战争纪念馆展出《吴印咸抗日战争时期摄影展览》,展出作品69幅
	巴西圣保罗和里约热内卢展出作品62幅
	《吴印咸摄影作品展》于内蒙古自治区通辽市展出,展出作品80幅
1992	《吴印咸摄影作品展》于深圳摄影大厦展出,展出作品160幅
	《吴印咸摄影作品及使用相机展》于中国第二届摄影节期间在北京展出,展出作品165幅
	参加为纪念中日邦交正常化20周年举办的《中日摄影名家20人联展》,展出作品12幅
1993	《吴印咸摄影作品展》于瑞士维拉博物馆展出,展出作品90幅
1997	《吴印咸摄影回顾展》在北京炎黄艺术馆展出,展出作品及生平、活动照片200余幅

Wu Yinxian was born on 21 September 1900 in Shuyang County, Jiangsu Province, and passed away on 7 September 1994 in Beijing. He was a famous Chinese photographer, and held positions as Leader of the Cinematographic Team of the Yan'an Eighth Route Army General Political Department Film - making Team (chairing the film - making work); at Northeast Film Studios he was Director of the Technical Department, Studio Vice - Director and Studio Director. He was Associate Dean and Head of Photography at the Beijing Film Academy, Film Board Adviser for the Ministry of Culture, Vice - Chairman and Honorary Chairman of the China Photographers Association; and Committee Member of the National Literary and Artistic Federation.

Mr. Wu Yinxian was the same age as the twentieth century, and he participated in and recorded many of the great historical events in the history of the Chinese Revolution. He used the film cameras and cameras at hand and, standing in the current of his era and of history, he faithfully recorded the great moments of the Chinese Democratic Revolution, the Socialist Revolution, and the periods of Construction and of Reform and Opening. In a career that spanned seventy years in the art of film and photography, he took tens of thousands of black - and - white and color photographs, shot seven feature films and five documentaries, and achieved national film prizes the Hundred Flowers Award and the Best Cinematography Award. He edited more than twenty monographs on the art of photography and held close to twenty solo photography exhibitions.

Personal photography exhibitions

1935	Exhibited 56 works in Shanghai Youth Association
1961	Works exhibited in the National Art Museum of China in Beijing, then toured to seven provinces and cities
1985	Sixty Years of Wu Yinxian's Photography Exhibition in the National Art Museum of China in Beijing, exhibited 310 works, then toured to more than 20 provinces, cities and regions
1988	Exhibited 43 works in New York International Center of Photography, the name of the Exhibition: Yan'an - The Birth Place of New China
	Exhibited 81 works in the 19th Les Rencontres d'Arles in Arles, France
	Exhibited 121 works in Retrospective Exhibition of Wu Yinxian's Photography in the 2nd Shanghai International Photography Exhibition
1989	Retrospective Exhibition of Wu Yinxian's Photography was exhibited in Urumqi, Xinjiang Province
1991	69 works were exhibited in Exhibition of Wu Yinxian's Photography during the Anti - Japanese War in the Memorial Museum of Chinese People's Anti - Japanese War
	62 works were exhibited in Sao Paulo and Rio de Janeiro, Brazil
	80 works were exhibited in Wu Yingxian Photography Work Exhibition in Tongliao, Inner Mogolia
1992	160 works were exhibited in Wu Yingxian Photography Work Exhibition in the Photography Building in Shenzhen
	165 works were exhibited in the Exhibition of Wu Yingxian's Photography Work and Cameras in Beijing during the 2nd Photography Festival of China
	12 works were exhibited in the Associated Exhibition of 20 Famous Chinese and Japanese Photographers in order to celebrate the 20th anniversary of the normalization of relations between China and Japan
1993	90 works were exhibited in Wu Yingxian Photography Work Exhibition in Villa Museum, Switzerland
1997	Retrospective Exhibition of Wu Yinxian's Photography was held in Yanhuang Art Museum in Beijing and showcased his works and more than 200 photos of his life

吴作人
Wu Zuoren
(1908 – 1997)

吴作人生于1908年11月3日，1997年4月9日逝世于北京，江苏省苏州市人。1926年入苏州工业专科学校建筑系，1927年至1930年初先后就读上海艺术大学、南国艺术学院及南京中央大学艺术系，师从著名画家徐悲鸿先生。1930年赴欧洲，先入巴黎高等美术学校，后考入比利时布鲁塞尔王家美术学院巴思天院长画室学习。入学第二年即在全院暑期油画大会考中获金奖和桂冠生荣誉。1935年回国在中央大学艺术系任教。1938年率战地写生团赴前方作画。1942年被教育部聘为终身教授。1943年至1944年，赴陕甘青地区写生，临摹敦煌壁画。1944年至1945年初赴康藏高原，作大量写生画，举行多次展览。1946年随徐悲鸿先生组建北平国立艺专，任教务主任和油画系主任。1950年中央美术学院成立后，一直担任教学和领导工作，曾任中央美术学院教务长、副院长、院长、名誉院长；中国美术家协会副主席、主席。1985年，法国政府文化部授予他"文学艺术最高勋章"。1988年，比利时国王授予他"王冠级荣誉勋章"。

Wu Zuoren was born on 3 November 1908 in Suzhou, Jiangsu Province, and passed away on 9 April 1997 in Beijing. He entered Architecture Department of Suzhou technical institute in 1926 and admitted to the Fine Arts Department of Shanghai Art University in 1927 and to South China Art Academy in 1928. Later he entered the Art Department of National Central University in Nanjing learning from famous painter Xu Beihong. In 1930 went to Europe for further studies with Xu Beihong's recommendation. He has studied in Paris Art College in France and Royal Fine Art Academy in Belgium learning from master Alfred Bastien, and got the "Best Student" award in his second year of Royal Academy. He graduated in 1935 from the Belgium Royal Academy of Fine Arts. After his return, he began to teach at the Central University. He lead a group of artists to create painting on the battlefront in 1938. He was tenured in 1942 by the Culture Ministry. He travelled to Gansu Province and Qinghai Province to imitate the Dunhuang frescoes and create paintings from 1943 to 1944. He went to Tibet creating sketches from 1944 to 1945 and the sketches have been exhibited many times. In 1946, he followed Xu Beihong to organize Peking National Art School, and was appointed professor and Dean of Studies. Since 1950 he had been Dean of Studies, Vice-president, President and Honorary President of the Central Academy of Fine Art; Vice Chairman and Chairman of China Artists' Association. He was awarded "Crown Medal" by the King of Belgium in 1988.

蒋兆和
Jiang Zhaohe
(1904 – 1986)

1904年5月9日生于四川泸州，1986年4月15日于北京逝世。16岁赴上海以画像和从事广告及服装设计为生，业余自修素描、油画和雕塑。后与徐悲鸿结识，受其写实主义主张和改革中国画思想的影响颇深，并受到30年代左翼文艺运动感召，从事进步文艺创作。抗日战争爆发后，投入抗日救亡宣传工作，绘制宣传画和爱国将领肖像。30年代上半叶，辗转于上海、南京、北京、重庆之间，从事美术教育和创作。1943年作《流民图》，高2米，长近20米，全图100余个人物形象，显示了作者宏观上把握矛盾冲突、把握社会现象的构思才能和水墨人物画方面的创造精神。蒋兆和长期从事美术教育，曾在许多院校担任教授，在教学上他致力于中国画教学的改革，其中国画的造型基础课及水墨人物写生课教学原则和实施方案自成体系，颇有影响。曾任中央美术学院教授，中国美术家协会理事、顾问等职。出版有《蒋兆和画集》、《蒋兆和画选》。

Born 9 May 1904 in Luzhou, Sichuan, he passed away on 15 April 1986, Beijing. At the age of 16 he went to Shanghai where he survived by drawing portraits and working in advertising and clothing design. In his spare time, he practiced sketching, oil painting and sculpture on his own. He later got to know Xu Beihong, whose advocacy of realism and ideas on reforming Chinese painting influenced him deeply, and he received the calling to the left - wing literature and art movement of the 1930s, and practiced progressive literary and artistic creation. After the Anti - Japanese War of Resistance broke out, he took part in the Anti - Japanese National Salvation propaganda work, painting propaganda posters and portraits of patriotic generals and leaders. In the first half of the 1930s, he was tossed between Shanghai, Nanking, Beiping and Chongqing, working in art education and creation. In 1943 he painted Refugees, 2 meters tall by 20 meters wide, with more than two hundred images of human figures, showing the artist's ideas on the macroscopic mastery of the contradictions and clashes, and mastery of social phenomena and the creative spirit of ink - and - wash paintings of human figures. For a long time, Jiang Zhaohe was active in art education, and he was a professor at a number of academies and schools. As a teacher, he focused on the reform of Chinese painting, including making his own system on the educational principles and implementation program of basic modeling classes for Chinese traditional painting and ink - and - wash human figure life - drawing classes, which was rather influential. He became professor at the Central Academy of Fine Arts, Director and Counselor of the Chinese Artists Association and also held other positions. Among his publications are: Collected Works by Jiang Zhaohe and Selected Works by Jiang Zhaohe.

靳尚谊
Jin Shangyi

河南焦作人。1953年毕业于中央美术学院绘画系；1957年结业于马克西莫夫油画训练班并留校在版画系教授素描课；1962年调入油画系第一画室任教。曾任中央美术学院院长、中国文联副主席。2003年担任北京国际美术双年展主席，2004年担任第十届全国美展总评委主任。现任中国美术家协会主席、中央美术学院教授。

从1958年起，他的油画作品不断参加全国美术展览，历史画多幅被革命历史博物馆收藏。1980年以后，他作为中央美术学院油画系第一工作室的主任与教授，以自己丰富的经验培养了许多人才，同时以大量肖像作品产生了广泛的社会影响，被评论家称为当代中国油画的代表画家。

主要展览

2005	靳尚谊艺术回顾展，中国美术馆，北京
2000	庆祝澳门回归——中国艺术大展，中国革命博物馆，北京
1999	第九届全国美展，中国美术馆，北京
1997	中国油画肖像百年展，中国美术馆，北京
1996	首届中国油画学会展，中国美术馆，北京
1995	中央美术学院油画系教师作品展，中国美术馆，北京
1994	第二届中国油画展，中国美术馆，北京
1992	第一届中国油画年展，中国香港
1991	深圳美术馆34周年美展，深圳美术馆，深圳
1990	中央美术学院油画雕塑作品展，新加坡
1988	现代中国优秀美术作品展，日本
1987	现代中国油画展，苏联
1986	中国当代油画展，中国美术馆，北京
1984	第六届全国美展，中国美术馆，北京

Born in Jiaozuo, Henan Province. Graduated from the Department of Painting of Central Academy of Fine Art in 1953. In 1957 he finished study in the oil painting courses offered by Konstantin M. Maksimov and stayed in the Department of Print to teach sketch course. In 1962, he was transferred to the No. 1 Studio in the Department of Oil Painting. He used to be the head of Central Academy of Fine Art and the vice-chairman of China Federation of Literature and Art Circles. In 2003, he was the director of the International Fine Art Biennial in Beijing. In 2004, he was the head of judges of the 10th National Art Exhibition. Now he is the chairman of Chinese Artists Association and the professor of Central Academy of Fine Art.

Since 1958, his oil paintings have kept participated in national art exhibitions. Many of his historical paintings are collected by the revolution and history museums. Since 1980, as the head and professor of the No. 1 Studio of the Department of Oil Painting of Central Academy of Fine Art, he has educated many talented people with his rich experiences. Meanwhile, a large amount of his portrait paintings have had broad social influences and he is considered one of the representative oil painters in China by the critics.

Selected Exhibitions

2005	*A Retrospective Art Exhibition of Jin Shangyi*, NAMOC, Beijing
2000	*Celebration of the Return of Macau-Chinese Art Exhibition*, Museum of Chinese Revolution, Beijing
1999	*The 9th National Art Exhibition*, NAMOC, Beijing
1997	*A Hundred Years of Chinese Oil Painting of Portraits*, NAMOC, Beijing
1996	*The 1st Exhibition of China Oil Painting Society*, NAMOC, Beijing
1995	*Works by the Teachers of the Department of Oil Painting of CAFA*, NAMOC, Beijing
1994	*The 2nd Exhibition of Chinese Oil Painting*, NAMOC, Beijing
1992	*The 1st Annual Exhibition of Chinese Oil Painting*, Hong Kong, China
1991	*The Art Exhibition of the 34th Anniversary of Shenzhen Art Museum*, Shenzhen Art Museum, Shenzhen
1990	*The Oil Painting and Sculpture Exhibition of Central Academy of Fine Art*, Singapore
1988	*Excellent Works of Art Exhibition of Modern China*, Japan
1987	*Chinese Modern Oil Painting Exhibition*, Soviet Union
1986	*Chinese Contemporary Oil Painting Exhibition*, NAMOC, Beijing
1984	*Chinese Modern Oil Painting Exhibition*, Nagoya, Japan

陈逸飞
Chen Yifei
(1946 – 2005)

陈逸飞1946年4月14日生于浙江宁波，2005年4月10日逝世于上海，浙江镇海人。1965年毕业于上海美术专科学校，入上海画院油画雕塑创作室，曾任油画组负责人。60-70年代创作了《金训华》《黄河颂》《占领总统府》《踱步》等知名的优秀油画。1980年赴美国，在纽约从事油画创作，曾在华盛顿、纽约、东京等地举办个人展览。其作品被中国美术馆、中国人民革命博物馆和国内外藏家广泛收藏。并先后在纽约国际画展、新英格兰现代艺术中心、史密斯艺术博物馆和布鲁克林博物馆展出。

主要展览

2010	"纪念陈逸飞逝世五周年"系列展，陈逸飞艺术基金会、上海美术馆，上海
2003	陈逸飞个展，蒙特卡罗，摩纳哥
2000	现代雕塑回顾展，皇家花园，巴黎，法国
1999	"跨世纪"个人画展，玛勃洛画廊，英国
1998	陈逸飞个展，法国
1997	威尼斯双年展，意大利
1996	陈逸飞个展，玛勃洛画廊，英国
	陈逸飞回顾展，上海博物馆、中国美术馆
1992	香港国际艺术博览会，中国香港
1990	陈逸飞个展，西武，日本
1985	陈逸飞个展，科克伦艺术博物馆，华盛顿，美国
1983	陈逸飞个展，哈默画廊，纽约，美国

Chen Yifei was born on 14 April 1946 in Ningbo Zhejiang Province his Ancestral Home is Zhenhai Zhejiang Province. He passed away on 10 April 2005 in Shanghai. He graduated from Shanghai Fine Arts Academy in 1965. Chen headed the oil painting studio at the Shanghai Painting Academy. In the 1960s and 1970s Chen painted several iconic masterpieces and received numerous awards. In 1980, Chen moved to New York where he continued working as an oil painter. He had solo shows in Washington DC, New York, Tokyo and Europe. His works are collected by the National Art Museum of China, China People's Revolution Museum and collectors internationally. He had exhibitions at the Hammer Galleries in New York, New England Modern Art Center, Smith College Museum of Art, the Brooklyn Museum, the Solomon R.Guggenheim Museum in New York and Bilbao in Spain.

Selected exhibitions

2010	*Commemoration Exhibition Series of The 5th Anniversary of the Death Of Chen Yifei,* Chen Yifei Art Foundation, Shanghai Museum, Shanghai
2003	*Solo Exhibition of Chen Yifei,* Monte-Carlo, Monaco
2000	*Retrospective Exhibition of Modern Sculpture,* Imperial Garden, Paris, France
1999	*Solo Exhibition "Trans-century",* Marlborough Gallery, Britain
1998	*Solo Exhibition of Chen Yifei,* France
1997	*Venice Biennale,* Italy
1996	*Solo Exhibition of Chen Yifei,* Marlborough Gallery, Britain
	Retrospective Exhibition of Chen Yifei, Shanghai Museum, National Art Museum of China
1992	*Hong Kong International Art Fair,* Hong Kong, China
1990	*Solo Exhibition of Chen Yifei,* Seibu, Japan
1985	*Solo Exhibition of Chen Yifei,* Cochran Art Museum, Washington, USA
1983	*Solo Exhibition of Chen Yifei,* Hammer Gallery, New York, USA

吴冠中
Wu Guanzhong
(1919 – 2010)

吴冠中1919年出生于江苏宜兴，2010年6月25日逝世于北京。1936年入国立杭州艺专习西画，兼学中国画及水彩画。1946年以美术类总分第一的成绩考取"中法交换留学"公费生，赴法国巴黎国立高等美术学院学习油画。1950年归国，曾先后任教于中央美术学院、清华大学营建系、北京师范大学、北京艺术学院、中央工艺美术学院、清华大学美术学院。1991年被法国文化部授予"法国文化艺术最高勋位"。2002年当选为法兰西学院艺术院终生通讯院士。2010年病逝于北京。

主要展览

2007	沧桑入画——吴冠中艺术展，中国美术学院美术馆，杭州
2005	吴冠中艺术回顾展，上海美术馆，上海
2004	情感、创新——吴冠中水墨里程，巴黎联合国教科文组织，巴黎，法国
1999	吴冠中画展，国家文化部，北京
1997	"叛逆的师承——吴冠中"专题展，香港艺术馆，中国香港
1993	走向世界——吴冠中油画水墨速写展，塞纽奇博物馆，巴黎，法国
	吴冠中四十年速写展，斯民艺苑、新加坡文物馆，新加坡
1992	吴冠中：二十世纪的中国画家，大英博物馆，英国
1989	吴冠中画展，中华文化基金会，旧金山，美国
	"吴冠中——一个当代中国艺术家"巡展，美国
1987	吴冠中回顾展，香港艺术中心，中国香港
1983	八十年代中国画展，中国美术家协会，北京
1979	吴冠中绘画作品展，中国美术馆，北京
1978	吴冠中作品展，中央工艺美术学院，北京

Wu Guanzhong was born in 1919 in Yixing, Jiangsu Province and passed away on 25 June 2010 in Beijing. Studied western painting in National Hangzhou Art School since 1936. In 1946, got the qualification as government-supported "exchange student between China and France" with the highest score in fine arts and went to ENSB in Paris, France to study oil painting. In 1950, he returned to China and taught successively in Central Academy of Fine Arts, Tsinghua University, Beijing Normal University, Beijing Art Institute, Central Academy of Art and Design and Academy of Fine Arts in Tsinghua University. In 1991, he was endowed the "highest order in art and culture" by the Department of Culture of France. In 2002, he was elected as the life academician of French Academy of Fine Arts. In 2010, he died of illness in Beijing.

Selected Exhibitions

2007	*Picture of Vicissitudes-Wu Guanzhong Art Exhibition*, Museum of China Academy of Art, Hangzhou
2005	*A Retrospective Exhibition of Wu Guanzhong*, Shanghai Art Museum, Shanghai
2004	*Emotion, Renovation-The Mileage of Wu Guanzhong's Ink and Wash*, UNESCO, Paris, France
1999	*Wu Guanzhong Painting Exhibition*, Department of Culture, Beijing,
1997	*Rebellious Succession of Teachings*, Hong Kong Art Museum, Hong Kong, China
1993	*Open to the World-Ink and Wash Sketches byWu Guanzhong*, Paris, France
	Forty Years of Sketches by Wu Guanzhong, Soobin Art Gallery, Singapore Antique Museum, Singapore
1992	Wu Guanzhong: Chinese Painter of the 20th Century, The British Museum, Britain
1989	Painting Exhibition of Wu Guanzhong, Chinese Culture Foundation, San Francisco, USA
	Wu Guanzhong-A Chinese Contemporary Artist, USA
1987	*A Retrospective Exhibition of Wu Guanzhong*, Hong Kong Art Center, Hong Kong, China
1983	*Chinese Paintings from the 1980s*, Chinese Artist Association, Beijing
1979	*Wu Guanzhong Painting Exhibition*, NAMOC, Beijing
1978	*Works by Wu Guanzhong*, Central Academy of Art and Design, Beijing

孟禄丁
Meng Luding

1962	出生于河北保定
1987	毕业于中央美术学院
1990	就读于德国卡斯鲁赫国立美术学院
	现生活、工作于北京

展览

2010	伟大的天上的抽象，中国美术馆，北京
2009	意派——世纪思维，今日美术馆，北京
	向祖国汇报——新中国美术60年，中国美术馆，北京
2008	意派：中国"抽象"艺术三十年，la Caixa Forum美术馆，巴塞罗那、马德里，西班牙
	孟禄丁艺术展，广东美术馆，广州
2006	1978年以来中国大陆油画，台北市立美术馆，台北
1993	中国油画双年展，中国美术馆，北京
1991	不和塞尚玩牌，亚太艺术博物馆，加里福尼亚，美国
1989	中国现代艺术展，中国美术馆，北京
1988	中国油画人体艺术大展，中国美术馆，北京
1987	第一届中国油画展，上海展览中心，上海
1985	国际青年年美展，中国美术馆，北京

1962	Born in BaoDing, HeiBei Province, China
1987	Graduated from Central Academy of Fine Arts, Beijing, China
1990	Studied in the National Academy of Fine Arts, Karlsruhe, Germany
	Currently lives and works in Beijing, China

Selected Exhibitions

2010	*The Great Celestial Abstraction - Chinese Art in 21st Century*, the National Museum of Fine Arts, Beijing, China
2009	*YiPai - Century Thinking*, Today art Museum, Beijing, China
2008	*Chinese Abstract Art in Last 30 Years*, La Caixa Forum, Barcelona and Madrid, Spain
	Meng Luding Art Exhibition, Guangdong Museum of Art, Guangzhou, China
2006	*The Oil Painting of Mainland China since 1978*, Taipei Fine Arts Museum, Taibei, China
1993	*China Oil Painting Biennial Exhibition*, the National Museum of Art, Beijing, China
1991	*I don't Want to Play Cards with Cezanne*, Pacific Asia Museum, Pasadena, U.S.A
1989	*China / Avant - Garde Art Exhibition*, the National Art Museum, Beijing, China
1988	*Oil Painting Exhibition of Human Body*, the National Museum of Fine Arts, Beijing, China
1987	*The First Chinese Oil Painting Exhibition*, Shanghai Exhibition Center, Shanghai, China
1985	*Exhibition for International Year of Youth*, the National Museum of Art, Beijing, China

张群
Zhang Qun

1962	生于内蒙古包头市
1979	就读于中央美术学院附中
1983	进入中央美术学院油画系第一画室，师从靳尚谊先生，并获得学士学位
1986	作为中国青年艺术家代表团成员访问日本
1987	执教于首都师范大学美术系
1988	获加拿大Elizabeth Greenshield艺术基金会赞助艺术家
1988	作为客座艺术家赴加拿大班芙艺术中心（Banff Centre）
1993	成为加拿大华人艺术家协会理事
	现为自由艺术家

主要作品及展览

2010	9人当代艺术展，青岛美术馆，中国
	北京一号地金螳螂国际艺术中心主题展，北京，中国
2009	建国六十周年优秀作品展，中国美术馆，中国
2007	澳门艺术展，中国澳门
1998	系列作品展示，Co-Art Gallery，加拿大
1997	无声拍卖，The Richmond Art Gallery，加拿大
1996	此地并非彼处，温哥华Art Gallery，温哥华美术馆，加拿大
1995	和田女，中国台湾
1994	美国东西方艺术中心展，洛杉矶，美国
1990	门系列——对流，Woodwords现代艺术展，温哥华，加拿大
1989	门系列——走出，加拿大班芙艺术中心个展，Walter Philips画廊，加拿大
1986	祈祷——肖像系列，中央美术学院学生毕业展，中国
1985	前进中的中国青年画展，中国美术馆，中国
1983	静物，中央美术学院学生作品展，中国

1962	Born in Baotou, Inner Mongolia, China
1979	Studied in the Attached Middle School of Central Academy of Fine Arts, China
1983	Entered the First Studio of the Department of Painting of Central Academy of Fine Arts, learned from Jin Shangyi and got the Bachelor's Degree
1986	Visited Japan as a member of the Delegation of Young Chinese Artists
1987	Taught in the Department of Fine Art of Capital Normal University, China
1988	Won support from Elizabeth Greenshield Art Foundation of Canada
1988	Went to Banff Centre of Canada as guest artist
1993	Became the trustee of Chinese Artist Association of Canada
	Now is freelance artist

Selected Works and Exhibitions

2010	*Nine Artists Contemporary Art Exhibition,* Qing Dao Art Museum, China
	Theme exhibition of Beijing Yihaodi Gold Mantis International Art Center, Beijing, China
2009	*60th Anniversary of the Founding of the P.R.C. Excellent Work Exhibition,* National Art Museum of China
2007	*Macau Art Exhibition,* China Macau
1998	*Series Work Show,* Co - art Gallery, Canada
1997	*Silent Auction,* Richmond Art Gallery, Canada
1996	*Here, not There,* Vancouver Art Gallery, Canada
1995	*Hetian Girl,* China Taiwan
1994	*The American Art Center Exhibition of East and West in Los Angeles,* U.S.A.
1990	*Woodwords Contemporary Art Exhibition,* Vancouver, Canada
1989	*The Solo Exhibition of Banff Centre,* Walter Philips Gallery, Canada
1986	*The Graduation Exhibition of the Students of Central Academy of Fine Arts,* Beijing, China
1985	*The Exhibition of Marching Chinese Youth,* NAMoC, China
1983	*The Work Exhibition of the Students of Central Academy of Fine Arts,* Beijing, China

肖鲁
Xiao Lu

1962	出生于浙江杭州
1984	毕业于北京中央美术学院附中
1988	毕业于杭州浙江美术学院
	现生活、工作于北京

精选个展

2006　开火，Ethan Cohen Fine Arts，纽约，美国

精选群展

2011　红色，10号赞善里画廊，香港
　　　爱与希望，伊比利亚当代艺术中心，北京
　　　回溯与偏移：《体外的心脏》系列展2011·北京，时代美术馆，北京
　　　时代精神，佛罗里达海岸大学画廊，美国
2010　终结水墨画，大象艺术空间，中国台湾
　　　绿色态度：2010后尚北京时装艺术展，三里屯Village，北京
2009　暖冬计划，正阳艺术区，北京
　　　泰康收藏摘要，泰康空间，北京
　　　女人与行为艺术，La Bellone，布鲁塞尔，比利时
　　　城市的女人2009，Stara Elektrarna，卢布尔雅那，斯洛文尼亚
　　　中华人民共和国60周年书画（当代）艺术成果展，北京饭店，北京
　　　看画、听画，斯民国际艺苑，新加坡白兔中国当代艺术收藏首展，白兔美术馆，悉尼，澳大利亚
　　　意派：世纪思维，今日美术馆，北京
　　　还乡，林大艺术中心，北京
　　　反光，西湖美术馆，杭州；墙美术馆，北京
　　　中国现代艺术展―十周年纪念"文献展"，墙美术馆，北京
　　　中国现代艺术展―十周年纪念"七宗罪"展映式，今日美术馆，北京
2008　七宗罪，雁南艺术机构，杭州
　　　中国行动，格罗宁根艺术博物馆，荷兰
2007　抱虎过山，久画廊，北京
　　　长征计划五周年回顾展，长征空间，北京
　　　'85新潮：中国第一次当代艺术运动，尤伦斯当代艺术中心，北京
　　　七宗罪，北京现在画廊，上海
　　　龙的变身：当代摄影展，创意广场，北京；中国广场，纽约
　　　新锐策展人计划：头发的故事，TSI当代艺术中心，北京
　　　中国行为艺术图片，映艺术中心，北京
　　　温普林中国当代艺术档案发布展：王德仁、肖鲁、张念，零空间，北京
　　　长征计划：延安，长征空间，北京
2006　双性社会中性的女性，当代唐人艺术中心，曼谷，泰国
　　　画幅决定态度：首届5×7（平遥）照相双年展，平遥，山西；TSI当代艺术中心，北京
　　　冷能，表画廊，北京
　　　长征计划：延安，抗大宾馆，延安
2005　以身观身：中国行为艺术文献展，澳门艺术博物馆
2004　越界语言2004"音量调节"，时态空间，北京
2003　城市幻觉与感知，季节画廊，新加坡
2002　长征：一个行走中的视觉展示，纽约，美国
1998-2001　缘起：全球观念艺术20世纪50年代至80年代，纽约、波士顿、芝加哥、迈阿密，美国；欧洲
1998-2000　蜕变突破：中国新艺术，纽约、旧金山、西雅图，美国；悉尼，澳大利亚；墨西哥；中国香港
1993　中国当代艺术六人展，YZ空间，澳大利亚
1992　皇帝的新衣，Irving画廊，悉尼，澳大利亚
1991　十二个中国现代艺术家，悉尼大学，澳大利亚
1989　中国现代艺术展，中国美术馆，北京

1962	Born in Hangzhou, China
1984	Graduated from the Subsidiary School of Central Academy of Fine Arts, Beijing, China
1988	Graduated from Zhejiang Academy of Fine Arts, Hangzhou, China
	Currently lives and works in Beijing, China

Selected Solo Exhibition

2006	*Open Fire*, Ethan Cohen Fine Arts, New York, U.S.A

Selected Group Exhibitions

2011	*Red hot*, 10 Chancery Lane Gallery, Hong Kong, China
	Love and hope, Iberia Center for Contemporary Art, Beijing, China
	Heart Outside Body - Exhibition of Oversea Chinese Artists, Times Art Museum, Beijing
	ShiDai JingShen, The Main Gallery of Florida Gulf Coast University, U.S.A
2010	*Back to the essence*, Da Xing Art space, China
	Green Attitude - ARfT Fashion Art Exhibition 2010, Sanlitun Village, Beijing, China
2009	*Warm Winter Programme*, ZhengYang Art zone, Beijing, China
	A Selection of Taikang Art Collection, Taikang Space, Beijing, China
	Women and performance, La Bellone, Bruseel, Belgium
	City of Women 2009, Stara Elektrarna, Ljubljana, Slovenia
	The Art Achievement Exhibition in Commemoration of the 60th Anniversary of the Founding of the People's Republic of China, Grand ballroom of the Beijing Hotel, China
	Art - Look or Listen?, SooBin Art Int'L, Singapore
	The White Rabbit First Collection Show, White Rabbit Gallery, Sydney, Australia
	Yi Pai - Century Thinking, Today Art Museum, Beijing, China
	Coming Home, Linda Gallery, Beijing, China
	Reflective, West Lake Art Museum, Hangzhou; Today Art Museum, Beijing, China
	Twenty - year Anniversary of China ∕ Avant - Garde Exhibition "Documentary Exhibition", Wall Art Museum, Beijing, China
	Twenty - year Anniversary of China ∕ Avant - Garde Exhibition: Seven Sins, Today Art Museum, Beijing, China
2008	*Seven Sins*, Yan Nan Art, Hangzhou, China
	China Action, Groninger Museum, Netherland
2007	*Carrying Tigers Over Mountains*, Permanence Gallery, Beijing, China
	Long March Project 5 Year Retrospective, Long March Space, Beijing, China
	'85 New Wave: The Birth of Chinese Contemporary Art, UCCA, Beijing, China
	Seven Sins, Beijing Art Now Gallery, Shanghai, China
	Dragon's Evolution, China Square, New York, U.S.A
	New Curator Project: The Story of Hair, TSI Contemporary Art Center, Beijing, China
	China's Performance Art photography, Inter Art Center & Gallery, Beijing, China
	Wen Pulin Archive of Chinese Avant - Garde Art: Wang Deren, Xiao Lu, Zhang Nian, Zero Field, Beijing, China
	Long March Project: Yan'an, Long March Space, Beijing, China
2006	*Women in A Society of Double - sexuality*, Tang Contemporary Art, Bangkok, Thailand
	Size Decides Attitude: 1st 5×7 Picture - taking Biennale Project, Pingyao, Shaanxi; TSI Contemporary Art Center, Beijing, China
	Cold Energy, PYO Gallery, Beijing, China
	Long March Project: Yan'an, Yan'an, China
2005	*Inward Gazes - Documentaries of Chinese Performance Arts*, Museu de Arte de Macau, Macau
2004	*Transborder Language 2004 - Volume Control*, The Spaciousness, Beijing, China
2003	*Urban Illusions and Perceptions*, Art Seasons, Singapore
2002	*The Long March: A Working Visual Display*, New York, U.S.A
1998-2001	*Global Conceptualism: Point of Origin, 1950s - 1980s*, New York, Boston, Chicago and Miami, U.S.A; Europe
1998-2000	*Inside Out - New Chinese Art*, New York and San Francisco, U.S.A; Sydney, Australia; Mexico; Hong Kong, China
1993	*Six Contemporary Chinese Artists*, YZ Space, Sydney, Australia
1992	*Emperor New Clothes*, Irving Gallery, Sydney, Australia
1991	*Twelve Contemporary Chinese Artists*, University of Sydney, Sydney, Australia
1989	*China ∕ Avant - Garde Art Exhibition*, National Art Museum of China, Beijing, China

王广义
Wang Guangyi

1957	出生于哈尔滨
1984	毕业于浙江美术学院
	现生活、工作于北京

精选个展

2008	视觉政治学：王广义个展，何香凝美术馆，广东
	冷战美学：王广义，
	L.T.B基金会美术馆，伦敦，英国
2007	王广义，Thaddaeus Ropac 画廊，巴黎，法国
2006	王广义个展，Arario 画廊，首尔，韩国
2004	王广义个展，Urs Meile 画廊，卢塞恩，瑞士
2003	王广义，Enrico Navarra 画廊，巴黎，法国
2001	王广义个展：信仰的面孔，斯尼艺苑，新加坡
1997	王广义个展，立特曼画廊，克劳斯，巴塞尔，瑞士
1994	王广义个展，汉雅轩画廊，中国香港
1993	王广义个展，白拉芙画廊，巴黎，法国

精选群展

2011	纸上美术馆，伊比利亚当代艺术中心，北京
2010	建筑之维：2010年中国当代艺术邀请展，中国美术馆，北京
2009	国家遗产：一项关于国家思想产生的视觉史方案，曼彻斯特大学美术馆，曼彻斯特，英国
	何香凝美术馆OCT当代艺术中心，深圳
2008	中国当代美术二十年，东京国立新美术馆、大阪国立国际美术馆、名古屋爱知县美术馆，日本
2007	'85新潮：第一次中国当代艺术运动，尤伦斯当代艺术中心，北京
2006	展开的现实主义，1978年以来的中国大陆油画，台北市立美术馆，中国台湾
	从"极地"到"铁西区"：东北当代艺术展
	1985-2006，广东美术馆，广州
	麻将：中国当代艺术希克收藏展，汉堡美术馆，汉堡，德国
2005	麻将：中国当代艺术希克收藏展，伯尔尼美术馆，伯尔尼，瑞士
2004	无错误过程，泰康顶层空间，北京
2002	首届广州三年展：重新解读(1990-2000)，广东美术馆，广州
	巴黎-北京：中国当代艺术展，皮尔卡丹文化中心，巴黎，法国
2001	被移植的现场，何香凝美术馆，深圳
	多元城市：亚洲流动艺术展，汉堡美术馆，德国
2000	二十世纪中国油画展，中国美术馆，北京
1999	蜕变与突破：中国新艺术，卡斯蒂利亚当代艺术博物馆，蒙特利，墨西哥
	塔克玛艺术博物馆，西雅图；Henry艺术画廊，华盛顿；旧金山亚洲艺术博物馆，旧金山，美国
1998	中国！现代艺术巡回展，柏林世界文化宫，德国
1997	数字与神话：20世纪艺术回顾展，
	斯图加特国家美术馆，德国
1996	第二届亚太当代艺术三年展，昆士兰美术馆，澳大利亚
1995	亚洲新艺术展，中国、韩国、日本巡展
1994	第二十二届圣保罗双年展，圣保罗，巴西
1993	第四十五届威尼斯国际艺术双年展，威尼斯，意大利
	后八九中国新艺术：来自中国的新艺术，牛津现代艺术博物馆，英国
	后八九中国新艺术：来自中国的新艺术，香港艺术中心，中国香港
1989	中国现代艺术展，中国美术馆，北京

1956	Born in Harbin, Heilongjiang Province, China
1984	Graduated from Zhejiang Academy of Fine Arts, Zhejiang, China
	Currently lives and works in Beijing, China

Selected Solo Exhibitions

2008	*Visual Politics, Solo Exhibition of Wang Guangyi*, He Xiangning Art Museum, Guangdong, China
	Cold War Aesthetics, Wang Guangyi, Institute of Louisse Blouin Foundation, London, U.K
2007	*Wang Guangyi*, Galerie Thaddaeus Ropac, Paris, France
2006	*Wang Guang Yi Solo Exhibition*, Gallery Arario, Seoul, Korea
2004	*Wang Guang Yi Solo Exhibition*, Gallery Urs Meile, Lucerne, Switzerland
2003	*Wang Guang Yi*, Gallery Enrico Navarra, Paris, France
2001	*Wang Guangyi Solo Exhibition*, Face of Faith, Soobin Art Int'L, Singapore
1997	*Wang Guangyi Solo Exhibition*, Gallery Klaus Littmann, Basel
1994	*Wang Guangyi Solo Exhibition*, Hanart TZ Gallery, Hong Kong, China
1993	*Wang Guangyi Solo Exhibition*, Dellet Gallery, Paris, France

Selected Group Exhibitions

2011	*Museum on Paper*, Iberia Center for contemporary Art, China
2010	*The Constructed Dimension, 2010 Chinese Contemporary Art Invitational Exhibition*, National Art Museum of China, Beijing, China
2009	*State Legacy, A Visual History Project On The State Concept*, The Holden Gallery,Manchester, U.K;OCT Contemporary Art Terminal of He Xiangning Art Museum, Shenzhen, China
2008	*Avant - Garde China: Twenty Years of Chinese Contemporary Art*, The National Art Center, Tokyo; The National Museum of Art, Osaka; Aichi Prefectural Museum of Art, Nagoya, Japan
2007	*'85 New Wave - The Birth of Chinese Contemporary Art*, UCCA, Beijing, China
2006	*The Blossoming of Realism*, The Oil Painting of Mainland China Since 1978, Taipei Fine Art Museum, Taiwan, China
	From "The Frigid Zone" to "The Old Industrial Area" , Northeast Contemporary Art Exhibition of China 1985 - 2006, Guangdong Museum of Art, Guangzhou, China
	Mahjong: Contemporary Chinese Art from the Sigg Collection, Hamburger Kunsthalle, Hamburg, Germany
2005	*Mahjong, Contemporary Chinese Art from the Sigg Collection*, Kunstmuseum Bern, Bern, Switzerland
2004	*New Boundaries*, Taikang Top Space, Beijing, China
2002	*The First Guangzhou Trienniale - Reinterpretation: A Decade of Experimental Chinese Art (1990 - 2000)*, Guangdong Museum of Art, Guangzhou, China
	Paris - Pekin, Chinese Contemporary Art Exhibition, Espace Pierre Cardin, Paris, France
2001	*Transplantation in Situ*, He Xiangning Art Museum ,Shenzhen, China
	Polypolis - Art from Asian Pacific Megacities, Hamburger Kunsthaus, Hamburg, Germany
2000	*20th Century Chinese Oil Painting Exhibition*, National Art Ggallery, Beijing, China
1999	*Inside Out, New Chinese Art*, Museo de Art Contemporaneo, Monterrey, Mexico; Tacoma Art Museum, Seattle; The Henry Art Gallery, Washing D.C., San Francisco Museum of Modern Art and The Asian Art Museum of San Francisco, San Francisco, U.S.A
1998	*China! , Touring Exhibition*, Haus der Kulturen der Welt, Berlin, Germany
1997	*Magie der Zahl - In der Kunst des 20 Jahrhunderts*, Staatsgalerie, Stuttgart, Germany
1996	*The Second Asia - Pacific Triennial of Contemporary Art*, Queensland, Australia
1995	*New Asian Art Show: China*, Korea, Japan Touring Exhibition
1994	*22nd International Biennial of Sao Paulo*, Sao Paulo, Brazil
1993	*45th International Art Exhibition Venice Biennale - Cardinal Points of the Arts*, Venice, Italy
	China's New Art, Post-1989, New Art from China, Museum of Modern Art, Oxford, U.K
	China's New Art, Post-1989, Hong Kong Arts Centre and City Hall, Hong Kong, China
1989	*China / Avant - Garde Art Exhibition*, National Art Museum of China, Beijing, China

余友涵
Yu Youhan

1943	出生于上海
1973	毕业于中央工艺美术学院
	现生活、工作于上海

精选个展

2008	新抽象画，上海艺博会，世贸商城，上海
2004	沂蒙山风景，香格纳H空间，上海
1999	啊！我们，香格纳画廊，上海
1998	余友涵，Sonne画廊，柏林，德国
1996	余友涵，Maison de la Chine，巴黎，法国

精选群展

2010	Made in popland，国立当代美术馆，韩国
	改造历史：2000-2009的中国新艺术，特别文献展，国家会议中心，北京
2009	意派：世纪思维——当代艺术展，今日美术馆，北京
	中国项目——三十年：中国当代艺术收藏，昆士兰美术馆，澳大利亚
	麻将：中国当代艺术希克收藏展，Peabody Essex博物馆，马萨诸塞州，美国
2008	墙上的字：中国80、90年代新现实主义和前卫艺术，格罗宁根博物馆，荷兰
	红色之外：中国当代艺术希克收藏展，米罗基金会，塞罗纳，西班牙
2007	85新潮：第一次中国当代艺术运动，尤伦斯当代艺术中心，北京
2006	见证，上海当代艺术名家邀请展，蓝色空间画廊，成都
2005	学而时习，沪申画廊，上海
2004	身体，现代艺术博物馆，马赛，法国
2003	念珠与笔触，北京东京艺术工程，东京画廊，北京
2002	巴黎——北京：中国当代艺术展，皮尔卡丹文化中心，巴黎，法国
2001	上海之星，CASULA艺术中心，悉尼，澳大利亚
2000	"Futuro"：中国当代艺术展，当代艺术中心，澳门
1997	面孔与身体：90年代的中国艺术，鲁道夫美术馆，布拉格，捷克；OTSO美术馆，埃斯波，芬兰
1996	追昔：中国当代绘画展，Fruitmarket画廊，爱丁堡，英国
1995	变化：中国现代艺术展，哥德堡艺术博物馆、云雪平市立美术馆，瑞典
	来自中心的国家：1979年以来的中国前卫艺术展，圣莫尼卡艺术中心，巴塞罗那，西班牙
1994	第二十二届圣保罗双年展，圣保罗，巴西
1993	第四十五届威尼斯国际艺术双年展，威尼斯，意大利
	后89中国新艺术，香港艺术中心，中国香港
1991	物质，北京、南京、重庆
1989	中国现代艺术展，中国美术馆，北京
1988	今天，上海美术馆，上海
1986	上海第一届凹凸展，徐汇区文化馆，上海
	上海美术馆落成展，上海美术馆，上海

1943	Born in Shanghai, China
1973	Graduated from the Central Academy of Art & Design, Beijing, China
	Currently lives and works in Shanghai, China

Selected Solo Exhibitions

2008	*New Abstract Paintings - Yu Youhan Solo Exhibition*, Shanghai Art Fair, Outstanding Artists Section, Booth E21, Art Fairs ShanghaiMART, Shanghai, China
2004	*Yu Youhan, Landscape of Yi Meng Shan*, ShanghART H - Space, Shanghai, China
1999	*Ah! Us*, ShanghART Gallery, Shanghai, China
1998	*Yu Youhan*, Gallery Sonne, Berlin, Germany
1996	*Yu Youhan*, Maison de la Chine, Paris, France

Selected Group Exhibitions

2010	*Made in popland*, National Museum of Contemporary Art, Korea
	Reshaping History: Chinart from 2000 - 2009, Special Documenta, China National Convention Center, Beijing, China
2009	*Yi Pai - Century Thinking A Contemporary Art Exhibition*, Today Art Museum, Beijing, China
	The China Project - Three Decades: The Contemporary Chinese Collection, Queensland Art Gallery, Australia
	Mahjong: Contemporary Chinese Art from the Sigg Collection, Peabody Essex Museum, Salem, Mass, U.S.A
2008	*Writing on the Wall*, Chinese New Realism and Avant - Garde in the Eighties and nineties, The Groninger Museum, Groningen, The Netherlands
	Red Aside, Contemporary Chinese Art from the Sigg Collection, The Joan Miró Foundation, Barcelona, Spain
2007	*'85 New Wave - The Birth of Chinese Contemporary Art*, UCCA, Beijing, China
2006	*Witness*, Blue Dreamland Gallery, Chengdu, China
2005	*Study Practice*, Shanghai Gallery of Art, Shanghai, China
2004	*Chine, le corps partout? (China, the body everywhere?)*, Museum of Contemporary Art, Marseilles, France
2003	*Prayer Beads and Brush Strokes*, Beijing Tokyo Art Projects, Dashanzi, Beijing, China
2002	*Paris - Pekin*, Chinese Contemporary Art Exhibition, Espace Pierre Cardin, Paris, France
2001	*Shanghai Star*, Casula Art Centre, Sydney, Australia
2000	*Future Chinese Contemporary Art*, Contemporary Art Centre, Macau
1997	*Faces and Bodies of the Middle Kingdom, Chinese Art of the 1990'*, Galerie Rudolfinum, Prague, Czech; OTSO Gallery, Espoo, Finland
1996	*Reckoning with the Past, Contemporary Chinese Painting*, Fruitmarket Gallery, Edinburgh, U.K
1995	*Change - Chinese Contemporary Art*, Konsthallen Goetaplatsen, Goeteborg, Sveden
	Des Pais del Centre, Avantguardes Artistiques Xineses, Santa Monica Art Centre, Barcelona, Spain
1994	*22nd International Biennial of Sao Paulo*, Brazil
1993	*45th International Art Exhibition Venice Biennale - Cardinal Points of the Arts*, Venice, Italy
	China's New Art, Post-1989, Hong Kong Arts Centre and City Hall, Hong Kong, China
1991	*Materials*, Beijing, Nanjing, Chongqing, China
1989	*China Avant - Garde Art Exhibition*, National Art Museum of China, Beijing, China
1988	*Today*, Shanghai Art Museum, Shanghai, China
1986	*First Shanghai Concave - Convex Exhibition*, Xuhui Cultural Centre, Shanghai, China
	Inauguration Exhibition of the Shanghai Art Museum, Shanghai Art Museum, Shanghai, China

韩磊
Han Lei

1967	出生于河南开封
1989	毕业于中央工艺美术学院
	现生活、工作于北京

精选个展

2010	照相法：韩磊 + 摄影，玛吉画廊，马德里，西班牙
	间隔：韩磊摄影展，泰康空间，北京
	未雨绸缪：韩磊摄影个展，M97画廊，上海
2009	照相法：韩磊 + 摄影，伊比利亚当代艺术中心，北京
2008	沼泽：韩磊个展，西五画廊，北京
2007	影像复兴：韩磊摄影展，J.Chen画廊，台湾
	韩磊摄影展，汉雅轩，香港
2006	Where is China? 韩磊摄影展，现在画廊，北京
	Pagoda：韩磊摄影展，Loft画廊，巴黎，法国
2005	肖像：韩磊，Polaris画廊，巴黎，法国
	韩磊摄影展，Leda Fletcher画廊，日内瓦，瑞士
2003	陌生：韩磊摄影展，亦安画廊，上海
1997	疏离：韩磊摄影展，北京，中国；柏林，德国；赫尔辛基，芬兰

精选群展

2010	趣味的共同体：2000年以来的中国当代艺术，当代美术馆，圣地亚哥，智利
	摄影劫：中国艺术家在第二届马德里摄影节，伊比利亚当代艺术中心，北京
2009	连州国际摄影节，广东
2008	在瓦伦西亚55天．中国当代艺术展，现代艺术博物馆，瓦伦西亚，西班牙
2007	目测距离：当代中国摄影8人展览，关山月美术馆，深圳
	中国当代艺术展，光州美术馆，光州，韩国
2006	连州国际摄影节，连州
	中国先锋20年，四方美术馆，南京
2005	巴黎摄影博览会，巴黎，法国
	城市：重视——2005广州摄影双年展，广东美术馆，广州
2004	罗马摄影节，罗马，意大利
	旧金山国际摄影博览会，旧金山，美国
2003	神游，泰康顶层空间，北京
	第一届罗马摄影节，罗马，意大利
2002	金色的收获：中国当代艺术，国立当代美术馆，克罗地亚
	面对真实，中国艺术文件仓库，北京
2001	当代中国摄影及录像艺术，前波画廊，纽约，美国
2000	21世纪的城市：西门子文化项目，法兰克福、东京、纽约；德国、日本、美国
1999	心声：当代中国摄影，Cypress画廊、BC空间画廊，美国
1998	铁路与人，Studio画廊、艺术中心，旧金山，美国
1996	来自中国的15个工作室，慕尼黑，德国
1995	布鲁塞尔国际艺术节，布鲁塞尔，比利时
1994	中国当代摄影：大陆、香港、台湾，香港艺术中心，中国香港

1967	Born in Kaifeng, Henan Province, China
1989	Graduated from Central Academy of Craft and Design, Beijing, China.
	Currently lives and works in Beijing, China

Selected Solo Exhibitions

2010	*Han Lei: Ruptura Breakthrough*, Magee Art Gallery, Madrid, Spain
	In Between: Han Lei Solo Exhibition, Taikang Space, Beijing, China
	The Light of Day: Han Lei Solo Exhibition, M97 Gallery, Shanghai, china
2009	*Image Tricks: Han Lei + Photography*, Iberia Center for Contemporary Art ,Beijing, China
2008	*Swamp, Han Lei Solo Exhibition*, C5 Art, Beijing, China
2007	*Renaissance of Photography: Han Lei Photography Exhibition*, Gallery J. Chen, Taiwan, China
	Photography by Han Lei, Hanart TZ Gallery, Hong Kong, China
2006	*Where is China? Han Lei Photography*, Art Now Gallery, Beijing, China
	Pagoda: Han Lei Photography, Gallery LOFT, Paris, France
2005	*Portraits: Han Lei*, Gallery Polaris, Paris, France
	Han Lei Photography, Gallery Leda Fletcher, Geneva, Switzerland
2003	*Strange*, Aura Gallery, Shanghai, China
1997	*Alienation*, Hippolyte Gallery, Helsinki, Finland; Podwell Gallery, Berlin, Germany;
	China Art Archives & Warehouse, Beijing, China

Selected Group Exhibitions

2010	*Community of Tastes, Chinese Contemporary Art Since 2000*, Museo de Arte Contemporaneo, Santiago, Chile
	Kalpastival of Photography, Iberia Center for Contemporary Art, Beijing, China
2009	*Lianzhou International Photo Festival*, Lianzhou, Guangdong, China
2008	*55 Days in Valencia: Chinese Art Meeting*, Instituto Valenciano de Arte Moderno, Valencia, Spain
2007	*Distance Estimated by Eyes Photography of Eight Chinese*, Guan Shanyue Art Museum, Shenzhen, China
	Chinese Contemporary Art Exhibition: The New Wind from China, Gwangju Museum of Art, Gwangju, Korea
2006	*Lianzhou International Photo Festival*, Lianzhou, Guangdong, China
	Chinese Contemporary Photography for 20 Years, Square Gallery of Contemporary Art, Nanjing, China
2005	*Paris Photo*, Paris, France
	Viewing the City, Guangzhou Photo Biennial, Guangdong Museum of Art, Guangzhou, China
2004	*Rome Photography Festival*, Rome, Italy
	San Francisco International Photographic Art Exposition, San Francisco, U.S.A
2003	*Spiritual Tour*, Taikang Top Space, Beijing, China
	Rome Photography Festival, Rome, Italy
2002	*Golden Harvest: Chinese Contemporary Art*, Croatia National, Croatia
	Facing Reality, China Art Archives & Warehouse, Beijing, China
2001	*Disorientation: Photography and Video in China Today*, Chambers Fine Art, New York, U.S.A
2000	*Cities of the 21st Century: Siemens Cultural Program*, Frankfurt, Germany; New York, U.S.A
1999	*A Visible Spirit: Contemporary Photography from the People's Republic of China*, Cypress College Photography Galleries, California, U.S.A.
1998	*Railways and People*, Art Center and Studio Gallery, San Francisco, U.S.A
1996	*China: Aktuelles aus 15 Ateliers*, Reithalle, Munich, Germany
1995	*International Art Festival of Brussels*, Brussels, Belgium
1994	*Contemporary Photography from Mainland China*, Taiwan and Hong Kong, Hong Kong Arts Centre, Hong Kong, China

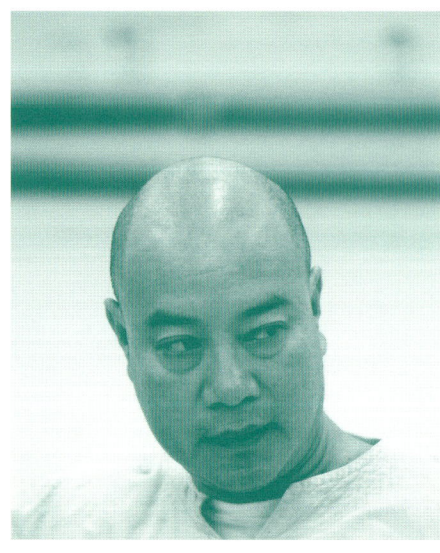

叶永青
Ye Yongqing

1958	出生于云南昆明
1982	毕业于四川美术学院
	现任教于四川美术学院

精选个展

2011	非关鸟事：叶永青画展，形而上画廊，台北，中国台湾
2010	时间的穿行者：叶永青黄桷坪二十年，坦克仓库·重庆当代艺术中心，重庆
2009	画·图：叶永青精品收藏展，寒舍空间，台北，中国台湾
2008	迷涂症：叶永青艺术之旅，香港艺术中心，中国香港
	画鸟：矛盾与现实，纽约中国广场，纽约，美国
2007	画个鸟！，方音空间，北京
	一只忧伤的鸟，Artside画廊，首尔，韩国
2006	单飞，蓝色空间画廊，成都
2005	涂你个鸦，上海张江艺术馆，上海
2001	叶永青，上海香格纳画廊旋宫50，上海
2000	叶永青，中国当代，伦敦，英国
1999	叶永青个展，慕尼黑凯琳萨克斯画廊，德国
1995	生活在历史中，奥格斯堡工作室，德国
1989	叶永青个展，北京法国使馆文化处，北京

精选群展

2011	中国式书写，今日美术馆，北京
2010	改造历史，国家会议中心，北京
2009	布拉格双年展，布拉格，捷克
2008	个案：艺术史中的艺术家，北京圣之空间，北京
2007	从西南出发：当代艺术展，广东美术馆，广州
2006	诗意现实：对江南的再解读，南京南视觉美术馆，南京
2005	未来考古学：第二届中国艺术三年展，南京博物院，南京
2004	妄想的侧面：方力钧、岳敏君、叶永青画展，沪申画廊，上海
2003	开放的时代，中国美术馆，北京
2002	广州艺术三年展，广东美术馆，广州
2001	中国艺术梦，红楼艺术中心，伦敦，英国
2000	二十世纪中国油画大展，中国美术馆，北京
1999	1999中国艺术，Limn画廊，旧金山，美国
1998	新中国艺术，四方观象台画廊，蒙特利尔，加拿大
1997	刘炜、叶永青联展，中央美术学院画廊，北京
1996	首届上海美术双年展，上海美术馆，上海
1995	来自中心之国，莫尼卡美术馆，巴塞罗那，西班牙
1994	中国艺评家年度提名展，中国美术馆，北京
1993	89后中国新艺术展，香港艺术中心，中国香港；现代艺术博物馆，悉尼，澳大利亚
1992	92年中国油画艺术展，民族文化宫，北京
1990	法国现代艺术国际博览会，巴黎大皇宫美术馆，巴黎，法国
1989	现代艺术大展，中国美术馆，北京

1958	Born in Kunming, Yunnan Province, China
1982	Graduated from Sichuan Fine Arts Institute, Chongqing, China
	Currently Professor at Sichuan Fine Arts Institute, China

Selected Solo Exhibitions

2011	*Ye Yongqing Beyond the Bird*, Metaphysical Art Gallery, Taipei, China
2010	*Time Permeants - Ye Yongqing's Art in Huangjueping for Twenty Years*, Tank Loft · Chongqing Comtemporary Art Center, Chongqing, China
2009	*Beyond Graffiti - Ye Yongqing Solo Exhibition*, My Humble House Art Gallery, Taipei, China
2008	*As Free As a Bird*, Hong Kong Arts Centre, Hongkong, China
	Paint a Bird: Paradox and Reality, China Square Gallery, New York, U.S.A
2007	*To Paint a Bird!*, Fun Art Space, Beijing, China
	A Wounded Bird, Gallery Artside, Seoul, Korea
2006	*Solo Flight*, Blues Dreamland Gallery, Chengdu, China
2005	*Scribble*, Shanghai Zhangjiang Art Museum, Shanghai, China
2001	*Ye Yongqing*, ShanghART, Shanghai, China
2000	*Ye Yongqing*, China Contemporary, London, U.K
1999	*Ye Yongqing Solo Exhibition*, Gas Studio, U.K
1995	*To Live in History*, China Art Studio, Augsberg, Germany
1989	*Ye Yongqing*, French Embassy in Beijing, China

Selected Group Exhibitions

2011	*Expression of Chinese Contemporary Art*, Today Art Museum, Beijing, China
2010	*Reshaping History - ChinArt from 2000 to 2009*, CNCC, Beijing, China
2009	*Prague Biennial*, Prague, Czech
2008	*Case Studies of Artists in Art History*, SZ Art Centre, Beijing, China
2007	*Embarking from the Southwest - Contemporary Art Exhibition*, Guangdong Museum of Art, Guangzhou, China
2006	*Poetic Realism: A Reinterpretation of Jiangnan*, RCM Art Museum, Nanjing, China
2005	*Future Archaeology of Chinese Art Triennial*, Nanjing Museum of Art, Nanjing, China
2004	*Ye Yongqing, Fang Lijun and Yue Minjun*, Shanghai Gallery of Art, Shanghai, China
2003	*Opening Era*, National Art Museum of China, Beijing, China
2002	*Guangzhou Triennale*, Guangdong Museum of Art, Guangzhou, China
2001	*The Dream of Chinese Art*, Red Building Art Centre, London, U.K
2000	*Chinese Oil Painting in the 20th Century*, National Art Museum of China, Beijing, China
1999	*Art from China*, LIMN Gallery, San Francisco, U.S.A
1998	*China's New Art Exhibition Observatoire 4ed Montreal*, Montreal, Canada
1997	*Liu Wei and Ye Yongqing*, Gallery of the Central Academy of Fine Arts, Beijing, China
1996	*First Shanghai Art Biennale*, Shanghai Art Museum, Shanghai, China
1995	*Avant - guard Artisiques Xineses*, Santa Monica Art Centre, Barcelona, Spain
1994	*The Annual Exhibition of Works of Artists Nominated by Art Critics*, National Art Museum of China, Beijing, China
1993	*Post 89 New Art from China*, Hong Kong Arts Centre, Hong Kong, China; Museum of Contemporary Art, Sidney, Australia
1992	*China Oil Painting Exhibition*, Beijing Minority Cultural Palace, China
1990	*French Modern Art Expo*, Grand Palace Fine Arts Museum, Paris, France
1989	*China Avant - guard*, National Art Museum of China, Beijing, China

丁乙
Ding Yi

1962	出生于中国上海
1990	毕业于上海大学美术学院
1983	毕业于上海市工艺美术学校
	现生活、工作于上海

精选个展

2011	丁乙·十示，Waldburger 画廊，布鲁塞尔
2010	《丁乙·荧光色》——新画册发布酒会，上海民生现代美术馆，上海
2008	十示 1989-2007：丁乙个展，博洛尼亚当代美术馆，博洛尼亚，意大利
2007	丁乙，KARSTEN GREVE 画廊，巴黎，法国
2006	经纬线：丁乙十年回顾展（1996-2006），香格纳 H 空间，上海
2005	丁乙·十示，IKON 美术馆，伯明翰，英国
2004	十示：丁乙作品展，中国艺术文件仓库，北京
2003	丁乙：十示系列，URS MEILE 画廊，卢塞恩，瑞士
2000	丁乙：布上荧光绘画，中国艺术文件仓库，北京
1998	十示 1989-1998：丁乙作品展，国际艺苑美术馆，北京
1997	1997 丁乙作品展，上海美术馆，上海
1996	丁乙，十五·红色，香格纳画廊主空间，上海
1995	丁乙纸本展，GALLERIA DEGLI ARCHI，科米索，意大利
1994	丁乙抽象艺术展，上海美术馆，上海

精选群展

2011	决绝：一个抽象媒体群展，Boers-Li 画廊，北京
2010	事物状态：中比当代艺术展，中国美术馆，北京
2009	麻将：中国当代艺术希克收藏展，Peabody Essex 博物馆，马萨诸塞州，美国
2007	'85 新潮：第一次中国当代艺术运动，尤伦斯当代艺术中心，北京
2006	超设计，第六届上海双年展，上海美术馆，上海
2005	麻将：中国当代艺术希克收藏展，伯尔尼美术馆，伯尔尼，瑞士
2004	无错误过程，泰康顶层空间，北京
2003	念珠与笔触，北京东京艺术工程，北京
2002	首届广州三年展：重新解读，广东美术馆，广州
2001	2001 横滨三年展，横滨，日本
2000	不合作方式，东廊艺术，上海
1999	玛雅双年展，玛雅市艺术中心，玛雅，葡萄牙
1998	每天：第十一届悉尼双年展，悉尼当代艺术博物馆，悉尼，澳大利亚
1997	引号：中国现代绘画展，国家美术馆，新加坡
1996	96 上海美术双年展，上海美术馆，上海
1995	来自中心的国家：1979 年以来的中国前卫艺术展，圣莫尼卡艺术中心，巴塞罗那，西班牙
1994	抽象艺术六人展，汉雅轩画廊，中国香港
1993	第四十五届威尼斯国际艺术双年展，威尼斯，意大利
1991	中国艺术研究文献（资料）展，北京、南京、重庆、东北地区
1989	中国现代艺术展，中国美术馆，北京
1988	今日艺术作品展，上海美术馆，上海
1986	上海第一届凹凸展，上海徐汇区文化馆，上海
1985	现代绘画六人展，复旦大学，上海

1962	Born in Shanghai, China
1990	Graduated from Academy of Fine Arts in Shanghai University, China
1983	Graduated from Shanghai Arts & Crafts Institute, China
	Currently lives and works in Shanghai, China

Selected Solo Exhibitions

2011	*DING YI - Appearance of Crosses*, Galerie Waldburger, Brussels
2010	*Ding Yi Fluorescence - New catalogue release cocktail party*, Minsheng Art Museum, Shanghai, China
2008	*Appearance of Crosses from 1989 - 2007*, Solo Exhibition of Ding Yi, Museo d'Arte Moderna di Bologna, Bologna, Italy
2007	*DING Yi*, Galerie Karsten Greve, Paris, France
2006	*Graticule, Ding Yi's Works from 1989 to 2006*, ShanghART H - Space, Shanghai, China
2005	*Ding Yi, Appearance of Crosses*, Ikon Gallery, Birmingham, U.K
2004	*Crossed Vision, Works by Ding Yi*, China Art Archive & Warehouse, Beijing, China
2003	*DING Yi: Appearance of Crosses*, Galerie Urs Meile, Lucerne, Switzerland
2000	*Ding Yi: Fluorescence Paint on Tartan*, China Art Archive & Warehouse, Beijing, China
1998	*Ding Yi: Crosses '89 - '97*, International Art Palace, Beijing, China
1997	*Ding Yi: Crosses '97*, Shanghai Art Museum, Shanghai, China
1996	*15 x Red, New Works on Paper by DING Yi*, ShanghART Gallery, Shanghai, China
1995	*Ding Yi: Opere su Carta (Paper Works of Ding Yi)*, Galleria Degli Archi, Comiso, Italy
1994	*Exhibition of Ding Yi's Abstract Art Works*, Shanghai Art Museum, Shanghai, China

Selected Group Exhibitions

2011	*Breaking Away, An Abstract Art Exhibition*, Boers - Li Gallery, Beijing, China
2010	*The State of Things*, Contemporary Art from China and Belgium, National Art Museum of China, Beijing, China
2009	*Mahjong: Contemporary Chinese Art from the Sigg Collection*, Peabody Essex Museum, Salem, Mass, U.S.A.
2007	*'85 New Wave - the Birth of Chinese Contemporary Art*, UCCA, Beijing, China
2006	*6th Shanghai Biennale - Hyper Design*, Shanghai Art Museum, Shanghai, China
2005	*Mahjong: Contemporary Chinese Art from the Sigg Collection*, Kunstmuseum Bern, Bern, Switzerland
2004	*New Boundaries*, Taikang Top Space, Beijing, China
2003	*Prayer Beads and Brush Strokes*, Beijing Tokyo Art Projects, Dashanzi, Beijing, China
2002	*The First Guangzhou Trienniale - Reinterpretation: A Decade of Experimental Chinese Art (1990 - 2000)*, Guangdong Museum of Art, Guangzhou, China
2001	*Yokohama 2001: International Triennale of Contemporary Art*, Yokohama, Japan
2000	*Uncooperative Approach (Fuck Off)*, Eastlink Gallery, Shanghai, China
1999	*BM99, Bienal da Maya*, Maya Art Center, Portugal
1998	*Every Day, 11th Biennale of Sydney*, Museum of Contemporary Art etc., Sydney, Australia
1997	*Quotation Marks, Chinese Contemporary Paintings*, National Art Museum, Singapore
1996	*1st Shanghai Biennale*, Shanghai Art Museum, Shanghai, China
1995	*Des Pais del Centre, Avantguardes Artistiques Xineses*, Santa Monica Art Centre, Barcelona, Spain
1994	*Abstract Works by Six Artists*, Hanart TZ Gallery, Hong Kong, China
1993	*45th International Art Exhibition Venice Biennale - Cardinal Points of the Arts*, Venice, Italy
1991	*Documentary Exhibition of China Art Research*, Beijing; Nanjing; Chongqing; Dongbei Area, China
1989	*China / Avant - Garde Art Exhibition*, National Art Museum of China, Beijing, China
1988	*Exhibition of Today's Art*, Shanghai Art Museum, Shanghai, China
1986	*First Shanghai Concave - Convex Exhibition*, Xuhui Cultural Centre, Shanghai, China
1985	*Exhibition of Modern Art by Six Artists*, Fudan University, Shanghai, China

张晓刚
Zhang Xiaogang

1958	出生于云南昆明
1982	毕业于中国四川美术学院
	现生活、工作于北京

精选个展

2010	16:9，今日美术馆，北京
2009	张晓刚：灵魂上的影子，昆士兰美术馆，昆士兰，澳大利亚
	史记，佩斯北京，北京
2008	中国绘画——张晓刚，鲁道夫美术馆，布拉格，捷克
	修正，佩斯威尔斯登画廊，纽约，美国
2007	张晓刚，萨拉·希尔顿美术馆，坦佩雷，芬兰
2006	Home——张晓刚，北京公社，北京
	张晓刚展，东京艺术中心，东京，日本
	失忆与记忆，Artside画廊，首尔，韩国
2005	张晓刚2005，Max Protetch，纽约，美国
2004	时代的脐带——张晓刚绘画，香港艺术中心，中国香港
2003	失忆与记忆，法兰西画廊，巴黎，法国
2000	张晓刚2000，Max Protetch，纽约，美国
1999	同志，法兰西画廊，巴黎，法国
1997	血缘：大家庭1997，中央美术学院画廊，北京

精选群展

2011	溪山清远，亚洲艺术博物馆，旧金山，美国
2010	北京-哈瓦那：新中国当代艺术革命，古巴国家美术馆，哈瓦那，古巴
	改造历史：2000-2009年的中国新艺术，国家会议中心，北京
	云端：亚洲当代艺术大展，索卡艺术中心，北京
	中国当代艺术30年历程：绘画篇(1979-2009)，民生现代美术馆，上海
	面具之下，沃尔索尔新艺术美术馆，英格兰沃尔索尔，英国
	建构之维：2010中国当代艺术邀请展，中国美术馆，北京
	Cafam生活／艺术季·2010，中央美术学院美术馆，北京
2009	十九个游戏，梯级艺术中心，北京
	给马可波罗的礼物，威尼斯国际大学，威尼斯，意大利
	INAMANIA，阿肯当代美术馆，哥本哈根，丹麦
2008	个案：艺术史和艺术批评中的艺术家，圣之空间，北京
	我们的未来：尤伦斯基金会收藏展，尤伦斯当代艺术中心，北京
	前卫中国：中国当代美术二十年，日本国立新美术馆，东京；日本国立国际美术馆，大阪，日本
	墙上的字：中国80、90年代新现实主义和前卫艺术，格罗宁根博物馆，格罗宁根，荷兰
2007	中国：面向现实，维也纳当代艺术博物馆，维也纳，奥地利
	开放的中国艺术，国立俄罗斯博物馆，圣彼得堡，俄罗斯
	从西南出发，广东美术馆，广州
2006	今日中国：中国当代艺术的转世魅影，路德维希美术馆，维也纳，奥地利
	展开的现实主义：1978年以来的中国大陆油画，台北市立美术馆，中国台湾
2005	起飞：OCAT当代艺术典藏展，何香凝美术馆，深圳
2004	第五届上海双年展，上海美术馆，上海
2002	广州三年展，广东美术馆，广州
2001	第三届Mercosul双年展，巴西
2000	"人+间"光州国际当代艺术双年展，光州，韩国
1999	蜕变与突破：中国新艺术，纽约P.S.1当代艺术中心、旧金山现代艺术博物馆，美国
1996	第二届亚太地区当代艺术三年展，昆士兰美术馆，昆士兰，澳大利亚
1995	第四十六届威尼斯双年展，威尼斯，意大利
1994	第二十二届圣保罗双年展，圣保罗，巴西

1958	Born in Kunming, Yunnan Province, China
1982	Graduated from Sichuan Academy of Fine Arts, Chongqing, China
	Currently lives and works in Beijing, China

Selected Solo Exhibitions

2010	*16:9*, Today Art Museum, Beijing, China
2009	*Zhang Xiaogang Shadow in Soul*, Queensland Art Gallery, Queensland, Australia
	The Record, Pace Beijing, Beijing, China
2008	*Chinese Painting, Zhang Xiaogang*, Galleria Rudofinum, Prague, Czech
	Revision, PaceWildenstein, New York, U.S.A
2007	*Zhang Xiaogang*, Sara Hilden Art Museum, Tampere, Finland
2006	*Home: Zhang Xiaogang*, Beijing Commune, Beijing, China
	Zhang Xiaogang Exhibition, The Art Centre Of Tokyo, Japan
	Amnesia and Memory, Artside Gallery, Souel, Korea
2005	*Zhang Xiaogang 2005*, Max Protetch, New York, U.S.A
2004	*Umbilical Cord of History Paintings by Zhang Xiaogang*, Hong Kong Art Center, Hong Kong, China
2003	*Forget and Remember*, Gallery of France, Paris, France
2000	*Zhang Xiaogang 2000*, Gallery of Max Protetch, New York, U.S.A
1999	*Les Camarades*, Gallery of France, Paris, France
1997	*Bloodline: the Big Family 1997*, CAFA Gallery, Beijing, China

Selected Group Exhibitions

2011	*Pure Views*, Asian Art Museum, San Francisco, U.S.A
2010	*Beijing - Havana - Nueva Revolucion del Arte Contemporaneo Chino*, National Art Museum of Cuba, Havana, Cuba
	Reshaping History: China Art from 2000 to 2009, CNCC, Beijing, China
	Clouds - Power of Asian Contemporary Art, Soka Art, Beijing, China
	Thirty Years of Chinese Contemporary Art 1979 - 2009, Minsheng Art Museum, Shanghai, China
	Behind the Mask, New Art Gallery Walsall, England, U.K
	The Constructed Dimension, National Art Museum of China, Beijing, China
	Life Art Festival Contents, Gallery of Central Academy of Fine Art, Beijing, China
2009	*19 Games: A Chinese Contemporary Art Exhibition*, T Art Centre, Beijing, China
	A Gift to Marco Polo, Venice International University, Venice, Italy
	Inamania, Arken Museum of Modern Art, Copenhagen, Denmark
2008	*Case Studies of Artists in Art History and Art Criticism*, SZ Art Centre, Beijing, China
	Our Future: The Guy and Myriam Ullens Foundation Collection, UCCA, Beijing, China
	Avant - Garde China: Twenty Years of Chinese Contemporary Art, Roppongi, Minatoku, Tokyo, Japan
	Writing on the Wall: Chinese New Realism and Avant - Garde in Eighties and Nineties, Groningen, Netherlands
2007	*China Facing Reality*, Museum Modern Kunst Stiftung Ludwing Wien, Vienna, Austria
	From Southeast, Guangdong Museum of Fine Art, Guangzhou, China
2006	*China Now*, SAMMLUNG ESSL Museum, Vienna, Austria
	The Blossoming of Realism - The Oil Painting of Mainland China since 1978, Taipei Fine Arts Museum, Taiwan, China
2005	*Take Off - An Exhibition of the Contemporary Art Collection*, He Xiangning Art Museum and Contemporary Art Terminal, Shenzhen, China
2004	*Shanghai Biennial*, Shaunghai Art Museum, Shanghai, China
2002	*TRIENNIAL of Guangzhou*, GuangDong Art Museum, China
2001	*The Third Mercosul Bienal*, Porto Alegre, Brazil
2000	*Man+SPACE*, Kwangju Biennale 2000, Kwangju, Korea
1999	*Inside Out:New Chinese Art*, P.S.I. Contemporary Art Center New York, Modern Art Museum of San Francisco, U.S.A
1996	*2nd Asia Pacific Triennial of Contemporary Art*, Queensland, Australia
1995	*The 46th Venice Biennial*, Venice, Italy
1994	*Chinese Contemporary Art at Sao Paulo - 22nd International Biennial of Sao Paulo*, Sao Paulo, Brazil

曾梵志
Zeng Fanzhi

1964	出生于湖北武汉
1991	毕业于湖北美术学院
	现生活、工作于北京

精选个展

2010	曾梵志，外滩美术馆，上海
2009	曾梵志：首个美国个展，ACQUAVELLA 画廊，纽约
2008	太平有象：曾梵志，香格纳画廊，北京
2007	理想主义，新加坡美术馆，新加坡
2006	英雄：曾梵志个展-06迈阿密·巴塞尔艺术博览会，美国
2005	曾梵志的绘画，汉雅轩画廊，中国香港
2004	看景——1989-2004，曾梵志的绘画，何香凝美术馆，深圳
2003	我/我们1991-2003曾梵志油画展，上海美术馆，上海
2001	面具之后，香格纳画廊主空间，上海
1998	曾梵志：1993-1998，中央美术学院画廊，北京
1995	曾梵志：假面，汉雅轩画廊，中国香港
1990	曾梵志作品展，湖北省美术院美术馆，武汉

精选群展

2011	聚变·当代艺术展，艺元空间，武汉
2010	中国当代艺术三十年，民生现代美术馆，上海
2009	第53届威尼斯双年展：制造世界，La Biennale，威尼斯，意大利
2008	我们的未来：尤伦斯基金会收藏展，尤伦斯基金会，北京
2007	第二届美术文献展，湖北省艺术馆，武汉
2006	恒动：当代艺术对话，上海当代艺术馆，上海
2005	麻将：希克的当代艺术收藏展，伯尔尼美术馆，伯尔尼，瑞士
2004	无错误过程，泰康顶层空间，北京
2003	画廊邀请展，上海美术馆，上海
2002	巴黎-北京：中国当代艺术展，皮尔卡丹文化中心，巴黎，法国
2001	新形象：中国当代绘画二十年大型巡回展，中国美术馆，北京；上海美术馆，上海；广东美术馆，广州；四川省美术馆，成都
2000	Futuro：中国当代艺术展，澳门当代艺术中心，澳门
1998	中国当代艺术，Nikolaus Sonne Fine Arts，柏林，德国
1997	引号：中国现代绘画展，国家美术馆，新加坡
1996	中国！现代艺术展巡回展，波恩当代艺术博物馆，德国
1995	从国家意识形态出走：中国新艺术，国际文化中心，汉堡，德国
1994	中国批评家提名，中国美术馆，北京
1993	后八九中国新艺术，香港艺术中心，中国香港
1992	九十年代中国美术[油画]双年展，广州

1964	Born in Wuhan, Hubei Province, China
1991	Graduated from Hubei Academy of Fine Arts, China
	Currently lives and works in Beijing, China

Selected Solo Exhibitions

2010	*Zeng Fanzhi*, Shanghai Rockbund Art Museum, Shanghai, China
2009	*Zeng Fanzhi*, Acquavella Gallery, New York, U.S.A
2008	*Tai Ping You Xiang, Zeng Fanzhi solo exhibition*, ShanghART Gallery, Beijing, China
2007	*Zeng Fanzhi Idealism*, National Art Museum, Singapore
2006	*Hero, Zeng Fanzhi solo exhibition*, Art Basel Miami 06, Miami, U.S.A
2005	*Paintings by Zeng Fanzhi*, Hanart TZ Gallery, Hong Kong, China
2004	*Scapes 1989 - 2004, the Paintings of Zeng Fanzhi*, He Xiangning Art Museum, Shenzhen, China
2003	*I / We, 1991 - 2003, The Painting of Zeng Fanzhi*, Shanghai Art Museum, Shanghai, China
2001	*Raw Beneath the Mask*, ShanghART Gallery, Shanghai, China
1998	*Zeng Fanzhi Works 1993 - 1998*, CAFA Gallery, Beijing, China
1995	*Behind the Mask*, Hanart TZ Gallery, Hong Kong, China
1990	*Zeng Fanzhi*, Hubei Institute of Fine Arts Gallery, Wuhan, China

Selected Group Exhibitions

2011	*Fusion · Contemporary Art Exhibition*, Yiyuan Space, Wuhan, China
2010	*Thirty Years of Chinese Contemporary Art*, Minsheng Art Museum, Shanghai, China
2009	*53rd Venice Biennial, Making World*, La Biennale, Venice, Italy
2008	*Our Future, The Guy & Myriam Ullens Foundation Collection*, Ullens Foundation, Beijing, China
2007	*Wuhan 2nd Documentary Exhibition of Fine Arts*, Hubei Museum of Art, Wuhan, China
2006	*Art in Motion*, MoCA, Shanghai, China
2005	*Mahjong, Contemporary Chinese Art from the Sigg Collection*, Kunstmuseum Bern, Bern, Switzerland
2004	*New Boundaries*, Taikang Top Space, Beijing, China
2003	*Invitational Gallery Exhibition*, Shanghai Art Museum, Shanghai, China
2002	*Paris - Pekin, Chinese Contemporary Art Exhibition*, Espace Pierre Cardin, Paris, France
2001	*Towards a New Image, Twenty Years of Chinese Contemporary Painting*, The National Art Museum of China, Beijing; Shanghai Art Museum, Shanghai; Guangdong Art Museum, Guangzhou; Sichuan Modern Art Museum, Chengdu, China
2000	*Futuro Chinese Contemporary Art*, Contemporary Art Centre, Macau
1998	*Chinese Contemporary Art*, Nikolaus Sonne Fine Arts, Berlin
1997	*Quotation Marks, Chinese Contemporary Paintings*, National Art Museum, Singapore
1996	*China!, Touring Exhibition*, Kunstmuseum Bonn, Germany
1995	*Beyond Ideology: New Art from China*, Haus der Kulturen der Welt, Hamburg, Germany
1994	*Exhibition of Works Selected By Art Critics*, China Art Gallery, Beijing, China
1993	*China's New Art, Post-1989*, Hong Kong Arts Centre and City Hall, Hong Kong, China
1992	*Guangzhou Biennial, Oil Painting of the Nineties*, Convention Centre, Guangzhou, China

李山
Li Shan

1942	出生黑龙江兰西
1963	毕业于黑龙江大学
1964	就读于上海戏剧学院
	现生活、工作于上海

精选个展

2007	南瓜计划：李山、张平杰生物艺术作品展，香格纳画廊，上海
	人类的进化已到尽头：李山之阅读，李山个展，香格纳H空间，上海
2006	阅读：2003-2005照片，香格纳H空间，上海
2004	李山近期小作品展，香格纳画廊，上海
2002	阅读：李山新作品展，香格纳画廊主空间，上海
2001	李山：子非鱼，顶层画廊，上海
1990	个展，上海戏剧学院，上海

精选群展

2010	Made in popland，国立当代美术馆，韩国
2009	意派：世纪思维——当代艺术展，今日美术馆，北京
2008	2008法国国际当代艺术博览会，巴黎大皇宫，巴黎
2007	85新潮：第一次中国当代艺术运动，尤伦斯当代艺术中心，北京
2006	虚拟的爱，上海当代艺术馆，上海
2005	墙：中国当代艺术二十年展，奥尔布莱特·诺克斯美术馆、纽约州立大学布法罗分校美术馆，纽约，美国；中华世纪坛艺术馆，北京
2003	打开天空：多伦当代美术馆开幕展，上海多伦现代美术馆，上海
2002	首届广州三年展：重新解读，广东美术馆，广州
2001	上海之星，Casula艺术中心，悉尼，澳大利亚
2000	"Futuro"：中国当代艺术展，澳门当代艺术中心，澳门
1998	蜕变与突破：来自中国大陆、香港、台湾的新艺术展，亚洲协会美术馆、纽约P.S.1当代艺术中心、旧金山当代艺术博物馆、TACOMA美术馆、亨利美术馆，美国；蒙特雷当代美术馆，墨西哥；香港艺术馆，中国香港
1997	面孔与身体：90年代的中国艺术，鲁道夫美术馆，布拉格，捷克；OTSO美术馆，埃斯波，芬兰
1995	来自中心的国家：1979年以来的中国前卫艺术展，圣莫尼卡艺术中心，巴塞罗那，西班牙
1994	第二十二届圣保罗双年展，圣保罗，巴西
1993	第四十五届威尼斯国际艺术双年展，威尼斯，意大利
	后八九中国新艺术，香港艺术中心，中国香港
1992	相遇：第九届卡塞尔文献展外围艺术展，卡塞尔，德国
1989	中国现代艺术展，中国美术馆，北京
1988	上海第二届凹凸展：最后的晚餐，上海美术馆，上海
1987	转变中：来自上海的现代绘画，香港艺术中心，中国香港
1986	上海第一届凹凸展，上海徐汇区文化馆，上海
	上海美术馆落成展，上海美术馆，上海
1983	83阶段：绘画实验展览，复旦大学，上海
1982	描绘中国梦：改革后中国艺术30年，北安普顿史密斯女子学院、波士顿市政厅、纽约布鲁克林博物馆，美国

1942	Born in Lanxi, Heilongjiang Province, China
1963	Graduated from Heilongjiang University, China
1964	Graduated from Shanghai Theater Academy, China
	Currently lives and works in Shanghai, China

Selected Solo Exhibitions

2007	*The Pumpkin Project, Li Shan & Zhang Pingjie Bio - Art Exhibition*, ShanghART Gallery, Shanghai, China
	Li Shan, ShanghART H - Space, Shanghai, China
2006	*Reading, Photoworks 2003 - 2005*, ShanghART H - Space, Shanghai, China
2004	*Li Shan - Small New Works*, ShanghART Gallery, Shanghai, China
2002	*Reading, the New Works by Li Shan*, ShanghART Gallery, Shanghai, China
2001	*Li Shan: Thou Are Not the Fish*, A Room with a View, Shanghai, China
1990	*Solo Exhibition*, Shanghai Theater Academy, Shanghai, China

Selected Group Exhibitions

2010	*Made in popland*, National Museum of Contemporary art, Korea
2009	*Yi Pai - Century Thinking A Contemporary Art Exhibition*, Today Art Museum, Beijing, China
2008	*FIAC 2008*, Booth B12, Art Fairs Grand Palais, Paris, France
2007	*'85 New Wave - The Birth of Chinese Contemporary Art*, UCCA, Beijing, China
2006	*Fiction@Love / Forever Young Land*, the Museum of Contemporary Art, Shanghai, China
2005	*The Wall - Reshaping Contemporary Chinese Art*, UB Art Gallery, UB Anderson Gallery and Albrigh - Knox Art Gallery, University at Buffalo Art Galleries, Buffalo, New York, U.S.A; Millennium Art Museum, Beijing, China
2003	*Open Sky - Grand Opening of Shanghai Duolun Museum of Modern Art*, Duolun Museum of Modern Art, Shanghai, China
2002	*The First Guangzhou Triennale - Reinterpretation: A Decade of Experimental Chinese Art (1990 - 2000)*, Guangdong Museum of Art, Guangzhou, China
2001	*Shanghai Star*, Casula Art Centre, Sydney, Australia
2000	*Futuro Chinese Contemporary Art*, Contemporary Art Centre, Macau, China
1998	*Inside Out, New Chinese Art, Exhibition of Art from China*, Taiwan and Hong Kong, Asia Society Galleries; PS1, New York; SFMoMA / Asian Art Galleries, San Francisco; Museo de Arte Contemporaneo, Monterrey, Mexico; Tacoma Art Museum and the Henry Art Gallery, Seattle, U.S.A; Hong Kong Museum of Art, Hong Kong, China
1997	*Faces and Bodies of the Middle Kingdom, Chinese Art of the 1990'*, Galerie Rudolfinum, Prague, Czech; OTSO Gallery, Espoo, Finland
1995	*Des Pais del Centre, Avantguardes Artistiques Xineses*, Santa Monica Art Centre, Barcelona, Spain
1994	*22nd International Biennial of Sao Paulo*, Brazil
1993	*45th International Art Exhibition Venice Biennale - Cardinal Points of the Arts*, Venice, Italy *Chinese Art: Post-1989*, Marlborough Gallery, London, U.K
1992	*Encountering the Others - Projektgruppe Stoffwechsel*, Dokumenta Kassel, Kassel, Germany
1989	*China / Avant - Garde Art Exhibition*, National Art Museum of China, Beijing, China
1988	*Second Concave - Convex Installation Exhibition*, the Last Supper, Shanghai Art Museum, China
1987	*A State of Transition, Contemporary Painting from Shanghai*, Asian Fine Arts at the Hong Kong Arts Centre, Hong Kong, China
1986	*First Shanghai Concave - Convex Exhibition*, Xuhui Cultural Centre, Shanghai, China Inauguration Exhibition of the Shanghai Art Museum, Shanghai Art Museum, Shanghai, China
1983	*Art and Experiment of 83 (Stage'83: Paintings Experiments)*, Fudan University, Shanghai, China
1982	*Painting the Chinese Dream, Chinese Art 30 Years after the Revolution*, Smith College, Boston City Hall, Brooklyn Museum, U.S.A

张大力
Zhang Dali

1963	出生于黑龙江哈尔滨
1987	毕业于北京中央工艺美术学院
	现生活、工作于北京

精选个展

2011	新口号，艺莱·克莱因画廊，纽约，美国
2010	第二历史，广东美术馆，广州
2009	无所不在，何香凝美术馆，深圳
2008	口号，Kiang画廊，亚特兰大，美国
2007	种族，中国当代画廊，纽约，美国
2006	第二历史，Walsh Gallery，芝加哥，美国
2005	升华：中国历史图片档案，北京公社，北京
2004	张大力新作展，中国当代艺术画廊，伦敦，英国
2003	AK-47，特拉盖托画廊，威尼斯，意大利
2002	头条，中国当代艺术画廊，伦敦，英国
2000	AK-47，四合苑画廊，北京
1999	对话与拆，四合苑画廊，北京
	对话，中国当代艺术画廊，伦敦，英国
1994	革命与暴力，5号画廊，波伦尼亚，意大利
1993	张大力水墨作品展，5号画廊，波伦尼亚，意大利
1989	张大力水墨画展，中央美术学院画廊，北京

精选群展

2011	第五十四届威尼斯双年展，丹麦馆，威尼斯，意大利
2010	原始拷贝：1839年至今的雕塑摄影，现代艺术美术馆，纽约，美国
2009	历史的图像：中国当代艺术邀请展，深圳美术馆，深圳
2008	重新看亚洲，世界文化宫，柏林，德国
2007	现在中国，CoBrA现代美术馆，阿姆斯特丹，荷兰
2006	第六届光州双年展，光州，韩国
2005	来自中国的新摄影和录像，维多利亚和阿尔伯特美术馆，伦敦，英国
2004	过去与未来之间：中国当代摄影展，国际摄影中心，纽约，美国
2003	罗马国际摄影节：中国艺术联展，Arte del Borghetto画廊，罗马，意大利
2002	第一届广州三年展，广东美术馆，广州
2001	中国当代摄影展，摄影美术馆，赫尔辛基，芬兰
2000	不合作方式，东廊，上海
1999	中国摄影展，巴尔德学院，纽约，美国
1998	第十一届塔林三年展，塔林，爱沙尼亚
1997	W^2+Z^2：多媒体幻灯展，中央美术学院画廊，北京
1995	地球的组成，歌德学院，都灵，意大利
1993	腐化艺术，纳维勒文化空间画廊，波伦尼亚，意大利
1992	中国艺术家联展，印章画廊，帕都瓦，意大利
1991	纸上作品展，城市画廊，费拉拉，意大利
1989	北京现代艺术沙龙：水墨画展，首都博物馆（孔庙），北京
1987	三人画展，中山公园兰花室，北京

1963	Born in Harbin, Heilongjiang Province, China
1987	Graduated from National Academy of Fine Arts and Design, China
	Currently lives and works in Beijing, China

Selected Solo Exhibitions

2011	*New Slogan*, Eli Klein Fine Art, New York, U.S.A
2010	*The Second History*, Guangdong Museum of Art, Guangzhou, China
2009	*Pervasion*, He Xiangning Art Museum, Shenzhen, China
2008	*Slogans*, Kiang Gallery, Atlanta, U.S.A
2007	*Chinese Offspring*, Chinese Contemporary Gallery, New York, U.S.A
2006	*Zhang Dali: A Second History*, Walsh Gallery, Chicago, U.S.A
2005	*Sublimation*, Beijing Commune Gallery, Beijing, China
2004	*New Works by Zhang Dali*, Chinese Contemporary Gallery, London, U.K
2003	*AK - 47*, Galleria Il Traghetto, Venice, Italy,
2002	*Headlines*, Chinese Contemporary Gallery, London, U.K
2000	*AK - 47*, The Courtyard Gallery, Beijing, China
1999	*Dialogue and Demolition*, The Courtyard Gallery, Beijing, China
	Dialogue, Chinese Contemporary Gallery, London, U.K
1994	*Rivoluzione e Violenza*, Galleria Studio 5, Bologna, Italy
1993	*Zhang Dali: Pitture a Inchiostro*, Galleria Studio 5, Bologna, Italy
1989	*Wash Painting Exhibition by Zhang Dali*, Gallery of the National Academy of Fine Arts, Beijing, China

Selected Group Exhibitions

2011	*Speech Matters, 54th Biennale of Venice*, Denmark Pavilion, Venice, Italy
2010	*The Original Copy: Photography of Sculpture, 1839 to Today*,
	The Museum of Modern Art, New York, U.S.A
2009	*Images from History*, Shenzhen Art Museum, Shenzhen, China
2008	*Re - imagining Asia*, House of World Cultures, Berlin, Germany
2007	*China Now*, CoBrA Museum of Modern Art, Amsterdam, Netherlands
2006	*Gwangju Biennnale 6th Edition Fever Variations*, Gwangju, Korea
2005	*New Photography and Video from China*, Victoria and Albert Museum, London, U.K
2004	*Between Past and Future*, ICP, New York, U.S.A
2003	*Festival Internazionale di Roma, L'Officina - Arte del Borghetto*, Rome, Italy
2002	*The First Guangzhou Triennial*, Guangdong Museum of Art, Guangzhou, China
2001	*Contemporary Chinese Photography*, Finland Museum of Photography, Helsinki, Finland
2000	*Fuck Off*, Eastlink Gallery, Shanghai, China
1999	*Chinese Contemporary Photography*, Bard College, New York, U.S.A
1998	*11th Tallinn Triennial*, Tallinn, Estonia
1997	*W² + Z², Multi - media and video Exhibition*,
	Gallery of the Central Academy of Fine Arts, Beijing, China
1995	*La Formazione della Terra*, Goethe Institute Gallery, Torino, Italy
1993	*Arte Deperibile*, Spazio Cultura Navile, Bologna, Italy
1992	*Collettiva di Artisti Cinesi*, Il Sigillo Gallery, Padova, Italy
1991	*Pittura su Carta*, Galleria Comunale, Ferrara, Italy
1989	*Wash Paiting Salon in Peking*, Capital Museum (Confucius Temple), Beijing, China
1987	*Three Men Show*, Sun Yat - sen Park, Beijing, China

方力钧
Fang Lijun

1963	生于河北邯郸
1989	毕业于中央美术学院
	现生活、工作于北京

精选个展

2011	编年记事：方力钧文献展，西安建筑科技大学建筑学院，西安
2010	方力钧，今日美术馆，北京
2009	生命之渺：方力钧创作25年展＆像野狗一样生活：1963-2008方力钧文献档案展，台北市立美术馆，中国台湾
2008	方力钧，鲁道夫美术馆，布拉格，捷克
2007	方力钧个人作品展，上海美术馆，上海
2006	方力钧：版画与素描，Kupferstichkabinett美术馆，柏林，德国
2004	方力钧，Prüss & Ochs 画廊，柏林，德国
2002	北京和大理之间，Ludwig Forum Für Internationale Kunst Aachen，德国
2001	方力钧，亚洲当代艺术，柏林，德国
2000	方力钧作品展，斯民艺苑，新加坡
1998	方力钧作品展，阿姆斯特丹城市博物馆，阿姆斯特丹，荷兰
	方力钧作品展，Max Protetch 画廊，纽约，美国
1996	方力钧作品展，日本基金会，东京，日本
1995	方力钧作品展，Bellefroir 画廊，巴黎

精选群展

2011	未来通行证：2011年威尼斯双年展平行专题展，Abbey of San Gregorio，Palazzo Mangilli - Valmarana，威尼斯，意大利
2010	建构之维：2010年中国当代艺术邀请展，中国美术馆，北京
2009	见微知著，威尼斯双年展中国馆，威尼斯，意大利
2008	前卫·中国：中国当代艺术二十年展，国立国际美术馆，大阪，日本
2007	后解严与后八九：两岸当代艺术对照，国立台湾美术馆，中国台湾
2006	变种：华人当代艺术的双轨衍变，台北美术馆，中国台湾
2005	第二届中国当代艺术三年展，南京博物院，南京
2004	身体中国，奥赛现代艺术博物馆，马赛，法国
2003	Alors, la Chine，蓬皮杜中心，巴黎，法国
2002	广州当代艺术三年展，广东美术馆，广州
	方力钧／约尔格·伊门道夫，上海现代画廊，上海
2001	Mercsul双年展，Mercsul，巴西
2000	当代中国肖像，法郎索瓦·密特朗文化中心，法国
1999	开放的边界，第四十八届威尼斯双年展，威尼斯，意大利
1998	透视：中国新艺术，亚洲社会博物馆，纽约，美国
1997	光州双年展，光州，韩国
1996	与中国对话，路得维希广场，亚琛，德国
1995	幸福幻想，日本基金会，东京，日本
1994	圣保罗双年展，圣保罗，巴西
1993	东方之路，威尼斯双年展，意大利
1992	中国新艺术展，悉尼新南威尔士美术馆、布里斯班昆士兰美术馆、巴拉瑞特市立美术馆、堪培拉艺术学校美术馆，澳大利亚
1991	方力钧＆刘炜作品展，北京
1989	中国现代艺术展，中国美术馆，北京
1984	第六届全国美术展，广州

1963	Bone in Handan, Hebei Province, China
1989	Graduated at from Central Academy of Fine Arts, Beijing, China
	Currently lives and works in Beijing, China

Selected Solo Exhibitons

2011	*Chronology - Fang Lijun Documenta*, Xi'an University of Architecture and Technology, Xi'an, China
2010	*Fang Lijun*, Today Art Museum, Beijing, China
2009	*Endlessness of life: 25 Years Retrospect of Fang Lijun, Living Like A Wild Dog 1993 - 2008*, Taipei Fine Art Museum, Taiwan, China
2008	*FANG LIJUN* , Rudolf Art Museum, Prague, Czech
2007	*Fang Lijun Solo Exhibition*, Shanghai Art Museum, Shanghai, China
2006	*Fang Lijun - Holzschnitte und Zeichnungen*, Kupferstichkabinett Staatliche Museum zu Berlin, Berlin, Germany
2004	*Fang Lijun*, Prüss & Ochs Gallery, Berlin, Germany
2002	*Fang Lijun, Between Beijing & Dali, Woodcuts & Paintings 1989 - 2002*, Ludwig Forum für Internationale Kunst Aachen, Germany
2001	*Fang Lijun, New Woodcuts & Paintings*, Prüss & Ochs Gallery, Berlin, Germany
2000	*Fang Lijun*, Soobin Art Gallery, Singapore
1998	*Fang Lijun*, Stedeljik Museum, Amsterdam, Netherlands
	Fang Lijun, Max Protetch Gallery, NYC, U.S.A
1996	*Fang Lijun, Human Images in an Uncertain age*, The Japan Foundation, Tokyo, Japan
1995	*Fang Lijun*, Galerie Bellefroid, Paris, France

Selected Group Exhibitions

2011	*Future Pass Collateral Event of the 54th Venice Biennial*, Abbey of San Gregorio, Palazzo Mangilli - Valmarana, Venice, Italy
2010	*Construction Dimension - 2010 Chinese Contemporary Art Invitation Exhibition*, The National Art Museum of China, Beijing, China
2009	*The Chinese Pavilion at the 53rd International Art Exhibition Venice Biennale See a World in Grain of Sand*, Giardini, Arsenale, Venice, Italy
2008	*Avant-Garde China:Twenty Years of Chinese Contemporary Art*, The National Museum of Art, Osaka, Japan
2007	*Post-Martial Law V.S. Post - '89:The Contemporary Art in Taiwan And China*, National Museum of Fine Arts, Taiwan, China
2006	*Change*, Taipei Museum, Taiwan, China
2005	*China Contemporary Art*, Nanjing Museum, Nanjing, China
2004	*China, The Body Everywhere?*, Museum of Contemporary Art, Musée d'Orsay Marseilles, France
2003	*Alors, la Chine*, Pompidou Center, Paris, France
2002	*Guangzhou Triennial 2002*, Guangdong Museum of Art, Guangzhou, China
	Fang Lijun & Jörg Immendorff, Shanghai Contemporary Albrecht, ochs & Wei, Shanghai, China
2001	*Bienal de Artes*, Visuais do Mercosul, Porto Alegre, Brazil
2000	*Portrait of China Contemporaries*, Espace Culture Francois Mitterand, France
1999	*Aperto, The 48th Venice Bennial*, Venice, Italy
1998	*Inside Out: New Chinese Art*, Asia Society, New York, U.S.A
1997	*The 1st Kwangju Biennial*, Kwangju, Korea
1996	*Begegnungen mit China*, Ludwig Forum. Aachen, Germany
1995	*Visions of Happiness - Ten Asian Contemporary Artists*, The Japan Foundation, Tokyo, Japan
1994	*Chinese Contemporary Art at San Paulo*, 22nd International Biennale of San Paulo, Brazil
1993	*Passagio ad Oriente*, 45th Biennale di Venezia, Italy
1992	*New Art from China / Post - Mao Product*, Art Gallery of New South Sales, Sydney; Queensland Art Gallery, Brisbane; City of Ballarat Fine Art Gallery, Ballarat; Canberra School of Art Gallery, Canberra, Australia
1991	*Fang Lijun and Liu Wei Private Exhibition*, Beijing, China
1989	*China Avant - Garde Art Exhibition*, China Art Gallery, Beijing, China
1984	*6th National Art Exhibition*, Guangzhou, China

刘小东
Liu Xiaodong

1963	出生于辽宁
1988	获中央美术学院油画系学士学位
1999	毕业于康普鲁登塞大学美术学院
	现生活、工作于北京

精选个展

2010	盐官镇：刘小东，Mary Boone画廊，纽约，美国
	金城小子：刘小东个展，尤伦斯当代艺术中心，北京
2009	痕迹：刘小东文献展，角度画廊，北京
2008	青藏高原和北京女孩：刘小东新作，Mary Boone画廊，纽约，美国
2007	生命的富足：中国当代艺术家刘小东影集1984-2006，东8时区，北京
	刘小东2007，诚品画廊，中国台湾
2006	温床：刘小东一张画的项目，唐人画廊，曼谷，泰国
	三峡项目：刘小东作品，亚洲美术馆，旧金山，美国
	刘小东：写生，广东美术馆，广州
2005	儿时的朋友都胖了，Loft画廊，巴黎，法国
2004	金门碉堡艺术展：18个个展，金门碉堡艺术馆，中国台湾
	三峡大移民和三峡新移民，环碧堂画廊、中国艺术文件仓库，北京
2003	生存状态，诚品画廊，中国台湾
2002	刘小东在东海，东海大学艺术中心，中国台湾
2001	刘小东，Loft画廊，巴黎，法国
2000	刘小东1990-2000，中央美术学院美术馆，北京
	刘小东，LIMN画廊，旧金山，美国
1990	刘小东，中央美术学院画廊，北京

精选群展

2011	纸上美术馆：12位华人艺术家，伊比利亚当代艺术中心，北京
2010	巡回排演，第八届上海双年展，上海美术馆，上海
2009	第十届哈瓦那双年展，古巴
2008	中国21世纪，Palazzo delle Esposizioni美术馆，罗马，意大利
2007	中国制造，路易斯安那美术馆，哥本哈根，丹麦
2006	接触地带：2006悉尼双年展，悉尼，澳大利亚
2005	墙：中国当代艺术二十年，中华世纪坛艺术馆，北京
2004	龙族之梦：中国当代艺术展，爱尔兰现代美术馆，爱尔兰
2003	中国怎么样？，蓬皮杜艺术中心，巴黎，法国
2002	广州艺术三年展：中国实验艺术十年(1990-2000)，广东美术馆，广州
2001	中国当代艺术，新加坡美术馆，新加坡
2000	上海、海上：上海双年展，上海美术馆，上海
1997	第四十七届威尼斯双年展，意大利，威尼斯
1994	东西相遇，发现博物馆，康州，美国
1993	后89中国新艺术展，马尔堡画廊，伦敦，英国
1991	二十世纪中国艺术展，中国美术馆，北京
1989	中国现代艺术大展，中国美术馆，北京

1963	Born in Liaoning Province, China
1988	Bachelor of Fine Arts in oil Painting, Central Institute of Fine Arts, Beijing, China
1999	Graduated from Academy of Fine Arts, University of Complutense, Madrid, Spain
	Currently lives and works in Beijing, China

Selected Solo Exhibitions

2010	*Liu Xiaodong: Hometown Boy*, UCCA, Beijing, China
	Liu Xiaodong: Yan'GuanTown, Mary Boone Gallery, New York, U.S.A
2009	*Traces: Liu Xiaodong*, Angle Gallery, Beijing, China
2008	*Qinghai - Tibet Plateau & Beijing Girls: New Paintings by Liu Xiaodong*, Mary Boone Gallery, New York, U.S.A
2007	*Liu Xiaodong 1984 - 2006*, Time Zone 8, Beijing, china
	Liu Xiaodong Solo Exhibition 2007, Eslite Gallery, Taiwan, China
2006	*Hot Bed - A Painting Project by Liu Xiaodong*, Tang gallery, Bangkok, Tailand
	The Three Gorges Project - Painting by Liu Xiaodong, Asian Art Museum of San Francisco, U.S.A
	Liu Xiaodong's new works:Domino, Xin Beijing Gallery, Beijing, China
	Liu Xiaodong:Painting from Life, Art Museum of Guangdong, China
2005	*Childhood Friend Getting Fat*, LOFT Gallery, Paris, France
2004	*Three Gorges: Displaced Population & Three Gorges: Newly Displaced Population*, Chinablue Gallery & CAAW Beijing, China
	Eighteen Soldiers Between Mainland and Taiwan, Bunker Museum of Contemporary Art Jinmen, China Taiwan, China
2003	*Liu Xiao Dong*, Eslite Gallery, Taiwan, China
2002	*Liu Xiao Dong*, Art Center of Donghai University, Taiwan, China
2001	*Liu Xiao Dong*, LOFT Gallery, Paris, France
2000	*Liu Xiaodong 1990 - 2000*, Museum of Central Academy of Fine Arts, Beijing, China
	Liu Xiao Dong and His Time, LIMN Gallery, San Francisco, U.S.A
1990	*Liu Xiao Dong*, Gallery of Central Academy of Fine Arts, Beijing, China

Selected Group Exhibitions

2011	*Museum on Paper: Twelve Chinese Artists*, Iberia, Beijing, China
2010	*Rehearsal, 2010 Shanghai Biennale*, Shanghai Art Museum, Shanghai, China
2009	*10th Havana Biennial*, Cuba
2008	*China 21Century*, Palazzo delle Esposizioni, Roma, Italy
2007	*Made in China*, Israel Museum, Jerusalum, Israel
2006	*Zones of Contact - 2006 Biennale of Sydney*, Sydney, Australia
2005	*The Wall - Reshaping Contemporary Chinese Art*, Millennium Art Museum, Beijing, China
2004	*Dreaming of the Dragon's Nation - Contemporary Art Exhibition from China*, Irish Museum of Modern Art, Irish
2003	*Alors, La Chine?*, Centre Pompidou, Paris, France
2002	*A Decade of Experimental Chinese Art - Guanzhou Triennial*, Art Museum of Guangdong, Guangzhou, China
2001	*China Art Now*, Singapore Art Musuem, Singapore
2000	*Shanghai Spirit*, Shangai Biennial Art Exhibition, Shanghai, China
1997	*47th Venice Biennial Art Exhibition*, Venice, Italy
1994	*Between East and West: Transformation of Chinese Art in the Late 20th Century*, The Discover Museum, CT, U.S.A
1993	*New Art from China: Post 1989*, Marlborough Gallery, London, U.K
1991	*20th Century China*, Art Museum of China, Beijing, China
1989	*Chinese Avant - garde Art Exhibition*, Art Museum of China, Beijing, China

曾浩
Zeng Hao

1963	出生于云南昆明
1989	毕业于北京中央美术学院
	现生活、工作于北京

精选个展

2010	盛夏：曾浩画展，天安时间当代艺术中心，北京
2008	曾浩个展，玛蕊乐画廊，米兰，意大利
2006	环顾：曾浩个展，外滩三号沪申画廊，上海
	曾浩和他的新画，Fredericks&Freiser 画廊，纽约，美国
2005	2005年11月19日下午5点01分：曾浩作品展，何香凝美术馆，深圳
	关系：曾浩个展，第雅画廊，中国台湾
2004	曾浩作品展，Meymac 艺术中心，法国
2003	曾浩作品展，loft 画廊，巴黎，法国
1997	曾浩个展，中央美术学院画廊，北京

精选群展

2010	改造历史 2000-2009 年的中国新艺术，国家会议中心，北京
2009	制造世界：第五十三届威尼斯国际艺术双年展——见微知著，威尼斯，意大利
2007	中国：面对现实，当代美术馆，奥地利
2006	柏拉图和他的七种精灵，何香凝美术馆，深圳
2005	第二届布拉格双年展：第二视角，国家美术馆，布拉格，捷克
2004	无错误过程，泰康顶层空间，北京
2003	新生代后革命，炎黄艺术馆，北京
2002	第二十五届圣保罗双年展，圣保罗，巴西
2001	尘世与天堂之间，PMMK 现代艺术博物馆，比利时
	火锅，奥斯陆现代艺术中心，挪威
	下一代：亚洲当代艺术，德雷斯美术馆，法国
	第一届成都双年展，成都现代艺术馆，成都
2000	社会：上河美术馆第二届学术邀请展，上河美术馆，成都
	皮肤与空间，当代艺术中心，米兰，意大利
1999	瞬间：二十世纪末中国实验艺术展，The David and Alfred Smart 美术馆，芝加哥大学、俄勒冈大学艺术博物馆，美国
	中国 1999，Lmin 画廊，旧金山，美国
1998	迷惑：当代中国绘国和摄影，Canvas World Art & Gallerie Serieuze，阿姆斯特丹，美国
	三张年轻的脸，汉雅轩，香港、台北
	两性平台，泰达当代艺术博物馆，天津
1997	来自15个中国艺术家工作室的作品，巴塞尔，瑞士；东京，日本；慕尼黑，德国
1996	中国现在！巴塞尔，瑞士；东京，日本；慕尼黑，德国
1994	广州美术学院油画系作品双年展，广州美术学院，广州
1992	第二届中国当代艺术文献资料展，广州
	90年代中国艺术油画双年展，中央大酒店展览中心，广州

1963	Born in Kunming, Yunnan Province, China
1989	Graduated from Central Academy of Fine Art, Beijing, China
	Currently Lives and works in Beijing, China

Selected Solo Exhibitions

2010	*Summer: a solo exhibition by Zeng Hao*, Beijing Center for the Arts, Beijing, China
2008	*Zeng Hao Solo Exhibition*, Primo Marella Gallery, Milano, Italy
2006	*Looking Around, Zeng Hao Solo Exhibition*, Shanghai Gallery of Art, Shanghai, China
	Zeng Hao and His New Painting, Fredericks & Fraser Gallery, New York, U.S.A
2005	*5:01 pm, 19.11.2005, Works by Zeng Hao*, He Xiang Ning Art Museum, Shen Zhen, China
	Relations, Zeng Hao Solo exhibition, Robert and Li Art Gallery, Taiwan, China
2004	*Zeng Hao's Works*, Meymac Art Center, France
2003	*Zeng Hao's Works*, Loft Gallery, Paris, France
1997	*Zeng Hao Solo Exhibition*, Gallery of Central Academy of Fine Art, Beijing, China

Selected Group Exhibitions

2010	*Reshaping History, ChinArt from 2000 to 2009*,
	China National Convention Center, Beijing, China
2009	*Making Worlds, 53rd Venice Biennial, What is to come*, Chinese Pavilion, Venice, Italy
2007	*China: Facing Reality*, Museum Modern Kunst Stiftung, Ludwig Wien, Wien, Austria
2006	*Plato and His Seven Spirits*, He Xiang Ning Museum, Shenzhen, China
2005	*Prague Biennale 2*, National Art Museum, Prague, Czech
2004	*New Boundaries*, Taikang Top Space, Beijing, China
2003	*New generation and Post Revolution*, Yanhuang Art Museum, China
2002	*The 25th Sao Paulo Biennial*, Sao Paulo, Brazil
2001	*Between Earth and Heaven*, PMMK Museum of Modern Art, Ostende, Belgium
	Hot Pot, Kunstermes Hus, Oslo, Norway
	Next generation, Art Contemporary D'asie, Passage de Retz, France
	The 1st Chengdu Biennial, Chengdu Contemporary Art Museum, Chengdu, China
2000	*Society, The 2nd Academic Exhibition of the Upriver*, Upriver Museum, Chengdu, China
	Skin and Space, Contemporary Art Center, Milan, Italy
1999	*Transience, Chinese Experimental Art at the End of the Twentieth Century*,
	The David and Alfred Smart Museum of Chicago University, Chicago, U.S.A
	China 1999, Limn Gallery, San Francisco, U.S.A
1998	*Confused:Guess the Future*, Amsterdam, Holland
	Three Young Faces, Hanart TZ Gallery, Hongkong, Taipei, China
	Two Sexual Flat Roof, Taida Contemporary Art Museum, Tianjin, China
1997	*Works from 15 Chinese artists' studio*, Basel, Switzerland; Tokyo, Japan; Munich, Germany
1996	*China Now!*, Basel, Switzerland; Tokyo, Japan; Munich, Germany
1994	*The 2nd Exhibition of Guangzhou Fine Arts Academy Oil Painting Department*,
	Guangzhou Fine Arts Academy, Guangzhou, China
1992	*The 2nd Exhibition of Chinese Contemporary Art Documentation*, Guangzhou, China
	90's Guang Zhou Oil Painting Biennial, Guangzhou, China

蔡国强
Cai Guo-Qiang

1957	生于福建泉州
1985	毕业于上海戏剧学院
	现生活、工作于美国纽约

精选个展

2010	农民达芬奇，外滩美术馆，上海，中国
	地中海游记，当代美术馆，尼斯，法国
2009	我想要相信，古根汉姆美术馆，毕尔巴鄂，西班牙
2008	我想要相信，古根汉姆美术馆，纽约，美国
2007	不合时宜：舞台1，西雅图美术馆，西雅图，美国
2006	蔡国强在屋顶：透明纪念碑，大都会博物馆，纽约，美国
	撞墙，古根海姆美术馆，柏林，德国
2005	黑彩虹，现代美术馆，瓦伦西亚，西班牙
2004	不合时宜，马萨诸塞州当代美术馆，北亚当斯，美国
2003	爆炸事件：中央公园上空的光轮，亚洲协会美术馆，纽约，美国
2002	蔡国强的茶室：向冈仓天心致敬，箱根雕刻之森美术馆，神奈川，日本
2001	水墨写生表演，当代艺术馆与孙中山中国古典园林，温哥华，加拿大
2000	蔡国强，卡地亚当代艺术基金会，巴黎，法国
1999	我是千年虫，维也纳美术馆，维也纳，奥地利
1997	文化大混浴：为20世纪作的计划，皇后美术馆，纽约，美国

精选群展

2010	第十七届悉尼双年展：距离的美，悉尼，澳大利亚
2009	第十届哈瓦那双年展：全球时代的融合与抵抗，哈瓦那，古巴
2008	血在纸上：书的艺术，维多利亚和艾伯特美术馆，伦敦，英国
2007	旅程：测绘中国艺术当中的地与心，大都会博物馆，纽约，美国
2006	从时间出发：典藏中的当代艺术，现代美术馆，纽约，美国
2005	翻译，当代艺术中心东京宫，巴黎，法国
2004	第二十六届圣保罗双年展：自由的领地，圣保罗，巴西
2003	间，蓬皮杜文化艺术中心，巴黎，法国
2002	第三届蒙特利尔双年展，蒙特利尔，加拿大
2001	人类的高原：第四十九届威尼斯双年展，阿森纳卡斯特罗花园，威尼斯，意大利
2000	分享异国情调：第五届里昂双年展，当代美术馆，里昂，法国
1999	全面开放：第四十八届威尼斯双年展，军械库，威尼斯，意大利
1998	创伤：当代艺术中的民主与救赎，现代美术馆，斯德哥尔摩，瑞典
1997	未来、现在、过去：第四十七届威尼斯双年展，阿森纳卡斯特罗花园，威尼斯，意大利
1996	第二十三届圣保罗双年展：普遍性，圣保罗，巴西
1995	超国度文化：第46届威尼斯双年展，洛林广场，威尼斯，意大利
1994	暗黑之心，欧特罗库勒慕勒美术馆，荷兰
1993	沉默的力量，现代美术牛津美术馆，英国
1992	寻找宇宙树：亚洲当代美术之旅，县立现代美术馆，琦玉，日本
1991	非常口：中国前卫艺术展，香椎火车站旧址及三菱地产展览馆，福冈，日本
1990	献给昨天的中国明天，普罗旺斯布利也尔，法国
1989	第十六届国际现代艺术AU展，东京都美术馆，东京，日本
1987	第五十五届日本独立艺术协会纪念展，东京都美术馆，东京，日本
1985	蔡国强与吴红虹：绘画，家庭一日画廊，日本
	上海与福建青年现代美术联展，福州美术馆，福州

1957	Born in Quanzhou, Fujian Province, China
1985	Graduated from Shanghai Theatre Academy, China
	Currently lives in New York, U.S.A

Selected Solo Exhibitions

2010	*Peasant Da Vincis*, Rockbund Art Museum, Shanghai, China
	Travels in the Mediterranean, Museum of Modern and Contemporary Art, Nice, France
2009	*I Want to Believe*, Guggenheim Bilbao, Spain
2008	*I Want to Believe*, Solomon R. Guggenheim Museum, New York, U.S.A
2007	*Inopportune: Stage One*, Seattle Art Museum, Seattle, U.S.A
2006	*Cai Guo - Qiang on the Roof: Transparent Monument*, Metropolitan Museum of Art, New York, U.S.A
	Head On, Deutsche Guggenheim, Berlin, Germany
2005	*On Black Fireworks*, Institut Valencia d'Art Modern (IVAM), Valencia, Spain
2004	*Inopportune*, Massachusetts Museum of Contemporary Art, North Adams, U.S.A
2003	*An Explosion Event: Light Cycle Over Central Park*, Asia Society Museum, New York, U.S.A
2002	*Cai Guo - Qiang's CHADO Pavilion: Homage to Tenshin Okakura*,
	Hakone Open - Air Museum, Kanagawa, Japan
2001	*Performing Chinese Ink Painting*, Contemporary Art Gallery and Dr. Sun Yat - Sen Classical
	Chinese Garden, Vancouver, Canada
2000	*Cai Guo - Qiang*, Fondation Cartier pour l'art contemporain, Paris, France
1999	*I Am the Y2K Bug*, Kunsthalle Wien, Vienna, Austria
1997	*Cultural Melting Bath: Projects for the 20th Century*, Queens Museum of Art, New York, U.S.A

Selected Group Exhibitions

2010	*The Beauty of Distance: Songs of Survival in a Precarious Age*, 17th Biennale of Sydney, Sydney, Australia
2009	*Meeting Point*, 10 th Havana Biennial, Havana, Cuba
2008	*Blood on Paper: The Art of the Book*, Victoria and Albert Museum, London, Britain
2007	*Journeys: Mapping the Earth and Mind in Chinese Art*, Metropolitan Museum of Art, New York, U.S.A
2006	*Out of Time: A Contemporary View*, Museum of Modern Art, New York, U.S.A
2005	*Translation*, Palais de Tokyo, Paris, France
2004	*26th Bienal de São Paulo: Free Territory*, Pavilhão Ciccillo Matarazzo, Parque do Ibirapuera, São Paulo, Brazil
2003	*Alors, la Chine?*, Centre National d'art et de culture Georges Pompidou, Paris, France
2002	*3th Biennale de Montréal*, Montréal, Canada
2001	*Plateau of Humankind, 49th Venice Biennale*, Giardini di Castello, Arsenale, Venice, Italy
2000	*Sharing Exoticisms. 5th Lyon Biennale d'art contemporain*, Musée d'Art Contemporain de Lyon, Lyon, France
1999	*Looking for a Place: The Third International Biennial*, SITE Santa Fe, New Mexico, U.S.A
1998	*Wounds: Between Democracy and Redemption in Contemporary Art*, Moderna Museet, Stockholm, Sweden
1997	*Future, Past, Present, 47th Venice Biennale*, Giardini di Castelo, Arsenale, Venice, Italy
1996	*23th Bienal Internacional de São Paulo: Universalis*, Pavilhão Ciccillo Matarazzo, Parque do Ibirapuera, São Paulo, Brazil
1995	*TransCulture, 46th Venice Biennale*, Palazzo Giustinian Lolin, Venice, Italy
1994	*Heart of Darkness*, Kröller - Müller Museum, Otterlo, Holland
1993	*Silent Energy*, Museum of Modern Art Oxford, Britian
1992	*Encountering the Others: The Kassel International Art Exhibition*, various sites, Hannover - Münden and Kassel, Germany
1991	*Exceptional Passage: Chinese Avant - Garde Artists Exhibition*, Mitsubishi - jisho Artium and Kashii Former Train Yard, Fukuoka, Japan
1990	*The 7th Japan Ushimado International Art Festival*, Ushimado, Okayama, Japan
1989	*16th International Modern Art AU Show*, Tokyo Metropolitan Art Museum, Tokyo, Japan
1987	*55th Memorial Exhibition of Dokuritsu Art Association*, Tokyo Metropolitan Art Museum, Tokyo, Japan
1985	*Cai Guo - Qiang and Hong Hong Wu: Paintings*, Quanzhou Art Gallery, Japan
	The Shanghai and Fujian Youth Modern Art Joint Exhibition, Fuzhou City Museum, Fuzhou, China

刘野
Liu Ye

1964	出生于北京
1984	毕业于北京工艺美术学校
1989	毕业于中央美术学院
1994	毕业于柏林艺术学院
	现生活、工作于北京

精选个展

2009	Leave me in the Dark，Sperone westwater画廊，纽约
2007	迷恋，Johnen+schoettle画廊，科隆
	刘野，伯尔尼美术馆，瑞士
2006	诱惑，Sperone westwater画廊，纽约
2005	刘野，Tomio Koyama画廊，东京

精选群展

2009	Fat Art之目耳计划，今日美术馆，北京
	Chinamania，丹麦阿肯美术馆，丹麦
	Metropolis Now!，子午线国际中心，华盛顿，美国
2008	快城快客：第七届上海双年展，上海美术馆，上海
	Facing China：福瑞德收藏展，Akureyri 美术馆，冰岛
	艺术批评中的艺术家，北京圣之空间艺术中心，北京
	2008年度马爹利非凡艺术人物，广东美术馆，广州；上海美术馆，上海；今日美术馆，北京
	China-Facing Reality，中国美术馆，北京
2007	Rockers Island-Olbricht Collection，Folkwang美术馆，埃森，德国
	麻将，中国当代艺术希克收藏展，萨尔茨堡美术馆，奥地利
	China-Facing Reality，维也纳现代美术馆，奥地利
2006	麻将：中国当代艺术希克收藏展，汉堡美术馆，汉堡，德国
2005	麻将：中国当代艺术希克收藏展，伯尔尼美术馆，伯尔尼，瑞士
	一卡通，顶层空间，北京
	刘野／金田胜一，Frank Schlag & Cie画廊，埃森，德国
2004	虚拟的爱，台北当代艺术馆，中国台湾
	龙族之梦，爱尔兰现代美术馆，都柏林，爱尔兰
	板起面孔，多伦现代美术馆，上海
2003	左手右手：中德当代艺术家联展，798时态空间，北京
	中国当代艺术巡展，路德维希博物馆，布达佩斯，匈牙利
	惦记，北京东京艺术工程，北京
	中国当代艺术巡展，罗马当代艺术博物馆，罗马
2002	巴黎-北京：中国当代艺术展，皮尔卡丹空间，巴黎
	中国当代艺术巡展，Kueppersmuehle Sammlung Grothe博物馆，杜伊斯堡，德国
	第一届中国当代艺术三年展，广州艺术博物院，广州
	中国当代艺术展，雷克亚未克美术馆，冰岛
2001	第一届成都双年展，成都现代美术馆，成都
	透明不透明，De Markten，布鲁塞尔，比利时
2000	刘野与毛焱，中国当代画廊，伦敦，英国
	上海美术馆收藏展，上海美术馆，上海
1998	是我：中国当代艺术的一个侧面，故宫太庙，北京
	蒙德里安在中国，国际艺苑美术馆，北京
1995	世说新语，国际艺苑美术馆，北京

1964	Born in Beijing
1984	Graduated from School of Arts & Crafts, Beijing
1989	Graduated from Central Academy of Fine Arts, Beijing
1994	Graduated from Hochschule der Kunst Berlin
	Currently lives and works in Beijing

Selected Solo Exhibitions

2009	*Leave Me in the Dark*, Sperone Westwater, New York, U.S.A
2007	*Liu Ye*, Kunstmuseum Bern, Bern, Switzerland
	Infatuation, Johnen + Schoettle, Colonge, Germany
2006	*Temptations*, Sperone Westwater, New York, U.S.A
2005	*Project room*, Tomio Koyama Gallery, Tokyo, Japan

Selected Group Exhibitions

2009	*Music to My Eyes - The First Exhibition of FAT ART*, Today Art Museum, Beijing, China
	Chinamania, Arken Museum of Modern Art, Ishoj, Demark
	Metropolis Now! A Selection of Chinese Contemporary Art, Meridian International Center, White - Meyer House (Cafritz Galleries), Washington DC, U.S.A
2008	*7th Shanghai Biennale*, Shanghai Art Museum, Shanghai, China
	Facing China - The Fu Ruide Collection, Akureyri Municipal Art Museum, Akureyri, Iceland
	Martell Artists of the Year Exhibition, Er - sha, Island; Guangdong Museum of Art, Guangzhou, China; Shanghai Art Museum, Shangai, China; Beijing Today Art Museum, Beijing, China
	China - Facing Reality, National Art Museum of China, Beijing, China
2007	*Rockers Island, Works from the Olbricht Collection*, Museum Folkwang, Essen, Germany
	Mahjong: Contemporary Chinese Art from the Sigg Collection, Salzburg Art Museum, Austria
	China - Facing Reality, Vienna Contemporary Art Museum, Austria
2006	*Mahjong: Contemporary Chinese Art from the Sigg Collection*, Hamburger Kunsthalle, Germany
2005	*Mahjong, Chinese Contemporary art of Sigg's collection*, Kunstmuseum Bern, Switzerland
	A Cartoon, Taikang Top Space, Beijing, China
	Liu Ye, Kaneda Schowichi, Gallery Frank Schlag & Cie, Essen, Germany
2004	*Fictional Love - Ultra New Vision in Contemporary Art*, Museum of Contemporary Art, Taipei, China
	Dreaming of the Dragon Nation, Irish Museum of Modern Art, Dublin, Ireland
	Stone Face, Duolun Museum of Modern Art, Shanghai, China
2003	*Left Hand, Right Hand*, 798 Space Art & Culture Co. Ltd, Beijing, China
	ChinArt, Ludwing Museum, Budapest, Hungary
	ChinArt, Museo Arte Contemporanea di Roma, Rome
	Lifetime, Beijing Tokyo Art Projects, Beijing, China
2002	*Paris - Pekin*, Espace Pierre Cardin, Paris, France
	ChinArt, Museum Kuppersmuehle Sammlung Grothe, Duisburg, Germany
	The First Trienal of Chinese Arts, Guangdong Art Museum, Guangzhou, China
	Chinese Contemporary Art, Reykjavic Art Museum, Iceland
2001	*The First Chengdu Biennale*, Chengdu, China
	Transparence Opacity, De Markten, Brussel, Belgium
2000	*Liu ye and Mao Yan*, Chinese Contemporary Ltd, London, U.K
	A Selection From Collection, Shanghai Art Museum, Shanghai, China
1998	*It's Me!*, Forbidden City Taimiao, Beijing, China
	Mondrian in China, Art Gallery of the International Palace in Beijing, China
1995	*New Anecdotes of Social Talk*, Art Gallery of International Palace, Beijing, China

周铁海
Zhou Tiehai

1966	出生于上海
1987	毕业于上海大学美术学院
	现生活、工作于上海

精选个展

2011	甜点：部长，文华东方，中国香港
2010	甜品：周铁海艺术展，上海当代艺术馆，上海
2008	周铁海个展，PKM画廊，首尔，韩国
2006	Ego，Art&Public画廊，日内瓦，瑞士
	周铁海：油画2006，Frank Schlag & Cie.画廊，埃森，德国
2004	1989-2003作品展，香格纳画廊，上海
2003	周铁海新作品展，Marella Arte Contemporanea，米兰，意大利
2001	艺术家不在这里，香格纳画廊，上海
2000	第三十一届巴塞尔艺术博览会，瑞士
	安慰药：瑞士，东京原美术馆，日本
1999	不要怕犯错误，香格纳画廊，上海
1998	边界线的那边，Bernhard Schindler画廊，伯尔尼，瑞士
	周铁海，荷兰鹿特丹美术馆，荷兰
1996	太物质、太精神，北京中央美院画廊，北京

精选群展

2011	一堆热情，香格纳画廊，上海
2010	日以继夜或美术馆可为之若干事，上海外滩美术馆，上海
2009	资产阶级化了的无产阶级：当代艺术展在松江，松江创意工坊，上海
2008	我们的未来：尤伦斯基金会收藏展，尤伦斯基金会，北京
2007	真实的东西：来自中国的当代艺术，泰特美术馆，利物浦，英国
2006	第五届亚太当代艺术三年展，昆士兰当代美术馆，澳大利亚
2005	麻将：中国当代艺术希克收藏展，伯尔尼美术馆，伯尔尼，瑞士
2004	上海双年展：影像生存，上海美术馆，上海
2003	那么，中国呢？，蓬皮杜艺术中心，巴黎，法国
2001	生活在此时：29位中国当代艺术家作品展，汉堡火车站当代美术馆，柏林，德国
2000	媒体城市，汉城大都会美术馆，韩国
1999	第四十八届威尼斯国际艺术双年展，Aperto Over All，威尼斯，意大利
1998	现代文化的声誉，悉尼现代文化交流中心，澳大利亚
1997	移动中的城市1，分离派美术馆，维也纳，奥地利；
	移动中的城市2，CAPC当代艺术博物馆，波尔多港，法国；
	移动中的城市3，纽约P.S.1当代艺术中心，美国
1996	上海传真：让我们谈谈钱，国际传真艺术展，
	华山美校画廊，上海
	以艺术的名义：中国当代艺术展，刘海粟美术馆，上海
1995	猿，上海华山美术学校，上海
1986	"M"：行为＆观念艺术展，上海虹口文化艺术中心，上海
	创造行动，复旦大学，上海
1984	寒假作品展，上海美术学校，上海

1966	Born in Shanghai, China
1987	Graduated from Fine Arts College of Shanghai University, China
	Currently lives and works in Shanghai, China

Selected Solo Exhibitions

2011	*Desserts - Le Ministre*, Mandarin Oriental, Hong Kong, China
2010	*Desserts, ZHOU Tiehai*, MoCA Shanghai, Shanghai, China
2008	*Zhou Tiehai*, PKM Gallery, Seoul, korea
2006	*EGO*, Art&Public, Geneva, Switzerland
	Zhou Tiehai:Oil paintings 2006, Galerie Frank Schlag & Cie., Essen, Germany
2004	*Works 1989 - 2003*, ShanghART Gallery, Shanghai, China
2003	*Zhou Tiehai*, Marella Arte Comtemporanea, Milan, Italy
2001	*Zhou Tiehai - the Artist Isn't Here*, ShanghART Gallery, Shanghai, China
2000	*Art 31 Basel, Art Statement Solo Presentation Zhou Tiehai Scrolls*, Art Fairs Switzerland
	Placebo Swiss, Hara Museum, Tokyo, Japan
1999	*Don't be Afraid to Make Mistakes*, ShanghART Gallery, Shanghai, China
1998	*Beyond the Borderline*, Galerie Bernhard Schindler, Bern, Switzerland
	Zhou Tiehai, Kunsthal Rotterdam, Netherlands
1996	*Too Materialistic, Too Spiritualized*, CAFA Gallery, Beijing, China

Selected Group Exhibitions

2011	*A Pile of Passion*, ShanghART Gallery, Shanghai, China
2010	*By Day By Night or Some special Things a Museum Can Do*,
	Rockbund Art Museum, Shanghai, China
2009	*Bourgeoisified Proletariat, Contemporary Art Exhibition in Songjiang*,
	Shanghai Songjiang Creative Studio, Shanghai, China
2008	*Our Future, The Guy & Myriam Ullens Foundation Collection*,
	Ullens Foundation, Beijing, China
2007	*The Real Thing, Contemporary Art from China*, Tate Liverpool, U.K
2006	*The 5th AsiaPacific Triennial of Contemporary Art (APT5)*, Gallery of Modern Art,
	Queensland Art Gallery, Australia
2005	*Mahjong, Contemporary Chinese Art from the Sigg Collection*,
	Kunstmuseum Bern, Bern, Switzerland
2004	*5th Shanghai Biennale - Techniques of the Visible*, Shanghai Art Museum, Shanghai, China
2003	*Alors la Chine?*, Centre Pompidou, Paris, France
2001	*Living in Time, 29 Contemporary Artists from China*, National galerie in Hamburger, Germany
2000	*Media City*, Seoul, Korea
1999	*48th International Art Exhibition Venice Biennale, APERTO over ALL*, Venice, Italy
1998	*Modern Culture's Fame, Modern Culture Communications*, Sydney, Australia
1997	*Cities on the Move 1*, Exhibition of Asian art, Secession, Vienna, Austria
	Cities on the Move 2, CAPC, Musee d' Art Contemporain, Bordeaux, France
	Cities on the Move 3, P.S.1 Contemporary Art Center, New York, U.S.A
1996	*Shanghai Fax: Let's Talk about Money, International Fax Art Exhibition*,
	Shanghai Huashan Professional School of Art Gallery, Shanghai, China
1995	*Ape*, Huashan Art School, Shanghai, China
1986	*"M", Performance & Conceptual Art Exhibition*, Hongkou District Cultural Centre, Shanghai, China
	Critical Action, Fudan University, Shanghai, China
1984	*Students Exhibition*, Fine Art School of Shanghai University, Shanghai, China

洪浩
Hong Hao

1965	出生于北京
1985	毕业于中央美术学院附中
1989	毕业于中央美术学院
	现生活、工作于北京

精选个展

2009	洪浩：负部，北京公社，北京
2007	洪浩之雅集，前波画廊，纽约，美国
2004	洪浩作品，LOFT画廊，巴黎，法国
	洪浩展，Base画廊，东京，日本
2003	洪浩作品在阿尔勒国际摄影节，阿尔勒，法国
2000	世说新语及其他，精艺轩，温哥华，加拿大
	景象中国，四合院画廊，北京

精选群展

2010	此处彼处之间：当代摄影的通道，大都会美术馆，纽约，美国
2009	第三届广州国际摄影双年展2009，广东美术馆，广州
2008	书、书架，现代美术馆，纽约，美国
2007	旅程，大都会美术馆，纽约，美国
2006	H+Y：一件作品之泰康计划，泰康顶层空间，北京
2005	城市重视：2005广州国际摄影双年展，广东美术馆，广州
2004	过去将来：中国当代摄影，国际摄影中心，纽约，美国
2003	念珠与笔触，东京艺术工程，北京
2002	首届广州当代艺术三年展，广东美术馆，广州
2001	第十六届亚洲国际艺术展，广东美术馆，广州
2000	海上、上海：2000上海双年展，上海美术馆，上海
1999	爱：中国当代摄影和录像，99东京立川国际艺术节，东京，日本
1998	蜕变与突破：中国新艺术展，亚洲协会美术馆、纽约P.S.1当代艺术中心、旧金山现代艺术博物馆，美国
1997	不易流行：中国现代艺术与环境之视线，东京、大阪、福冈，日本
	面孔与身体：90年代的中国艺术，Rudolfinum美术馆，布拉格，捷克
1995	变化：来自中国的现代艺术，艺术博物馆，哥德堡，瑞典
	世说新语，国际艺苑美术馆，北京
1994	中国当代艺术方案展，翰墨画廊，北京
1993	后八九中国新艺术展，香港艺术中心，中国香港；悉尼当代美术馆，悉尼；Marlborough画廊，伦敦，英国
1992	'92亚洲国际艺术展，会议展览中心，中国香港
1988	第十九届阿尔勒国际摄影节，阿尔勒，法国

1965	Born in Beijing, China
1989	Graduated from the Central Academy of Fine Arts, Beijing, China
	Current Lives and works in Beijing, China

Selected Solo Exhibitions

2009	*Bottom*, Beijing Commune Beijing, China
2007	*Hong Hao's Elegant Gathering*, Chambers Fine Art, New York, U.S.A
2004	*Hong Hao*, Base Gallery, Tokyo, Japan
	Hong Hao's Reading Room, Chambers Fine Art, New York, U.S.A
2003	*Hong Hao at Rencontres d'Arles 2003*, Arles, France
2000	*Scenes from the Metropolis*, The CourtYard Gallery, Beijing, China
	Suspended Disbelief, Art Beatus Gallery, Vancouver, Canada

Selected Group Exhibitions

2010	*Between Here and There: Passages in Contemporary Photography*, The Metropolitan Museum of Art, New York, U.S.A
2009	*2009 Guangzhou International Photography Biennale*, Guangdong Museum of Art, Guangzhou, China
2008	*Book / Shelf*, The Museum of Modern Art, New York, U.S.A
2007	*Journeys: Mapping the Earth and Mind in Chinese Art*, The Metropolitan Museum of Art, New York, U.S.A
2006	*One Work: the Taikang Project of Hong Hao + Yan Lei*, Taikang Top Space, Beijing, China
2005	*Reviewing the City:2005 Guangzhou International Photography Biennale*, Guangdong Museum of Art, Guangzhou, China
2004	*Between Past and Future, New Photography and Video from China*, International Center of Photography, New York, U.S.A
2003	*Prayer Beads and Brush Strokes*, Beijing Tokyo Art Projects, Beijing, China
2002	*First Guangzhou Triennial*, Guangdong Museum of Art, Guangzhou, China
2001	*The 16th Asian International Art Exhibition*, Guangdong Museum of Art, China
2000	*Shanghai Biennale*, Shanghai Art Museum, China
1999	*Love: Chinese Contemporary Photography and Video International*, Arts Festival, Tachikawa, Japan
1998	*Inside Out: New Chinese Art*, Asia Society and P.S.1Contemporary Art Center, San Francisco Museum of Modern Art, U.S.A
1997	*Immutability and fashion: Chinese Contemporary Art in the Midst of Changing Surroundings*, Tokyo / Osaka / Fukuoka, Japan
	Faces and Bodies of the Middle Kingdom, Chinese Art of the 90's, Gallery Rudolfinum, Prague, Czech
1995	*Changes: Modern Art from China*, Art Museum of Gothenburg, Sweden
	New Anecdotes of Social Talk, Art Gallery of Beijing International Art Palace, Beijing, China
1993	*China's New Art, Post-1989*, Hong Kong Art Center, Hong Kong; Museum of Contemporary Art, Sydney; Australia Marlborough Fine Art, London, U.K
1992	*Art Asia'92 Infomation*, Hong Kong Convention And Exhibition Center, Hong Kong, China
1988	*19'es Rencontres Internationales de la Photographie*, Arles, France

刘韡
Liu Wei

1972	出生于北京
1996	毕业于中国美术学院
	现生活、工作于北京

精选个展

2011	三部曲：刘韡个展，民生美术馆，上海
2010	转换的时代：刘韡，CAN Foundation，首尔，韩国
2009	对！这就是全部，Boers-Li画廊，北京
	被遗忘的经验，Galerie Hussenot，巴黎，法国
2007	徘徊者，Boers-Li画廊，北京
	爱它、咬它，中国艺术文件仓库与Boers-Li画廊合作举办，北京
2006	刘韡专有，北京公社，北京
	紫气，Grace Li画廊，苏黎世，瑞士
	爱它、咬它，比翼画廊，上海
2005	刘韡个展，四合苑艺术空间，北京

精选群展

2010	Dreamlands，蓬皮杜中心，巴黎，法国
	上海双年展：巡回排演，上海
2009	中坚：新世纪中国八个艺术的关键形象，尤伦斯当代艺术中心，北京
2008	消耗：釜山双年展，釜山，韩国
	与后殖民说再见：第三届广州三年展，广州
	趣味的共同体，伊比利亚当代艺术中心，北京
	我们的未来，尤伦斯当代艺术中心，北京
	麻将：中国当代艺术希克收藏展，伯克利美术馆，伯克利，美国
	中国电站Ⅲ，卢森堡大公现代艺术博物馆，卢森堡
2007	第九届里昂双年展，里昂，法国
	中国电站Ⅱ，Astrup Fearnley现代美术馆，奥斯陆，挪威
2006	第四届首尔媒体艺术双年展，首尔美术馆，首尔，韩国
2005	第五十一届威尼斯双年展，威尼斯，意大利
	麻将：中国当代艺术希克收藏展，伯尔尼美术馆，伯尔尼，瑞士
	第一届南京三年展，南京
	第二届广州三年展，广州
2004	影像生存：上海双年展，上海
	在过去和未来之间：来自中国的新摄影和录像，国际摄影中心及亚洲协会，纽约，美国
2003	第五系统：后规划时代的公共艺术——第五届深圳雕塑展，何香凝美术馆，深圳
2002	首届广州三年展，广州美术馆，广州
2001	后感性：狂欢，北京电影学院，北京
	非线性叙事：新媒体艺术节，中国美术学院展览馆，杭州
	附体，印象画廊，杭州；比翼艺术中心，上海；
	藏酷新媒体艺术空间，北京
	香港国际影像节，环境博物馆，香港
2000	家？：当代艺术提案展，月星家具广场，上海
	肖像、人物、一对和一组，比翼艺术空间，上海
1999	超市，上海广场，上海
	北京在伦敦，ICA当代艺术中心，伦敦，英国
	后感性：异形与妄想，芍药居地下室，北京
	香港国际影象节，环境博物馆，中国香港

1972	Born in Beijing, China
1996	Graduated from the National Academy of Fine Arts, Hangzhou, China
	Currently lives and works in Beijing, China

Selected Solo Exhibitions

2011	*Trilogy*, Minsheng Art Museum, Shanghai, China
2010	*Diversion Era: Liu Wei*, CAN Foundation, Seoul, Korea
2009	*Yes, That's All!*, Beors - Li Gallery, Beijing, China
	The Forgotten Experience, Galerie Hussenot, Paris, France
2007	*The Outcast*, Boers - Li Gallery, Beijing, China
	Love It, Bite It, China Art Archives and Warehouse in association with Boers - Li Gallery, Beijing, China
2006	*Property of Liu Wei*, Beijing Commune, Beijing, China
	Purple Air, Grace Li Gallery, Zurich, Switzerland
	Love It, Bite It, BizArt, Shanghai, China
2005	*Liu Wei Solo Exhibition*, Courtyard Gallery, Beijing, China

Selected Group Exhibitions

2010	*Dreamlands*, Centre Pompidou, Paris, France
	Shanghai Biennale: Rehearsal, Shanghai Art Museum, Shanghai, China
2009	*Breaking Forecast - 8 Key Figures of China's New Generation Artists*, UCCA, Beijing, China
2008	*Expenditure: Busan Biennale*, Busan, Korea
	Farewell to Postcolonialism: Third Guangzhou Triennial, Guangzhou, China
	Community of Tastes, Iberia Center for Contemporary Art, Beijing, China
	Our Future, Ullens Center for Contemporary Art, Beijing, China
	Mahjong: Contemporary Chinese Art from the Sigg Collection, Berkeley Art Museum, Berkeley, U.S.A
	China Power Station 3, Mudam Luxembourg, Luxembourg
2007	*The History of A Decade That Has Not Yet Been Named, Ninth Lyon Biennale*, Lyon, France
	China Power Station: Part II, Astrup Fearnley Museet for Moderne Kunst, Oslo, Norway
2006	*The 4th Seoul International Media Art Biennale*, Seoul Museum of Art, Seoul, Korea
2005	*51 Venice Biennale*, Venice, Italy
	Mahjong: Contemporary Chinese Art from the Sigg Collection, Kunstmuseum Bern, Bern, Switzerland
	The First Nanjing Triennial, Nanjing, China
	Second Guangzhou Triennial, Guangzhou, China
2004	*Techniques of the Visible*, Shanghai Biennial, Shanghai, China
	Between Past and Future: New Photography and Video From China, International Center of Photography; Asia Society New York, U.S.A
2003	*The Fifth System: Public Art in the Age of Post - Planning*, The Fifth Sculpture Exhibition in Shenzhen, Hexiangning Art Museum, Shenzhen, China
2002	*The First Guangzhou Triennial*, Guangdong Museum of Art, Guangzhou, China
2001	*Post - Sense Sensibility: Spree*, Beijing Film Academy, Beijing, China
	Non - Linear Narrative, Gallery of National Academy of Fine Arts, Hangzhou, China
	Mantic Ecstasy, Impression Gallery, Hangzhou; Bizart Art Center, Shanghai; Loft New Media Art Space, Beijing, China
	Hong Kong International Video Festival, Museum of Circumstance, Hong Kong, China
2000	*Home?, Contemporary Art Project*, Yuexing Furniture Warehouse, Shanghai, China
	Portraits, Figures, Couples, and Groups, BizArt, Shanghai, China
1999	*Art for Sale*, Shanghai Plaza, Shanghai, China
	Beijing in London, Institute of Contemporary Art, London, U.K
	Post - Sensibility: Alien Bodies and Delusion, Shaoyaoju, Beijing, China
	Hong Kong International Video Festival, Museum of Circumstance, Hong Kong, China

颜磊
Yan Lei

1965	出生于河北
1999	毕业于中国美术学院
	现生活、工作于北京、香港

精选个展

2009	追光（升级版），尤伦斯当代艺术中心，北京
2008	追光Aspen，Aspen美术馆，美国
	追光：颜磊个展，新北京画廊，北京
2007	颜磊个展，RMG画廊，美国纽约
	狗星计划，常青画廊，圣基米亚诺，意大利
	支柱，沪申画廊，上海
2006	特醇：香港，香港艺术中心，中国香港
2005	特醇，麦勒画廊，瑞士
2003	上升空间，麦勒画廊，瑞士
2002	颜磊个展，Loft画廊，巴黎，法国
2001	国际山水，中国艺术文件仓库，北京
1999	在资本主义前沿，香港Most，中国香港
1995	入侵，北京儿童艺术剧院，北京

精选群展

2009	事物状态：中比当代艺术交流展，比利时皇家美术馆，比利时
2007	第十届伊斯坦布尔双年展，土耳其
	第十二届卡塞尔文献展，德国
2006	一件作品·洪浩+颜磊，泰康顶层空间，北京
2005	麻将：希克个人收藏展，泊尔尼美术馆，瑞士
2004	找不到北，尼斯Villa Arson当代艺术中心、塞特当代艺术中心，法国
2003	紧急地带，第五十届威尼斯双年展，意大利
	中国怎麽样？，蓬皮杜艺术中心，巴黎，法国
	第五系统：后规划时代的公共艺术——第五届深圳当代雕塑展，何香凝美术馆，深圳
2002	都市营造：上海双年展，上海美术馆，上海
	大都市肖像学：第二十五届圣保罗双年展，圣保罗，巴西
	暂停：第四届光州双年展，光州，韩国
2001	Polypolis：东南亚当代艺术展，汉堡艺术宫，德国
1999	开放的真实，泰曼谷大学博物馆，泰国
1998	影像志异，上海大学美术馆，上海
	是我！，北京紫禁城太庙，北京
1997	新亚洲、新城市、新艺术：中韩当代艺术展，上海当代美术馆，上海
1996	现象与影像，中国美术学院画廊，北京
1995	后'89中国新艺术，温哥华艺术画廊，加拿大
1994	中、港、台摄影艺术展，香港艺术中心，中国香港
1993	后'89中国新艺术，香港艺术中心，中国香港
1989	中国现代艺术展，中国美术馆，北京

1965	Born in Hebei Province, China
1999	Graduated from China Academy of Art, China
	Currently lives and works in Beijing and Hong Kong, China

Selected Solo Exhibitions

2009	*Sparkling Upgraded*, UCCA, Beijing, China
2008	*Sparkling: Aspen*, Aspen Museum of Art, Colorado, U.S.A
	Sparkling Yanlei Solo Exhibition, Xin Beijing Art Gallery, Beijing, China
2007	*Yanlei Solo Exhibition*, Robert Miller Gallery, New York, U.S.A
	Dogzstar Project, Gallery Continua, San Gimignano, Italy
	Support, Shanghai Gallery of Art, Shanghai, China
2006	*Super Lights - Hong Kong*, HK Art Centre, Hong Kong, China
2005	*Super Lights*, Galerie Urs Meile, Luceme, Switzerland
2003	*Climbing Space*, Galerie Urs Meile, Luceme, Switzerland
2002	*Yan Lei Solo Exhibition*, Galerie Loft, Paris
2001	*International Scenery*, China Art Archives & Warehouse, Beijing, China
1999	*At the Frontiers of Capitalism*, Museum of Site, Hong Kong, China
1995	*Invasion*, Beijing Junior Art Theatre, Beijing, China

Selected Group Exhibitions

2009	*The State of Things: The Exchanging of Contemporary Art between China and Belgium*, BOZAR, Belgium
2007	*10th International Istanbul Biennial*, Istanbul, Turkey
	12 Documenta, Kassel, Germany
2006	*One Work: Hong Hao and Yan Lei*, Taikang Top Space, Beijing, China
2005	*Mahjong - Chinese Contemporary Art from the Sigg Collection*, Kunstmuseum Bern, Switzerland
2004	*A l'Est du Sud de l'Ouest, Villa Arson*, Nice and Crac - Centre National d'Art Contemporain, Sète, France
2003	*Zones of Urgency, 50th Biennale di Venezia*, Italy
	Alors, la Chine, Centre Pompidou, Paris
	The Fifth System: Public Art in the Age of Post - Planning, 5th Shenzhen Contemporary Sculpture Exhibition, He Xiangning Art Museum, Shenzhen, China
2002	*Cidades, 25th Sao Paulo Biennale*, Sao Paulo, Brazil
	The First Guangzhou Triennial, Guangdong Museum of Art, China
	Pause, The Fourth Gwangju Biennale, Korea
2001	*Polypolis: Contemporary Art from South East Asia*, Kunsthaus, Hamburg, Germany
1999	*Unveiled Reality, Contemporary Chinese Photography*, Chulalongkorn University, Bangkok, Thailand
1998	*China Maze*, Gallery OTSO, Espoo, Finland
	Images Telling Stories (Beautiful like Materialism), Shanghai University Art Museum
1997	*It's Me*, Tai Temple of the Forbidden City, Beijing, China
1996	*New Asia, New City, New Art '97, China - Korean Contemporary Art Exhibition*, Shanghai Contemporary Art Museum, Beijing, China
1995	*Phenomenon and Image*, Gallery of Zhejing Academy of Fine Arts, Hangzhou, China
1994	*China's New Art: Post '89*, Vancouver Art Gallery, Canada
1993	*Contemporary Photography from Mainland China, Hong Kong and Taiwan*, Hong Kong Arts Centre, Hong Kong, China
1989	*China / Avant - Garde*, China Art Museum, Beijing, China

阳江组
Yangjiang Group

创于2002年

成员

郑国谷，1970年生于阳江
陈再炎，1971年生于阳春
孙庆麟，1974年生于阳江

精选个展

2006　鼠牛虎兔龙蛇，泰康顶层空间，北京
2002　你去看书法还是量血压？，世界机构，阳江
　　　公元2002年在上海阳江有大事发生，香格纳画廊，上海

精选群展

2009　第十届里昂双年展，里昂，法国
2008　白夜生长，Bonniers艺术中心，斯德哥尔摩，瑞典
　　　马、羊、猴、鸡、狗、猪，第三十九届巴塞尔博览会，巴塞尔，瑞士
　　　松园：艺术无限，第三十九届巴塞尔艺术博览会，巴塞尔，瑞士
　　　'85以来现象与状态系列展之三：广州站——广州当代艺术特展，广东美术馆，广州
2007　第十二届卡塞尔文献展，卡塞尔，德国
　　　中国欢迎你：愿望、努力、新身份，格拉茨，奥地利
　　　真实：中国当代艺术，利物浦泰特现代美术馆，利物浦，英国
2006　第五届深圳国际水墨画双年展：水墨、生活、趣味——要想甜加点盐，何香凝美术馆，深圳
　　　鼠牛虎兔龙蛇，北京
　　　迷乱之城，北京
　　　渗：意境与幻想——第二届当代水墨空间，广州美术馆，广州
2005　黑极生像，深圳
　　　跟我来！中国当代艺术展，东京森美术馆，日本
　　　第二届国际三年展，广东美术馆，广州
2004　颠倒的过去，东亚当代艺术展，圣地亚哥美术馆，美国
　　　A L'estdu sud de L'ouest，国立当代艺术中心、尼斯／赛特艺术中心，法国
2003　自制天堂，Le Parvis当代艺术中心，法国
　　　主场、客场，现实迷宫，深圳
2002　巴黎-北京，皮尔卡登剧场，巴黎
　　　光州双年展，光州，韩国

Created in 2002

Members:

	Zheng Guogu
1970	Born in Yangjiang, Guangdong Province, China
	Chen Zaiyan
1971	Born in Yangchun, Guangdong Province, China
	Sun Qinglin
1974	Born in Yangjiang, Guangdong Province, China

Selected Solo Exhibitions

2006	*Mouse Cow Tiger Hare Dragon Snake*, Taikang Top Space, Beijing, China
2002	*Are you going to enjoy calligraphy or measure blood pressure?*, World Organization, Yangjiang, Guangdong, China
	In Shanghai 2002, Yangjiang some event occurring, Shanghart Gallery, Shanghai, China

Selected Group Exhibitions

2009	*Biennales de Lyon 2009 - The Spectacle of the Everyday*, Lyon, France
2008	*Sprout from White Nights*, Bonniers Konsthall, Stockholm, Sweden
	Horse, Goat, Monkey, Rooster, Dog, Pig, Art Statements, Art 39 Basel, Basel
	Pine Tree Garden, Art Unlimited, Art 39 Basel, Basel, Switzerland
	Exhibition Series Third About Artistic Phenomena and Situations Since 1985:Guangzhou Station - Special, Guangdong Museum of Art, Guangzhou, China
2007	*Documenta 12*, Kassel, Germany
	China Welcomes You: Desires, Struggles, New Identities, Kunsthaus Graz, Graz, Astria
	The Real Thing: Contemporary Art from China, Tate Modern Liverpool, U.K
2006	*Int ernational Ink Biennale of Shenzhen :Ink,Life, Taste - To Sugar Add Some Salt'*, He Xiangning Museum of Art, Shenzhen, China
	Mouse Cow Tiger Hare Dragon Snake, Beijing, China
	Infiltration · Idylls and Visions, the second Contemporary Ink - wash Space, Guang Zhou, China
2005	*Black Extreme Vigorous Figurative*, Shenzhen, China
	Follow Me!, Contemporary Art of China, Moro Art Museum, Tokyo
2004	*Past in Reverse: Contemporary Art of East Asia*, San Diego Museum of Art, San Diego, U.S.A
	A l1ouest du sud de l1est, Center of Contemporary Art, Sète / Villa Arson in Nice, France
2003	*Fabricated Paradises*, Le Parvis Centre of Contemporary Art, France
	Place of host / Place of guest, Realistic maze, Shenzhen, China
2002	*Paris - Pekin*, Espace Pierre Cardin, Paris, France
	Guangju Biennual, Guangju, Korea

郑国谷
Zheng Guogu

1970	出生于广东阳江
1992	毕业于广州美术学院
	现生活、工作于广东

精选个展

2008	2008年纪念牌匾：雷曼兄弟门，2008巴塞尔艺术博览会，迈阿密，美国
	百年老树再长一遍：郑国谷近期新作，前波画廊，纽约
	加工厂，当代唐人艺术中心，北京
2007	郑国谷，Barbara Gross画廊，德国
	香港城市惊喜发掘：郑国谷新作，中国香港
	巴塞尔：郑国谷新画展，瑞士
2006	鼠牛虎兔龙蛇，泰康顶层空间，北京
2005	惑：它来自阳江，Grace Alexander当代艺术画廊，瑞士
2004	郑国谷：我家是你的博物馆，维他命空间，广州
2003	照片作品1997-2000，香格纳画廊，上海
2002	在上海：你去看书法还是量血压，上海
2001	郑国谷：世界正压缩，广东
2000	多维：郑国谷，中国艺术文件仓库，北京
	郑国谷：一个多维在上海，比翼空间，上海

精选群展

2009	第十届里昂双年展，里昂，法国
2008	向后殖民说再见，第三届广州三年展，广东美术馆，广州
2007	第十二届卡塞尔文献展，卡塞尔，德国
	真实：来自中国的当代艺术，利物浦泰特现代美术馆，英国
2006	第五届深圳国际水墨画双年展，何香凝美术馆，深圳
2005	第二届广州三年展，广州
	跟我来！新世纪初中国艺术，Mori美术馆，东京，日本
2004	天下，安特威普当代美术馆，比利时
2003	第五系统：后规划时代的公共艺术，何香凝美术馆，深圳
2002	光州双年展，光州，韩国
2001	城市俚语：珠江三角洲的当代艺术，何香凝美术馆，深圳
	生活在此时：29位中国当代艺术家作品展，柏林汉堡火车站当代美术馆，柏林，德国
2000	不合作方式，东廊，上海
1999	后感性异形与妄想，北三环路十号地下室，北京
	观念、感性与色彩，中国艺术文件仓库，北京
1998	98巴黎影像双年展，国立摄影中心，巴黎，法国
	台北双年展，台北美术馆，中国台湾
	移动中的城市，纽约P.S.1当代艺术中心，美国
1997	移动中的城市2，维也纳，奥地利
1996	可能性：与大尾象联合展，广州
1994	第三届中国现代艺术文献展，上海
	瀚墨新艺术特展，广州
	没有空间：与大尾象联合展，广州

1970	Born in Yang Jiang, Guangdong Province, China
1992	Graduated from Guangzhou Academy of Fine Art, China
	Currently lives and works in Guangdong, China

Selected Solo Exhibitions

2008	*Zheng Guogu: Commemorative Plaque 2008: Lehman Brothers Gate*, Art Basel Miami Beach 2008, Miami, U.S.A
	Hundred - Year - Old Tree Blooms Again, Recent Works by Zheng Guogu, Chambers Fine Art, New York, U.S.A
	Processing Factory, Tang Contemporary Art Center, Beijing, China
2007	*Zheng Guogu*, Barbara Gross Gallery, German
	HONG KONG, Surprise Urban Discoveries, New Works by Zheng Guogu, Hong Kong, China
	Basel: New Paintings by Zheng Guogu, Switzerland
2006	*Mouse Cow Tiger Hare Dragon Snake*, Taikang Top Space, Beijing, China
2005	*Puzzle, It is from Yangjiang*, Grace Alexander Contemporary Art Gallery, Switzerland
2004	*My Home is Your Museum*, Vitamin Creative Space, Guangzhou, China
2003	*Photo works 1997 - 2000*, ShanghART, Shanghai, China
2002	*Are You Going to Enjoy Calligraphy or Measure Blood Pressure?*, Shanghai, China
2001	*Zheng Guogu: The Compressing World*, Yang Jiang Guang Dong, China
2000	*Zheng Guogu: More Dimensional*, China Art Archives and Warehouse, Beijing, China
	Zheng Guogu: More Dimensional, Shanghai at BizArt Space, Shanghai, China

Selected Group Exhibitions

2009	*Biennales de Lyon 2009 - The Spectacle of the Everyday*, Lyon, France
2008	*Farewell to Post - Colonialism, The Third Guangzhou Triennial*, Guangdong Museum of Art, Guangzhou, China
2007	*Documenta 12*, Kassel, Germany
	The Real Thing: Contemporary art from China, Tate Modern Liverpool, U.K
2006	*International Ink Biennale of Shenzhen :Ink ,Life, Taste - To Sugar Add Some Salt*, He Xiangning Museum of Art, Shenzhen, China
2005	*The Second Guangzhou Triennial - BEYOND: An Extraordinary Space of Experimentation for Modernization*, Guangdong Museum of Art, Guangzhou, China
	Follow me! Chinese Art at the Threshold of the New Millennium, Mori Art Museum, Tokyo, Japan
2004	*All Under Heaven*, Museum of Contemporary Art Antwerp, Antwerp, Belgium
2003	*The Fifth System: Public Art in the Age of Post Planning*, Shenzhen, China
2002	*Gwangju Biennial*, Gwangju, Korea
2001	*City Slang*, HeXiangning Art Museum, Shenzhen, China
	Living in Time, 29 Contemporary Artists from China, Hamburger Bahnhof, Museum für Gegenwart, Berlin, Germany
2000	*Fuck Off*, Donglang Gallery, Shanghai, China
1999	*Post - Sense Sensibility Alien Bodies & Delusion*, Basement in the Third Ring Road, Beijing, China
	Concepts, Colors and Passions, China Art Archives and Warehouse, Beijing, China
1998	*Biennial de l'imago Paris 98*, Centre National de la Photographie, Paris, France
	Taipei Biennial, Taipei Fine Arts Museum, Taiwan, China
	Cities on the Move 3, P.S.1 Contemporary Art Centre, New York, U.S.A
1997	*Cities on the Move 2*, Wiener Secession, Austria
1996	*Possibility, Installation Exhibition with The Big Tail Elephant Group*, Guangzhou, China
1994	*The Third Exhibition of Chinese Contemporary Art Documentation*, Shanghai, China
	Hanmo New Art Special Show, Guangzhou, China
	No Room, with the Big Tail Elephant Group, Guangzhou, China

黄永砯
Huang Yong Ping

1954	出生于福建厦门
1982	毕业于浙江美术学院
	现生活、工作于法国巴黎

精选个展

2011	诺丁汉当代美术馆个展，诺丁汉，英国
2010	砚台：永久室外装置，维埃卉镇教堂庭院，格罗宁根，荷兰
2009	方舟2009，小奥古斯丁礼拜堂，巴黎国立高等美术学院，巴黎，法国
2008	占卜者之屋，尤伦斯当代艺术中心，北京，中国
2007	占卜者之屋，温哥华美术馆，加拿大
2006	占卜者之屋，北亚当斯当代艺术中心，马萨储塞，美国
2005	占卜者之屋，沃克艺术中心，明尼阿波利斯，美国
2003	意大利狗，博蒙公众画廊，卢森堡
2002	玄武、艺术和公众，日内瓦，瑞士
2000	太公钓鱼——愿者上钩，杰克提敦画廊，纽约，美国
1999	鹤足鹿迹，当代艺术中心，北九州，日本
1998	天平秤，德阿普基金会，阿姆斯特丹，荷兰
1997	羊祸，卡地亚当代艺术基金会，巴黎，法国
1996	三步九迹，马赛市艺术家工作室，马赛，法国
1995	药房，福洛门和彼特曼画廊，巴黎，法国
1994	中国手洗衣店，新当代美术馆，纽约，美国
1993	108签和龟桌，独孤城堡学院，斯图加特，德国
1992	占卜者之屋，福洛门和彼特曼画廊，巴黎，法国
1991	再现红十字，瞬间医院，巴黎，法国
1990	苔图，阿维侬艺术学院，阿维侬，法国

精选群展

2011	世界属于你们，格拉切宫，威尼斯，意大利
2010	万人谱：2010光州双年展，光州，韩国
2009	制造世界，第五十三届威尼斯双年展，威尼斯，意大利
2008	中国电站Ⅲ，大公现代美术馆，卢森堡
2007	'85新潮：中国当代艺术的诞生，尤伦斯当代艺术中心，北京
2006	艺术的力量，巴黎大皇宫，法国
2005	对位：从美术物件到雕塑，罗浮宫，巴黎，法国
2004	圣保罗双年展，圣保罗，巴西
2003	Z.O.U——紧急地带，第50届威尼斯双年展，威尼斯，意大利
2002	首届广州三年展——重新解读(1990-2000)，广东美术馆，广州
2001	黄永砯&沈远，魁北克当代艺术中心，加拿大
2000	上海、海上：上海双年展，上海美术馆，上海
1999	第四十八届威尼斯国际艺术双年展，法国国家馆，威尼斯，意大利
1998	雨果仓斯奖1998，苏荷古根海姆博物馆，纽约，美国
1997	移动中的城市，分离派博物馆，维也纳，奥地利
1996	面对历史，蓬皮杜中心，巴黎，法国
1995	第六届费巴赫三年展，维也纳现代艺术博物馆，奥地利
1994	边界之外——艺术与生活1952／1994，蓬皮杜中心，巴黎，法国
1993	沉默的力量，牛津现代艺术博物馆，英国
1992	私人通道，巴黎，法国
1991	卡内基国际三年展，卡内基美术馆，匹茨堡，美国
1990	卡地亚当代艺术基金会工作室，卡地亚当代艺术基金会，普罗旺斯，法国
1989	大地魔术师，蓬皮杜中心和拉维列特大厅，巴黎，法国
	中国现代艺术展，中国美术馆，北京
1986	厦门达达，厦门市群众艺术馆，厦门
1983	当代艺术五人展，厦门市文化宫，厦门

1954	Born in Xiamen, Fujian Province, China
1982	Graduated from Zhejiang Academy of Fine Arts, Hangzhou, China
	Currently lives and works in Paris, France

Selected Solo Exhibitions

2011	*Nottingham Contemporary Solo Exhibition*, Nottingham Contemporary, U.K
2010	*Inkstone, permanent outdoor installation*, Vierhuizen churchyard, Groningen, Netherlands
2009	*Arche 2009*, Chapelle des Petits Augustins, Ecole Nationale Supérieure des Beaux - Arts, Paris, France
2008	*House of Oracles*, UCCA, Beijing, China
2007	*House of Oracles*, Vancouver Art Gallery, Canada
2006	*House of Oracles*, MOCA, North Adams, Massachusetts, U.S.A
2005	*House of Oracles*, Walker Art Center, Minneapolis, U.S.A
2003	*Un Cane Italiano*, Galerie Beaumontpublic, Luxembourg
2002	*Xian Wu, Art & Public*, Geneva, Switzerland
2000	*Taigong Fishing*, Willing to Bite the Bait, Jack Tilton Gallery, New York, U.S.A
1999	*Crane's legs*, Deer's tracks, Project Gallery, Kitakyushu, Japan
1998	*HUANG Yong - Ping*, De Appel, Amsterdam, Holland
1997	*Péril de Mouton*, Fondation Cartier pour l'Art contemporain, Paris, France
1996	*Trois Pas, Neuf traces*, Atelier d'Artistes de la Ville de Marseille, France
1995	*Pharmacie*, Galerie Fromen & Putman, Paris, France
1994	*Chinese Hand - Laundry*, New Museum of Contemporary Art, New York, U.S.A
1993	*1&108*, Akademie Schloss Solitude, Stuttgart, Germany
1992	*La maison d'augure*, Galerie Froment & Putman, Paris, France
1991	*Réapparition de La Croix - Rouge*, Hôpital Ephémère, Paris, France
1990	*HUANG Yong - Ping*, L'Ecole des Beaux - arts d'Avignon, France

Selected Group Exhibitions

2011	*Le Monde vous Appartient*, Palazzo Grassi, Venice, Italy
2010	*10000 Lives*, Gwangju Biennale 2010, Gwangju, Korea
2009	*Fare Mondi / Making Worlds*, 53rd Venice Biennale, Venice, Italy
2008	*China Power Station III*, Musée d'Art Moderne Grand - Duc Jean, Luxembourg
2007	*85' New Wave*, The Birth of Chinese Contemporary Art, UCCA, Beijing, China
2006	*La Force de l'Art*, Grand Palais, Paris, France
2005	*Contrepoint*, de l'objet d'art à la sculpture, Musée du Louvre, Paris, France
2004	*Sâo Paulo Biennial 26*, Sâo Paulo, Bresil
2003	*Z.O.U - Zone of Urgency*, The 50th Venice Biennal, Venice, Italy
2002	*Reinterpretation: A Decade of Experimental Chinese Art (1990 - 2000)*, Guangzhou Triennale, Guangdong Museum of Art, China
2001	*Huang Yong Ping & Shen Yuan*, Contemporary Art Center, Québec, Canada
2000	*Biennal Shanghai*, Shanghai Museum of Art, Shanghai, China
1999	*The 48th Venice Biennale, Jean - Pierre Bertrand et Huang Yongping*, French Pavillon, Venice, Italy
1998	*Hugo Boss Prize 1998*, The Guggenheim Museum Soho, New York, U.S.A
1997	*Cities on the Move*, Secession, Wien, Austria
1996	*Face à l'Histoire*, Centre Georges Pompidou, Paris, France
1995	*6 Triennal Felbach 1995*, Museum Moderner Kunst Stiftung Ludwig Wien, Austria
1994	*Hors - Limites, (L'Art et la Vie 1952 / 1994)*, Centre Georges Pompidou, Paris, France
1993	*Silent Energy*, Museum of Modern Art, Oxford, U.K
1992	*Parcours Privés 1992*, Paris, France
1991	*Carnegie International 1991*, The Carnegie Museum of Art, Pittsburg, U.S.A
1990	*Chine Demain Pour Hier*, Pourrières, France
1989	*Magiciens de la Terre*, Centre Georges Pompidou et Grande Halle de la Villette, Paris, France
	China Avant - Garde, China National Art Gallery, Beijing, China
1986	*Xiamen 86 Neo - Dada Exhibition of Modern Art*, Xiamen Hall of Culture, China
1983	*Exhibition of Five Artists*, Cultural Palace of Xiamen, Xiamen, China

汪建伟
Wang Jianwei

1958	生于四川
1987	毕业于浙江美术学院
	现生活、工作于北京

精选个展

2011	黄灯，尤伦斯当代艺术中心，北京
2009	时间·剧场·展览，今日美术馆，北京
2008	人质，上海证大现代美术馆，上海
	征兆：汪建伟大型剧场作品展，何香凝美术馆
	OCT当代艺术中心，深圳、上海
2007	交叉感染，Hebbel am ufer，柏林，德国
	三岔口，前波画廊，纽约，美国
2006	躲闪，外滩三号沪申画廊，上海
	飞鸟不动，Arario画廊，北京
2005	飞鸟不动，前波画廊，纽约，美国
2004	巨人，亚太当代艺术中心，悉尼，澳大利亚
2002	汪建伟个展，沃克艺术中心，美国
1994	种植-循环，四川
1992	汪建伟个展，香港艺术中心，中国香港
1991	汪建伟个展，民族文化宫，北京

精选群展

2009	国家遗产：一项关于视觉政治史的研究，Holden画廊，曼彻斯特大学，英国
	国家遗产：一项关于视觉政治史的研究，何香凝美术馆OCT当代艺术中心，深圳
2008	中国动力站（第三站），卢森堡现代美术馆，卢森堡
2007	中国-面对现实，维也纳现代艺术美术馆，奥地利
2006	显微学，澳门当代艺术馆，澳门
2005	第二届广州三年展，广州美术馆，广州
2004	现代中国，现代艺术博物馆，纽约，美国
2003	第五十届威尼斯双年展，威尼斯，意大利
2002	第二十五届圣保罗双年展，圣保罗双年展馆，巴西
2001	生活在此时，柏林汉堡火车站美术馆，德国
2000	上海国际双年展，上海美术馆，上海
1999	移动的城市，Louisiana当代博物馆，哥本哈根，丹麦；纽约P.S.1当代艺术中心，美国；Hayward画廊，伦敦，英国
1998	移动的城市展，波尔多现代艺术馆，法国
1997	第九届日本山形国际电影纪录片节，山形，日本
	又一次长征：中国当代艺术1997展，布瑞德，荷兰
	第十届文献展，卡塞尔，德国
1996	第二届亚太地区当代艺术三年展，昆士兰美术馆，澳大利亚
1995	'95光州双年展，光州，韩国
1994	中、韩、日'94北京国际交感艺术展，首都师范大学美术馆，北京
1993	后89中国新艺术展，香港艺术中心，中国香港

1958	Born in Sichuan Province, China
1987	Graduated from Zhejiang Academy of Fine Arts, China
	Lives and works in Beijing, China

Selected Solo Exhibitions

2009	*Time · Theathre · Exhibition*, Today Art Museum, Beijing, China
2008	*Hostage*, Zendai Museum of Modern Art, Shanghai, China
	Symptom, A Large Work by Wang Jianwei, OCT Contemporary Art Terminal of He Xiangning Art Museum, Shenzhen, Shanghai, China
2007	*Cross Infection Hebbel am Ufer*, Berlin, Germany
	Dilemma: Three Way Fork in the Road, Chambers Fine Art, New York, U.S.A
2006	*Dodge*, Shanghai Gallery of Art, Shanghai, China
	A Flying Bird is Motionless, Arario, Beijing, China
2005	*A Flying Bird is Motionless*, Chambers Fine Art, New York, U.S.A
2004	*Giant steps*, Asia - Australia Arts Centre, Sydney, Australia
2002	*Wang Jianwei*, Walker Art Center, U.S.A
1994	*Accomplish Circulation - Sowing and Harvesting*, Sichuan Province, China
1992	*Wang Jianwei*, Hong Kong Art Center, Hong Kong, China
1991	*Wang Jianwei*, Cultural Palace of Nationalities, Beijing, China

Selected Group Exhibitions

2009	*State Legacy: Research in the Visualisation of Political History*, Manchester Metropolitan Universtity, U.K
	State Legacy: Research in the Visualisation of Political History, OCT Contemporary Art Terminal of He Xiangning Art Museum, Shenzhen, China
2008	*China Power Station (Part 3)*, Mudam Luxembourg, Luxembourg
2007	*China Facing Reality*, Museum Moderner Kunst Stiftung Ludwig Wien, Vienna, Austria
2006	*Micrology*, The Museum of Modern Art, Macao
2005	*The Second Guangzhou Triennial*, Guangzhou Museum of Art, China
2004	*China Now*, The Museum of Modern Art, New York, U.S.A
2003	*The 50th Venice Biennale*, Venice, Italy
2002	*The 25th Sao Paulo Biennale*, National Representation, Sao Paulo, Brazil
2001	*Living in time*, Nationalgalerie im Hamburger Bahnhof , Berlin, Germany
2000	*Shanghai Biennale 2000*, Shanghai Art Museum, China
1999	*Cities on the Move*, Louisiana Museum of Modern Art, Humlebaek, Denmark; P.S.1 Contemporary Art Center, New York, USA; Hayward Gallery, London, U.K
1998	*Cities on the Move*, Secession, Vienna, Austria; Musee d'art Contemporary de Bordeaus, France
1997	*Yamagata International Documentary Film Festival'97*, Yamagata, Japan
	Another Long March: China Conceptual Art'97, Breda, Holland
	The 10th Documenta, Kassel, Germany
1996	*The Second Asia - Pacific of Contemporary Art Triennial*, Brisbane, Australia
1995	*95 Kwang - ju Bienneal - InfoArt*, Kwang - ju City, Korea
1994	*94 Beijing International COM - ART Show*, The Art Museum of Capital Normal University, Beijing, China
1993	*China's New Art, Post-1989*, Hong Kong Arts Center, Hong Kong, China

王兴伟
Wang Xingwei

1969	出生于辽宁沈阳
1990	毕业于沈阳大学师范学院
	现生活、工作于北京

精选个展

2008	王兴伟个人展，麦勒画廊，北京
2007	大划船，麦勒画廊，北京
	大划船，麦勒画廊，卢森，瑞士
2004	交织的梦，麦勒画廊，瑞士
2003	过继，香格纳画廊，上海
2001	还在画画：王兴伟和陈丹青，中国艺术文件仓库，北京
1996	男性浪漫英雄史之尘，中央美术学院画廊，北京

精选群展

2010	中国当代艺术三十年历程1979-2009，民生现代艺术馆，上海
2009	事务状态：中比当代艺术交流展，比利时皇家美术宫，布鲁塞尔，比利时
2008	开幕展，白南准艺术中心，首尔，韩国
2007	麻将：中国当代艺术希克收藏展，萨尔茨堡现代博物馆，奥地利
2006	从"极地"到"铁西区"：东北当代艺术展1985-2006，广东美术馆，广州
	第六届上海双年展，上海美术馆，上海
2005	麻将：中国当代艺术希克收藏展，伯尔尼美术馆，伯尔尼，瑞士
2004	里里外外：中国当代艺术展，里昂当代艺术馆，法国
2003	布拉格双年展，布拉格，捷克
2002	首届广州当代艺术三年展，广东美术馆，广州
2001	自届成都双年展，成都
2000	不合作方式，东廊，上海
1999	第四十八届威尼斯双年展，威尼斯，意大利
	观念、颜色和激情，中国艺术文件仓库，北京
	中国现代艺术基金会收藏展，根特，比利时
	创新I，中国艺术文件仓库，北京
	改变视觉，Hof 88美术馆，阿尔默洛，荷兰
	来自中国的新绘画，油画国际艺术画廊，阿姆斯特丹，荷兰
1998	是我！紫禁城工人文化宫，北京
	中国五千年，古根海姆美术馆，毕尔巴鄂，西班牙
	偏执，北三环东路十号地下室，北京
1997	里昂当代艺术双年展，里昂，法国
1996	中国现在，立特曼文化项目中心，巴塞尔，瑞士；帕库广场和麒麟艺术，东京，日本
	中国：15个艺术家的工作室，Artcircolo艺术项目有限公司，慕尼黑，德国
	追昔：中国当代绘画，水果市场画廊，爱丁堡，英国
1994	阶段测验，中央美术学院画廊，北京

1969	Born in Shenyang, Liaoning Province, China
1990	Graduated from the Shenyang Normal University, China
	Currently lives and works in Beijing, China

Selected Solo Exhibitions

2008	*Wang Xingwei Solo Exhibition*, Galerie Urs Meile, Beijing - Lucerne, Beijing, China
2007	*Wang Xingwei - Large Rowboat*, Galerie Urs Meile, Beijing - Lucerne, Beijing, China
	Wang Xingwei - Large Rowboat, Galerie Urs Meile, Beijing - Lucerne, Lucerne, Switzerland
2004	*Interlinked Dreams*, Galerie Urs Meile, Beijing - Lucerne, Lucerne, Switzerland
2003	*Fostered Art*, ShanghArt Gallery, Shanghai, China
2001	*Still Paint - Wang Xingwei & Chen Danqing*, China Art Archives&Warehouse, Beijing, China
1996	*The Dust of the Romantic History of Male Heroism*, Museum of the Central Academy of Fine Arts, Beijing, China

Selected Group Exhibitions

2010	*The Official Opening of Minsheng Art Museum - Thirty Years of Chinese Contemporary Art 1979 - 2009*, Minsheng Art Museum, Shanghai, China
2009	*The State of Things, Brussels / Beijing*, Bozar Centre for Fine Arts, Brussels, Belgium
2008	*Opening Exhibition*, Nam June Paik Art Center, Seoul, Korea
2007	*Mahjong, Chinesische Gegenwartskunst aus der Sammlung Sigg*, Museum der Moderne, Salzburg, Austria
2006	*From Polar Region to Tiexi District - Contemporary Art in Northeastern China 1985 - 2006*, Guangdong Museum of Art, Guangzhou, China
	6th Shanghai Biennale, Shanghai Art Museum, Shanghai, China
2005	*Mahjong, Chinesische Gegenwartskunst aus der Sammlung Sigg*, Kunstmuseum Bern, Berne, Switzerland
2004	*The Monk and the Demon, Contemporary Chinese Art*, Musée d'Art Contemporain, Lyon, France
2003	*Prague Biennale*, Prague, Czech
2002	*The 1st Guangzhou Triennial*, Guangdong Museum of Art, Guangzhou, China
2001	*The First Chengdu Biennale*, Chengdu Modern Art Museum, Chengdu, China
2000	*Fuck Off*, EastLink Gallery, Shanghai, China
1999	*D'APERTutto, La Biennale di Venezia, 48. Esposizione Internationale d'Arte*, Venice, Italy
	Concepts, Colors and Passions, China Art Archives & Warehouse, Beijing, China
	Modern China Art Foundation Collection, Caermersklooster - Provinciaal Centrum voor Kunst en Cultuur, Gent, Belgium
	Innovations Part I, China Art Archives & Warehouse, Beijing, China
	Changing Views, Kunsthal Hof 88, Almelo, Netherlands
	China's High Potentials Canvas, Canvas International Art, Amsterdam, Netherlands
1998	*It's Me!*, Workers' Cultural Palace, Forbidden City, Beijing, China
	China Five Thousand Years, Guggenheim Art Museum, Bilbao, Spain
	Opportunists, Basement in the North Third Ring No.10, Beijing, China
1997	*Biennale d'Art Contemporain de Lyon*, Lyon, France
1996	*China Now*, Littmann Kultur Projekte, Basel, Switzerland; Parco Square and Kirin Art, Tokyo, Japan
	China - Aktuelles aus 15 Ateliers, Artcircolo Kunstprojekt GmbH, Munich, Germany
	Reckoning with the Past - Contemporary Chinese Painting, Fruitmarket Gallery, Edinburgh, U.K
1994	*Put to Trial*, Museum of the Central Academy of Fine Arts, Beijing, China

没顶公司
MadeIn

MadeIn(没顶文化有限公司)是由徐震在2009年创立于上海的文化有限公司。公司致力于艺术创造、制作、传播、支持以及策划,是一个多功能的复合式文化有限公司。

精选个展

2011	意识形状,长征空间,北京
	意识形状,伯尔尼美术馆,伯尔尼,瑞士
2010	不要把信仰挂在墙上,长征空间,北京
	看见自己的眼睛,IKON美术馆,伯明翰,英国
	There are new species! What do you suppose they are called? Fabien Fryns Fine Art,洛杉矶,美国
	蔓延到北京:没顶公司出品,香格纳画廊,北京
2009	蔓延到上海:没顶公司出品,香格纳在淮海路796号,上海
	MadeIn: Seeing One's Own Eyes, Europalia.China, S.M.A.K.,根特,比利时
	孤独的奇迹:中东当代艺术展,James Cohan画廊,纽约,美国
	看见自己的眼睛:中东当代艺术展,香格纳画廊,上海
	看见自己的眼睛:中东当代艺术展,香格纳H空间,上海

精选群展

2011	香格纳群展,香格纳画廊,上海
	一堆热情,香格纳画廊,上海
	怎么办?,恒庐美术馆,杭州
2010	一个接一个:香格纳画廊群展,香格纳画廊,上海
	香格纳桃浦展库,香格纳桃浦展库,上海
	巡回排演·第八届上海双年展2010,上海美术馆,上海
	有效期2010,香格纳H空间,上海
	香格纳群展,香格纳画廊主空间,上海
	中国当代艺术三十年,民生现代美术馆,上海
	个人前线,IA32 Space,北京
	丛林:中国当代艺术生态管窥,站台中国,北京
	冬季群展,香格纳画廊,北京
2009	中坚:新世纪中国艺术的八个关键形象,尤伦斯艺术中心,北京
	自由自在,Waldburger画廊,布鲁塞尔,比利时
	图像的新态度,当代唐人艺术中心,北京
	资产阶级化了的无产阶级:当代艺术展在松江,松江创意工坊,上海

MadeIn is a company established in the year 2009 in Shanghai by Xu Zhen. The firm expands its diversity on the creation, support, spread and curation of art.

Selected Solo Exhibitions

2011	*Physique of Consiousness*, Long March Space, Beijing, China
	Physique of Consciousness, Kunsthalle Bern, Bern, Switzerland
2010	*Don't Hang Your Faith on The Wall*, Long March Space, Beijng, China
	Seeing One's Own Eyes, Ikon Gallery, Birmingham, U.K
	There are new species! What do you suppose they are called?,
	Fabien Fryns Fine Art, Los Aageles, U.S.A
	Spread, by MadeIn at ShanghART Beijing, ShanghART Beijing, China
2009	*Spread, New Exhibition Produced by MadeIn*, ShanghART, Shanghai, China
	MadeIn, Seeing One's Own Eyes, Europalia.China, S.M.A.K., Gent, Belgium
	Lonely Miracle: Middle East Contemporary Art, James Cohan Gallery, New York, U.S.A
	Seeing One's Own Eyes, Middle East Contemporary Art Exhibition, Space #1,
	ShanghART Gallery, Shanghai, China
	Seeing One's Own Eyes, Middle East Contemporary Art Exhibition, Space #2,
	ShanghART H - Space, Shanghai, China

Selected Group Exhibitions

2011	*A Pile of Passion*, ShanghART Gallery, Shanghai, China
	How we to do?, Heng Lu Art Museum, Hangzhou, China
2010	*One by one, ShanghART Group Show*, ShanghART Gallery, Shanghai, China
	ShanghART Taopu, ShanghART Taopu Warehouse, Shanghai, China
	Rehearsal: 8th Shanghai Biennale 2010, Shanghai Art Museum, Shanghai, China
	Useful Life 2010, ShanghART H - Space, Shanghai, China
	Thirty Years of Chinese Contemporary Art, Minsheng Art Museum, Shanghai, China
	Personal Frontier, IA32 SPACE, Beijing, China
	Jungle: A Close - up Focus on Chinese Contemporary Art Trends,
	Platform China, Beijing, China
2009	*Breaking Forecast, 8 Key Figures of China's New Genration Artists*, UCCA, Beijing, China
	Footloose, Galerie Waldburger, Brussels, Belgium
	The New Attitude of Image, Tang Contemporary Art Center, Beijing, China
	Bourgeoisified Proletariat, Contemporary Art Exhibition in Songjiang, Shanghai, China
	Songjiang Creative Studio, Shanghai, China

蔡东东
Cai Dongdong

1978	出生于甘肃
1996	入伍
2002	学习于北京电影学院
	现生活、工作于北京

个展

2010	51m²：6#蔡东东，泰康空间，北京

群展

2011	第三届特尔纳当代艺术奖获奖作品展，罗马，意大利
	蔡东东 × 葛磊 × 苏文祥 × 赵耍，以太空间，北京
	51m²：16位年轻艺术家，泰康空间，北京
	第三方第三幕，站台中国，北京
	重庆国际当代摄影邀请展，重庆
2009	领升：2009中国美术批评家提名展，北京当代美术馆，北京
	Youth，中国广场，纽约
2008	超自然：中国当代影像，纽约，美国
	透视，香港当代唐人艺术中心，香港
	史迹·造像，环碧堂画廊，北京
	外象，三影堂摄影艺术中心，北京
2007	态度，东廊画廊，上海
2006	中国－台湾当代摄影家邀请展，韩国
2005	城市－重视·广州国际摄影双年展，广东美术馆，广州

1978	Born in Gansu Province, China
1996	Join the Army
2002	Studied in Beijing Film Academy, Beijing, China
	Currently lives and works in Beijing, China

Solo Exhibition

2010	*51m²: 6#Cai Dongdong*, Taikang Space, Beijing, China

Group Exhibitions

2011	*Terna Prize 03 for Contemporary Art*, Rome, Italy
	Cai Dongdong × Ge Lei × Su Wenxiang + Zhao Yao, Aether Art Space, Beijing, China
	51m²: 16 Emerging Chinese Artists, Taikang Space, Beijing, China
	The Third Party · Act 3, Platform China, Beijing, China
2009	*2009 Chinese Art Critics Nominating Exhibition*, Museum of Contemporary Art Beijing, Beijing, China
	Youth, New York China Square, New York, U.S.A
2008	*China's Contemporary Photography in the New Century*, Art Gate Gallery, New York, U.S.A
	See Through, Tang Contemporary Art, Hong Kong, China
	Fabricating Images from History, Chinablue Gallery, Beijing, China
	Outward Images, Three Shadows Photography Center, Beijing, China
2007	*Attitude*, Eastlink Gallery, Shanghai, China
2006	*China and Taiwan Contemporary Photography*, Donggang Photography Museum, Korea
2005	*Re - viewing*: Guangzhou International Photo Biennale, Guangdong Museum of Art, Guangzhou, China

胡向前
Hu Xiangqian

1983	出生于广东雷州
2007	毕业于广州美术学院
	现生活、工作于北京

个展

2010	51m²：7#胡向前，泰康空间，北京
	身体美术馆／Sweet and Sweat，24小时艺术中心——北领地当代艺术中心，达尔文，澳大利亚
2009	用膝盖思考，观察社，广州

群展

2010	王郁洋＆胡向前：有机体，尤伦斯当代艺术中心，北京
	伟大的表演，佩斯北京，北京
2009	资产阶级化了的无产阶级——当代艺术在淞江，淞江创意园，上海
	档案，奥沙画廊，香港
2008	广州站：广东当代艺术展，广东美术馆，广州
	我的身体是你的战场，非艺术中心，上海
2007	中国发电站 II，Astrup Fearnley现代美术馆，奥斯陆，挪威
	Slash Fiction，Gasworks，伦敦，英国
2006	都市状态，爱沙尼亚国家美术馆，塔林，爱沙尼亚
	从昌岗路出发，广东美术馆时代分馆，广州
	中国第一届独立电影展，巴黎，法国
2005	未来考古学：第二届中国三年展，南京博物馆，南京

1983	Born in Guangdong Province, China
2007	Graduated from Guangzhou Academy of Fine Arts, Guangzhou, China
	Currently lives and works in Beijing, China

Solo Exhibitions

2010	*51m²: 7#Hu Xiangqian*, Taikang Space, Beijing, China
	Body as a Museum / Sweet and Sweat, 24hr Art, Northern Territory Centre for Contemporary Art, Darwin, Australia
2009	*Knee - Jerk Reaction*, Observation Society, Guangzhou, China

Group Exhibitions

2010	*Wang Yuyang & Hu Xiangqian: Organisms*, UCCA, Beijing, China
	Great Performance, Pace Beijing, Beijing, China
2009	*Bourgeoisified Proletariat: Contemporary Art in Songjiang*, Songjiang Creative Studio, Shanghai, China
	Biography, Osage Gallery, Hong Kong, China
2008	*Guangzhou Station: the Contemporary Art in Guangzhou*, Guangdong Museum of Art, Guangzhou, China
	My Body is Your Battleground, Fei Art Center, Shanghai, China
2007	*China Power Station Part II*, Astrup Fearnley Museum of Modern Art, Oslo, Norway
	Slash Fiction, Gasworks, London, U.K
2006	*Urban Situation*, Estonian National Museum of Art, Tallinn, Estonian
	The Road from Changgang, Guangdong Museum of Art, Guangzhou, China
	The 1st Independent Chinese Film Exhibition, Paris, France
2005	*A Future of Antiquity: The 2nd Chinese Triennial*, Nanjing Museum, Nanjing, China

刘窗
Liu Chuang

1978	出生于湖北
2001	毕业于湖北美术学院
	现生活、工作于北京

个展

2010	51m² : 13#刘窗，泰康空间，北京

群展

2011	51m² : 16位年轻艺术家，泰康空间，北京
2010	中国发电站，Pinacoteca Giovanni e Marella Agnelli，都灵，意大利
	SH Contemporary发现：价值重构，上海展览中心，上海
	研究与理论，Kwadrat，柏林，德国
	军械库博览会2010，纽约，美国
	线索，Boers-Li画廊，北京
2009	就在拐角，箭厂空间，北京
	永久移民，传承——项目空间，深圳
	世代：比耶稣年轻，新美术馆，纽约，美国
2008	失眠摄影展，比翼艺术空间，上海
	永葆青春，Anne + Art Project，巴黎，法国
	调解，波兹南双年展，波兹南，波兰
	暂停，Para / Site Art Space，香港
	没有要讲的故事，唐人画廊，北京
	乡愁，T空间，北京
	物异，玛吉画廊，北京
	癫狂北京，PKM画廊，北京
	神话之界，外滩三号，上海
2007	同人小说，Gasworks，伦敦，英国
	在深圳，艺术方位，深圳
	中国发电站 II，Astrup Fearnley现代美术馆，奥斯陆，挪威
2005	未来考古学：第二界中国艺术三年展，南京博物院，南京
2004	任何地方：艺术、移民、乌托邦，马其顿当代美术馆，希腊
	物体系：无为，维他命空间，西班牙全球艺术博览会，马德里，西班牙
2003	第五系统：后规划时代的公共艺术，第五界深圳国际公共艺术展，何香凝美术馆，深圳

1978	Born in Hubei Province, China
2001	Graduated from Hubei Institute of Fine Arts, China
	Currently lives and works in Beijing, China

Solo Exbihition

2010	*51m²: 16#Liu Chuang*, Taikang Space, Beijing, China

Group Exbihitions

2011	*51m²:16 Emerging Chinese Artists*, Taikang Space, Beijing, China
2010	*China Power Station*, Pinacoteca Giovanni e Marella Agnelli, Turin, Italy
	Studies & Theory, Kwadrat, Berlin, Germany
	Trailer, Boers - Li Gallery, Beijing, China
	Armory Show 2010, New York, U.S.A
2009	*Just Around the Corner*, Arrow Factory, Beijing, China
	Permanent Migrants, Inheritance - Shenzhen, Shenzhen, China
	The Generational: Younger Than Jesus, New Museum of Contemporary Art, New York, U.S.A
2008	*Insomnia. Photographs Exhibition*, Biz - Art Art Center, Shanghai, China
	Forever Young, Anne + art project, Paris, France
	Poznan Mediations International Biennale Of Contemporary art, Poznan, Poland
	Terminus, Para / Site Art Space, Hong Kong, China
	There Is No Story To Tell, Tang Gallery, Beijing, China
	Homesickness, T Space, Beijing, China
	Delirious Beijing, PKM Gallery, Beijing, China
	Realms of Myth, Shanghai Gallery Of Art, Shanghai, China
2007	*China Power Station: Part II*, Astrup Fearnley Museum of Modern Art, Oslo, Norway
	In Shenzhen, J&Z Gallery, Shenzhen, China
	Slash fiction, Gasworks, London, U.K
2005	*The 2nd Triennial of Chinese Art: Archaeology of the Future*, Nanjing Museum, Nanjing, China
2004	*Any Place Any - Art, Immigration, Utopia*, Macedonian Museum of Contemporary Art, Thessaloniki, Greece
	Object System: Doing Nothing, Vitermin Creative Space, ARCO2004, Madrid, Spain
2003	*The Fifth System: Public Art in the Age of Post - Planning, The 5th Shenzhen International Public Art Exhibition*, He Xiangning Art Museum, Shenzhen, China

马秋莎
Ma Qiusha

1982	出生于北京
2005	毕业于中央美术学院
2008	毕业于美国阿尔弗雷德大学
	现生活、工作于北京

个展

2010	51m² : 12# 马秋莎，泰康空间，北京
2009	马秋莎，北京公社，北京
2008	矛盾的热情，Fosdick Nelson 画廊，阿尔弗雷德，美国
2007	盒子的空间，空间的盒子，泰康顶层空间，北京

群展

2011	51m² : 16位年轻艺术家，泰康空间，北京
	建筑形式，北京公社，北京
2010	伟大的表演，佩斯北京，北京
	媒体风貌——东部地带，韩国文化中心，利物浦，英国
	幕：中国录像艺术的三代，UTS画廊，悉尼，澳大利亚
	没有可售的灵魂，泰特现代美术馆，伦敦，英国
	Move On Asia 2010，Loop画廊，首尔，韩国
	调节器：第二届今日文献展，今日美术馆，北京
	七个年轻艺术家，北京公社，北京
	蝴蝶效应：两岸四地艺术交流计划，何香凝美术馆，深圳
2009	工作坊：艺术家是如何工作的，伊比利亚当代艺术中心，北京
	TNA艺术节，波特兰当代艺术学院，波特兰，美国
	私人空间，24小时艺术中心——北领地当代艺术中心，达尔文，澳大利亚
	首届三影堂摄影奖2008-2009作品展，三影堂摄影艺术中心，北京
	亚洲地图，CIGE中国国际画廊博览会，北京
2008	BCA艺术市集，天安时间当代艺术中心，北京
	风景的拓扑，玛吉画廊，北京；马德里，西班牙
	一切皆有可能，CCRN，卢森堡
	描绘食物，Walsh画廊，芝加哥，美国
	潜活：公寓日志，大未来画廊，北京
	机械器官，A9空间，北京
2007	刷新：中国青年艺术家，上海证大现代艺术馆，上海；阿拉里奥画廊，北京
	自动对焦：15件录像作品展，苏州工艺美院美术馆，苏州
	无界，南京圣划艺术中心，南京
	南方六十秒录像节，爱尔兰
	未来艺术节：中国录像单元，维尔纽斯，立陶宛
2006	2006女性电影节，台北，中国台湾
	第35届鹿特丹国际电影节，鹿特丹，荷兰
2005	当绯闻遭遇粉饰，东大名创库艺术中心，上海
	一卡通，泰康顶层空间，北京
	九百二十公斤，上海多伦现代美术馆，上海
	未来考古学：第二届中国艺术三年展，南京博物院，南京

1982	Born in Beijing, China
2005	Graduated from Central Academy of Fine Arts, Beijing, China
2008	Graduated from Alfred University, New York, U.S.A
	Currently lives and works in Beijing, China

Solo Exhibitions

2010	*51m²: 12#Ma Qiusha*, Taikang Space, Beijing, China
2009	*Ma Qiusha*, Beijing Commune, Beijing, China
2008	*Ambivalent Enthusiasm*, Fosdick - Nelson Gallery, New York, U.S.A
2007	*The Space of Box, the Box of Space*, Taikang Top Space, Beijing, China

Group Exhibitions

2011	*51m²:16 Emerging Chinese Artists*, Taikang Space, Beijing, China
	Constructing Form, Beijing Commune, Beijing, China
2010	*Great Performance*, Pace Beijing, China
	Media Landscape - Zone East, Contemporary Urban Centre - Liverpool Biennial / Korean Cultural Centre UK
	Mu: Screen - Three Generations of Chinese Video Art, UTS Gallery, Sydeny, Australia
	No Soul For Sale 2010, Tate Modern, London, U.K
	Move on Asia 2010, Loop Gallery, Seoul, Korea
	Negotiations, The Second Today's Documents, Today Art Museum, Beijing, China
	Seven Young Artists, Beijing Commune, Beijing, China
	The Butterfly Effect, An Artistic Communication Project of Cross - Strait Four - Regions, He Xiangning Art Museum, Shenzhen, China
2009	*Work in Progress: How Do Artists Work?* Iberia Center for Contemporary Art, Beijing, China
	2009 Time - Based Art Festival, Portland Institute For Contemporary Art, Portland, U.S.A
	Personal Space, 24 HR Art - Northern Territory Contemporary Art Centre, Darwin, Australia
	First Annual Three Shadows Photography Award Exhibition, Three Shadows Photography Art Centre, Beijing, China
	China International Gallery Exposition 2009 - Mapping Asia, Beijing, China
2008	*The MARKET: New Year Gifts from 60 Young Artists*, Beijing Center for the Arts at Legation Quarter, Beijing, China
	Landscape Topology, Magee Gallery, Beijing, China; Madrid, Span
	Anything is Possible, CCRN, Luxembourg
	Portraying Food (or the Absence of It), Walsh Gallery, Chicago, U.S.A
	Hidden Life: Apartment Diary, Lin&Keng Gallery, Beijing, China
	Mechanism Organism, A9 Space, Beijing, China
2007	*Refresh: Emerging Chinese Artists*, Shanghai Zendai Museum of Modern Art, Shanghai; ARARIO, Beijing, China
	Focus Automatically: 15 Video Art Works, Suzhou Art & Design Technology Institute, Suzhou, China
	Without Boundaries, Shenghua Art Center, Nanjing, China
	Southern 60 second festival, Ireland
	Next Festival 2007 - Special Chinese video art program, Vilnius, Lithuania
2006	*2006 Women Make Waves Film Festival*, Taipei, China
	35th International Film Festival Rotterdam, Rotterdam, The Netherlands
2005	*Rumor Décor*, DDM warehouse Art Center, Shanghai, China
	A Cartoon, Taikang Top Space, Beijing, China
	920 Kilograms, Shanghai Duolun Museum of Modern Art, Shanghai, China
	Archaeology of the Future: the 2nd Triennial of Chinese Art, Nanjing Museum, Nanjing, China

裴丽
Pei Li

1985	出生于江苏常州
2008	毕业于中国美术学院
2008	学习于北京电影学院

个展

2010	51m² : 9#裴丽，泰康空间，北京

群展

2011	梦眼：来自中国的影像艺术，悉尼，澳大利亚
	FAT ART 2011，今日美术馆，北京
	51m² : 16位年轻艺术家，泰康空间，北京
	分分秒秒，泰康空间，北京
2010	东京"Cool艺术"媒体艺术节，横滨，日本
	第十一届北京电子音乐节，中央音乐学院，北京
	轨迹与质变：60周年院庆当代艺术邀请展，北京电影学院，北京
2009	FAT ART之"目耳计划"，今日美术馆，北京
	"从零开始"中国新媒体实验电影艺术联展，北京
	中国青年艺术家实验电影(影像)作品展，北京
	群落：宋庄国际艺术节，北京
2008	水木境天：北京电影学院国际新媒体三年展，北京电影学院，北京
	中国美术学院新媒体系毕业作品展，中国美术学院，杭州
2007	进进出出：杭州首次纯互动装置展，杭州

1985	Born in Changzhou, Jiangsu Province, China
2008	Graduated from China Academy of Art, Hanghou, China
2008	Studing in Beijing Film Academy, Beijing, China

Solo Exhibition

2010	*51m²: 9#Pei Li*, Taikang Space, Beijing, China

Group Exhibitions

2011	*Eye of the Dream: Video Art form China Exhibition*, Sydney, Australia
	FAT ART 2011, Today Museum, Beijing, China
	51m²: 16 Emerging Chinese Artists, Taikang Space, Beijing, China
	Present Continuous Past(s), Taikang Space, Beijing, China
2010	*Tokyo Downtown Cool Media Festival*, Tokyo, Japan
	Track and Changing in Quality: 60th anniversary of Beijing Film Academy Cont, Beijing, China
2009	*Fat Art: Music to My Eyes*, Today Art Museum, Beijing, China
	From Scratch: China's New Media Experiments Exhibition, Beijing, China
	Chinese Young Artists Exhibition of Experimental Film, Beijing, China
	"Community" Fifth Cultural & Arts Festival of Songzhuang, Beijing, China
2008	*Water, Wood, Environment, Sky, Beijing Film Academy International New Media Art Exhibition*, Beijing, China
	New Media Art Graduation Exhibition, China Academy of Art, Hangzhou, China
2007	*Input Output: Interaction Art Exhibition*, Hangzhou, China

苏文祥
Su Wenxiang

1979	出生于安徽宣城
2002	毕业于蚌埠高等专科学校
	现生活、工作于北京

个展

2009	51m^2：2＃苏文祥，泰康空间，北京

群展

2011	蔡东东×葛磊×苏文祥×赵要，以太空间，北京
	51m^2：16位年轻艺术家，泰康空间，北京
2010	北京之声：在 起或孤芳自赏，佩斯北京，北京
	亚洲路标：丰田计划，伊比利亚当代艺术中心，北京
2009	工作坊：艺术家是如何工作的，伊比利亚当代艺术中心，北京
	再实验：智性与意志的重申，798艺术区，北京
	Polaroid，站台中国当代艺术机构，北京
	变卦，艺术通道画廊，北京
2008	物是·当代艺术中的物主题，玛吉画廊，北京
	Clinch／Cross／Cut展，巴塞尔，瑞士
2007	业余社会：偏离中的展览，非艺术中心，上海
	无界，南京圣划艺术馆，南京
2006	再生，海口当代艺术馆，海口
	高档货：来自上海，新凯旋门顶层，巴黎，法国
2005	亚洲交通·磁力悬浮，上海证大现代艺术馆，上海
	当绯闻遭遇粉饰，东大名创库，上海
	玖佰贰拾公斤，上海多伦现代美术馆，上海
	未来考古学：第二届中国艺术三年展，南京博物院，南京
	回到未来：上海艺术，内部空间，波兹南，波兰；浮士德美术馆，汉诺威，德国
2004	自动购物机器，苏州工艺美院桃花坞展厅，苏州
	费非飞，上海多伦现代美术馆，上海
	下一站系列当代艺术展，南京圣划艺术中心，南京
2003	电解质，南京圣划艺术中心，南京

1979	Born in Xuancheng, Anhui Province, China
2002	Graduated from Bengbu College, Anhui, China
	Currently lives and works in Beijing, China

Solo Exhibition

2009	*51m^2: 2#Su Wenxiang*, Taikang Space, Beijing, China

Group Exhibitions

2011	*Cai Dongdong × Ge Lei × Su Wenxiang × Zhao Yao*, Aether Art Space, Beijing, China
	51m^2: 16 Emerging Chinese Artists, Taikang Space, Beijing, China
2010	*Beijing Voice: Together or Isolated*, Pace Beijing, Beijing, China
	Asian Landmark - Toyota Art Project, Iberia Center for Contemporary Art, Beijing, China
2009	*Work in Progress: How Do Artists Work?*, Iberia Center for Contemporary Art, Beijing, China
	Re - experimentation: a reaffirmation of will and enlightenment, 798 Art Zone, Beijing, China
	Polaroid, Platform China Contemporary Art Institute, Beijing, China
	Transformation Hexagram, Art Channel Gallery, Beijing, China
2008	*Thinghood: the Object - related Theme in Contemporary Art*, Magee Art Gallery, Beijing, China
	Clinch / Cross / Cut - Team 404 & John Armleder, Basel, Switzerland
2007	*Self - taugaht Society: Exhibition in Deviation*, Fei Contemporary Art Center, Shanghai, China
	Without Boundaries, Nanjing Shenghua Art Center, Nanjing, China
2006	*Regenesis*, Haikou Museum of Contemporary Art, Haikou, China
	High Art from Shanghai, Roof of la Grande Arche de la Défense, Pairs, France
2005	*Asian Traffic (Magnetism - Suspension)*, Zendai Museum of Modern Art, Shanghai, China
	Rumor Décor, DDM warehouse Art Center, Shanghai, China
	920 Kilograms, Shanghai Duolun Museum of Modern Art, Shanghai, China
	Archaeology of the Future: The 2nd Triennial of Chinese Art, Nanjing Museum, Nanjing, China
	Back into Future: Shanghai Arts, Inner Space, Poznan, Poland; Kunsthalle Faust, Hanover, Germany
2004	*Automat*, Suzhou Art & Design Technology Institute, Suzhou, China
	Fei, fei, fei, Shanghai Duolun Museum of Modern Art, Shanghai, China
	Next Station - Overflow, Nanjing Shenghua Art Center, Nanjing, China
2003	*Electrolyte*, Nanjing Shenghua Art Center, Nanjing, China

王思顺
Wang Sishun

1979	出生于湖北武汉
2005	毕业于湖北美术学院
2008	毕业于中央美术学院
	现生活、工作于北京

个展

2010　51m²：4#王思顺，泰康空间，北京

群展

2011	51m²：16位年轻艺术家，泰康空间，北京
	占领舞台——回放，外滩18号，上海
2010	一切都是浮云，艾可画廊，上海
	心境，上海当代艺术馆，上海
	雕塑：隋建国和他的几个学生，A4画廊，成都
	丛林，站台中国，北京
	留住时间：中国当代艺术群展，艺术公社，香港
	反复：两岸四地青年艺术家作品展，全艺社当代艺术中心，北京
	寄居蟹，荔空间，北京
	楼上的青年，时代美术馆，北京
	什么是叙事？，A4画廊，成都
	我是……，天安时间当代艺术中心，北京
	向前一小步，798创意广场，北京
	给力，荔空间，北京
2009	全手工，天安时间当代艺术中心，北京
	时间的能量，昌阿特画廊，北京
	流feeling，艺术通道，北京
	中国意向，曲江当代艺术中心，西安
	再实验：智性与意志的重申，798创意广场，北京
	摆摊，宋庄尚堡美术馆，北京
	岸，月亮河美术馆，北京
2008	前夕，中央美术学院艺术通道画廊，北京
	Updating青年艺术季，墙美术馆，北京
	地震，艺术通道画廊，北京
	造谣，非艺术中心，上海
	北京bs1美术馆2008年度艺术提名展，bs1美术馆，北京
	断舌，梯空间，北京
	物是：当代艺术中的物主题，玛吉画廊，北京
	独白，水木当代艺术空间，北京
2007	缺席，创意正阳艺术区，北京
	形迹，凹凸空间，北京
2006	隔岸点火，独角视觉，北京

1979	Born in Wuhan, Hubei Province, China
2005	Graduated from Hubei Institute of Fine Arts, China
2008	Graduated from Central Academy of Fine Arts, Beijing, China
	Currently lives and works in Beijing

Solo Exhibition

2010	*51m²: 4# Wang Sishun*, Taikang Space, Beijing

Group Exhibitions

2011	*51m²: 16 Emerging Chinese Artists*, Taikang Space, Beijing, China
	Taking over the Stage - Reperform, Bund18, Shanghai, China
2010	*Floating Clouds*, Galleria Dell's ARCO, Shanghai, China
	Reflection of minds, MoCA Shanghai, Shanghai, China
	Sculpture: Sui jianguo and his students, A4 Gallery, Chengdu, China
	Jungle, Platform China Contemporary Art Institute, Beijing, China
	The Time Being Kept - Group Exhibition of Chinese Contemporary Artists, Artist Commune, Hong Kong
	Recurrence, Afa Beijing Contemporary Art Centre, Beijing, China
	Soldier crab I , Li - space, Beijing, China
	Youth at upstairs: nomination exhibition by young critics 2010, Time art museum, Beijing, China
	What is narrative?, A4 Gallery, Chengdu, China
	I am, Beijing Center for the Arts, Beijing, China
	Little step forward, 798 Originality Square, Beijing, China
	Wasabi, Li - space, Beijing, China
2009	*In the making*, Beijing Center for the Arts, Beijing, China
	Energy of time, Chang Art Gallery, Beijing, China
	Feeling, Art Channel, Beijing, China
	China Revisualized & The Banner of Urban Culture Xi'an Qujiang Iternationalontemporary Art Festival, Qujiang Cntenporary Art Center, Xi'an, China
	Re - experimentation: areaffirmation of will and enlightenment - Young Artists Promotional Exhibition, 798 Originality Square, Beijing, China
	Stall, Songzhuang Shangbao Art Museum, Beijing, China
2008	*Eve*, Art Channel, Beijing, China
	Updating, Wall Art Museum, Beijing, China
	Earthquake, Art Channel, Beijing, China
	Slander, Fei Contemporary Art Center, Shanghai, China
	Beijing bs1 Museum 2008 Art Nomination Exhibition, Beijing bs1 Museum, Beijing, China
	Tongue Breake, T Space, Beijing, China
	Thing Hood, Magee Art Gallery, Beijing, China
	Monologue, Shui Mu Contemporary Art Space, Beijing, China
2007	*Absent*, Creativity in the Sun Art, Beijing, China
	Evidence, Unevenness Space, Beijing, China
2006	*Burning A Fire from the Other Side of the River*, Unicorn - vision, Beijing, China

王郁洋
Wang Yuyang

1979	出生于黑龙江哈尔滨
2004	毕业于中央戏剧学院
2008	毕业于中央美术学院
	现生活、工作于北京

个展

2010	虫洞，Perth Horse Cross，英国
	51m² : 16#王郁洋，泰康空间，北京
2009	一张画，中央美术学院美术馆
	虫洞，Boers-Li画廊，北京
2008	尘归尘，CPU：798，北京

群展

2011	51m²:16位年轻艺术家，泰康空间，北京
2010	王郁洋＆胡向前：有机体，尤伦斯当代艺术中心，北京
	2010冬奥会世界交流展，温哥华，加拿大
	分享主义：2010大声展，北京
	控Con当代艺术家联展，5楼艺术空间，广州
	Transmediale全球艺术家提名奖，柏林，德国
	仁川国际电子艺术节，仁川，韩国
	心镜：上海当代艺术馆文献展 III，上海当代艺术馆，上海
2009	中国！中国！中国！
	视觉艺术博物馆，诺里奇，英国
	发现，铸造艺术馆，北京
	黑板，香格纳画廊，上海
	实境·异想，现代画廊，台中，中国台湾
	热身，民生现代美术馆，上海
	中国青年媒体艺术展，宁波美术馆，宁波
2008	中国！中国！中国！斯特罗兹宫博物馆，佛罗伦萨，意大利
	穷，Boers-Li画廊，北京
	囧，上海多伦现代美术馆，上海
	第三届南京三年展，南京博物院，南京
	失眠，比翼艺术中心，上海
	上海电子艺术节，徐家汇广场，上海
2007	可持续幻想，阿拉里奥，北京
	中德交流项目，工人体育场，北京
2006	首届学院实验艺术文献展，中央美术学院，北京
	时间，中央美术学院，北京
2003	再造798，时态空间，北京
2002	无题，中央戏剧学院，北京
	后感性内幕，七色光剧场，北京

1979	Born in Haerbin, Heilongjiang Province, China
2004	Graduated from Central Academy of Drama, Beijing, China
2008	Graduated from Central Academy of Fine Arts, Beijing, China
	Currently lives and works in Beijing, China

Solo Exhibitions

2010	*Worm Hole*, Perth Horse Cross, UK
	51m²: 16# Wang Yuyang, Taikang Space, Beijing, China
2009	*One Painting*, Art Museum of Central Academy of Fine Arts, Beijing, China
	Worm Hole, Boers - Li Gallery, Beijing, China
2008	*Dust is Dust*, CPU 798, Beijing, China

Group Exhibitions

2011	*51m²: 16 Emerging Chinese Artists*, Taikang Space, Beijing, China
2010	*Wang Yuyang & Hu Xiangqian: Organisms*, UCCA, Beijing, China
	Sharism, Get it Louder 2010, Beijing, China
	"Control Con" Contemporary Art Exhibition, 5 Art Space, Guangzhou, China
	Transmediale Global Artist Award nomination, Berlin, Germany
	Incheon International Digital Art Festival 2010, Incheon, Korea
	ReFlection of Minds - MoCA Shanghai Envisage III, MoCA, Shanghai
2009	*China China China!!!*, Sainsbury Centre for Visual Arts, Norwich, U.K
	Found, Foundry Museum, Beijing, China
	Blackboard, ShanghART Gallery, Shanghai, China
	Reality Fantasy, Modern Art Gallery, Taizhong, China
	Warm Up, Minsheng Art Museum, Shanghai, China
	Media Exhibition - Chinese Young Artists, Ningbo Art Museum, Ningbo, China
2008	*Cine Cine Cine!!!*, Strozzina Palazzo Strozzi, Florence, Italy
	Poorism, Boers - Li Gallery, Beijing, China
	Jiong, Duolun Museum of Modern Art, Shanghai, China
	The 3rd Nanjing Triennial, Nanjing Museum, Nanjing, China
	Insomnia, BizArt, Shanghai, China
	Final Cut: Shanghai E - Arts Festival, Xujiahui Plaza, Shanghai, China
2007	*Sustainable Imagination*, Arario, Beijing, China
	German Night, Goethe Institute, Beijing, China
2006	*Breathe*, Central Academy of Fine Art, Beijing, China
	Time, Central Academy of Fine Art, Beijing, China
2003	*Reproduce 798*, Beijing, China
2002	*Untitled*, Central Academy of Drama, Beijing, China
	Revealing: Post Sense and Sensibility, Seven Color Theatre, Beijing, China

辛云鹏
Xin Yunpeng

1982	出生于北京
2007	毕业于中央美术学院
	现生活、工作于北京

个展

2011	慢走，莼翠空间，北京
2010	51m² : 8#辛云鹏，泰康空间，北京

展览

2011	It's All True，Morono Kiang画廊，洛杉矶，美国
	我喺启德机场隔离等你话我知！1a空间，中国香港
	51m² : 16位年轻艺术家，泰康空间，北京
2010	Move，Morono Kiang画廊，洛杉矶，美国
	Our Maps，谷歌地图＆东方视觉"嘿！社会"论坛＆荔空间，北京
2009	嘿市－嘿板报，宋庄美术馆，北京
	随身携带，OV画廊，上海
	各搞各的，台北当代艺术馆，台北，中国台湾
2008	中国幻想，铸造艺术馆开幕展，北京
	清理臭水河－集体行动，黑桥，北京
	过来！中国当代艺术展，荔空间，北京
	第一展，荔空间，北京
	我的七天，奥沙画廊，马尼拉，菲律宾
	打鸟，梯空间，北京
	记忆是味觉，首尔，韩国
	乌托邦的边界，今日美术馆，北京
2007	相信未来，宋庄TS1美术馆，北京
	￥%……@￥！＃饿￥日－当代艺术展，当代唐人艺术中心，北京

1982	Born in Beijing, China
2007	Graduated from Central Academy of Fine Arts, Beijing, China
	Currently lives and works in Beijing, China

Solo Exhibitions

2011	*Take Care*, Chun Cui Art, Beijing, China
2010	*51m^2: 8# Xin Yunpeng*, Taikang Space, Beijing, China

Group Exhibitions

2011	*It's All True*, Morono Kiang Gallery, Los Angeles, U.S.A
	I Am Here Beside Kai Tak Waiting For You!, 1a Space, Hong Kong, China
	51m^2: 16 Emerging Chinese Artists, Taikang Space, Beijing, China
2010	*Move*, Morono Kiang Gallery, Los Angeles, U.S.A
	Our Maps, Google Map & iONLY & Li - Space, Beijing, China
2009	*Hey Markets*, Songzhuang museum, Beijing, China
	Carry - on Items, Oriental Vista Gallery, Shanghai, China
	Spectacle - To Each His Own, Museum of Contemporary Art Taipei, Taipei, China
2008	*Chinese Fantasies*, Found Museum, Beijing, China
	Clean Up River - Collective Activities, Black Bridge, Beijing, China
	We Shall Overcome, Li - Space, Beijing, China
	First Exhibition, Li - Space, Beijing, China
	My Seven Days, Osage Gallery, Manila, Philippines
	Hunting Birds, T - Space, Beijing, China
	Memory is Taste, Seoul, Korea
	The Borders of Utopia, Today Art Museum, Beijing, China
2007	*Trust the Future*, Songzhuang TS1 Museum, Beijing, China
	¥%……@¥！#饿¥日, Tang Contemporary Art, Beijing, China

徐渠
Xu Qu

1978	生于江苏盐城
2002	毕业于南京艺术学院美术学院
2007	毕业于德国布伦瑞克造型艺术学院
	现生活、工作于北京

个展

2010	51m²：11#徐渠，泰康空间，北京

群展

2011	视觉的结构，成都A4当代艺术中心，成都
	51m²：16位年轻艺术家，泰康空间，北京
2010	工作坊：传播的图与转译的像，伊比利亚当代艺术中心，北京
2009	两岸四地青年艺术家展，全艺社，北京
2008	Clinch／Cross／Cut展，New Jerseyy画廊，巴塞尔，瑞士
	XXQQ Record 3:22，Art Recorders，39 Art Basel，巴塞尔，瑞士
	Format 40展，Kunstverein Emmerich e.V.Deutschland，埃姆里希，德国
	Meisterschülerausstellung，HBK，布伦瑞克，德国
	Jahresgaben 08／09，Kunstverein Braunschweig，布伦瑞克，德国

1978	Born in Yancheng, Jiangsu Province, China
2002	Graduated from Nanjing Art Institute, China
2007	Graduated from Braunschweig University of Art, Germany
	Currently lives and works in Beijing, China

Solo Exhibition

2010	*51m²: 13# Xu Qu*, Taikang Space, Beijing, China

Group Exhibitions

2011	*Visual Structure*, A4 Contemporary Arts Center, Chengdu, China
	51m²: 16 Emerging Chinese Artists, Taikang Space, Beijing, China
2010	*Work In Spreading: Images of Circulation and Retranslation*,
	IBC for Contemporary Art, Beijing, China
2009	*Recurrence, Exhibition of Young Artists from Cross - Strait Regions*, AAF, Beijing, China
2008	*Clinch／Cross／Cut*, New Jerseyy Gallery, Basel, Switzerland
	XXQQ Record 3:22, Art Recorders, 39th Art Basel, Basel, Switzerland
	Copy and Paste, Braunschweig, Germany
	Format 40, Kunstverein Emmerich e.V. Deutschland, Emmerich, Germany
	Meisterschülerausstellung, HBK, Braunschweig, Germany
	Jahresgaben 08／09, Kunstverein Braunschweig, Braunschweig, Germany

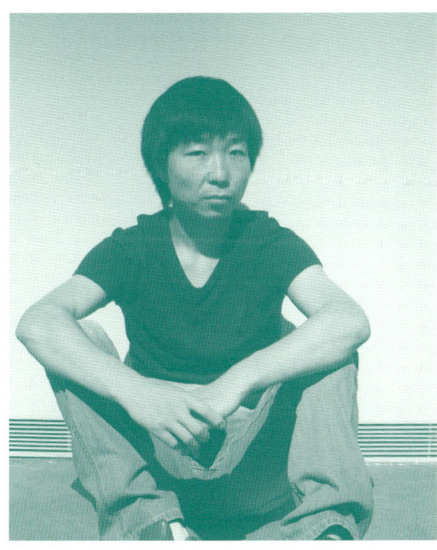

闫冰
Yan Bing

1980	出生于甘肃天水
2007	毕业于中央美术学院
	现生活、工作于北京

个展

2010	51m²：14#闫冰，泰康空间，北京
2009	温度，尤伦斯当代艺术中心，北京

群展

2011	51m²：16位年轻艺术家，泰康空间，北京
2010	游戏：中国青年艺术家，白盒子艺术馆，北京
	工作坊：传播的图与转译的像，伊比利亚艺术中心，北京
	一而二、二而一，莼萃空间，北京
	是与否，OFF Space，北京
2009	时间的能量，昌阿特画廊，北京
	空白展——制造生活，中间艺术馆，北京
2008	离艺术还有多远 II，Our Space，北京
2006	离艺术还有多远 I，雨画廊，北京

1980	Born in Tianshui, Gansu province, China
2007	Graduated from Central Academy of Fine Arts, Beijing, China
	Currently lives and works in Beijing, China

Solo Exhibitions

2010	*51m²: 14# Yan Bing*, Taikang Space, Beijing, China
2009	*Temperature*, UCCA, Beijing, China

Group Exhibitions

2011	*51m²: 16 Young Emerging Chinese Artists*, Taikang Space, Beijing, China
2010	*Games: Young Chinese Artists*, White Box Museum of Art, Beijing, China
	Work in Progress: Images of Circulation and Retranslation, Iberia Center for Contemporary Art, Beijing, China
	Two Sides of the Same Coin, Pure Space, Beijing, China
	Yes Or No, Off Space, Beijing, China
2009	*Energy of Time*, Chang Art Gallery, Beijing, China
	Blank - Making Life, Inside - Out Art Center, Beijing, China
2008	*How Far From Art II*, Our Space, Beijing, China
2006	*How Far From Art I*, Rain Gallery, Beijing, China

赵要
Zhao Yao

1981	出生于四川省泸县
2004	毕业于四川美院
	现生活、工作于北京

个展

2010	51m²: 3#赵要,泰康空间,北京

群展

2011	刀锋,弗里曼特尔艺术中心,弗里曼特尔,澳大利亚
	51m²: 16位年轻艺术家,泰康空间,北京,中国
2010	七个年轻艺术家,北京公社,北京,中国
	灵魂不可出卖,泰特现代美术馆,伦敦,英国
	移动的亚洲影像展,LOOP艺术中心,首尔,韩国;
	Para / Site艺术空间,中国香港
	媒体风貌——东部地带,韩国文化中心,伦敦,英国
	发现——价值重构:关于艺术、社会及其体系,上海艺术国际博览会,上海展览中心,上海
	心镜:上海当代艺术馆文献展III,上海当代艺术馆,上海
2010	大声展:分享主义,三里屯SOHO,北京
	调节器:第二届今日文献展,今日美术馆,北京
	概念之酶,A4艺术中心,成都
2009	艺术北京主题展:艺术突破——诗意·日常,农业展览馆,北京
	资产阶级化了的无产阶级——小制作,上海松江创意工坊,上海
	再实验:智性与意志的重申——青年艺术家推荐展,798艺术中心,北京
	工作坊:艺术家如何工作,伊比利亚当代艺术中心,北京
2008	小制作第五回,小平画廊,上海
	灰化肥发灰:当代艺术展,上海
	幸福对撞机艺术展,东坝艺术区,北京
	梦想与现实,月亮河艺术区,北京
2007	影子炼金术:第三届连州国际摄影年展,连州,广东
2006	入境:中国无章美学,上海当代艺术馆,上海
	六张照片和一个小房间,长征空间,北京
2005	当绯闻遭遇粉饰,东大名创库,上海
	景观:"世纪"与"天堂"——第二届成都双年展,成都世纪城,成都
	未来考古学:第二届中国三年展,南京
2004	双城计,重庆、香港
2003	悬而未决影像展,重庆

1981	Born in Lu County, Sichuan Province, China
2004	Graduated from Sichuan Fine Arts Institute, China
	Currently lives and works in Beijing, China

Solo Exhibition

2010	*51m^2: 3# Zhao Yao*, Taikang Space, Beijing, China

Group Exhibitions

2011	*The Knife's Edge*, Fremantle Arts Centre, Fremantle, Australia
	51m^2: 16 Emerging Chinese Young Artists, Taikang Space, Beijing, China
2010	*Seven Young Artists*, Beijing Commune, Beijing, China
	No Soul for Sale, Tate Modern Museum, London, U.K
	Move on Asia 2010, Alternative Space LOOP, Seoul, Korea; Para / Site Art Space, Hong Kong, China
	Media Landscape - Zone East, Korean Cultural Centre, London, U.K
	SH Contemporary - Discovery: Revalue, Shanghai Exhibition Center, Shanghai, China
	Reflection of Minds: MoCA Shanghai Envisage III, Museum Of Contemporary Art, Shanghai, China
	Sharism: Get It Louder 2010, Sanlitun Village SOHO, Beijing, China
	Negotiations: The 2nd Taday's Documents, Today Art Museum, Beijing, China
	Conception as Enzyme, A4 Contemporary Arts Center, Chengdu, China
2009	*Poetic - Daily: Chinese Young Artist Exhibition, the thematic project "Art Unforbidden" of Art Beijing 2009*, National Agriculture Exhibition Center, Beijing, China
	Bourgeoisified Proletariat, Small Production, Shanghai Songjiang Creative Studio, Shanghai, China
	Re - experimentation: A Reaffirmation of Will and Enlightenment - Young Artists Promotional Exhibition, Beijing, China
	Work in Progress: How Do Artists Work?, Iberia Center for Contemporary Art, Beijing, China
2008	*The 5th Small Productions Event*, Shopping Gallery, Shanghai, China
	Hui Hua Fei Fa Hui Art Exhibition, Shanghai, China
	Happy Collider Art Exhibition, Dong Ba County, Beijing, China
	Dream & Reality Art Exhibition, Moon River Museum of Contemporary Art, Beijing, China
2007	*The Alchemy of Shadows: the 2nd Lianzhou International Photo Festival*, Lianzhou, Guangdong, China
2006	*Entry Gate: Chinese Aesthetics of Heterogeneity*, Museum of Contemporary Art, Shanghai, China
	Six Photos and A Small Room, Long March Space, Beijing, China
2005	*Rumor Decor*, Video & Photograph Exhibition, DDM Warehouse, Shanghai, China
	Spectacle: "Century" and "Paradise" - the 2nd Chengdu Biennale, Chengdu Century City, Chengdu, China
	Archaeology of the Future - the 2nd Triennial of Chinese Art, Nanjing Museum, Nanjing, China
2004	*A Plan about Two Cities*, Chongqing / Hong Kong, China
2003	*Suspense: Video & Photograph Exhibition*, Chongqing, China

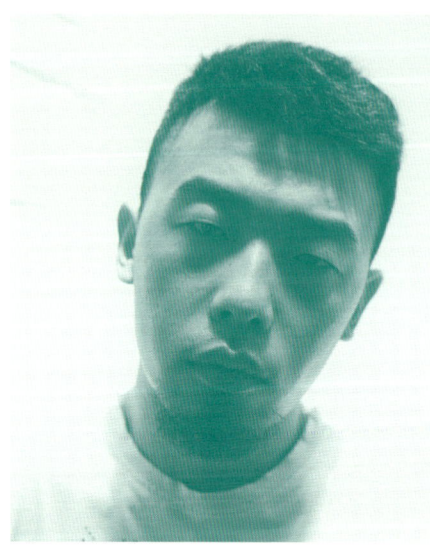

赵赵
Zhao Zhao

1982	出生于新疆石河子
2004	毕业于新疆艺术学院
	现生活、工作于北京

个展

2011	游走，亚历山大画廊，柏林，德国
2009	51m² 1# 赵赵，泰康空间，北京
2008	大泉沟，中国艺术文件仓库，北京

群展

2011	1+1 两岸四地艺术交流计划，何香凝美术馆，深圳
	自选动作，荔空间，北京
	51m²：16位年轻艺术家，泰康空间，北京
2010	心境：第三届上海当代艺术馆文献展，上海当代艺术馆，上海
	概念之酶，A4画廊，成都
	分享主义：2010大声展，北京、上海
	3＋X，中国艺术文件仓库，北京
	无名站：中国、澳大利亚当代艺术展，伊比利亚当代艺术中心，北京
	断章取义，梯空间，北京
	动起来！，荔空间，北京
	表征的重负，奥沙画廊，香港
	也是个地儿，C空间，北京
	档案，奥沙画廊，香港
2009	艺术新经济，奥沙画廊，上海
	私人空间，24小时艺术中心——北领地当代艺术中心，达尔文，澳大利亚
	工作坊：艺术家是如何工作的，伊比利亚当代艺术中心，北京
2008	癫狂北京，PKM画廊，北京
	失眠，比翼艺术中心，上海
	风景的拓扑，玛吉画廊，北京；马德里，西班牙
	断舌，梯空间，北京

1982	Born in Shihezi, Xinjiang, China
2004	Graduated from the Xinjiang Institute of Arts, China
	Currently lives and works in Beijing, China

Solo Exhibitions

2011	*Naked Walking*, Alexadner Ochs Galleries, Berlin, Germany
2009	*51m²: 1# Zhao Zhao*, Taikang Space, Beijing, China
2008	*Da Quan Gou*, China Art Archives&Warehouse, Beijing, China

Group Exhibitions

2011	*1 + 1 Art Exchange Program in Four Places: Mainland*, Hong Kong, Taiwan and Macau, He Xiangning Museum, Shenzhen, China
	Freestyle, Li Space, Beijing, China
	51m²: 16 Emerging Chinese Artists, Taikang Space, Beijing, China
2010	*Reflection of Minds: MoCA Shanghai Envisage III*, Shanghai, China
	Conception as Enzyme, A4 Gallery, Chengdu, China
	Sharism: Get It Louder 2010, Sanlitun Village SOHO, Beijing, China
	3 + X, China Art Archives&Warehouse, Beijing, China
	No - Name Station: China / Australia Contemporary Art Exhibition, Iberia Center for Contemporary Art, Beijing, China
	Moving!, Li Space, Beijing, China
	The Burden of Representation, Osage Gallery, Hong Kong, China
	Also Space, C Space, Beijing, China
	Archives, Osage Gallery, Hong Kong, China
2009	*Art Economies Beyond Pattern Recognition*, Osage Gallery, Shanghai, China
	Personal Space, 24hr Art - Northern Territory Contemporary Art Centre, Darwin, Australia
	Work in Progress - How Do Artists Work, Iberia Center for Contemporary Art, Beijing, China
2008	*Delirious Beijing*, PKM Gallery, Beijing, China
	Insomnia, Biz - art Art Center, Shanghai, China
	Landscape Topology, Magee Art Gallery, Beijing, China; Madrid, Spain
	Interpret Out of Context, T Space, Beijing, China

公司简介

泰康人寿保险股份有限公司系1996年8月22日经中国人民银行总行批准成立的全国性、股份制人寿保险公司，公司总部设于北京。

自成立以来，泰康人寿一直重视公司治理结构的不断完善。2000年11月，全面完成经国务院同意、保监会批准的外资募股工作，建立了国际化的公司治理结构。

在以董事长兼首席执行官陈东升为核心的专业化、国际化的管理团队领导下，泰康人寿发展迅速。截至2010年底，泰康人寿总资产近3000亿元，净资产超134亿元，偿付能力充足率超170%，当年利润超20亿元。2010年，泰康人寿主动防范风险，深化调整结构，坚持专业化方向和价值管理，实现业务稳健成长，全年保费规模达867.65亿元。2009-2010年，泰康人寿连续两年荣列"中国企业500强"百强企业。

截至2010年底，泰康人寿在全国设立了北京、上海、湖北、山东、广东等35家分公司（含筹建），269家中心支公司，形成了完整的服务网络，累计服务过的个人和机构客户近5400余万，累计赔付客户近720万人次，累计赔付金额近70亿元。

2006至2007年，经保监会批准，泰康人寿先后设立了泰康资产管理有限责任公司和泰康养老保险股份有限公司两家子公司。泰康资产是国内资本市场大型机构投资者之一，其综合投资收益率连续8年保持领先优势。2010年，泰康资产管理的投连进取型与货币避险型账户净值处同类保险投连账户净值领先地位，并连续两年蝉联"21世纪金贝奖"最佳资产管理团队大奖。泰康养老与泰康资产拥有企业年金受托人、账户管理人、投资管理人三项资格，形成了"三位一体"的企业年金服务体系。2010年，泰康养老在业务规模和价值业务成长上取得重大突破，累计年金到账历史性突破百亿，并首度摘得"第一财经金融价值榜"最佳市场竞争力养老金公司殊荣。

2009年11月19日，经保监会批准，泰康人寿获得中国保险行业第一个养老社区投资试点资格。2010年3月，泰康之家投资有限公司正式成立，正稳步推进泰康养老社区建设。

未来，泰康人寿将坚持深耕寿险产业，建立人寿保险、健康保险、企业年金、资产管理和养老社区五大核心业务板块，为广大客户提供"从摇篮到天堂"持续一生的全方位金融保险服务。

Corporate Profile

Taikang Life Insurance Co., Ltd. is a nationwide shareholding life insurance company approved by the People's Bank of China with official documents Yin Fu [1996] No.36 and Yin Fu [1996] No.254. The Company's registered capital is 852,197,070 RMB yuan. Headquartered in Beijing, the Company has 19 shareholders which include domestic and foreign enterprises as China National Foreign Trade Transportation (Group) Corp, Wumei Holdings Inc, China Guardian International Auctions Co., Ltd., The Goldman Sachs Group, Inc., Tetrad Ventures Pet., Ltd. and so on.

Since its establishment in 1996, with the philosophy of "to be steady and innovative", Taikang Life has been developing stably along the path of "Professionalism, standardization and internationalization". The company takes the demand of customers as its orientation, and actively engages in product innovation and improvement of service quality. Taikang Life advocates the modern life style of youth, health, fashion and happiness, and promotes the idea of modern consumption and family value. The Company takes the lead in introducing "Taikang Family Protection Plan" which realizes the goal of "One Policy Covering the Whole Family". Through bringing forward new products according to the demand of the market, a complete product series is formed which covers term and whole life insurance, insurance for serious diseases, pension, medical insurance, junior insurance, accident insurance, insurance for women's diseases, high protection insurance, participating insurance, unit - linked insurance, universal insurance and so on. The Company's two subsidiaries Taikang Asset Management Co., Ltd. and Taikang Pension & Insurance Company own certificates of annuity fund trustee, account manager and administrator of annuity investment, which form the "three in one" annuity service system of the Company

Through more than 10 years development, Taikang Life has formed a complete business system and a distribution network covering the country. The scope of the insurance business and the managed assets keeps growing, and the operation efficiency has been increased steadily. By the end of 2009, the company has set up 35 branches in areas including Beijing, Shanghai, Hubei, Shandong and Guangdong, and 269 sub - branches throughout the country. Through the individual insurance sales force, the group insurance sales force, and professional and concurrent business agencies, the Company provides comprehensive products and services to 25 million customers.

By the end of 2010, the Company's total assets was 293.475 billion RMB yuan, and the after - tax profit was 2.095 billion RMB yuan. The Company's solvency rate was over 170% The market share is 8.26%. Taikang Life was on the list of China's Top 500 Enterprises for year 2009 and 2010.

书名中文：图像·历史·存在	Chinese Title: 图像·历史·存在
书名英文：IMAGE · HISTORY · EXISTENCE	English Title: IMAGE · HISTORY · EXISTENCE
出品人：泰康人寿保险股份有限公司	Producer: Taikang Life Insurance Co., Ltd.
主编：陈东升、范迪安	Chief Editors: Chen Dongsheng, Fan Di'an
执行主编：唐昕、于歌	Executive Editors: Tang Xin, Yu Ge
责任编辑：苏文祥、许崇宝	Responsible Editors: Su Wenxiang, Xu Chongbao
文字整理：王婷婷、刘娜	Editors: Wang Tingting, Liu Na
翻译：Archibald McKenzie、陈早、戴伟平	Translators: Archibald McKenzie, Nicole Chen, Dai Weiping
中文校对：许晖	Chinese Proofread: Xu Hui
英文校对：吕静静、毛卫东	English Proofread: Lv Jingjing, David Mao
设计：吐毛球平面设计	Design: TOMEETYOU GRAPHIC

展览题目：图像·历史·存在——泰康人寿保险股份有限公司成立15周年艺术品收藏展

Exhibition Title: IMAGE · HISTORY · EXISTENCE
- TAIKANG LIFE 15th ANNIVERSARY ART COLLECTION EXHIBITION

主办：中国美术馆、泰康人寿保险股份有限公司	Organizers: National Art Museum of China, Taikang Life Insurance Co., Ltd.
总策划：陈东升、范迪安	Chief Curators: Chen Dongsheng, Fan Di'an
展览策划：唐昕	Curator: Tang Xin
项目管理：苏文祥、许崇宝	Project Managers: Su Wenxiang, Xu Chongbao
项目协调：王婷婷、于歌	Project Coordinators: Wang Tingting, Yu Ge
宣传统筹：宁文	Communication Director: Karma Douzi
行政助理：刘娜	Administrative Assistant: Liu Na
展览地点：中国美术馆	Venue: National Art Museum of China
展览时间：2011年8月20日至9月7日	Duration: 20 / 08 / 2011 - 07 / 09 / 2011

致谢：

全体参展艺术家

Thanks to:

All the Artists

黄专先生	殷双喜先生	刘刚先生	Mr. Huang Zhuan	Mr. Yin Shuangxi	Mr. Liu Gang
富井玲子女士	龚云表先生	林琳女士	Ms. Reiko Tomii	Mr. Gong Yunbiao	Ms. Lin Lin
巫鸿先生	田霏宇先生	冷林先生	Mr. Wu Hong	Mr. Philip Tinari	Mr. Leng Lin
皮力先生	尹吉男先生	刘礼宾先生	Mr. Pi Li	Mr. Yin Jinan	Mr. Liu Libin
王林先生	鲍栋先生	董冰峰先生	Mr. Wang Lin	Mr. Bao Dong	Mr. Dong Bingfeng
萧开愚先生	卢迎华女士	朱青生先生	Mr. Xiao Kaiyu	Ms. Carol Yinghua Lu	Mr. Zhu Qingsheng
刘淳先生	张夕远女士	滕宇宁女士	Mr. Liu Chun	Ms. Zhang Xiyuan	Ms. Teng Yuning
朱朱先生	欧美琳女士	万捷先生	Mr. Zhu Zhu	Ms. Madeleine O'Dea	Mr. Wan Jie
萧岭女士	凯伦·史密斯女士		Ms. Nataline Colonnello	Ms. Karen Smith	
郑乃铭先生	岳鸿飞先生		Mr. Nai-ming Cheng	Mr. Robin Peckham	

中国嘉德国际拍卖有限公司	China Guardian Auctions Co., Ltd.
雅昌企业（集团）有限公司	Artron Enterprises (Group) Limited.
乌斯麦勒画廊	Galerie Urs Meile
香格纳画廊	ShanghART Gallery

图书在版编目（CIP）数据

图像·历史·存在：泰康人寿保险股份有限公司成立
15周年艺术品收藏展 / 泰康空间编. —北京：文化艺术
出版社，2011.8
ISBN 978-7-5039-5161-9

Ⅰ.①图… Ⅱ.①泰… Ⅲ.①艺术品－收藏－中国
②艺术品－鉴赏－中国 Ⅳ.①G894

中国版本图书馆CIP数据核字〔2011〕第150887号

图像·历史·存在
——泰康人寿保险股份有限公司成立15周年艺术品收藏展

编　　者	泰康空间
责任编辑	蔡宛若
装帧设计	吐毛球平面设计
出版发行	文化藝術出版社
地　　址	北京市东城区东四八条52号　100700
网　　址	www.whyscbs.com
电子邮箱	whysbooks@263.net
电　　话	（010）84057666　84057660（总编室）
	（010）84057696　84057698（发行部）
经　　销	新华书店
印　　刷	北京雅昌彩色印刷有限公司
版　　次	2011年8月第1版
印　　次	2011年8月第1次印刷
开　　本	1194×889毫米 1/8
印　　张	50
字　　数	200千字
书　　号	ISBN　978-7-5039-5161-9
定　　价	498.00元

版权所有，侵权必究。印装错误，随时调换。